ALSO BY NORMAN BOGNER

NOVELS
In Spells No Longer Bound
Spanish Fever
Seventh Avenue
The Madonna Complex
Making Love
The Hunting Animal
Snowman
Arena
California Dreamers
To Die in Provence

PLAYS
The Match
The Waiters

SCREENPLAY
Privilege

Honor
Thy Wife

Norman Bogner

A TOM DOHERTY ASSOCIATES BOOK
NEW YORK

This is a work of fiction. All the characters and events portrayed in this book are either products of the author's imagination or are used fictitiously.

HONOR THY WIFE

Copyright © 1999 by No Inc.

A Forge Book
Published by Tom Doherty Associates, LLC
175 Fifth Avenue
New York, NY 10010

www.tor.com

Forge® is a registered trademark of Tom Doherty Associates, LLC.

ISBN: 0-812-57556-3
Library of Congress Catalog Card Number: 99-26077

First edition: August 1999
First mass market edition: May 2000

Printed in the United States of America

0 9 8 7 6 5 4 3 2 1

For my beloved Bettye
The music of your laughter never sounded sweeter.

&

For Alexander, Nicholas, and Jonathan
Love, Dad

Love is an ideal thing, marriage a real thing.
A confusion of the real and the ideal never goes
  unpunished.

—GOETHE

Book I

THE EMPIRE OF
THE HEART

Trapped between the Willamette River and the Columbia headwaters, the smoky acid rain swirling from the sawmills and tanning plants in Port Rivers had a sleety razor chill. It slashed over the roofs of wharf taverns and clacked over the tarps of the fishing barges that thumped against their moorings. Lead weights seemed to be falling from the sky and the air was filled with the murky discharge of fumes that blurred and clouded shop windows in Old Town. Freighted by stunted storage buildings and sullen tenements, hobo camps, embedded like rust, flourished inside abandoned terraced shanties. The only visible light elusively crept out of the marine works where men with welding torches seared a steel hull. The hissing flames formed an amber specter over their ghostly masks.

Earl Raymond appeared to emerge from this catacomb. It was a few days before Christmas and Earl had no reason to celebrate this or any other season as he limped across the street away from the hissing exhaust of the bus. He lowered his head in the wind and his gait was as crooked as the corroded stanchions supporting the embankment at the ancient bus terminal. It hadn't given way and that was a mercy. The road was as slick as eel skin, and Earl navigated past a series of troughs, wary of deep sinkholes. They were a scandal the locals—about a hundred thousand of them to judge by the last census—constantly griped about. The council would eventually refill them by spring to avoid prison.

The neighborhood mutated without warning and gushed into a gentrified square that had once been home to nineteenth-century traders in tea and spices who had established a northwest outpost for the Orient. Along the restored square, under period gas lamps that had been electrified, building after building arrogantly displayed the burnished shields of lawyers, brokers, and scheming financial privateers once more afloat.

With his long hair matted to his forehead, his nose running, and water dripping down his neck, Earl wove like a drunk. A skidding car almost hit him and for a moment he didn't care what happened. The way his luck was running, the driver probably had no insurance and Earl would wind up disfigured as well as crippled. A six-five geek with a mashed-potato face who could palm a basketball but could no longer dribble the length of the court. Earl was twenty-seven, and according to his doctor, his future was behind him.

The only law firm to take his call and actually speak to him was Brett & Conlan, which was located in the heart of Buccaneer Square. The building housed two offices: a babble of accountants' names on the ground floor, and Brett & Conlan in the penthouse. Renovated to the sconces, even the old pine banisters had been stripped and marine-varnished; the carpet itself was the crisp green of cash. The gated elevator was an Otis reproduction and it whispered up to the second story like a Rolls-Royce.

Without enthusiasm, Terry Brett had mentioned on the phone that he seldom did a personal injury case. He specialized in murder and mayhem. It was a slim opening, but Earl decided to drive down the lane like the old days when a championship game was on the line. Terry would give him a straight answer and wouldn't demand a retainer. Not that it much mattered. Earl had twelve bucks and change in his pocket, about enough for forty minutes of a happy hour.

In the waiting room, he cautiously eased himself down on an old English green leather sofa, trying to get comfortable. His knee was still locking. When he canted it on the table, he could hear the floating cartilages crunching, like the sound a drinker made chomping stale bar peanuts.

Terry came out a few minutes later. He still wore blue button-down Oxfords and penny loafers. His rep tie was askew, but his navy flannel suit was well cut and he seemed to be doing very well. The magazine subscriptions were in his name and the fancy lettered plaque outside was polished brass. The office trumpeted money.

"Well, Earl, sorry to have to pull you out in this freaking weather, but it was the only time I had."

"I know what you're thinking—I look like shit."

"Nah, you just smell like Gorgonzola," Terry replied.

"Right now I'd settle for a hunk of it and a beer."

"Ah, come on."

Terry smiled at him and pushed back his long, straight, blond hair, which had fallen over his broad forehead. He had always been strikingly good-looking, with a moody expression, a grand Irish lantern jaw, and a retroussé nose. His patrician bearing proclaimed a man in harmony with himself. His sharp, lustrous hazel eyes exuded the confidence of attainment. He stood opposite Earl, and although Terry himself was an even six feet tall, and broader than his former college roommate, there was still something of that imperial trait conveyed by very tall men like Earl. But late nights and booze had puffed dark pouches under Earl's cloudy, gray cat eyes and bloated his soft baby face into bacon fat.

Terry affably led him along the corridor. "Can't be that bad, Earl. I've finished all my other appointments. Let's play catch-up."

Earl stared at Terry enviously. Terry was still the clean-cut, glad-hander Earl had known at USC. He had a greater maturity, and his hair covered part of his ears, which was as far as he went to accommodate sixties, hippie fashion. He had been one of those professionally smart scholarship boys who always knew the right thing to say.

"So, Earl, what's the news from the front?"

"If the knee had my sack moves, I'd be playing point guard in the all-star game. Instead, I'm pouncing on retired cheerleaders and falling off the bed. I tell you . . ."

Terry laughed. "No more hot, scented towels on a tray?"

"Yesterday's news," Earl said with a snarl.

"You haven't changed. Come on in."

A plump, young woman with a pretty face craned her neck behind Terry. Earl's remark embarrassed him but not her. She gave him an abashed smile.

"This is Georgie Conlan, my associate. Earl Raymond."

She glowed with eagerness when Earl took her chubby, dimpled hand in his long Herculean fingers and allowed it to vanish in his palm.

"I saw you break the state record when you played us at Salem. Fifty-six points," she said.

"Five-six, easy eleven," Earl said, talking to imaginary dice in his fist and winding up for a roll at a craps table. "Come to me, baby."

"Georgie does our domestic work," Terry said. "Maybe she can come up with a rich divorcée with *Playboy* stats for you." He winked at Georgie. "When we roomed together, Earl was very fussy about that sort of thing. I spent my senior year sleeping in some booster's car while the master entertained the morning glories in his playpen."

"Hey, Georgie, I'm not so particular any more. She can be in a wheelchair, long as she's got a trust fund. Better yet, I'd like her husband dead, or being hunted by cannibals in Borneo."

Terry tweaked his lustful partner. "I hope you're taking this down, Georgie."

"Fast as I can. We're known for pleasing our clients. I'll see what I can do," she said, watching the onetime All-American basketball player grimace as he hobbled ahead of her partner.

Georgie looked them over, like a judicious housewife at the market. Double destruction, Mr. Inside and Mr. Outside. What havoc they must have wrought in sunny California with sorority sisters clamoring for Earl's paws and Terry's charm. She envied the girls. As a divorce lawyer, her days and nights were spent listening to tales of man's inhumanity to woman and yet she dreamed of virile brutes like Earl flinging her over a bare shoulder and heaving her on a bed. In court, though, her soft, melodic voice had a growl when she churned bedroom Apaches into sausage meat.

A few minutes later, Georgie knocked on Terry's office door to say good night and catch another glimpse of the renowned basketball star. But Earl was indignantly poring over legal documents and pointing to X rays curling over Terry's desk. She wanted to invite Earl out for a drink, but the spark was lost.

"Sorry to interrupt." Terry looked grateful. "I just got a call. The Arnold case is settled."

"Which one was that?"

"You met him. Chris Arnold, that navigator in the Merchant Marines who retained me for his divorce from the airline princess. He died aboard ship of appendicitis and was buried."

"Victory at sea."

"Do I have to return the retainer to his estate?" she asked.

"Not with Mr. Arnold wrapped in a flag."

She handed Earl a towel. His hair was still dripping. He draped it around his neck and nodded brusquely. With a sigh, she left.

Earl resumed his tirade. "You won't represent me as an act of friendship—on the come?"

Terry presumed that he was Earl's last resort and he had burned out all of the college contacts he had owned during his balmy campus days. Prospective clients like Earl Raymond were a nuisance.

"Jesus, Terry, it's only a few calls for you."

"Not exactly, Earl." Pondering how he could unload him, Terry thought quickly. "Hey, did you try getting in touch with Billy Klein about this? He's in L.A."

"Rich Billy! You've got to be kidding." Apparently, Earl had tried Terry's law school drone. "When a lawyer carries a crocodile attaché case, he either has a salami sandwich inside or his black book with hookers' numbers." Invariably the hurt child when he didn't get his way, Earl flapped his arms. "I don't get it, Ter. We were roomies, buddies."

Terry halfheartedly sorted through the crumpled maze

Earl had made of his documents, the daydreams of a score.

"With all this material, you can really get your teeth into Jonah Wolfe."

"What? Who the hell's he?"

"The owner of the Los Angeles Stars. He never paid me my disability insurance when I was injured. And I was covered!" Earl commenced a disjointed tale of betrayal. "Jonah's responsible. I treated him like a friend. My pal. He was a meatpacker from Milwaukee. Makes the Wolfe Dog. You could puke from the shit he churns out for the supermarkets."

Still demurring, Terry tried another approach. "It's the hours I've got to put in. They'll have some big gun against you in L.A."

"A big gun against us? I'm not afraid of a big gun."

"You used to be one yourself," Terry said kindly, but Earl took it in the wrong way. "Look, I don't want to bust my ass and have you wind up with five grand and no expenses."

"Five big ones would mean a lot to me."

"I'd give you maybe a month or two before you've blown it. Then what? Working as a bouncer in some club. Earl, you have two skills: screwing and dunking a basketball."

"Former skills."

Earl's arms and legs appeared to retract like landing gear. Behind the close-set gray eyes and the sodden, shoulder-length hair, Terry saw a frightened young boy still living in a realm of old triumphs and dog-eared scrapbooks. Terry realized he had been too severe.

"This could be—I don't know—like a landmark case," he said.

"I like the sound of that. You always thought big," Earl responded, as he unleashed his coiled body, stood upright, spanning the room with his arms extended as though he was going for a rebound after a missed foul shot.

"It's a total crapshoot. Could take years to work it out."

Years! Years! No one liked that plural. He paused, hoping to discourage Earl. The minute a client came into a lawyer's office with a grievance and moldy papers, he was already counting his money. "We'd have to go to the appellate court and appeal if we should lose. . . . If I were to take a case like this, I'd have to be prepared to sue the bastard forever."

Earl knew all about Terry's reputation. He'd heard about it from other lawyers in town who'd already turned him down. One of the old courthouse pros had said: "You get involved with that Terry Brett, it's like dancing with a bear." In five years, he'd won acquittals in a dozen murder cases, made fifty thousand on an arson-extortion setup, and developed an uneasy reputation for knowing how to investigate a case so that the jury felt he probably knew the color of a witness's panties. He was thorough and witty, which gave his briefs an incisiveness that stirred up the city's clubby, old-time firms but endeared him to judges.

"You see, Earl, I'd have to make Jonah Wolfe's life as miserable as your knee feels. This isn't a quick buck for a nuisance suit. You're crippled and it happened when you were on the job. You went up for a rebound in training camp and you were fouled." Terry was merely spinning wheels as he pretended to outline the case for Earl. He concluded, "Actually, I've never done an insurance tort. Let me think it over."

"Least come down to the hospital and talk to my doctor. He'll tell you."

"I've got your number."

"Don't leave it too long, Ter. I have no unemployment left . . . no disability." Earl sucked in his breath, expanding his chest, firing a water pistol. "Maybe this kind of case is too tough for you."

Terry ignored the lamentable jibe. It compounded desperation and self-pity, typical of Earl's style.

"What puzzles me is that the club should have had you covered for an injury and an ensuing disability."

"They did. But try collecting from an insurance company."

"*Did* you?" A note of surprise had crept into Terry's voice.

"They told me to tell my story walking. Isn't that something? Like I made it all up, malingered. Please, I'm doing therapy at Good Samaritan. I beg you, do something."

"Earl, this isn't like writing you a term paper. Do you understand that?"

"I've got twelve bucks in my pocket. I can't even take a dump with all the codeine I chug-a-lug."

Terry locked up the office, saw Earl out, and gave him a fifty-dollar bill. But Earl, who always played good defense and clung to his man like a crab, followed him down to the garage. He was tapping his fingers on the roof of Terry's new Shelby Mustang.

"How's your dad?"

"He asks about you," Terry replied, lying.

"Give him my best and . . . well, I owe him an apology. You probably don't remember. I was going to get him a ticket to the NCAA championship final. But you know me"—a hapless smirk crossed his face—"I laid it on a piece of tail."

"He'll understand."

"Yeah, he's a man's man. In the meantime, counselor, how do I eat?"

Terry's car crawled out of the narrow garage, wheeling around some big-assed Lincolns, but Earl was trailing him and holding on to the open window like a beggar in a foreign film.

"Where're you living?"

"Hanging off the rim out of bounds."

"Try getting a job, Earl. I'll even write you a reference."

"I have to *prove* I can't work, counselor."

"You got me there, pal."

2

Terry lived with his father in a spacious white-shingled Cape Cod house on four acres in Port Rivers. The nape of the property hung over the Willamette River, forming a small inlet. Terry and Pat, martinis in hand, sometimes fished naked in the summer from the end of their lawn. When Terry parked the car, he stood for a moment in the feathery mist looking at the place. The rain gutter he and Pat had installed worked like a charm. The cones on the high Douglas firs bounced through the drainpipe like bowling balls hooking down the alley for a strike. He would dry them in the storehouse, then lay them on the fire. He liked the smell they gave off and their hypnotic crackling sounds.

The TV was on to the news, and Yankee pot roast emitted the comforting aroma of familiarity, of home. Pat leaned through the kitchen hatch. "It's a whiskey evening, but fix me a vodka."

"You must be seeing Milly tonight."

"Yeah, when I've got scotch on my breath Milly leaves me out in the cold or sends me to bed with the dog." The amorous contractor stretched. "Milly's got her accountant over at her place. Seems she was a little light on the payroll tax and some weasel from the IRS read her the riot act."

Milly Canfield was a childless widow who owned a popular coffee shop and dinner house downtown near the courts. She had been Pat's lady for the past decade. They'd always been sweet on each other. And Pat, with a young boy to raise, was tired of doing his bonking covertly with the ladies whose houses he was remodeling. He wanted someone respectable like Milly, who he could bring home to sit down with his son at the table. Terry mused. They were an American love story: Milly made sublime meatloaf and paid strict attention to the reckless moods of his father's pecker.

"This IRS clown was keeping tabs on the waitresses' tips, too."

"I guess the government's running short on napalm and Agent Orange," Terry said, lightly grazing the ice cubes in the cocktail shaker with dry vermouth. He had been classified 4F for the army and he passionately hated the Vietnam War.

"Well, somebody's got to pay Dow Chemical and whoever else makes that shit."

A Fighting Seabee in World War II, Pat was outraged by current events. America's safety was not at stake or he would have taken up arms. He had come back from the war prematurely gray. For years it bothered him. But now the color meshed with his weathered face. Even the broken nose he had acquired boxing in the service blended with his personality.

"If there's a problem, tell Milly I'll talk to the bastard and subpoena *his* expense account."

We're blowing up the world, Terry thought. *And Milly is being hounded by the IRS. What next?* LBJ had sent combat troops to Vietnam and resumed the bombing after Ho Chi Minh rejected the president's offer of unconditional surrender. The student revolt on college campuses had resulted in massive sit-ins. A panel of blowhard lard-asses were on screen, giving their opinions of the new offensive.

"I've had enough of their bullshit," Pat said. He and Terry touched glasses and sat down at the kitchen bar.

"Anything new down the office?"

"Georgie's bringing in cases. She has this theory that from Thanksgiving to New Year's the divorce rate soars. High season."

Pat's gravelly Camel laugh vibrated in the room.

"It's the cheaters' girlfriends, they get fed up and won't be lied to any more. They're tired of the holidays alone while the guy spews out all that guilt drivel about his kids. So they put the heat on, seal up the mousetrap.

Either get rid of the old lady or you don't get any honey on your drumstick."

"Sounds like a strong brief."

Pat poured them fresh drinks before the ice watered the vodka in the shaker.

"Earl Raymond stopped by."

"What did that creep want? Freebie legal advice, I'll bet. And have you sue someone."

"You got it, but actually it's a little more complicated."

Pat got up and fixed their plates. "Well, Terry, since I'm a bullshitter from time to time, I don't get along with four-flushers like Earl."

"Really, I wasn't aware of that facet of your character." They both enjoyed a needle. "Earl asked me to apologize about the championship ticket you didn't get some years back."

"I'm glad to hear that. I didn't want Earl to go to the grave with that on his conscience."

"One of his unconquered centerfolds got your seat."

"I can understand a guy being horny. But if he'd have told me that like a man, I wouldn't have objected. It was ignoring it, like it never happened, that got me in an uproar. In any event, I hexed him. He had the apple all night long. It looked like a tennis ball stuck in his throat when he was shooting fouls."

Flower-power protesters at singing sit-ins took over the TV screen and Terry changed the channel, stopping at a college basketball game. He and his father watched avidly.

"Got any plans over Christmas?"

"I might drive up to Bend and go skiing for a few days."

"Alone?" Pat's tone had an unexpected edge.

"Why not?"

"Aren't you seeing someone?"

"Not at the moment."

"Won't you be bringing anyone to our Christmas bash?"

"I thought I'd hang out with you and tag along to Seacliff to see Milly's family." His father nodded, but

Terry noticed he was troubled. "Something wrong?"

"What about Joanne Van Wyck? I've always liked her. You sure know her old man owns half the county. Imagine him as a client."

"Oh, give it up, Pat. You and Joanne have been measuring me for a tux since I can remember."

"Hey, is there something wrong with marriage?"

"You and Milly seem to be doing fine without a ceremony."

"Oh, come on, we're different, no kids in our future."

Terry considered the bohemian attitude his father had adopted about promiscuity, which contradicted his own behavior. It made a puzzling pairing with his moralistic expectations for Terry.

"I might never get married. Who knows? Cases I hear about from Georgie . . . child custody fights and whatnot, don't make it very appealing. Georgie has this strange, professional approach that it's just the dissolution of a partnership. I mean, some of these people were in love once."

"You prefer murder, Ter?"

"In some ways I do," Terry said after a moment. "It's more focused. Unless the person's certifiable, there's a reason behind it. In domestic battles it's always, he said, she did. When one of them is screwing around, it makes it easier to find the bad guy. But, Jesus, half the time, it's someone just getting bored with life and that winds up as mental cruelty on the complaint sheet."

He cleared the table and started the dishwasher while Pat carried their coffee into the pine-paneled den and switched on the big TV to the game without sound. Pat threw a log on the fire and stared at it for a moment.

"Thing is, I'd like to see you settled down with a good woman. I want grandchildren while I can still walk around without tubes sticking out of me. You know, hunt and fish with them. It's been lonely for us, Ter, 'specially you."

"I hadn't noticed."

"Do you know what you're looking for?"

"Yeah, I think so. . . . Someone I can't live without.

I'm always compromising with lawyers and the goddamn courts. Yes, Pat, I do know what I want."

Terry realized he had always been somewhat inhibited. Perhaps it was growing up without a mother and the fact that Pat took such inordinate pains to keep his promiscuity private. They had always talked openly, but something from the equation was missing: the spell that flourished when there was the scent of a woman in the house, her hair in the sink, crumpled tissues with lipstick blots, soft clothes on top of the washer. Pat had never sent him out of the house on a fool's pizza mission so that he could plow some fox while pretending to plan her kitchen. Until Milly had become a fixture, Pat had carried circumspection to the point of oppression.

For a period Terry's decorous stance had relaxed when he roomed with Earl. Now locked in the mid-sixties, wherever he looked, there were girls in miniskirts and T-shirts that revealed their breasts. It was all too easy, too accessible. He saw this revolution as defiling his beliefs in privacy and the subtle secrets cherished between a man and woman who loved each other. He wondered what would remain of the country after the politics of dope and unconstrained sex had cut across the grain of everything he believed in. It was a free-for-all, and he had turned his back on this vulgar mood of the streets.

The lawyer cornered Pat. "Could you live without Milly?"

Pat pushed his glasses up on his wind-burned forehead, rubbed his eyes, and squirmed uncomfortably.

"If she got taken in an accident, car or plane crash, that sort of thing, I guess so."

"That's not what I meant."

"I understand what you meant. And, yes, I felt that way about your mother. But after she died, I thought, thank God, I'll never go through it again."

Terry was talking about rapture and realized it sounded somewhat embarrassing for grown men to explore their feelings.

"But one time, Pat, it's worth the grief, isn't it?"

Reluctantly, Pat nodded. "Yes, it is . . . if you want to live in hell."

It was almost eleven when Terry pushed the lamp on his desk away from his eyes. He had a rezoning configuration spread out on the floor, which his client wanted to develop into a shopping center; the police sheet on an armed robbery suspect whose wife had hired him was next. A photo of the pistol-whipped victim was attached. Terry would plead the thief guilty. The bastard deserved some time.

He got up from his swivel chair and felt a sudden twinge in his calf. His body seemed to freeze and for a moment he thought he would scream. He rolled on the sofa, raised his trouser leg, and massaged the thin, flaccid calf muscle, which was filled with knuckle-sized knots.

Pat knocked on the door: "Ter . . ."

"Yeah."

"You okay? You're damn pale, man."

Pat had nursed him through his polio while watching his mother evaporate into an eighty-pound piece of ash. All the while bringing in a buck, subcontracting on junky spec houses, trading wedges of land instead of a fee until he got the parcel he had dreamed of at the water's edge with tall trees. But then Alma Brett had died and all his work had struck him as futile.

Terry stood up after a moment. "Just a spasm. My foot fell asleep."

"You sure?"

"Nothing to worry about."

His father seemed uncertain. "Okay. I'm off to Milly's. Just spoke to her. The IRS nailed her. She needs forty-seven hundred dollars' worth of consolation."

"I'll walk you down."

Pat got into his pickup. Somebody's copper bathroom sink was already acquiring an aged patina from the dripping canvas lean-to covering it. It would be green on installation.

"Comfort Milly in this time of need."

Pat broke into a coughing sputter of a laugh. "You

always knew about us in the old days, didn't you?"

"Get a move on. You don't keep a lady who makes pies and pot roast waiting."

After he pulled away, Terry reached into the backseat of his car, pressing his chin against the cold leather on the back of the seat to reach the envelope Earl had left with him.

It might have been the twinges in his leg, or the revived, amused interest in Earl's gallery of intrigues that made Terry look at his former roommate's medical receipts and expenses. Somebody had given Earl some free advice. He was charging to the Los Angeles Stars everything from Vicks Formula 44 to chicken dinners from the Colonel. On graph paper, list upon list of scraggly, zigzagging columns were littered with his hen-track comments and wayward sums.

As Terry was falling asleep, he saw an image of Earl's pure fluid motion, stealing the ball and breaking away down the court. Earl Raymond had been one of those golden young men, touched by the gods. Gliding silently, effortlessly toward the basket, like a ghost rider in the rain, Earl floated in a chariot of rainbows.

3

The following afternoon in court Terry reached an eighteen-month plea bargain with Paul Cisco, the assistant D.A., for his armed robber. The negotiation had taken less time than Terry had anticipated. For once, Cisco didn't sing an entire opera. Terry found himself with a few hours to kill just before his dinner date with the bartender at Tuck Lung's, a high-cheekboned Far Eastern angel, who had made it clear that romance was not out of the question.

In a spitting rain, Terry wandered over to Good Samaritan Hospital to meet Earl's orthopedic surgeon. In college, Earl had always been an eloquent and voluble spokesman for his ailments. Terry was convinced that Earl had never had a day in his life when he was not laid low by some illness. Now, with a legitimate cause to defend, Terry knew from experience, they'd all be there till midnight unless Earl was excluded.

The doctor's office was next to the physical therapy room. They scanned X rays and the surgical reports. Earl and another player had gone up for a rebound in training camp. Their legs had become entangled. Earl's knee had been twisted unnaturally even before it smashed on the wooden floor, tearing tendons, fragmenting the kneecap, and fissuring the cartilage disk and ligaments.

Dr. Flannigan, a cool, temperate man whose emotions had been removed in the operating room, was worn down by Earl's blandishments and pestered to death by his complaints.

"God knows Earl's a trial to anyone who gets close enough to listen to him. But still not even a man of his grand delusions ought to suffer this much without some compensation."

"Dr. Flannigan, I assume you and the hospital have more than a personal interest at stake."

"Try fifteen thousand and change in medical bills for openers. That doesn't include the hundred I loaned him today. But the fact is, Mr. Brett, I didn't think about the money when I operated." Terry restrained his skepticism. "I'm not being disingenuous with you. I saw Earl play in high school and college before he turned pro."

"Seems everyone did."

"Well, he was a gazelle and the state hero. On my recommendation, the hospital board agreed to carry him."

Terry glanced through the report. "You came in after the reconstruction surgery in L.A.?"

"Yeah, they tried to repair the anterior cruciate damage. Then there were other problems. I put in pins. They created a different kind of stress and not all of the bone splinters could be found. As for the cartilage, it's floating around like chicken feathers."

Terry thought the doctor would make a solid witness if he decided to take the case. He found his prospective client in the therapy room. Dark patches of stubble made Earl look like a pop singer on a drug bender.

Terry saw a girl struggling on the bars, her left leg bound in orthopedic wraps up to the thigh.

"Don't dog it. Come on, Allison, you can do it! Have you got piss in your blood!" Earl ranted at a girl staggering with the jerkiness of a marionette.

From behind, her waist-length blond hair swayed from side to side. Terry could now see her torment. Her teeth dug into her lower lip, sweat dripped into her eyes. She seemed in the throes of an awful labor. The pain twisted her face and Terry felt imprisoned by the agony of her effort. Collapsing on the floor, she might have been a hobo's bundle flung from a boxcar.

"You've got no guts!" Earl yelled.

Terry rushed over and helped her to her feet. It was an involuntary response. Her skin was wet, perspiration stained through her gray sweatshirt. He would have done it for anyone. She looked at him without gratitude.

"Who the hell're you, another doctor?" she hissed sourly at Terry. Her good leg was majestically contoured, firm as a piece of sculpture.

"Oh, shut up, Allison." Earl said. "This here is Terry Brett, my *attorney*."

"Sorry to have helped you, Allison." She gave off a damp scent of the woods, something wild and uncivilized. "I won't do it again."

She reached for her crutches, scowling at them. "I'm hitting the whirlpool, Earl." Her tone had evened out, but she still maintained an angry, defiant surliness. "See you tomorrow, if I must." She staggered to the exit of the therapy room.

"What happens when she stings someone, Earl?"

"I wouldn't want to know. Don't think there's antitoxin for it. How we doing, Terry?"

"Great. I filed a writ of certiori with the Supreme Court. Chief Justice Warren agreed to hear the case."

Earl was loping off, staggering over the plane of the floor as though it were mountain terrain. "Aw, come on, cut it out. Look, let me grab a shower and we'll talk."

"No, we won't. I've got a date."

Despite his inclination to flee, Terry sat on a bench and peered at the torture equipment: pulleys, bikes, bars, and machines. It still held a ghastly fascination for him. He had done rehab until he was fourteen for his polio. For an instant he thought he could hear the sound of his own cries reverberate through the sweaty tormented memories of chambers like this. It had been worth the struggle; he was no longer lame.

Earl had cleaned up—Colgate, Old Spice, a Levi's suit, the handle of a hairdresser's comb jutting out of his back pocket. The gunfighter was all business. They were out in the front of the hospital.

"Where do I stand?" Earl demanded as though he had Melvin Belli already lined up. "You going to take my case and get famous?"

"You forgot rich."

"Listen to me good. When we get to court Dr. Flannigan will go to hell for me . . . he likes me that much. Admires me. It's a kind of hero worship."

Terry raised the cuff of his raincoat. It was nearing seven. "How could he help himself?"

"You said, get a job. I did! I'm not getting paid, or on the books, mind you. Room and board, a couple of pain-killers is all."

Earl's spidery manipulations left him breathless with admiration. "At the hospital?"

"You got it. I'm living here now. Doc Flannigan had me put on unofficially as an assistant in rehab. That's what I was doing tonight with one of my patients. Man, I'm an expert at this."

"I didn't know Good Samaritan had a wing for visiting specialists. This could get you into more trouble if it comes out."

Earl laughed. "Don't worry, I gave them your office number. This time I sue on behalf of all the disabled people in the country."

"Ah, a class action suit. I've never litigated one of

those. It'll only take five to six years. Why don't I just turn my career over to you, Earl?"

Earl turned fractious. It was difficult to keep up with his quixotic mood swings. "Did you go through my notes?"

"I've already said I have a date with a gorgeous Asian lady. She loves 'Fool on the Hill.' "

"That's you. Always arrive late, Ter. It's like you've got more important things to do with your life instead of clocking in on the button for some woman. Remember, they're the enemy. Adam said so in the Garden of Eden."

"I think he said yes."

They were a few feet from the corner and Terry noticed Allison awkwardly maneuver her crutches to the bus shelter. Her bag strap was looped around her neck.

"She's still non-weight-bearing. What a pain in the ass that is," Earl informed him with a note of kinship. "Buy her a dinner. She lives on roots and stuff . . . Indian crap. I think she's part Chinook."

Terry was intrigued. "With all that blond hair, she doesn't look it."

"I'm not kidding you." Earl then returned to his favorite issue. "My notes, Ter, are important. They are the basis of *our* case."

"I didn't even glance at them and I'm not a cryptographer."

"Who?"

"Never mind. Look, Earl, I'm running very late."

"So am I."

A cream 3.8 Jaguar turned the corner and pulled up. They were as rare as good pastrami in the city. Terry curiously stepped toward the curb.

"Big, big date. An admirer of my former jump shot who does volunteer work at the hospital."

The car window slid halfway down and the woman's cigarette smoke trailed into the chilled air. A head in a scarf turned around. She saw Earl and he contemptuously turned his back.

"She's taking me home. Her husband's away. Third time and I haven't given it up to her."

"You don't drop your pants for anyone."

"Once they get a taste, they grab it like they're turning a doorknob. They have no shame."

"That's a very delicate assessment, Earl. I'll review your claim and be in touch. I have your new professional address."

Blinding rain pelted down with typical suddenness. A moment ago, they could see Mount Hood. Now even the cars were silhouettes.

"Okay, Ter, you want to blow my case. . . . Fine." Earl headed for the Jaguar. The woman and the wipers were twitching. He leaned in. Then in a limping slow-motion spin, he grabbed hold of Terry in a fury. "I want to tell you something that's long overdue. I'm not a quiz kid. But don't ever sell me short."

"I saw you play. How could I forget?"

"Okay. Then drop this cute stuff, taunting me like I was a half-wit."

Earl was still puffing when he got into the woman's car and Terry watched the woman dive on him, hitting the horn in her excitement. Earl certainly could play his hand, Terry thought. A date with a rich woman with everything to lose and finessing a guilt trip on him. How did he do it? Terry dashed into his car.

On a bench, oblivious to the drama, Allison was reading a paperback under the bus shelter light. Terry thought about blowing the horn, then rushed out.

"Can I drop you downtown?"

"I'll wait for the bus."

He could see only the word "Edge" on the book jacket.

"You know what it's like this time of night." She ignored him. "I guess you do." He was getting wetter. "You're being silly."

"Downtown won't help. This bus gets me close to the river."

"You're reading *The Razor's Edge*."

"Yes. Have you read it?" He shook his head. Her face was animated. "The hero travels to India and finds the meaning of life. I can't wait to go there." She smiled, filled with an adolescent soulful yearning. "I'll walk on water."

"Maybe I can drop you at the Bay of Bengal. Come on, get in."

Allison's crutches clashed when she rose to her feet. Terry opened the door for her and drove down to Chinatown. She played with the radio dial and through the static found Dylan's "Like a Rolling Stone." Her long hair splayed on the headrest and her expression was beatific, communing with tides, tuned to the stars. A space traveler, singing along with Dylan.

"India. . . . In the meantime, how about Chinese takeout? It'll be like training camp for you. You can work your way up gradually from Cantonese to the flames of Vindaloo."

"I don't care," she said curtly, dismissing him for interrupting.

Terry realized that he had a dilemma. He, a Caucasian, couldn't brazenly walk into Tuck Lung's with Allison slung on his arm and break his date. It was said Chinese women would poison anyone who threatened their rice. His problem was solved. Allison had no intention of leaving the car.

With her thigh blinking out of a slit of her green dragon silk dress and a phone pressed against her ear, Han Lee was frantically writing take-out orders on a pad. She caressed her ebony hair and waved him to a bench.

"I filling in. Okay, eat at bar? Dinner ready. I order Imperial Dynasty Feast for us. You don't mind when I have answer phone. Mr. Tuck coming nine. Then we free."

"You'll be all mine."

"We see. Name in Cantonese—'Butterfly.' "

Up close, Han Lee was older than he remembered. His lawyers' club came in once a month and over many drinks she had seemed as mysterious as Nancy Kwan, someone to be cherished in an affair. He had a martini and tried to figure out his next move. While working the phone, checking out orders, taking cash, and dealing fortune cookies—he couldn't believe it—Butterfly would flash past him and conduct an instant tête-à-tête that had the taint of a legal meeting. It took a few of these sorties before he realized that she was bartering—offering him a contingency screw!—to get her husband and children out of Shanghai.

She cursed obscurely. "Mr. Tuck can't come in."

"I'll take the food out," he said, relieved.

Gabbling through the kitchen hatch, she shortly thrust a carton filled with steaming white boxes in his arms and grabbed his money, ringing up the check she had already made out before he had appeared.

"Free midnight. You call me, you can't come."

He waited for his change and tipped her. It was worth five bucks never to see her again. Case settled.

The rain had stopped when he got to the car. Allison was reading her book under the interior light. He apologized for switching it off as they drove out of the city.

"You can get car sick, reading."

"Not on buses." She closed the book and sniffed the air. "Smells good. I hope you got some fish?"

"I don't think they'd have the nerve to leave it out of the Imperial Dynasty Feast. Don't you eat meat?"

"My cat likes fish. I eat anything."

She directed him over the Otter Rock Bridge to Hardtack Island, an industrial zone in which exiled machinery guarded the night. Volleys of water slammed the windshield so hard the wipers couldn't keep up and he had to crawl while the windows fogged with their breath and garlic bean sauce of such astounding pungency that he half expected junks to appear on the horizon. Their damp clothes reeked of Shanghai and mystery.

"I think your cat would follow me to the ends of the earth for a whiff of this."

"Just concentrate, Ted."

"It's Terry. I can talk and drive five miles an hour. Or if you want to pull over . . . ?"

She was apprehensive but insisted he go on. "Sorry I was rude. But there are these people around giving me problems." She touched his hand. "I don't mean to be so bitchy, but I don't want any harm to come to you."

He was beginning to feel unexpectedly tender toward her. Out of the corner of his eye, he watched her breathing. She wore no perfume or lipstick. When she had been doing therapy and disguised in a ballooning sweatshirt, Terry hadn't realized that she was so coarsely beautiful and big. With a broad nose and very light blond eyebrows that were almost invisible, she had the sensuality of a buxom French model who drove painters to absinthe and penury.

"How'd you break your leg?"

"Van backing out of McDonald's. Hit-and-run. Flipped me over. Broke the tibia and fibula. First time it didn't set well, so they had to operate again. You know: break it again and reset it." She sounded almost cheerful.

"Did the company offer you anything?"

"For what?"

"Pain, suffering, medical expenses."

"Well, the people in the van had just robbed the place with sawed-off shotguns and they were in some kind of hurry."

"That's an act of God. McDonald's is not responsible."

"Doesn't matter. Nobody cares about people like me," she said with blunt indifference. "And why should they?"

Through the tempest, skidding along trenches of mud, he found his new Mustang about to close in for an unexpected dip in the river. He was puzzled when she told him they had arrived. The rain had subsided, but she didn't wait for him to come around. She plunged her crutches into the oozing grass.

He picked up the carton of Chinese food and followed her. They were in the middle of nowhere. Then in the bite of his headlights, he saw her limping toward a tent.

She screamed, "Oh, shit, those fuckers came after me."

The rain against the canvas sounded harsh and violent. She had lighted a kerosene lamp. Inside, wooden crates were overturned, LPs were being pocked by water, and a blue ice chest lay over on its belly. Her sleeping bag had been slashed. As a final insult, a monster had cut the tent open at the top and the rain pivoted through the opening.

"You don't live *here*?"

"Oh, shut up!"

For a moment, it was like one of the vitriolic retorts he gave other lawyers in court and he didn't like it.

"How about coming over to my house? Hot or cold, Chinese food tastes good." Trying to get her mind off the damage, he added, "I'll heat it up if you like."

"Whatever you've got in mind, I don't fuck anyone for an egg roll."

"I don't blame you." He was galled but controlled his anger and persisted. "Can I drop you somewhere? Or maybe you'd like to eat in the car?"

"No, thanks very much, you can just screw yourself."

Looking over his shoulder, he started back to the car, stumbled, righted himself, and rushed back up to her. He grabbed her by the shoulders, whipping her around.

"Who the hell're you to be so contemptuous of me!"

She was shocked, then reacted quickly, raising her crutch to strike him. He caught her arm and they both fell, wrestling and rolling over each other down the bank. In an instant, a current of anxiety vaulted through his trembling arms and legs. He got to his knees, picked up her dirty wet crutches, and pointed the armrests at her. She took hold of them and yanked herself to her feet.

"Oh, I finally met a gentleman. I thought I was about due to hook up with the frog king."

"You can stay at my place, so let's stop this crap."

"Thanks. But I've got to hang in."

"Why?"

"Try to get my things back."

"I don't get it."

"You don't have to understand everything, Terry."

They staggered back to the gashed tent. Her sleeping bag had turned a blackish purple in the whipping rain gusts. He carried it into a corner and squeezed it like a mop. She was composed, slashing a metal comb through her dripping hair. Primeval mud caked her face.

"Come on, will you, please?"

She waved him away. "Earl tells me you're a hotshot

attorney. Well, let me give you some advice. Do yourself a favor and go home. I hate fucking lawyers."

Under his eiderdown and crisp sheets, he couldn't close his eyes. He rubbed his forehead where she had scratched him. Strands of her hair were still entwined around his wrist. His unwashed hands smelled of Allison.

I was ready to kill this woman. Why? What is the reason? What has she done?

Allison had cried herself to sleep and she awoke very early to the caw of gulls swooping and skidding over tendrils of garbage heaved into the river by fishing boats. As she surveyed the damage of the previous night, she had a moment of enlightenment. This would be her life and she must accept these circumstances without shrinking. As she brushed her teeth in boiled water, the armor of stoicism settled her down.

4

After a night of self-doubt and inner turmoil about his motives, Terry decided he must see Allison again. At daybreak, he was back on her island. He spotted her jousting on crutches patched with dried mud. A flare of sunlight highlighted her, scavenging under the bridge. She seemed like one of those unhinged people who combed the beach, then trolled with a metal pole for signals from Atlantis and had conversations with shells while searching for buried dimes. Newspaper trucks bulging with the early editions stacked on their tailgates rolled overhead. In the shallows of the river edge, she was staring at her bloated dead cat. Around its neck it had a rope on which a brick had been tied.

"You've got yourself *some* enemy there."

"So does he!"

"You're not afraid?"

"When I'm in the right, I have nothing to fear. It's always been that way for me. Anyway I am a collector of experiences." Her fatalistic poise fascinated him. The cat, she explained, had achieved satori. "We're all part of the same universal spirit. Maybe he'll come back as a man and know the Truth of Truth."

Terry was dressed for the office in a charcoal gray flannel suit and a beige cashmere overcoat that caught her eye. She touched the sleeve, rubbed it on her cheek.

"Is that your blanket?"

He was beginning to get a fix on her. Her magnetic compass had no north; the equator varied with her mood.

"An engagement present from a loving client. He owns a restaurant and some discount clothing outlets. He had his Annual Going Out of Business Sale once too often. The witness against him is his fence and the case is one of entrapment."

"So you got a coat out of it."

"I don't kiss and tell." He smiled. "My fees, of course."

"I thought you might be a cause lawyer who fought for what he believed in." Her tennis sneaker oozed mud. "Someone noble, a white knight."

"I don't mean to be impertinent or introduce you to structured thinking, but I represent clients in jeopardy, not causes. I'm your black knight."

Some devious scheme sprang into her eyes. She sucked the inside of her cheek. He'd been around many talented connivers and he recognized someone trying to play fox with the hunter. She wouldn't find hedgerows high enough to hide from him.

"Oh, I sure hoped so," she said. "Tell me, what are you going to do about that witness against your client?"

He trudged alongside her. His wingtips were filling with broken clam shell.

"Oh, I'll see if I can discredit him. That's what you do with discreditable people," he said nonchalantly.

"I guess I belong in that category."

"Maybe I can get you jury duty, then. Lately my voir dires—that's when I challenge people—seem to be filled with degenerates and I could use a wholesome all-American girl." He noticed that she perked up with his confident display of power. "My Captain Kidd will walk and live to trade his booty another day."

"Well, I'm glad Earl's in good hands. He can sure use someone with your moral principles."

"Why should I jump into a trench for him and not other people?"

"He has a righteous cause and he's been good to me. But I guess he didn't walk into your office with a big bulging envelope or some hot diamonds that you could give your girlfriend."

Terry let it go. They had reached the knifed teepee. In Allison's life, the cavalry was not on her side. She had been judged a renegade. Several of Tuck Lung's signature boxes had been emptied. Others appeared to have been—stored!

"I ate the fish. That goes off first," she explained, expertly lighting her Coleman stove.

"What do you think you're doing?"

"Heating it. Breakfast for you." She was pulling out spareribs that had lost their red number two dye and become as gray as men with a drinking problem. "They'll taste great."

It was too early to think lucidly or it could have been Allison's loony hardness. Maybe seeing her through the bars of a cell, discussing her crime, would have made him more comfortable and her more amenable.

"Why'd you come back?"

He cut right into the belly of it. "I suppose I feel threatened by you. Can we barter?" He had a sense of risk when he was close to her. "I have whiskey, you have wampum."

She winked. "Then you can take me out to breakfast."

"Milly's, it's near my office."

"Okay, but I need to shower first."

"Should I get some rainwater and heat it in a kettle?"

"No, you can wait and read girlie magazines." Her eyes crept over the dead cat. "I need to be alone with him and bury him properly."

*   *   *

An hour later, Terry was glancing through a *Reader's Digest* in the YWCA downtown. With a false ID, Allison had bullied her way in and demanded extra towels and a hairdryer for which he was forced to leave a twenty-dollar deposit and his driver's license.

Nearing eight, she came out smelling deliciously clean, wearing a cherry red duffel coat, khaki cords, and a fisherman's knit black turtleneck. Her sweeping hair was done in a pretty French roll, held fast by a tortoiseshell comb. Her eyes were clear now. He'd never know from looking at her that she'd passed the night outside.

She had devised a system that suited her outcast state. Bathing at the Y, collecting her clothes at an all-night launderette, insisting that her driver pass by some coffeehouses so she could see if anyone was hanging out that she could scrounge from.

After this visual field check, she said expansively, "Well, I'm ready for the world." Her manner was guarded but friendly. "I hear they have those great homemade pies at Milly's."

"If you behave, I'll introduce you to the creator of them."

"You know everybody, huh, Terry?"

"I'm connected, no question about it."

Christmas was a few days off and Milly's windows were festive with white sleighs and a Santa striding over a gingerbread cake. Through a channel of waitresses in Dutch maid outfits, hellos from them and the regulars, he guided Allison to a window booth toward the rear. Cinnamon, buttery fresh-baked bread, coffee perking, permeated the place. In the confines of the restaurant, it seemed that nothing in the world could possibly go wrong.

Paul Cisco, the assistant district attorney, along with his cohort, Sergeant Barney Laver, were having breakfast with Judge Barry Walsh at a nearby table. They peered over at Terry as Allison was settling in. Terry laid her crutches across the hat rack.

Allison ordered a slice of lemon meringue pie to start

with, followed by the loggers' pork chops and eggs, which she slathered with ketchup and Tabasco, making the plate resemble some smelting process.

On his way out, Judge Walsh was about to stop by. Terry thought he wanted to say something but had changed his mind. He merely squinted at them, whispered to Laver as they headed for the cashier.

Milly came out of the kitchen. She possessed an insinuating professional restaurant owner warmth, immaculately turned out in a green watchplaid suit, red blouse, and Santa earrings. With never a strawberry spark of hair out of place, it was beyond the scope of his imagination to visualize Milly perspiring or in the throes of an orgasm. Yet she and Pat had been getting it on for years. His father claimed she was peerless, a contortionist in the sack.

"Milly, this is Allison." A handshake was exchanged. For a moment, the owner was stymied as she regarded the crimson explosion on Allison's plate.

"Well, hon, you've got the fastest gun in town."

"He's not my lawyer. He hasn't proven himself yet."

"Oh, really?" Milly had been trying to be polite and butted her can in Allison's face. "You just missed your father, Ter. He had to go out to the spec house at River Cove. The subcontractors are at each other's throats again. Never give him a day's peace."

"Well, he's lucky you're here to console him."

"It's mutual. The damned tax man trimmed my tree good." A customer was waving and she was dashing. "Your father said if he comes around again, he'd grind him into my meatloaf."

Terry unnecessarily explained that Milly and Pat had been engaged in romance and repasts for eternity.

"She's been around since I was a kid," he said.

Allison chucked him under the chin. "You never wanted for pies."

"That's true. Have you?"

"Yes." She hit her toast with a wad of marmalade. "I was at the Tillamook Orphanage. Nothing was ever fresh there. Used to pick ants out of the strawberries, plums were rotten. A couple of kids died from the pork. We'd get all the slop they would throw away at the supermarkets. The bread was always stale, gray as death. Crackers tasted like wood shavings."

She fiddled his sympathies with the skill of a virtuoso. He decided not to press her. His lawyer's instinct told him she was ready to start spilling most of the beans. In any event, it was like questioning an alien.

"I ran away when I was fifteen. I go-go danced on and off and cocktail-waitressed."

"What about school?"

"I did pretty well until I left. I was one-six-two on the IQ test for idiots. I always loved art and reading. Read books all the time." She pulled her sodden novel from her backpack, thumbed to her place, and revealed that she was up to the part when the hero seeks a shining mystical knowledge, forsakes commerce and the heart-broken heiress in love with him for a higher goal.

"Would you think of going back to school? You know, take some extension courses at River State."

"No way to pay for it." Allison stirred her coffee reflectively, sloshing her saucer. "Thing is, Terry, what do you do with big tits and no education? Lean over a tie counter in a department store and suckle a lot of jerks? Or I could go to permanent wave college and chop hair. What a life . . . getting up in the morning, going to work wearing a painted smile. Unless you have a skill, it's a hopeless grind. I'd rather be an outsider."

What keenly affected him was that she was not complaining or sponging for sympathy. But it might have been easier if she behaved with waiflike naïveté. He would have preferred Allison helpless, distraught.

"What made you go off and live in a tent?"

"I didn't have much choice. Once my leg was broken . . . it never stopped raining. And I don't mean the weather."

"Couldn't you get unemployment insurance?"

She smoked French cigarettes and lit a Gitane, blowing a haze of acrid blue smoke across the table, and gave a husky laugh. "Yeah, sure. Try collecting for underage go-

go dancing and working bars! And no Social Security card. I finally got one when I turned eighteen." She inhaled deeply, letting the smoke flare out of her nostrils. "Since I broke my leg, the only job I was offered—if you could call it that—was with this jack-off who owns the Paradise Inn. Warren Paris. What a case. He offered me a hundred dollars to . . ." Her face screwed up in revulsion. "Never mind. Give me the tent life any day."

"Actually, I will see Warren Paris on the witness stand shortly."

"Stick it to him."

"I'll do my best."

Terry was due in court and running late but found that he could not pull himself away from her. His motives were not pure and for a moment he detested his cynical interest.

"So when I couldn't pay the rent, I got heaved out of my room and went to stay at the hostel. Seems I was the only woman there who hadn't been battered or raped. Then this motorcycle mamma wanted to get rough. Used to lean up from the lower bunk to eavesdrop under my nightie and offered to find me an old man to *care* for me."

He waited with anticipation but her worldly eyes marked him as a voyeur. Nothing would have surprised him. She was by her own admission a collector of experiences.

"Hah, wouldn't you like to know if I let her?"

He signaled for the check. "Not especially."

"Well, no, I didn't, and if I did, would I tell you? Fact is, I put a crutch through her head. She took forty stitches. And that gentleman, who was going to walk over, recognized me."

"Judge Walsh?"

"I had a problem with his holiness and he put me on probation. Anyway, I like living outdoors."

"Well, we'll have to find a tent repair shop for you."

"Bet they have them in India."

"I have no doubt."

Dropping her at one of her espresso hangouts, he asked if she could type or do secretarial work.

"Sure, but it bores me silly."

"What about filing or research? My associate does divorces and she's looking for an assistant. Georgie'd tell you what she needed and I'd explain how the law library worked. Show you around. You like to read, that's in your favor."

"I'll call you on that one. Let's see. Maybe something better'll come along."

Allison was everything he despised about this anarchic rock generation with their indolence and defiance. But somehow she had caressed him into an unsettling interest. He overcame his ambivalence and wrote his home address and phone number on a business card and she dropped it into her bag.

Forcing it more than he would have liked, he made a date with her for that evening but did not count on her showing up. In any event he knew where to find her. She'd made certain of it.

5

Judge Walsh was hearing the Aristedes case in the old courthouse and called a recess to confer with Terry and Paul Cisco. Cisco had a leonine head, capped by a layered roll of hair dribbling over his forehead, and this fostered an odd resemblance to a dusty piece of Roman statuary. His bison shoulders descended abruptly to a small torso and short legs. Sometimes Terry thought of him as an agitated boar, honking through the woods, blindly impaling his tusks into tree trunks.

They walked past the evidence: clothes racks loaded with coats and suits seized by the police. Apart from a few chilled regulars reserving their seats for the opening arguments in a murder trial that was to follow, only the *Port Rivers Citizen* crime reporter was in attendance.

Mr. Aristedes, Terry's client, was a mustached Greek whose five o'clock shadow was as opaque as a blackboard. He specialized in taking clothing stores and restaurants into bankruptcies of such complexity that no charge had ever stuck. To everyone in court these fine byzantine mosaics, created as they were from obscure Hellenic interconnections and interstices, were incomprehensible.

When Terry whispered to his client to pay attention, the Greek was still examining his Hialeah forecasts in the racing form. Aristedes was a compulsive longshot player. In his liquid brown eyes, a faraway ballet of golden Trojan horses danced. He made prodigious bets based on some Delphic formula. Constantly consulting with his armada of brigand relatives, he furiously waved a clenched fist at his son, demanding that he return to the phone in the corridor and check with the bookie.

Terry went to the bench with Paul Cisco, whose basso profundo in low register vibrated through the room.

"Please moderate your voice, Mr. Cisco," the judge said for perhaps the thousandth time.

"I am, your honor."

"Now, Paul, I don't understand the significance of why tearing out labels on these garments constitutes evidence of a crime."

"Well, sir, the price of a garment would be higher with, say, a Saks Fifth Avenue or Brooks Brothers label. It's their product and that's a retail endorsement of quality."

"Obviously." The judge turned to Terry.

"Judge Walsh, my client is accused of grand larceny for selling garments without a label. Now, it's a common practice for manufacturers who are making clothing for particular stores to remove the labels when they have an overrun or get a cancellation from the retailer in question. They then mark down the goods. Businessmen like Mr. Aristedes buy them at a discount."

"There are no receipts in this transaction," Cisco boomed.

"Aw, come on, Paul. What do you want, provenance for some overcoats? These people live in a cash world."

"Then it's a question for the Internal Revenue Service and not this court, Mr. Brett."

Terry pointed at a reedy man with dyed bluish-black hair and a long, twitching nose. Below his sallow, guttered forehead, his ash eyes were so deeply sunken in their sockets that, from a distance, they seemed glazed by cataracts. "Warren Paris sandbagged Aristedes because of a gambling debt."

"Aristedes bought goods that he knew were stolen," Cisco interjected. "The witness against him is Warren Paris, a known fence with two previous convictions. So Aristedes was clearly aware that he was getting hot merchandise."

"That's what's at issue, Mr. Cisco," the judge reminded him.

"If I may, your honor—" The judge nodded at Terry. "What seems to have occurred is that the supplier, Mr. Warren Paris, and my client had a disagreement."

"How'd the police come to raid the Greek's store?" the judge asked.

For a moment, Cisco was tongue-tied. "The authorities received an anonymous phone call."

"Anonymous, my eye. Mr. Paris called them," Terry said angrily.

"Are you suggesting that citizens aware of criminal activity shouldn't contact the police, Terry?" Cisco demanded with indignation. "Many of the crimes prosecuted by this office have their genesis in such information."

"Genesis or not, Mr. Cisco, you haven't proved that my client *knew* the clothing was stolen," Terry said.

"Well, he'd done business with Warren Paris before. He admitted that. It was a transaction based on experience and empiricism."

"Maybe he read Mr. Paris's mind," Terry countered.

As Cisco was about to begin one of his all-too-familiar fulminations, the judge tapped the bench with his knuckles.

"Mr. Cisco, I hope your office plans to bring a case

against Mr. Paris for setting us all up with a false criminal charge."

"Unfortunately, your honor, he was given immunity."

"Well, then, Mr. Cisco, I'm going to dismiss the state's case for lack of evidence. Next time you come before me, I'd like you to improve the quality of your witnesses."

The three jurists were all friendly, hunting and fishing together, comparing lures, wrangling for shots aside on the golf course, and having a drink at the end of cases. As the attorneys parted ways, Judge Walsh crooked a finger at Terry.

"Terry, that girl you were with at Milly's, is she a client?"

"We're discussing it." He was puzzled. "Is something pending?"

"There could be. She hasn't reported to her probation officer and she has no fixed address."

"I'll tell her there could be serious consequences."

"Do that, Terry. I'd hate to jail her over Christmas."

Terry left the sidebar and took his seat as Walsh intoned his decision.

"The court finds insufficient . . ."

At that moment, oblivious of the court's ruling, Aristedes's son barged through the big wooden doors like a fireman about to rescue someone from an inferno. Terry turned slightly and observed the young man giving the patriarch a double thumbs-up sign. Terry was suddenly engulfed by Aristedes's dancing family members and swarthy clansmen breathing garlic and kissing him. Terry gathered that something more important than his legal victory had occurred in Aristedes's life, for his client virtually levitated from his seat and shouted:

"We win! A double daily. I double, Mr. Brett. Phyllo win second race in photo finish."

"How much?"

"Sixteen thousand. Tonight, you come for dinner at my restaurant. We drink ouzo. We eat and dance. We dance, we eat."

"I have a lady I'm expecting to see."

"Good. Bring her. Plenty food . . . make love, too."

Terry packed up. "I'm sure I'd enjoy that."

"You must come. Bad luck in Greece when victory not celebrated."

Slouching against a wall in the corridor, Earl shook his head at Terry with scornful effrontery. He clutched a thick folder from which mashed, headless clippings were peeking.

"I brought along more evidence for my case against Jonah Wolfe and the Los Angeles Stars. Now I don't know if I should show it to you. I can't believe someone with your talent can waste his time with bullshit like this. Warren Paris is a bad guy to cross. You should've let the Greek drown. This case had nothing do with hot threads. Aristedes is a big bettor. Warren owes him a lot of money and he pulled this stunt because he wanted to welsh."

"You seem very well informed about the underworld, Earl."

"Warren likes me around."

"Everyone does."

In the street, shuffling beside Terry, Earl's scowling eyes matched the murky, darkening afternoon. The Salvation Army Band was singing carols outside Meir & Frank's Department Store and vendors were hawking trees on the corners.

"Well, Earl, I took your Mr. Paris apart. And I thought you of all people were smart enough not to criticize winners."

When Earl couldn't keep pace with Terry, he stopped beside a chestnut wagon, helped himself to a fistful, and growled. Terry stopped, walked back.

Earl flapped the folder in Terry's face. "Far as I'm concerned, Ter, your balls aren't big enough to take on someone of Jonah Wolfe's stature! You're a shark in a sinkhole."

"Find some ambulance chaser to listen to your crap!"

"You want to represent chickenshits like that Greek, then keep hustling." Earl's harangue cut through the festive charivari. "I'm through trying to help you!"

"Did I hear you right? Help me do what?"

"Get you into the big time."

In a dazzling display of fury, Earl dumped the folder on the hot coals and loped across the street. Terry's eyes followed Earl's crazy gait until he crossed into Clark Row, when he lost sight of the bobbing head. Terry rescued the singed envelope and knew the moment he touched it, he had made a ghastly mistake. He was left with the sensation of having swallowed food he was already suspicious of and then trying to bark it out of his throat.

6

Three dirty cups of cappuccino and a pack of unfiltered Gitanes littered the unwiped slate table in the coffeehouse. The jukebox was wailing the Beatles' "Eleanor Rigby" while Allison, the revolutionary, was at a corner table, reading a tattered copy of some fugitive scandal sheet whose agit-prop headline called for armed insurrection against the republic. On the wall behind her were blurry photos and mimeoed announcements of folk singers "Coming to Stradivarius," the name of this intellectuals' hangout. She glanced up with some surprise when Terry sat down.

"Hi, what're you doing here?"

"Didn't we have a date?"

She was embarrassed and curiously diffident; for an instant, he wondered how to pierce the wall of bravado.

"I thought you were being polite."

"Not exactly. Now that my office is closed, I thought maybe we could run a few more of your errands. Got any stuff at the cleaners?"

"Why're you being so defensive?"

"I'll tell you. After I left court, I had an extremely unpleasant conference with your therapist Earl."

"That was a downer. I saw him. He sure was steaming. Didn't even talk to me." She paused. "You lose?"

"No. Ref stopped it on cuts. TKO in the first round. Mr. Cisco couldn't continue."

"Wow. You kicked his ass." She reached for Terry's hand and slapped the palm. "You get a bop for that!"

"Do you want to stay here?"

"No, not really. Can we go somewhere for a drink?"

He reached for the check, but she stopped him and threw down a five-dollar bill. "I have money."

"My client invited us for dinner. Do you like noise and Greeks?"

"Greek food? I've never had it. Is it greasy?"

"Shall I call and ask?"

"Probably is. I love greasy food. What's the party for, anyway?"

"A banquet celebrating Greek freedom and race-horses."

"Will they smash glasses?"

"I would hope so. I'll be there to guarantee their legal rights."

"Terry, you're a party all by yourself."

And so was Allison. On the way to Aristedes's restaurant, he tried to keep his eyes off her and fell into a cozier role—officer of the court, purveyor of legal expertise, defender of the wronged. He told her about Judge Walsh's warning. She half listened, then drifted off into a meditative spaciness.

"I have a P.O. box. Isn't that a fixed address?"

"Only if you were actually, physically, living in the post office. Your tent is not on the RFD route."

"Yeah, I've got to do something about that."

She was worried and he regretted his bad timing. Sprinkles laminated the window and the wind furled the flag when he passed the central fire station and turned into Old Town with its last hint of the city's seafaring history. The old wharf taphouses were filled with rummy sailors and fishermen.

The sound of glasses breaking and Melina Mercouri seductively singing "Never on Sunday" informed them they had reached Piraeus. Terry held the door for Allison and they entered an asylum filled with dancing men with whale-tail mustaches. Bouzoukias twanged, a whole lamb was being spit-roasted over charcoal, and the air was densely humid with body odor. At long wooden tables, bottles of retsina stood like the columns of Corinth. The Glory that was Greece had found its Great Northwest outpost on the trade route.

Allison said: "This looks like it's going to be a howl. Smells good, too."

A man resembling Anthony Quinn blocked their way. "Sorry, this private party tonight."

Suddenly, Aristedes sprang forward, upsetting the choreography of the dancers for a moment, and spat out a torrential explanation in Greek. Allison leaned against Terry, trying to comprehend the babble.

"Many apologies, Mr. Terry Brett," the counterfeit Quinn said, bowing. "You very lucky for us. We all hit daily double." Apparently this was the cause of the revel and not Terry's courtroom triumph.

Within the troupe of male dancers, one glided to the floor, stooped, picked up with his lips a glass filled with wine, and without spilling a drop succeeded in drinking it. Applause and shoes stomping the floor greeted this Olympian feat. The gymnast bowed and resumed dancing.

"You want to dance the *Zeibekiko*. It is drunken man's celebration," Aristedes informed him, then tugged his arm before realizing he was also dragging Allison.

"A little later maybe," Terry said.

"Okay, I show you *Chasapiko*. It is butcherman's dance. Easier." He gave Allison a courtly bow. "Now you, Lady and Mr. Terry Brett, you enjoy." He wove a path through the celebrants, found places for them at the head table, and, with a flurry of lubricating compliments, introduced them to his flock.

Terry whispered, "Aristedes beat his new bookie for sixteen grand today while I was fighting to keep his ass out of prison. He couldn't have been less worried about his trial."

"Maybe there's a lesson to be learned," she said.

"Like what?"

"Get yourself Terry Brett to do your worrying."

From somewhere a wing chair and footstool appeared for Allison's comfort. A waiter filled short, stubby glasses with ouzo, chips of irregular ice, and water. With childlike enthusiasm, Allison flicked the glass.

"What a rush! I love the color it turns," she said of the pale milky transformation.

Allison's pleasure was so endearing that another chink in Terry's armor vanished. She had traded a Gitane for a ropy cigar, which she puffed on merrily. She was also a tireless toaster with the Greeks and a drinker of great lustiness. They switched to retsina with their orgy of charred pink lamb. She loved the bone and went at it with ferocity. Her lips drizzled fat and he wanted to lick them.

"I wish I could dance with them. When my leg's better, I'd like to come back and learn how to do it."

"It's reserved for the men."

"Oh, bullshit, this is America." She laughed and kissed him on the cheek. "You're supposed to be a knight of the court." She was serious and leaned on his shoulder for support. "Aren't you here to protect my rights, too?"

"When your leg's better, Allison, I want to dance with you all night."

"We'll see." She blinked and giggled without innocence. "I don't wear much when I dance."

"Good, deal the last one down and dirty."

"Ah, Ter, you don't want to tangle with me."

He didn't know how to resolve the issue of Allison's legal sleeping requirements without swallowing her with his hunger. Rain peeled off oncoming headlights and in silence he rambled around the Old Town streets in his car with her. He couldn't handle another turndown. When she asked to be dropped back at the Strad, a wave of morose indignation clouded his face and she tuned in to his mood.

"I know you want to play around with me."

He was befuddled by the warring emotions within him.

His eagerness to be with her yielded to disquiet about her survival and the fear that she could be headed for jail. "To tell the truth, Allison, what I had in mind wouldn't have put you under any obligation."

"I think I believe *you* believe what you're saying. But from the time I was five, men have been taking shots at me."

He helped her out of the car and followed her, watching the crutches skid on the icy pavement. Marijuana fumes engulfed them amid the yapping sounds of the coffee bar. A man with a mellow, stoned expression waved at her. He was lanky and tall. He wore a Che Guevara mustache and combat beret rakishly drooping over his left eye. He opened his arms, but Allison was suddenly guarded and she clawed the air like a spitting alley cat. The man's amicable smile gave way to alarm.

"Thanks for the ride, Terry. I've got to go see this bozo."

"Why?"

"He could've been one of my visitors the other night." She greeted danger as though it were a natural force and nothing to become alarmed about.

"Want me to stay? As your adviser."

"He'll need a lawyer when he hears what I have to say."

Terry refused to relinquish her and for a moment they appeared again to physically struggle. "Allison . . ."

"I know you want to help, but not now. This is strictly personal."

"When will I see you again?"

"I'll be in touch."

"I'm pushing," he said, irritated with himself for stating what was obvious.

"Guys do. But it's okay, I can see you're one of the good ones." She hugged him. "Don't worry, I'll be around."

He departed in a quandary of doubt, mostly about himself. Skidding home on the slick country roads, the sting of battling for a lost cause had entered his soul.

7

He was relieved to be on his own. His father was staying over at Milly's. He was in no mood to share the mortification of being rebuffed by Allison again. But he yearned for her. He lay on the sofa, watching TV, feeling worthless. After a while, he switched off a replay of a basketball game and sat in the darkness with an empty bottle of beer. He realized where he'd gone wrong. He had been pleading and she despised him. He had not been in a situation like this before, voracious, in desperate pursuit. The cool detachment so prized by his clients had deserted him. The girls he dated were only too willing to clasp hold of him. The only tactic that might have worked with Allison was indifference.

Any number of things separated them, particularly their upbringing. In the years after the death of his mother, Terry's childhood had been marked by such emotional sunlight and incandescent joy that he did not have to dwell on her loss. His inclination was to be open with people, except in his practice. Wariness was a natural reflex for Allison. Images of her topless on stage, radiating sex to the fantasy seekers who congregated in those clubs, taunted him.

Drifting into sleep, he became an imaginary voyeur of her past. He saw her naked. Her big firm breasts thrashing against each other to some strident rock 'n' roll blast of sound while the audience of workingmen with tattooed arms drooled or felt her up as she passed through the tables for tips. Years back, he had gone to a few smokers at those places and had seen a girl scooping bills off the stage by squeezing the lips of her vagina together. The gyrating pincer movement astonished and repelled him.

Allison . . . Allison . . . Have you had to do that?

Trapped by spectral naked, sweating, heavy male bodies entwined with hers, he heard echoes of questions in the subconscious mist of his dreams.

Glass . . . Glass . . . Glass was shattering in the chamber of his mind. The sound woke him, startled. Someone was in the house! Terry leaped out of bed and took his gun from the desk drawer.

Pat had not returned home. Once before, they had a visitor of this kind. Pat and he had reconnoitered on the landing. Terry had taken the backstairs and Pat the front. Both of them dead shots with their Commander .45s. They had sandwiched the burglar in the living room and he had pissed his pants when Pat said: "It's your turn. You shoot him, Terry."

"Sure."

The burglar had keeled over. They thought he'd had a stroke. The fire department had to revive him.

Terry's hearing was now acute, heightened by his angry sense of danger. On tiptoe, he clung to the wall that led into the laundry room and from there into the kitchen. If the intruder were there, he was lost, with nowhere to run or hide.

This time, I'm going to smoke this bastard, Terry told himself.

Looking behind him, he heard clopping sounds near the entry. With an agile move, he switched on the light and instantly assumed the two-handed shooting position.

"No! Don't! Shit, no, please!"

Allison trembled and with arms raised, stumbling, fell back against the door.

"You almost missed your birthday." He slipped on the safety. "Why didn't you ring the doorbell?"

"It didn't work." They stood there, staring at each other. Her skin was pallid, breathless with fright. "You scared me. My heart's exploding."

He led her into the kitchen and poured them monster shots of brandy. She took a long gulp, still shivering. He walked around her as though examining a big cat in the zoo.

"Is this the way it has to be?" he asked. "You make

the moves and I wait patiently. Is this your mating ritual?"

"I don't know. Something like that, I guess."

"Okay, I'm in your power," he said with a smile.

"Can I stay, then?"

"We don't take personal checks. Just let me have your Diner's Club and I'll run it through the machine."

"Actually, you're very funny."

"That's the way I disarm my conquests. Oh, and at four in the morning I never lose my sense of humor. How was the summit meeting?"

"Worked out just fine."

"You met the man who tore your place apart?"

"No, but I found out who was responsible," she announced, dead calm.

"You don't seem upset or vindictive."

" 'Vindictive'? Pardon?"

"I meant, you're not looking for revenge."

"Oh, I'll get even. But you can't bring back the dead. My cat will eat his eyes in the next world."

"That's seems like reasonable punishment."

"You know, I wouldn't mind some sleep."

He switched on the lights in the living room and observed her peering around with curiosity. It was a place of comfort, neat and warm, with occasional feminine touches. Last year Milly had taken over the role of interior decorator and picked out print curtains and the new tweed sofas. They blended in with dark brown leather armchairs facing each other in front of the massive copper-hooded fireplace. Overhead, a domed skylight created the effect of an atrium. He and his father had spent many evenings looking through the trees at the stars. It was a home meant for relaxing and conversation. A gleaming yew wood trolley held crystal decanters of liquor, and old, thick Waterford glasses that had been in his mother's family. Brightly wrapped gifts laced a fourteen-foot Christmas tree that was dwarfed by the high ceiling.

"Do you live alone?"

"No, with my father. Two bachelors."

"What about the pie lady?"

"They use her place when they're feeling romantic."

"How come?"

"My father's hypocritical sense of propriety. It's a heady cocktail . . . equal parts sham and self-preservation. But he's a charmer and they rule the world. He doesn't want to get married. My mother died when I was a kid; he used me as an excuse to avoid any kind of commitment with Milly. To tell the truth, I love him to death."

Allison explored the house. She was awestruck and appeared intimidated. "Your house is so beautiful."

"Yep. My father built it. Patrick Brett, he's the best contractor in the county. But he'll never get the big municipal jobs because he doesn't pay graft."

"Everything's so complicated when you're straight."

"And the other way?" He was going to say *her* way, but caught himself.

"It's very direct. You grab it and run."

They stood at the bottom of the staircase and she turned to look at the shattered door glass, the icicles hanging over the lock.

"Is your dad going to be very sore about this?"

"No, he'll send a glazier over from one of his jobs." Terry set down their brandy glasses. "How're you with stairs?"

"Up they're a problem, down I do fine. Dr. Flannigan promised I'll be able to use a cane real soon. My Christmas present and I can hardly wait for it."

He leaned her crutches against the mahogany banister post and lifted her in his arms. Her hands clasped the back of his neck and her fingers touched his hair. She let her head drop on his chest. Her body was solid and there was a scent of the Greek wine on her breath. Her breast huddled against his chest. He took the steps with lingering diligence, holding her close. His frustration momentarily subsided. In its place her intoxicating sweetness overcame him. He tenderly carried her into the guest bedroom and laid her on the bed. He stood over her for a moment staring as she curled up against the pillow.

"I'll go down for your crutches and the brandy. There's an ashtray on the table."

In a few moments he was back. He laid out a set of his pajamas, his red-striped robe, and a pair of jockey shorts. He opened a door, switched on the light, and pointed to a bathroom with a pine-surround bath and a mirrored stall shower.

"Is there anything else I can get you?"

She was almost tearful and he stroked her face, then lightly pressed his lips against her forehead.

She shook her head. "Terry, no one's ever been so kind."

" 'Night, Allison."

Like a circling hawk, he flew off, leaving elusive prey.

In the morning he heard Pat thundering in, followed by irate sounds of puzzled consternation.

"What the hell? Terry—Boy? You alive? Terrrrrr!"

Unshaven, hair tousled, in a thick woolen bathrobe, Terry loped out of the kitchen. He had put on coffee and was eating a fried egg sandwich.

"We've got a houseguest for Christmas, Pat."

"Don't tell me you dragged in that asshole, Earl."

"Would I bring home anyone you wouldn't like?"

"Aw, come on. Cut it out, Ter. What gives?"

"This girl I met. It's a little awkward."

His father was uncertain. "You serious?"

"Uh-huh." A piece of glass that Terry had missed sweeping up scrunched under Pat's boot. "Allison lost her footing."

"Long as she doesn't sue us," he said good-naturedly.

Pat was tickled, wrapped an arm around Terry, and they were boys together again. He amiably mocked his son. "They're breaking the doors down to get to you. All that malarkey about someone you can't live without. You're a real master of deceit."

"She's sort of a client."

Pat's shoulders heaved through guttural laughter and he sprayed the air with the ash of his Camel cigarette. "Oh, come on, Terry, you're talking to me. Was your lady late with her legal fees? Hey, I know what it's like when some little witch can't hack her kitchen remodel bill."

"It's nothing like that. She slept in the guestroom."

"You trying to make a good impression on me, or what?" He had lost interest. "In any case, with Christmas falling on Sunday, Milly decided to leave today. I've got to throw some gear in a bag, then we'll be driving over to Seacliff. Harry's shot·some wild goose for us. And those sauces Carol makes are what paradise is all about. Get yourself ready, we'll be leaving in an hour."

"Sorry, I won't be joining you"

"What? I don't get it, Terry. I put in a request for Carol to do the oyster stuffing for you. Bring your client along. There'll be plenty of food."

"Her name's Allison and I have to drive her over to Good Samaritan. She broke her leg and has to do physio-therapy."

Pat's emotions lived on the surface and he was having difficulty reconciling Terry's break in tradition with family plans. Milly also owned a small diner on the coast in Seacliff, which her brother Harry and his wife managed. It blossomed in the summer, but, apart from locals, was funereal in the baying winter winds. Since childhood, the Christmas Eve visit had become a ritual.

Puzzled, Pat said, "Okay, I'll tell them. No hard feelings."

Terry suspected that there were hard feelings, for Pat's proprietary interests had been threatened. "Bring my presents for Harry and Carol with you."

"Sure." His father was disappointed and perplexed. "They were counting on seeing you." After a moment of silence, Pat yielded. "What'd you get Milly for Christmas?"

"A cashmere twin set at Meir's."

"Oh, Christ, so did I!"

"You didn't tell me. She's got ten bathrobes. I couldn't do that to her again. Suppose I exchange mine?"

"You're the prince of sons."

Pat glanced up to the top of the stairs and saw Allison

standing at the top step. He turned an amused, cynical eye on Terry and whispered, "Got yourself a *Playboy* playmate there. Look-it, I'll be in and out and you and your client can continue your conference. See you Christmas morning."

Pat started up the stairs and Allison was moving down at the same time, hanging on to the banister with one hand and slanting the crutch with the other, forcing him back down.

"I'm sorry about your doorpane," she said.

"Don't bother about me, honey. I'm just Mr. Terry's handyman and chairman of the welcoming committee."

"Allison, this is Pat. And he's in a good mood."

There was no hand to grasp and he patted her shoulder in an awkward comradely fashion as though she'd made a strike in the tenth frame.

"How'd your problem go, Mr. Brett?" Pat was stymied. "The spec house you're building in River Cove."

"Just fine, honey. Everyone's suing everyone. Story of my life. That's why my boy's a lawyer."

"You're a master builder. Your house is a castle. Some day when I'm rich enough, I'd like you to build one for me."

"Cost plus fifteen percent for a *client* of Terry's. Find yourself a lot, and it's done."

"In India."

"India? Well, angel, I don't know if my license is good there. Maybe you don't need one. Pull the permits and I'll just put on a turban and we'll start pouring concrete. Forgive me, got to run now. Nice meeting you."

"Please tell Milly her pies are the best in the world."

Sucking in his gut, Pat ran his eyes up and down Allison as though appraising a good river-view property.

"She'll be glad to hear that, thank you, Allison," he said, puckering his lips into a smile. "You make yourself at home."

A fan of the slick move, the head feint without traveling, Terry was impressed by the way Allison dealt herself a pair of back-to-back aces with Pat. She picked up domestic trivia and used it as a spearhead. He guided his ward into the kitchen. She sat on a bar stool and poured herself some coffee. Terry hadn't seen her with a good night's sleep: the fatigue had been razed off her face. His ardor was restrained. He'd give her a little taste of his professional coolness.

"You okay?"

"Just fine. The bed was very comfortable."

"I'll be back in a minute."

Pat was ramming his plaid lumberjack and cords into a canvas bag when Terry walked into his bedroom.

"She's a lost kid, Pat."

"I just got off the boat from Dublin, I'll believe anything."

"I really like her," he said cautiously. "I don't know, there's something about her."

"Put her on a slice of toast and skip the jam. I'll see you Christmas morning, lover."

8

I recommend Lily of France," Selma said, her thick glasses dangling on an elastic cord. The plump manageress of the ladies' department at Meir's claimed to have ruined her eyesight examining miniature printed tags on ladies' undies. "It was Marilyn Monroe's brand."

"I didn't know she wore underwear."

"Don't get smart with me, Terry. Now you have to give me a size."

Terry extended his hands and made balls with his fists. "She's a good-size girl—woman."

"The cup is the key."

"Is this something numerical?" he asked. "Like an equation?"

"Try the alphabet—from B to D."

When Selma had been in Boys Wear, she used to measure his closed fist for socks by wrapping the heel and toe on it. She opened her palm and winked. "Come on,

Terry, I'm not going to tell anyone. Is it more than a handful? Apples or melons?"

"I'm not sure, Selma. Is bountiful a size?"

"Well, dear, you have no right to be buying her garments of this kind. This calls for further investigation on your part."

He had dropped Allison at the hospital and was due to pick her up shortly. Killing time, he had wandered through the store, finally exchanged Milly's twin set for a pair of gold earrings, and found himself with a large credit.

"I think I'll go with the negligée set and the Joy."

He. was pleased with himself. Allison could unwrap the perfume in front of the drop-in guests. The diaphanous black nightgown and matching top also included an inexplicit satin covering with an elastic waist that had the presumption of panties. This pink box he planned to present to her privately, augmenting her Christmas.

He had never bought a woman anything like it. It went with the three-day hard-on he'd been carrying around like a hunchback. He thought if Allison just smiled, it would erupt. Terry hid his booty in the trunk.

He reflected on their morning together at his house. The weather had been particularly serene, with glorious rainbow plaques of ice refracting the light from the river waves. Before they went downtown to the hospital, she trudged through the hoarfrost out to the point. Terry was watching her from inside while Pat's glazier cut the glass and Terry puttied it.

Terry locked up and backed his car to the edge so that she wouldn't have far to walk.

"I'd like a wigwam here."

"I'll see if my dad's got some pull." He was teasing her, then saw she was upset.

"*You.* You rich people have it all, so it doesn't matter what the fog is made of and that the air is poisoned. While you're barbecuing, people like me are drinking the water you piss in."

"I didn't mean it that way, Allison. The house is beautiful and I never take it for granted."

Ablaze with excitement, he drove from the department store back to the hospital to pick her up after her therapy. He spotted her huddled in her duffel coat at the bus stop bench, still plodding her way through the novel.

"Don't tell me you were going to leave?"

"I left you a note at the reception desk."

"What the hell're you talking about?"

"I'm sorry, I've got this draggy stuff to do. First down to the Greyhound station, then to drop off my cocktail outfits at the place I used to work in. It's all a lot of garbage. And I thought you'd be bored silly. After all, it is Christmas Eve."

"How were you going to get around?"

"The buses are running."

"Weren't you going to come back to the house?"

Allison was silent, and the downtown bus was turning into the curb stop. Its doors were already open. The driver craned his neck, saw her pick up her crutches, and squeezed out of his seat, ready to do his good deed and help her on.

"Allison!"

"I'm afraid of you." Terry's intensity mingled with outrage, and some foreign emotion she had not detected, a latent savagery, sprang out of him that made her freeze. "I don't want to mess you around. I'm so attracted to you, Terry. It makes me dizzy. It's never been this way—with anyone."

Had he heard right? Terry flushed, his skin felt bitten. *I must have her.*

As she vacillated, the bus driver was on the top step, listening. "Are you coming, young lady?"

"I'll catch the next one, thanks." The bus doors closed. "Terry, please let me go. You must have plans . . . parties . . . a lawyers' binge with a stripper jumping out of a cake."

"That's for stockbrokers."

"Not *just* them."

He nodded stoically and no longer had interrogatories about her hardscrabble life or previous employment.

"We'll do whatever errands you have to do, together. Okay?"

As he placed his arm on her shoulder, she moved it away and slid off his glove and pressed his warm palm against her cheek. He couldn't breathe. He eased her body close, savoring her mouth. He pressed his lips to her cheek and she turned away.

"Not now . . . I want us to be on our own and do things properly."

He parked outside the bus depot. She had some fugitive belongings, a bag in a locker, and she took the key out. He forcibly prevented her from going to pick it up.

"Stop giving me a hard time, Allison."

"I can do it," she protested. "It's no hassle. Another day or two and I won't need crutches."

"That's great news. Now sit tight, I'll be back in a minute with the queen's spoils."

"Terry, I want to talk to you about me."

Since the orphanage, she had existed in firetraps, trailers, crash pads—sleazy rooms she rented in apartments, subletting a sublet, which evolved into pyramid clubs of tenancy. Whoever the landlord seized in the hallway got nailed for rent.

"It's all going to be different for you now," he said, about to leave the car. She grabbed the tail of his coat, but he bolted out. The terminal was quiet on Christmas Eve, apart from a band of winos talking to themselves and waiting for handouts. A Salvation Army crew cornered him. Terry was feeling terrific and contributed a sawbuck to the collection and was blessed.

He found the lockers through this legion of lost, displaced loiterers, their loneliness affecting him, and he included Allison among them.

How can she live this way?

He returned from the bus station carrying a heavy black vinyl tote bag and slung it in the backseat.

He hugged her. "I got your precious cargo."

"Captain Kidd, the gentleman pirate."

"With his cutlass."

"I read about him in the old *Classic Comics*." And then

as he moved close to Allison, she held his face in her palms. "I want you to understand that pirates kill people even today."

Fueled by unrealized passion, Terry drove through the snow-caked road along the river with his treasure. Located about an hour north of Port Rivers through tongues of muddied dirt roads, the Paradise Inn overlooked a forgotten bay of the Columbia River. It had gone through a series of convulsions before its present rebirth. In the midst of timber country, it had been a trading post for the early settlers who came to the end of the Western Trail in their Conestoga wagons. Remnants of its conquered Indian civilization had been pacified and the white man had purchased bear skins, cured venison from the great deer herds, and stolen the giant salmon that once populated the waters.

There were any number of elements that made the region appealing: the Chinook would smoke the salmon with dark sugar over alder wood; the tantalizing spruce-fir-pine smells of the heroic rain forest, hooded by the Cascade Range; sunsets of such effulgence that the dancing river seemed to be adorned with a diamond and ruby necklace. Paradise Cove had always attracted individuals whose holistic visions of nature were by turns romantic and inconclusive.

Now its environs were something of an outdoor mission, attracting hippies who lived on antiwar ideals and the Beatles' music. Preaching the return to mother nature, they walked naked and foraged for food. These commune people preferred the growl of grizzly bears to working in stuffy offices and punching clocks.

At one time Allison had lived nearby and enjoyed guitar nights, listening to the magical insights of doped spellbinders explaining the sources of the universe, the meaning of life. Allison herself had been guilty of understanding everything about everything. The mysteries were all solved. With the snap and bark of daily life absent, nothing remained but to experience ecstasy.

Along the line, the Paradise Inn had been bought, sold

several times, traded and bartered, gone bankrupt, and had its character altered. It had been converted from a convivial haven for hunters and fishermen into a coruscating vision of splays of fuchsia neon light. The welcome mat was out for liberated encounter groups encouraged to cheat on their spouses and take part in revelries. The atmosphere was rife with plots of infidelity and wife swapping.

Terry had vaguely heard of the place. It was in an unincorporated hamlet and considered outlaw territory. Bikers rode in, raised hell, and on weekends the jukebox never stopped. For a price, the bikers' mamas would come to the rooms of those groups of hunters getting away from city life and their wives.

The Paradise Inn bar was about forty feet long with a massive mirror that seemed to magnify the packs of salesmen, groupies, hustlers, the commune dwellers, everyone on the make, everyone looking to get high. Terry had always avoided these hellholes with their scurfy, drugged residents. He saw in them the future, the ruin of families and dispossessed children.

Clattering in spike heels on a platformed stage, a pair of topless vampires in g-strings bounced around to piercing music. They were getting their fannies stroked by a crew of nail pounders who were sitting ringside below the dwarfish stage.

"Christ, what a meat market," Terry said.

"Everything is. Look, I told you not to come."

"I still don't know why the hell we're here."

"For me to get paid—and even. If you want to split, I can hang out here and crash with one of the girls."

"Don't be crazy."

She signaled one of the bartenders and Terry recognized him. Allison had met him at the Strad coffeehouse.

He swished over in a ballet pirouette. "Allison, you're wild. I hope you're not still sore?"

"No, Randy. Long as you explained the rules to Warren." He nodded and gestured to a figure at the rear of the bar. "It's all settled. You better not disappoint him."

"I'm here, aren't I?" Allison fired back. She stroked

Terry's neck. "Hang in like a good boy for a few minutes." Over the din, she shouted: "Set my friend up."

"I didn't know Warren Paris owned this place," Terry said.

"Yes." She giggled. "You did him in court, I intend to carve him up here. Then, my sweet, I'll rub your back and we'll watch *Holiday Inn* on TV and sing 'White Christmas' with Bing Crosby."

Allison squealed with laughter and her breasts bounced under the tight tank top. A characteristic furrowing of the brow and broad smile, which revealed slightly crooked teeth, accompanied her treacheries. Terry roped the vinyl bag around her neck. She looked adorable, a female St. Bernard. Allison was not beautiful, she was beyond that. He knew he had found the alluring girl he'd been subconsciously and dreamily searching for. And try as he might, he could not oppose the force of her emotional and physical gravity, which had altered the laws that balanced him. He witnessed his life slipping off its axis and was incapable of avoiding the collision.

Allison hugged him. "I won't be long, so don't go away."

After a third tequila shooter, Terry grew concerned and headed for the room he had seen Allison enter. He knocked on the door. Allison poked her head out. A flinty, abrupt smile crossed her face.

"Give me five more minutes."

She closed the door and he returned to the bar. Almost forty minutes later, banging back his fifth shooter, Terry became so angry he decided to leave. As he was signing his Diner's Club receipt, Allison reappeared and nuzzled up against him.

"We're off, Terry," she said with a weary grimace. She signaled the bartender. "Give me a bottle of Yukon Jack, Randy."

"You can't take it out."

"I know. It's to settle a bet about the proof."

Randy reached to the top shelf. "Here you go."

Allison took the bottle, reared back, and flung it

against the mirror behind the bar. People screamed and ducked as the glass shattered.

Warren Paris ran out of the office toward Allison. As though threatened by a lioness over a kill, his crouched bony figure, features distorted by rage, was hyenalike.

"You fucking bitch, I'll hack your head off for this," he said in a voice in which brutality and a nasal whinny combined in a savage authenticity.

Allison defiantly raised one of her crutches. "You're calling me a fucking bitch? I forgot to tell you, Warren, my cat asked to be remembered," she calmly added.

Warren Paris stared icily at her, immobilized by the spectators, who wondered if he were going to strike her. Terry burst between them.

"I see you got your little shark with you, Allison."

Allison picked up a shard of mirror glass from the bartop. "Listen, you scumhead, next time you want to take naked pictures of me walking on crutches, I'll cut your eyes to pieces." She flung the fragment on the floor and it spat on his shoes.

"Next time, Allison, I'll bring two bricks. One for you and one for your fucking lawyer."

"Here's my business card, Warren, or would you like me to stay and kick your ass through your teeth right here," Terry said, clenching his fists.

"Fuck you, Brett, and get out with that scavenger."

On the parking lot, the rush of cold air shocked Terry's system into cloudy sobriety. At his car, he swayed against Allison.

"Warren was the one who chopped up my tent. I was just returning the favor. When the Indian villages were burned to the ground, didn't they go after the white settlements?"

His blood roiled with outrage. "Yes, they did. I'm going back to deck him."

"Terry, give me the car keys, you've had too much to drink. My right leg's fine. I can brake and hit the gas."

"Maybe you're right. Warren's going to call the police. I'll be with you when they book you. The judge'll release you in my custody."

"Police? What're you talking about?"

"You're not afraid of Warren calling the cops?"

"With about a thousand tabs of acid sitting in his office? Plus betting slips. Not to mention his stable of hookers." Terry reeled against his car and clapped a hand against his forehead. "Get in," she commanded.

"What if he comes after you?"

She winked. "Well, you've been waiting to use that big .45 of yours on someone."

In the Mustang, Allison's mind switched gears. "What guts they've put into this baby," she said, tooling up to 110. "What a sweetheart. Sucks into the road like wet gravel."

"What was really going on with you and Warren?"

"Don't ask."

"I have to know if my suspicion is justified."

Her cheeks puffed out and she exhaled heavily. "These days, it's you do this for me and I'll do something for you. Along the way, people screw each other over. Can we please leave it now?"

"No. Warren wanted more than for you to pose for him, didn't he?"

She pulled into his driveway and tapped the steering wheel approvingly.

"Warren tried to burn me. I was holding the acid. He tried to beat me for it and not pay. I would've been left in the middle with some very bad dudes who live on the commune. I had to pour some vinegar in his coffee and see how he liked it."

"So naturally you gave me a tale from the *Arabian Nights* about returning your cocktail outfits."

"Warren thought the acid tabs were in my tent. But I'd already hidden them in the locker at the bus depot."

"That's why you got rid of me when you saw that bartender, Randy, in the Strad coffeehouse?"

"Yes. Randy came to tell me Warren would be willing to make peace and not kill me if I came across. I made sure he paid first."

"So in a sense you were running a kind of pizza delivery service."

"Don't get cute."

The effect of the tequila had evaporated and he blinked incredulously. "The drugs were in the bag I carried out from the bus locker."

After a moment, she nodded. "I do what I have to."

"But *I* brought them out and transported them in my car!"

"Goddamn it, Terry, I tried to stop you! To protect you. Don't you know? I was going to take the bus, wasn't I?" She was screaming and her smoky breath hissed against the window. "Wasn't I? I wouldn't involve you in this!"

9

As she drove up to his house, his brain churned with the knowledge that Allison was an outlaw. He had surmised as much but conveniently blocked it out. She had subjected him to the most extraordinary peril of his life and he had gullibly submitted. As a party to a trifling settlement between petty criminals, Allison could have ruined him. She had calmly set him up as her accomplice.

"Well, let's say good-bye, Terry. And please don't think too harshly of me. I'll shoot down to the Y and get a room. May I call a taxi? Is that okay with you?" she asked, as though the possibility of her coming into the house would require a momentous decision.

"At the rate we're going, I may kill you. I don't know what the hell to do with you."

"I could sleep in the car. If you don't trust me, take the keys."

"Damn you, Allison, cut it out!"

Her technique of baiting him was infuriating. Something about her behavior sucked him into a maze. He had no way of escaping, of finding daylight.

"Do you have the fixings for a chocolate milk shake?"

"What? What're you talking about?"

"Add a raw egg to it. It'll neutralize the booze. It's like the white cells attacking germs. I promise you, you won't have a hangover."

Once in the kitchen, Allison peered in the freezer and suggested Boston cream pie with the milk shake. They sat there like teenagers on an icebox raid. With whipped cream on her nose, Allison was no longer a maniac destroying the Paradise Inn, but a vagabond kid, paying back an adult who had abused her.

"You didn't meet Earl at the hospital?"

"No, we were both at the club. Earl is one of Warren's errand boys. He drives the girls home at night, collects bets—whatever Warren asks him. Well, when I had my accident, Earl took over. I had nobody and he proved to be a real friend. Recommended I go see Dr. Flannigan and he put me in physiotherapy."

Terry probed as though he had her on the stand. In court, this technique enabled him to provoke witnesses into indiscretions. Just get them angry enough.

"Question."

She shook her head and sighed. "If you really must."

"All those drugs. Do you have any idea what effect they can have on the people who buy them?"

"Where's this leading, Ter?"

"To some ill-defined area sometimes known as conscience and more generally morality."

"The Buddha had an explanation for my behavior. He called it: 'The craving for nonexistence.' "

"I suppose if a cop pulled us over and found the drugs, I could claim no contest, since it would be evident that I had a similar craving."

"Well, maybe you just do."

He was actually feeling better from the potions and energized by debate. He was going to wring her neck.

"You want to be evasive, fine. Just don't insult me with all this mystical trash."

Storm clouds raced into her blue eyes and he could see the pulse in her neck throb again. Her body was wrenched by tremors.

"Morality! Morality!" she shrieked, and the word

sounded like automatic gunfire. "When I was with my third foster family, living in a trailer park, the guys used to tail me to the shower house, beat their meat, and slosh their come on the window when I was inside. Man, I couldn't see daylight. So don't you preach morals to me."

Wounded, a rage of tears and frustration coursed down her cheeks. She wiped her face with the back of her hand. "I've lived in hostels. On the street with winos eating out of restaurant garbage bins. Morality," she said, seething, "that's for people like you who've never been in want."

"Allison, I'm sorry."

She tried to catch her breath. "I was a foundling. Do you know what that means? 'A deserted or abandoned child of unknown parentage.' I am an outcast. I want to be *reborn*. Is that so wrong? Ever since I can remember, I didn't want to be me. Never mind." She lunged to her feet. "Now this—oh, fuck it, nothing matters."

"For Chrissake, don't go. I want you to stay."

She seemed doubtful, then she slumped on the table, too exhausted to resist.

"Thank you. I appreciate it. But you can turn me out Christmas morning. You'd best protect your friends, and your sugar-coated daddy and the pie queen from dangerous little me."

No doubt about it, Allison was winning, spinning his world upside down. At every turn, she had some flippant rationalization or crafty intuition that slashed through his common sense. Her eyes were bloodred. But finally she gave him a contrite smile.

"I know I was wrong to do this, get you involved as a courier," she said. "But Jesus, don't you realize yet, I'd never do anything to hurt you. See, I trust you. Which I guess is more than you can say for me."

"I'm as confused as you are."

"Can I take some pie up to bed?"

He again helped Allison upstairs to the guest bedroom and left her. After he showered, he remembered he had her Christmas gifts in the car trunk. He put on a robe, grabbed his keys, and heard her splashing in the bath. He called through the door.

"Want a drink. Water? Anything?"

"No thanks, really, I'm fine."

He yearned to hold her, fix all the broken pieces within her. He carried the box upstairs and set it down outside the open door of her room.

She lay naked on the bed, balancing the pie plate on her navel and scooping out curls of cream with her fingers. The bedside table held a smoking water pipe with a red-hot ash of grass. She gave him a dazed, lambent, lazy smile and crooked her finger. Helen of Troy calling Paris. She was worth war, scorched earth. He stood bolted to the floor as she continued to beckon.

"Didn't you want to say good night?" Slowly, he went toward her and she dreamily touched his lips. "You like cream?"

"Yes. . . . Yes, I do."

His voice sounded as though it came from a different time dimension. Her tongue moved over his mouth, licking the cream, and their mouths were joined. He was almost paralyzed by the bewitchment of holding her and gliding his fingertips along her body and into the soft, damp rondures, the hidden crease of her thighs.

She reached through his robe and held the throbbing head of his penis.

"Is this all for me? My, oh, my, you're not going to be here very long. I hope you've got a good book to read. I may send you to bed early as punishment."

"I could get a bottle of Yukon Jack and you could christen it. Build up your arm."

"No, I don't think I want to do that. Terry Brett, you're bad."

"Company I'm keeping."

She laughed. "I want to be friendly, so very friendly."

His fingers danced along her hard flat stomach and paused on her silky wet clitoris.

"That feels so good."

He kissed her breasts, stroked the nipples, then clasped the buds with his lips. He couldn't get enough, rolling his tongue over them.

"Allison, you taste so sweet."

She twisted under him and they moved belly to belly, kissing with rushing intoxication. He roved into her, succumbing to the moist patch he felt. She carefully arched her legs over his shoulders and he moved his head between them, his tongue darting over the velvety sweet lips, and then inside her. Inebriated by desire, touched by madness, he was devouring her.

Her body quivered in shock and she cried out, started to coax, then pleaded with him to cease. He slowly raised his head and Allison kissed him with such a depth of trembling, longing, holding him, until he felt her tears running down his own face into his mouth.

"This is magic," she said, shuddering. "Love me, fuck me, fuck me, love me," she pleaded, her body flowing with shivers.

His desire bordered on derangement. He could barely get inside her.

"You're so tight."

She cautiously changed the angle of her leg and he thrust inside. Her silky, heavy, swinging breasts smothered him.

"Deeper, deeper," she crooned, a conspirator whispering a secret code. "I'm bad, punish me. . . . Give it to me. . . . Hurt me. . . ."

Her body seemed to rise up, meeting his in the air, and they meshed and pounded at each other in a savagely gorgeous rampage.

"Let it go," she cried. "Swamp me, please."

Frantically, grinding his teeth in the release from captivity, his body still barreling, he tightened up shuddering in the current of orgasm. Their arched forms, still churning, fell to earth like comets from the night sky and came to rest in some deep-burning crater. They felt glued together. Her thighs and short blond pubic hair were awash with pearls of his come.

She framed his face in her palms and smiled.

"Oh, what a shot. I feel like I was hit by a cannon." Her large, heated breasts pulsated provocatively. "You got me there, I don't know how many times." She kissed him tenderly for a long time. "Oh, Ter, Ter, I think I'm falling in love with you." His eyes fixed on her, swallowing and encompassing her. "You don't have to say anything."

Something of cataclysmic power had happened. He couldn't regain his speech and remained suspended as she insinuated herself inside him until she had become his world.

It's never been this way, he thought. He felt himself retreating, pulling away, troubled, fearful of covenants. Attempting to conceal the clash within himself, he went to the corridor, shook his head, perplexed, and brought in her present. He laid it at her feet.

"Thank you. But it's not Christmas yet. I'd like to wait and open it with your dad and Milly here."

"You would, wouldn't you? Now, Allison, do as I say!"

Like a suspicious cat investigating, scenting, Allison nuzzled the box against her body. She slid the ribbon down and cautiously peeked inside. She held up the nightdress and flounced the negligée around her neck so that it had the effect of a boa. Then, she located the panties and appeared mystified.

"Is it a handkerchief or what?"

"I don't know, there should be instructions."

She tugged at the delicate elastic waistband. "I had you figured dead wrong. Oh, Terry, what a wonderful, horny little piggy you are. I'll wear these in the pocket of my jean jacket."

They were back to their mockery and he felt on more secure ground. Not to be outdone in the thoughtfulness department, Allison reached over for the sack that was her handbag.

"I gave that bastard Warren a beat count. I've got a little something for you, your dad. And I haven't forgotten Milly. I owe her for the pie."

"Acid tabs!" He waltzed around the room giddily. "I guess sooner or later I was going to be disbarred. Maybe now's as good a time as any. I'm still young enough to start a new career. Nothing that requires a license like a contractor. With you to guide me, prison's in my future."

"There's another less direct way of using the acid," she advised him with pedagogical enthusiasm, a sharing of cunning knowledge. He waited as though cajoling a witness who needed a short pause to remember the details of the scene of the crime. Allison's luminous eyes flamed with deviltry. "I could make up a batch of eggnog and you serve it to your guests."

"Oh, that sounds wonderful. Give me a minute and I'll check on what arrangements I can make for ambulances."

He came close to her and they smiled, enjoying their absurdity and their passion. They put their arms around each other and tightened their linked hands until they had squeezed out the realization of what this forbidding moment had begun to mean.

"You know what I'd really like for Christmas, Ter? For you to take Earl's case."

He was taken by surprise. "Have you got a good reason?"

"Yeah, we owe him for tonight and for whatever happens after."

After a moment's consideration, he said, "Okay, then you do something for me. Get rid of that acid and the grass. I don't want you stoned when we're together. I'm your trip, Allison, so enjoy it."

"If I can have you, I'll be your slave."

"I prefer you as an equal."

"That will take the rest of my life."

He placed his head in the cup of her warm shoulder and knew that now he might talk about rapture.

10

In the morning a silvery forge of snow crusted the lawn, and Allison was bursting with rhapsody and humming sweetly. It was as though nature had struck some private bargain of wish fulfillment finally for her and she was given this white Christmas. During the night they had entered a free-fall daze of love that glutted their senses. Anything seemed possible, except unhappiness. They were sitting on the porch, huddled under a blanket, drinking coffee, watching the wheat barges steam down the river into port.

"I'd give up a joint for a real sleigh ride—pulled by a horse," she said.

"We'll do it without the joint. And when your leg's strong enough, I'll take you skiing up at Mount Hood."

For some reason his remark disturbed her; she turned morose, but snapped herself out it. Their bodies were still smoldering and he kissed her.

"My body twitches every time you stroke me. It's driving me mad."

"Well, you found something to hate about me."

"No, Ter, I'm hooked on you."

"Allison, Allison, I'm delirious about you coming into my life."

"Yes, we have our land of milk and honey for the moment."

This gorging on each other with small intimate touches had become almost instinctive. He viewed the return of his father and Milly without enthusiasm. Later, Pat's rowdy subcontractors would come by for their bonuses and hang around for food and to tank up with the boss. His law partner, Georgie Conlan, would show up when the men were feeling good. Last Christmas, she had birddogged the concrete slabber, then played the flu game and not shown up at the office for days.

Maybe Allison's recipe for LSD punch wasn't such a bad idea after all. They'd go upstairs, make love, and walk around in the nude. They'd give this group of merrymakers something to conjure with when they came down. For himself, he despised drugs. He had smoked grass a few times at college and failed to find the kick. It made him lazy and inattentive. He felt like he was missing out on his life.

Around 8:00 A.M. Pat phoned from a gas station to tell him he was running late and wouldn't be back until noon. He and Milly would stop by the restaurant to pick up the party food. Terry's office service followed up, transmitting the messages of bail bondsmen. With an apologetic wave to Allison, Terry jotted down the names of clients in jeopardy. He was grateful not to be among them in the Port Rivers lockup. He imagined himself explaining to a lawyer how he'd been conned. No, he didn't know a damned thing about the thousand tabs of acid he'd collected from the bus station locker.

Even burglars and arsonists deserved to carve turkeys, he was told by several overwrought wives. While commiserating with them about the bleakness of their Christmas, Terry crossed himself.

Allison explored Terry's study, which was off the bow-shaped screened porch. It was warm inside the room and she slipped off the navy blue robe he had given her to wear. She touched the objects that were his: a paperweight on his desk, which was filled with flowers and snowflakes; a wooden file tray stacked with legal complaints; the thick buck clips holding notes. She was watchful, turning around every moment, wary of being surprised, startled. On a marble washstand that may have come from pioneers, Terry had assembled old bottles from pharmacies and relabeled them with the names of spirits.

Outside of a public library, she had never encountered such a vast number of books. Carefully arranged on floor-to-ceiling burled walnut shelves, she marveled at the dust-free set of leatherbound Harvard Classics, the *Britannica,* legions of dictionaries in foreign languages, and reference works. She slid the elegant wrought-iron ladder that was fixed with brass hinges along the ledge, just to see if it worked or was permanently stationed as an artifact for show. It moved without a creak.

On a counter, four or five feet of LPs stood erect, neatly arranged by the name of the composer. She roved from Bach to Vivaldi, finally arriving at a section for pop music—mostly Sinatra and big bands from the forties. At last she found something that revealed Terry had been touched by the 1960s: three Bob Dylan albums. But on the Dual turntable was Jackie Gleason's "Music for Lovers Only." She wondered how Bobby Hackett's lyrical trumpet would sound on the four Harmon Kardon speakers with the volume peaking on the Sansui tuner.

Still snooping, Allison listened to him talking on the hall phone. She decided not to experiment with his stereo equipment and instead turned the pages of Webster's to pass the time, checking on words she had underlined in her novel. She brought out her notebook and began to write and memorize words that flashed on the pages.

Suddenly, she felt sick to her stomach. She stifled a silent scream, which reverberated through her consciousness. A ghastly flash of reality snaked within her, like a summer vein of lightning that might have been miles away, then sundered a tree that fell across her path.

She was an intruder in the life of this orderly man whose very education served as a reproach to her own ignorance. She did not belong in his well-bred society. Her night and morning of elation with Terry crumbled. It had been the first time she had ever slept the night in a man's arms. Every experience before this had been furtive and bitter. Early on, she recognized that she was not somebody with a soul or feelings, but merely a commodity to be tossed away or changed like a razor blade.

Allison Desmond could never measure up to Terry Brett. He occupied a storied, privileged position, and this realization nourished her sense of unworthiness, scattering the happiness she had glimpsed. She had no business with a man who had a crown in his future.

It would have been a simple matter to cry at that moment and liberate the pain within her, but her strength had always emerged from the discipline of withholding pain until it rotted in her gut and ultimately vanished. The pure anarchy of this technique was her weapon and had proved to be her salvation. Remorse had never been allowed to last very long when she was trying to feed herself at a mission or a temporary shelter. Allison closed her eyes, silently repeating the *bija* mantra seed sounds of the Tantra she had learned when she lived in a Buddhist commune one stark winter when she was fifteen.

* * *

Terry crept in while Allison was entombed in her meditation. He quietly leaned against the bookcase, gazing at her. His bathrobe was on the floor, and from her abbreviated wardrobe, she was wearing only the mini-panties he had whimsically bought for her. Crumpled below her navel, they seemed merely an afterthought for modesty's sake, a painter's serendipitous brush stroke. The moonscape of her body, its dips and streaming bends, the harmonies of her flesh, almost made his heart stop. Terry had panned for gold and found the mother lode.

He discovered that Allison was a dedicated and assiduous keeper of word lists. She had his big Webster's spread out. In a black-and-white spotted school tablet, she had written out definitions of exotic words that she had collected from Maugham's *The Razor's Edge* as she bailed through it. "*Vindictive,* disposed to seek revenge." Her name was printed on the cover, but beside the address, she had written in block letters: "UNKNOWN."

Eventually, she sensed someone in the room, opened her bright eyes, and appeared fully recovered from her galactic flight as she glided back to earth. She smiled at him and the courtier bowed his head.

"You look very content," he said.

"It's good practice swimming against the tide."

"Which means? I think I could use a subtitle here."

"I'm utterly miserable and resigned to my destiny."

"You don't look it."

"Witches have their ways with truth," she said, and he kissed her tenderly.

"You must be enjoying this novel, making these notes."

"I mine books like you do. And this one is wonderful. My soul is expanding."

"I hate to interrupt your spiritual education but—"

"But what?" She stood up. "You know, my leg's feeling stronger."

"I have certain mystical healing powers."

Her lips parted, a sting on the horizon. "Just soil me at your pleasure. Drench me with your healing spray."

She constantly amused him. "Yes, that's part of the

cure. I don't brag about it or else they'd be lined up at my bedroom like Lourdes."

"Seriously now, I can get around without crutches. If I had a cane."

"We've got an old hickory one somewhere."

"Great, can I try it out?"

"First, Allison, we have to discuss attire—yours."

She snapped the elastic of her fire engine red panties. "I wouldn't think this is too risky for a contractor's Christmas bash."

He kissed her knee. "Not for me," he said with a sigh and another erection.

"My jeans are dirty. . . . Hey, I've got some stuff back in the tent."

"Something less scanty. A dress maybe?"

"I love driving your car. So let's roll," she replied, without his detecting her sadness, the loss of him staring at her future.

11

Under a dun sky and battered by the river wind, the collapsed tent might have been the ragged sail of a beached lifeboat from a shipwreck, with Allison the lone survivor. She and Terry foraged, grappling with the flapping canvas cheeks for her knickknacks, damp rotted books and records. He felt a renewed sadness for the hard days she had endured. In what was formerly her dining table, actually a metal trunk with mildewed souvenir stickers of faraway places, they packed a ragtag of her possessions. She was without complaint, another skin shed in the wasteland of her eighteen-year existence. She was walking with the cane and he was delighted by her progress.

"You're not coming back here," he magisterially informed her at the end of the pilgrimage. She was quiet and withdrawn again. Farewells were nothing new to her. "I want you to be with me."

"We'll see."

"No, we won't."

It was Christmas Day and he had no wish to cross swords with her again. The church bells tolled as they drove through town and he stopped off at St. Luke's. When they were inside, they stopped beside the font and paused during the singing of hymns, which sounded vaguely uplifting and mellifluous.

"Do you pray?" he asked.

She held his hand. "To a God unknown. . . . He must've heard me to bring you into my life."

She had left herself no path for retreat and his emotions were stirred by her candor. "I think we both owe him a debt. I'm Catholic, or used to be. I was six when my mother died of cancer. Her service was held here. Force of habit to come on Christmas," Terry said, lighting a candle and putting a hundred-dollar bill in the collection box. "Pat and I sort of lost it after she was gone. To see her shrink to nothing. Afterwards, I felt God had abdicated."

On the way back to his house, she spotted a baronial Tudor house at the end of River Cove on the point. When he told her that the owners were in Palm Beach, she asked if they might stop. They walked through the gate and into the back garden, which overlooked the river. An intricate maze with trimmed six-foot hedges undulated beside a platformed wrought-iron gazebo.

"This is the Van Wyck estate. I worked here one summer," he said as they toured the dream palace, beyond the means of the Bretts. "Must be a good ten or twelve years ago. The dock was rotting and my father got the job. We also built the boathouse. I dug ditches, laid some pipe, did the marine varnish." He boosted her up so that she could look at the sailboat in its winter nest. "Best summer tan I ever had."

"You are a gorgeous man. How some rich girl didn't get you by now is one of the wonders."

He thought of Joanne, the pining patrician daughter of the owner. "I keep a shotgun for that."

She peeked through the window at latitudes of fine English furniture and giddy chandeliers. "These people must own the world."

"Shipyards and mills. Very old money. Something we won't have to worry about. They built the River Cove Country Club. Even though they're loaded, the Van Wycks are good people."

"You actually know them?"

"I went to school with their kids."

"What happened to the pretty daughter?"

The question drew a chagrined smile from Terry. "What made you ask that?"

"I was fishing for stuff about you. Any comment?"

"We're just old friends."

"I'll bet. You used to gather old arrowheads with her, didn't you? Terry Brett, you heartbreaker. Poor girl must be about to drown herself in Palm Beach."

Allison's quickness, beyond mere street smarts, astounded him. She was like an agile lioness always on the hunt. When they returned to the more modest Brett spread, Terry brought out the crystal glasses and Lenox china. He dusted their long refectory dining table and set it for a buffet. Allison sat in the corner window seat, wiping water marks off the silverware. She looked up at him with a shyly innocent longing as though he had caught her out.

"I'll never forget this day and our Christmas Eve," she said, clasping at the memory and fearful of losing it.

"We'll have more and even better times."

"Don't make me cry."

He knew gracious days were not part of her history. He was neither naive nor given to maudlin speculation, but he couldn't help but wonder who had given her a doll or a toy for Christmas. She had crept into his heart and he felt in thrall to the helpless independence of this child-woman.

He carried her trunk into the guest room with a sense of resentment, for their intimacy was about to be fractured by convention. He wanted to be only with her and to embrace the solitude of lovers. But she was now detached and watchful. They heard a cavalcade of cars and voices in the driveway.

"I won't be long."

"Take as long as you like. I'll be at the bar. Oh, maybe, I'll have to run to the liquor store for some Yukon Jack."

"Smart-ass."

Terry changed into a gray tweed jacket, charcoal slacks, and blue shirt. He looked into the mirror and approved of the image. He brushed his blond hair straight back and smiled at himself. His hazel eyes were illuminated with a magic light, the current and knowledge of passion. He was so deliriously happy that he smiled at himself.

Terry sailed downstairs to check on things. The activities of the speedy technicians in the kitchen resembled those of a group of laboratory scientists on the verge of a great medical breakthrough; with its hams honeyed and cloved, the turkeys dusted with herbs and garlic and filled with Milly's incomparable sausage and raisin-chestnut stuffing, the ovens were at full throttle. Three of her kitchen staff were assisting her.

Pat had a highball in his hand and was toasting himself. Except for his split fingernails, he might have been taken for the owner of the Yankees or a beer baron, as he professionally surveyed the kitchen from the bar.

"Ready for a drink?"

"Sure," Terry said. "Merry Christmas, Dad."

"You look very well rested, Ter."

"You know me, twelve hours or I get cranky."

"Is your guest still here or did you shake her out of the sack and send her packing?"

"I thought I'd keep her around for a while. She helps me sleep."

"Well, you missed something special. We had great wild goose in that Madeira lingonberry sauce Carol makes. We did four bottles of Liebfraumilch and I asked Harry to get us a few cases." They raised their glasses and Pat's eyes twinkled. "But I guess you didn't need to drive over to Seacliff for goose. Well, you stuff her today and bundle her on her way. Okay?"

The hardy, masculine undertone offended Terry, broke the spell. This was not a time for camaraderie or sharing. He couldn't remember a time in his life when he'd ever thought of slapping his father.

"I'll leave right now. We'll go look for an apartment," Terry said.

Pat backed away, afraid Terry was about to throw his drink in his face. He was bewildered and hurt. "That's a little impulsive. Goddamn, Terry, I was just kidding. Trying to get a rise."

Standing in the threshold supported by her own gravity, Terry's velvet appeared. He didn't know which part of Allison to look at first. She had on a beige suede dress and dark russet knee-high boots, which must have been an ordeal to pull on. She had woven her flaxen hair in a crisscrossed web of braids on top of her head, forming a gold crown. She had on a pale pink lipstick, a touch of color on her cheeks. She might have been more beautiful if her illusion weren't so regal and dazzling.

Terry was overcome by the effect. Had he imagined this vision in the sweat-soaked girl struggling in the hospital rehab room with Earl barking at her? Her face was open, filled with curiosity, and she wrinkled her nose, sniffing the air, taking in the scents of the kitchen.

"I owe you an apology," Pat whispered. "I had no idea the other morning . . . this is movie star looks," he continued, pulling Terry aside in the alcove. "I'd've missed Harry's goose for her, too. And Carol could've poured her lingonberry sauce down the drain." He caught himself. "Sorry, I know you're touchy on the subject of Miss Allison. A little fatherly advice. Get used to it, my friend."

Allison walked toward them, a bit stiffly on the hickory cane, and Pat breathed her in like a fine wine.

"I'm delighted to see you, Allison. Terry must've been very persuasive to get you to share Christmas with us."

In an instant, he was kissing her cheeks in the Charles Boyer *Gaslight* style.

"How was your drive from Seacliff, Mr. Brett?"

"Please call me Pat. We had too much wine. I ran out of gas and had to call the Triple A."

"Milly must've been upset." She saw at the range the pie queen with a white hairnet shielding her Marcel. "She's like an all-seeing Indian goddess."

Mistress of the put-on, Terry winked at Allison.

"Jesus, if I ever said that to Milly, she'd think it was a marriage proposal." Pat stroked her cane. "This was once Terry's. He complains about me, but I don't throw anything out."

Her sapphire blue eyes filled with sympathy. "I didn't know."

"Terry suffered like a champ and never griped about the polio. You can't believe how he fought it. Broke my heart watching him in rehab." Pat chucked him under the chin. "Nobody can possibly realize what guts Terry has. He wouldn't ever quit."

"No more tales from the frontlines, Pat." Terry was relieved to find his voice. He was just about done in surveying his field of glory.

Allison turned to Terry and nodded. "Pat, does Milly allow people to talk to her while she's cooking?"

"You can do anything you like here, honey. Just be at home." A bargeload of people were heading toward them. " 'Scuse me, Allison." Pat hurried to greet people at the door.

"Terry, I thought this was going to be a quiet, cozy family Christmas."

"Maybe I misled you, darling. With my dad, Christmas is a working day and it's business as usual."

Terry nestled her in the alcove. They were out of sight of the guests for the moment. It was now time to plant his banner. He kissed her ear, and madly slipped his hand in her panties, and she gave his dick a tug.

"You've got me twitching again," she murmured.

"I'll see if they do room service. Allison, you're breathtaking."

"Thank you, sir. My passion is my task. Terry, I'm going to make you so happy."

"I love you, Allison," he whispered.

"What? You do? Do you know what you're saying?" She swayed and he held her back. "Jesus, even if you don't, it's pleasing to hear something like that when you're not in bed."

She stared at him and touched the healing pink scratch on his forehead.

"Our battle at the river. It all seems long ago when you were my enemy. I thought you were just another hound trying to brawn and bully me into submission. I sent packs of them home screaming for mama."

"Was I too tough?"

"It was the eggroll."

"I have to be a host, or give it a try," Terry said, breaking away from Allison for another Christmas open house at the Bretts. "I've known most of these clowns for years."

"Would you please put some more of those pinecones on the fire?" Allison asked. "I like the way they crackle."

"Allison, do you think you could love me?"

She held him close and lightly touched his lips with her finger.

"Terry, I wouldn't want to live without you." She fell into the corner of the alcove. "I'd take out a fucking brick wall and brick by brick hang them around my neck ... then plunge into the river and meet my maker."

"Do you mean it?"

"Yes," she said solemnly. "Now see to your guests."

They both reached for her cane and banged heads. He accompanied her into the kitchen and they stood back from the frothing pots.

"I'm going to watch Milly doing the turkeys. After I ran away from the institution, I boosted one of those birds from a supermarket. I cooked it at a hobo campfire under a railroad bridge. I didn't know the packers stuffed the giblets inside. I was surrounded by starving men and they wouldn't go near it. It was as though they'd gotten a whiff of Satan. And they booted me out. I really have to learn how to cook for you, my darling."

Swarms of people glutted the entrance. The living room was beginning to throb with some of Terry's civil clients planning on room additions. Terry was surprised. Pat had raided his client list. They were joined by Pat's plumbers in their fancy duds; a stray bail judge; carpenters carrying champagne; a hippie electrician, shunned by the others, wore a suit with a red T-shirt underneath that said, GET OUT OF VIETNAM. No one talked of the war. It was forbidden in the living rooms of *nice* people.

Rife with breathless scandals of domestic abuse and the insolvencies of divorce, Terry's law associate Georgie Conlan arrived. Her giggly party voice and her Persian lamb coat, the sleeves winged with mink, invaded the living room. Her cheeks were visibly contoured and her doughy face revealed a hitherto concealed bone structure. She was wearing one of the new chemises with a low-cut V-neckline and kid boots. Terry thought she would no longer continue to wince through her thirties, while her fruitful time was squandered on pies and berating every male she encountered.

Terry kissed Georgie. "You look absolutely lovely, madam."

"I'm on a new diet. I soaked my Oreo cookies in nitric acid and I've been drinking eight glasses of water a day. I live on boiled brown rice and sardines."

Terry was about to help her off with her fur coat, but Georgie pulled away.

In a harsh lawyerly tone, she said: "I'm not staying. I know it's a tradition since you made me your junior partner. But I only stopped by to pay my respects."

"The moratorium on your Judy Garland impression is over. Please, Georgie, don't go. What's the matter? Listen, Big Tony is on his way. I think you guys should make up. He's been miserable without you."

"Thank you for the memory of a bygone era. I hope Big Tony dies in one of his own cement foundations. Let it be after your father plants his trowel in his brainpan. *This* year, Terry, I have an escort."

"You do? Bring him in. Let's have a look."

Georgie sucked in her cheeks. "He's not welcome here."

Terry was astounded. "You're kidding. There are people here who've gone belly up rather than pay Pat's bills. It's Christmas Day, Georgie."

"Well, in that case, I hope that includes Mr. Earl Raymond. He's the gentleman who scored fifty-six points against Salem University and holds more professional scoring records than anyone."

"So I've heard. Are you both filing a lawsuit today or are you going to get smashed with the rest of us?"

"I have options."

Terry listened with disbelief to the cannonball romance that had occurred. Earl had put Georgie on a fasting regime, and, along the way, apparently taught her the cruel irresponsible delights of multiple orgasms.

"Now that Earl's on the hospital staff, he can probably prescribe opium and he'll have his patients bowling for Quaaludes."

"Terry, lay off Earl. You keep pounding at him and I don't like it," Georgie said. "Kick someone else's ass. The man's helpless."

In their three years of deep friendship and partnership, this was the most caustic exchange they'd had. Obviously, Earl had provided Georgie with an edited version of their encounter outside court with himself as the injured party. Terry had an aversion to bullies and to find himself larded with the charge angered him. Nonetheless, he soothed Georgie.

"No apologies necessary. Bring Earl in. Anyway, I want to talk to him." Terry was suddenly whirled around in the room by glad-handers and kisses from their wives. "Got to go, Georgie," he said through the friendly fire of visitors.

In the kitchen, Allison, the mistress of his destiny, was chatting with Milly, who was basting the turkeys and doing five other things with cool surgical aplomb.

"There's a rhythm to cooking," Milly was explaining to her admirer.

"I'm looking for a job, Milly. And I'd love you to teach me to cook in the restaurant. I don't think I can handle tables with a bum leg."

"In a pinch you'd have to."

"Then I would. Cooking is what excites me."

Milly removed her hairnet, patted her auburn fringe, gave herself a squirt of White Shoulders, and smiled at Allison. Unharried, Milly was a handsome, stately woman. "After the first of the year, come by. Let's join the fellas." As an afterthought she turned to one of her staff. "Mix the cornstarch with cold water before stirring it into the gravy. If I find a lump, you'll get one on your head!"

The living room had filled with seventy or eighty people. In the doorway, Pat in his seignorial posture was dealing out envelopes and gifts to those inspectors who had ignored the obtuse angles on his sinking bathroom tile floors and didn't force him to lay them again.

Missing nothing, Pat spotted Earl sidling in just about cuffed to Georgie's wrist, and gave him a curt nod.

Earl caught sight of Allison waving from the kitchen.

"Jesus, Ter, you've made Allison beautiful. Man, I'd never recognize her."

"What's the real story with her? What the hell is she into . . . with this acid and dope?"

Earl was baffled. "What are you talking about? She wouldn't even smoke a joint with me. She's totally fogged out on all this India mystical purity trash. White robes. Incense. It's curry time with her."

"Well, she was selling acid."

"A girl does what a girl has to do. Don't you and me know that by now?"

"A onetime shot?" Terry persisted. "Tell me!"

"I guess."

Earl had already profoundly influenced his life and Terry wanted to believe him.

"Is that it?" Earl nodded. "If you know anything else . . . I'd appreciate—" Terry left the subject as Allison and

Georgie approached them. "I've been telling Earl that I'll look into his claim against Jonah Wolfe."

Earl held his breath. "Prince Terry. I can't tell you what this means to me."

"When I've got a fix on the case, I'll probably have to go to Milwaukee."

"Why? The club's in L.A. and Jonah Wolfe lives there."

"I will circle his den. Find out about him. That's the way I operate."

Terry looked over to the women, who were talking up a storm. Georgie had the sisterhood knack of creating instant empathy.

"I see you two have met," Terry said.

"Sure have," Georgie replied with an ironic eye. "You're a real squirrel."

"Well, I have my best man, Earl, to thank for the smile on my face this Christmas."

Terry poured them fresh drinks. Someone was playing the piano and a quartet of drywallers were singing "What the World Needs Now Is Love." Terry cupped his hand around Allison's chin and kissed her nose.

Squinting at him in the distance and closing in was Paul Cisco. Terry reluctantly stole away from Allison. The men shook hands.

"I've got to say this for you, Terry. Of all the people I know, you have the greatest capacity for forming strange and dangerous alliances."

"Are you still carrying on about my Golden Greek? For Chrissake, Aristedes was railroaded by that two-bit bookie Warren Paris because he owed him money."

"I am not referring to that, Terence. My sermon on morality has a more personal bent on this holy day of the Lord's birth. I am not referring to the Greek. It's the blond bombshell beside Georgie. What is *she* doing here—with *you*?"

Terry hoped the nuisance of Allison's domicile was not at issue again. It was getting on his nerves.

"She is a guest like yourself, Paul."

Cisco poured himself a glass of champagne from one of the bottles on the buffet table.

"How'd you come to saddle up with her, Ter?"

"A mutual friend introduced us. Why the hell're you and Judge Walsh busting her chops?"

"Maybe to protect you."

Terry reached over him for the scotch bottle and refilled his glass.

"This is hard to believe."

"Remember that robbery at McDonald's on Labor Day?"

"Not really."

"They sold a lot of burgers that day, Terry. Fifteen grand's worth. And it was removed by two guys waving sawed-off shotguns at children and mothers."

"So what?"

"Well, the lady you were rubbing noses with was there."

"You have my attention, Paul."

"McDonald's is just off the interstate. You don't walk or bike there."

"Didn't they run her over, almost killing her?"

"Ah, so you have heard."

"Sure, she told me."

"She had no car and gave us some story about her date dumping her there after an argument. Now I ask you, Terry, would any man dump her?"

Terry was growing increasingly uncomfortable at the turn of the discussion, the innuendoes. "I know how infuriating she can be. Paul, do me a favor and stop the jousting. Bring out the broadsword."

"Miss Desmond was a most uncooperative witness, hostile and defiant."

"Some people get that way after they've been the victim of a hit-and-run. Lose their job. Get thrown out on the street because they can't pay the rent."

"The company offered a ten-grand reward. The young lady was shown mugs and couldn't identify anyone."

"What's so surprising about that? You know what eyewitnesses are worth. Especially when things happen fast.

She also happened to have been in shock."

"Notwithstanding your spirited defense, Sergeant Barney Laver adduced his own theory from the circumstances."

"And what did Barney adduce?"

"That she was the lookout."

"Bullshit. Barney couldn't catch a rat in a trap. After the arson case in which I discredited him, he hates me."

"Barney also says Port Rivers is swimming in LSD. Now a man of your potential and probity could wind up governor or senator of this state, Mr. Brett." Cisco gave him a clumsy hug. "Now I fucking well admire and respect you and I don't want you to ruin yourself by keeping low company with ladies who rotate their tits in sewer joints."

Terry cooled his anger. He had been taught at law school never to take offense when his belly was exposed.

"Thanks for the buildup, Paul."

"I'm off." Cisco called out for his wife, who was raping the seafood tray. "Unlike those of you in private practice, Christmas is a working day for me."

"You and my father. Where're you going now?"

"To make my rounds of the judges and kiss ass for a reversal if I can carol sweetly enough."

Terry walked with him to the Christmas tree and located a large rectangular box. He handed it over.

"It's too large to be a bomb."

"Shit, open it, Paul." Hands twitching over the green ribbon, then caressing the tissue paper, Cisco became starry-eyed and diffident when he discovered a beige cashmere overcoat. "Thirty-six short, Paul."

"I'm going to kill you one day, Terry. If this is stolen property from the Greek . . ." He examined the label and gave a little start. "Saks Fifth Avenue! How do you do it?"

"I don't kiss and tell, Mr. Cisco."

"Are there any more around?"

"Just one for Pat with a Lord & Taylor label."

"Goddamn, I may have to come back here with a search warrant," Paul said with a choked laugh.

Allison moved beside Terry and he interlocked their fingers and she pressed her hip against his.

"You've met Miss Desmond, I believe, Paul."

"Yes. Unfortunately, it's always been a municipal pleasure seeing her."

"I think I prefer social visits with you, sir."

"Let's try to keep it that way, then, Allison."

"Oh well, I guess I can call you Paul since we're having a drink." She banged her glass against Cisco's. "Merry Christmas." Allison noticed the coat draped on Paul Cisco's arm. "You must do your shopping at Greek restaurants," she said, mutinously pressing her bosom against Cisco. "Try it on and we'll see if it fits."

"Look," Cisco said in wrath, "your attorney and I butt heads in court. But we've been bosom buddies since we hung out our shingles. Even though we're on opposing sides, Terry's friendship is valuable to me."

"I'll do what I can to service it," Allison said tartly.

Cisco gathered his wife, and as they were leaving, she peered over her shoulder at Allison and encountered the new couple smiling at them. Having watched his angel in armed combat, Terry decided that she needed legal counseling.

"Do you ever give any ground, Allison?"

"Not when I'm standing on it."

Terry led her through the acreage of guests, until they reached the garden. Allison cuddled close to him.

"I like it out here, with the fog and the cold lightbeams of the fishermen's boats shrouding in."

Terry kissed her forehead. "I don't. Don't ever get fresh with Paul Cisco. He carries the failure of aspiration and it's an unstable condition."

"I understand. Now stop coaching me. I know how to behave with bullies."

12

The new year frivolously rolled in for Allison and Terry. All through January 1966 they were together, luxuriating in the recklessness of new love. The snow and ice shingles, the nightly clap of sleet dropping down from the eaves, were a matter of indifference to them. They were invariably in Terry's bedroom wrapped in each other's arms, toiling under the covers.

Terry was not even mildly curious about the McDonald's robbery. In fact, he decided he would not beat his chest or leap out of his socks if Allison admitted complicity. But somehow or other, Terry believed it would have been an exhausting and querulous face-off for anyone to silence her. If Allison had been a part of the McDonald's robbery—the exquisite setup diversion— she would have confessed to him. He had witnessed his lady riled at the Paradise Inn. Violence was not an element that would engage Allison's fears, as with most women. A pair of sawed-off shotguns or not, these cowboys would have to come up with some convincing reasons if they had run her down and put her out of action with a broken leg.

Terry's trust was complete, his doubts reconciled against her bare breasts each night. As he plunged deeper and deeper into the honeyed symphony of bliss, the emotion was no longer an exotic luxury but tangible. Allison's recovery was almost complete. She exercised at home and could walk without a cane. Milly had hired her as kitchen support and assigned her tasks, like cracking a gross of eggs for the breakfast cook, mixing pancake batter, and frying slabs of bacon.

Terry's practice slowed. Murder was seasonal; armed robbery stalled on the slippery roads; arson was just about impossible in the windy, pelting daily rains. Terry's caseload diminished as Georgie's increased with the profusion of divorces. According to Georgie, the hatred that New Year's Eve parties fertilized between married couples was simply wondrous for Terry. With a broad smile in the morning, after having worked till midnight, Georgie would be in before him and ask: "Am I'm pulling my weight as your junior partner?"

Come spring, he'd be visiting clients facing prison.

"Not only are you pulling it, you're losing it."

"The drama of Dr. Earl's diets."

"I'd say."

Terry found time to study Earl's claim, the exotica of torts, and the latest contract cases published in the law reviews. He slowly began to develop a strategy. It would be fruitless to take Jonah Wolfe to court. They'd be there for five years in a swamp of depositions, continuances, airy meaningless motions. To skin this cat, Terry was convinced he had to uncover something beyond the legal purview of claims and counterclaims.

And Earl was a dynamic witness, with one of those memories for specific details about himself that nurtured his case. Whether it was the name of a date on a one-night stand, or the cut of steak he ordered at dinners he mooched, the man was believable. Along the way, Earl virtually recreated Jonah Wolfe's personality and behavior patterns for Terry. It seemed that the sex-driven owner and the point guard had done some road work together, with Earl acting as bait for groupies. Jonah always provided suites at the hotel and was waiting with liquor and ludes.

But life was too placid for the former hoop star. This situation was remedied by a crisis that arose when one of Earl's wealthy ladies burst into the office and created a scene. She and Georgie came to blows while the hero back-doored them and hid in the men's room. Earl stayed there for hours smoking joints.

Terry acted as the go-between in the domestic situation.

But Georgie, now a size ten, was still a formidable opponent, and finally she whizzed past Terry and caught

Earl while he was combing his hair for the seventieth time.

"You will never again humiliate me professionally." She grabbed his address book as evidence, tore it into pieces, and flushed it down the toilet. Then she put her knee in his groin. "I will devote my life to ruining you. By the time I'm through with you, not even a state mental asylum will accept you. Do you follow me, Earl?"

Humiliated, Earl crept out with his head lowered. Winter shelter beckoned and he decided to snuggle with Georgie in her spacious new waterfront condo.

Terry and Allison saw them a few times a week for a movie or a dinner on Terry at the Surf Rider so that Earl could check things out at the bar while he guzzled a few dozen oysters and belted back scotches. On these occasions, Allison would sneak in a bottle of some sauce she concocted in Milly's kitchen. Since Terry was paying, Allison exacted compensation. Earl became the guinea pig for her champagne mustard butter on the grilled sturgeon. Like a pharmaceutical company testing a new drug, Earl was always there to volunteer his services. Georgie and Terry stuck to the menu.

With a number of intriguing, spicy, buckshot leads from Earl and the office slow, Terry was eager to travel to Milwaukee and begin an investigation of Jonah Wolfe. He would take Allison along on his journey to the Midwest. They would not be far from Chicago and he had friends there from law school whom he hadn't seen for some time.

He did not realize Allison had her own program. She was learning how to prepare roast loin of pork in Milly's kitchen with the magical meatloaf on the horizon. Allison was so conscientious that she worked a Saturday before Lincoln's Birthday. When he was around her, he couldn't concentrate. He didn't know whether to finish reading his case law research or stick his hand under her skirt. The previous night after her surprisingly good chicken and dumplings, they had made love on the dining room table. The lazy Susan was a casualty of his haste.

"That was a macrorogasm. Is that a word?" she inquired.

"I would say so," he replied. "I think we could double India's population with that blast." They converted the dinner napkins into loincloths and in this blithe primitive state picked up hunks of glass and carried on a conversation while she swept up and he held the dustpan. "Good thing it wasn't my mother's china salt and pepper shakers or Pat's crystal bowling award for his three hundred game."

"He'd chain us to an ice floe," she said, pausing to kiss him. "Ter, I've been thinking. . . . It'll be better for you to go to Milwaukee without me. I'm really making progress with Milly. She's spending a lot of time with me, teaching me everything. And I think she'd feel I was an ingrate if I swanned off now."

"You're manipulating me."

"Not at all, Terry. One day, I'll make money out of learning a skill. In any case, I prefer making pies to skunking acid tabs for Warren Paris."

"So do I, darling."

Terry caved in. He had a losing case with Allison. It would be best to leave the culinary apprentice at home. She distracted him too much.

There was, however, one person who did not share the couple's exhilaration. It had been silently building offstage and seemed to come out of nowhere. Pat brought the matter to a head when Allison was out working.

"I should've been consulted about Allison taking over the house and permanently moving in. I'm even signing for UPS packages for her. That's all I'm saying, Ter," Pat began.

"I've been buying art supplies for her and books on painting."

"She's rearranged your mother's sewing room."

"Nobody uses it, so I let her have it. She likes to paint and draw. What's the big deal?"

Terry could see he was in for an afternoon's crabbing. How could a woman who was painting, learning to cook professionally, exploring E. M. Forster and quoting from A Passage to India, adding to her word lists daily, stir controversy?

"I think Allison is damn near perfect."

"I don't care. I'm steaming. You are screwing your brains out in *our* home. Everywhere I look, there's Allison's underthings."

His father's ill humor was not entirely manufactured by Allison. Pat was being sued for his spec house and worried about losing his contractor's license. The gypsy subs he'd hired had sabotaged the plumbing and central heating system, then vanished into their next rip-off. Terry wondered if see-through panties atop the dryer and gurgling sounds in the middle of the night were doing his father in, creating insomnia.

"Allison is suddenly the boss here. I smelled grass the other day."

Terry heard the years of male bondage, the emotional sisal, snap. "I'll chew her out about that."

"I never let Milly move in. I always stayed at her place."

"I didn't stop you, *you* stopped yourself because you didn't want her to catch you romancing your other fillies. When you live a double life, you have to pay a price, so this sudden case of the virtues won't fly."

Pat had an innate talent for ignoring his own weaknesses. "It'd be a good idea to get yourselves an apartment."

"Slam dunk. Look, Allison's a wonderful person and I wouldn't have let her move in if there wasn't a legal reason as well. She had some trouble and the court demands that she have a domicile."

"Do me a favor, Ter. Spare me this bilge."

"Allison's working at Milly's and studying. I want to send her to college. She's already passed her high school equivalency. Pat, she has a hundred and sixty-two IQ."

"The label on her see-through bra said thirty-six D. Do you want to have this out?"

"Sure."

"This girl is lousing up our friendship. She's come between us. A father and son."

As Pat revealed his covert hostility, Terry realized that jealousy was at the root of his father's suit. He put on his deposition shoes. "Dad, what would you like me to do? I'm leaving for Milwaukee on a case. I'm pressed for time and can't look around for a place with her. I don't want to grab some dump. If you can hang on awhile longer, I'd be damned grateful."

Pat went into convulsions of thought. "I never moved a woman in."

"You've already told me that. I would've been happy to have someone you cared about living here. I love having a woman around." Terry wanted a summary judgment, have it tossed by the judge. "Look, Dad, Allison used to hang out with a bad crowd."

"Really? Well, she better not be entertaining them when you're away. Okay, she can stay. It'll be my Salvation Army contribution for next Christmas. And I want her to be private and keep out of my way."

"I don't think I can tell Allison that in quite those terms." Terry saw how distressed his father was and went outside their precedents for the first time. "Do this for me, please. I'd appreciate it."

For a moment Pat was speechless. He went to his pipe rack, found one he liked, and filled it with shag tobacco.

"Terry, don't give me some lecture about not being able to live without her."

Terry bowed his head; after a moment, he looked directly at his father.

"That's the point, Dad. I can't."

In the ice belly of winter, Terry took Allison away in the hope that this separation would defuse the situation at home. They drove along the Columbia River past the gorgeside waterfalls and down through the Mount Hood Loop. He had made reservations at Timberline Lodge.

An odd, unshakable sadness overtook Allison and her free-flowing humor was shaded by confusion. She stared out the window, a victim of frozen scenery. The holes in her parka had been patched and he had offered to take her shopping for a heavier coat. She merely shook her head and he could not insist.

"Allison, we'll find our own place when I get back.

You might start looking at the condos down at the riverfront."

"Let's see how it is with us when you come back from Milwaukee."

"Why wait?"

"Your father's a problem."

"What makes you say that?"

She shook her head and a rueful expression pinched her features. "I can tell. The last thing I would ever do is start trouble between you two."

"He's having a problem letting go. We've been bachelors and roomies for over twenty years and never a beef. We had it out as much as we ever had."

"Blood spilled?"

"I hope not. A few scratches maybe. I know him. He perked up when I had a friend of mine take his lawsuit for the spec house. How're you doing at Milly's?"

"I never thought having a straight job in the straight world would agree with me."

"Welcome to the middle class. Speaking of which, how about enrolling in River State for the spring semester?"

"I'd have to save up. Mr. Aristedes came into Milly's for breakfast the other day. He told me I can hang around his kitchen and learn something about the way Greeks use spices."

"Oh, forget that and listen to me. The point I was making is, you're one of the few people I've ever known who would really benefit from a college education." He sounded pompous, the guardian of a troublesome ward.

"The self is Brahman. I am on the path to enlightenment. I have faith, now I must develop skill through work, and then I will achieve knowledge."

"Which means you don't agree?"

"I like to study my own things. I don't want to have to bum out on all those required courses."

"You don't have to go for a degree. Take a few subjects that appeal to you."

"I'll think about it." After a moment, she said, "Is it

because I seem so dumb? I've always tried to watch my grammar."

"No, Allison. You're potentially brilliant. What I'm suggesting is that you'd kind of fill your toolbox by getting a formal education. You'd learn things you could call on *just* for you . . . always."

Allison was back to herself, smiling and cuddling against his shoulder. There was so much about her that he could not decipher and that continued to fascinate him.

He told her a bit of the history of the Timberline Lodge, which had been built by the Northwest's skilled craftsmen and artisans in the 1930s as part of President Roosevelt's national recovery project. It stood like a castle below the snow-covered pinnacle of Mount Hood. When they left the car, Allison gazed up, opening her arms as though to embrace it.

"This is so exciting, Ter. The Himalayas can't be any grander. And it's my first time ever—being away."

"From the city?"

"No, on a vacation. I've never stayed at a hotel. Like a guest."

"Wait till we go to Europe."

She stopped in her tracks. "You've been?"

"Yes. Let's see? Four or five times."

"You've been to Paris?"

"I never miss it."

"How? You just flew over?"

"Uh-huh. I spent three months in Geneva when they were selling a miracle polio cure. When that didn't work, I went to lots of other doctors in Europe. I think I cured myself, working out when I got home. In my junior year at S.C. they had an exchange program with Montpellier, which has a famous law school."

She was like a child shown a telescope. "You can speak French?"

"*Oui.*"

"Go on, say something in French."

They were walking through the rustic paneled lobby, its grand fireplace ablaze with Oregon pine. Guests at small tables nipped at sandwiches and drank tea. Follow-

ing the bellhop to the reception desk, he took her arm
and looked up at the kindly woman.

"*Bonjour, madame. Je m'appelle Terence Sean Brett.
Nous avons reservé votre grande suite.*"

"*Ahh, bienvenue, Monsieur Brett. Tout est prêt pour
vous and votre femme.*"

Allison had a moony smile. She laid her head on his
shoulder and whispered: "I should've let you buy me a
jacket. But don't worry, I saw a bunch of mink coats on
wooden pegs near the entrance."

"Don't even think that one through." He seized her
arm and as he was signing the large green leather book
said: "I have something better upstairs."

"Not purple panties for more vigor?" she asked, clinging to him in the elevator.

"Do I need more?"

"Dear God, no."

Despite Allison's worldly street sharpness, Terry found
in her a wealth of innocence that constantly enriched his
passion. The suite he'd reserved had a view of the mountain and the glittering frozen lake on the arced flanks,
which sparkled in the late afternoon sunlight.

He had ordered a bottle of Dom Pérignon, which was
already there, and he popped the cork and filled their
glasses. She dropped her canvas bag by the side of the
bed, then tested it like a wrestler.

"Oh, this is two out of three falls and a full press wins
it. I don't know why you picked this place. It must cost
a fortune. You're crazy. We passed a Holiday Inn with
a vacancy sign."

He lifted her off the bed and grasped her tapered fingers in his. Holding her close, he led her out to the terrace.

"I sure hope you like to drink champagne," he said,
tapping her glass.

"I'll cry if you don't stop."

"Allison, what's your favorite month?"

"Right this second. This moment. Let me die with *you*
in paradise."

"No, Allison, that's not good enough. You have to answer the question."

"Lawyers be damned. May, all right? May is my month. When I was a little girl, I read about Maia. She was a Roman goddess who was one of the stars. Maia had a son with Zeus and they named him Hermes." With perfect seriousness she said, "We will become them."

He was captivated by the explanation.

"I had another reason for picking Timberline."

"Tell me."

"My father proposed to my mother here ... in this room. Allison Desmond, will you marry me in May?"

Allison's body plunged forward over the redwood rail and he grasped her.

"I can't catch my breath. Oh, God, Terry, I think I'm going to faint." He hugged her. "You are my destiny."

Terry was so stunned by the power of his feeling for her, the flawless love, devoid of faultlines, that he yielded to the innocence of his captivity.

"You've got it wrong, Allison. You're *my* destiny."

They made love again and again until exhaustion mounted the throne. Allison was too excited to sleep. Terry lay curled against her bare shoulder and she timed his breaths like a metronome. It all seemed fantastic that such a man had fallen in love with her. The grave authenticity of his proposal and her acceptance had a hallucinatory effect on her. It struck her as inconceivable that her nomadic existence was at an end. Beckoning in the future was shelter, an actual home, the possibility of a clan, and conceiving their family. These thoughts filled her with reverence. As dawn crept into the room, she realized that in the nativity of this light she had been reborn.

13

Terry eventually worked out a representation contract with Earl. His new client was filled with resentment and animosity by the arrangement he proposed. Somewhat irritated, Terry was forced to elaborate.

"I want forty percent and expenses. It's called a contingency contract."

Earl frowned. "Strikes me as heavy."

"I'm prepared to sue Jonah Wolfe's ass off—the NBA, the Players' Association. All of them, if I have to. I want you to understand something, Earl. Incurring the hatred of powerful people carries a risk which I'm prepared to take. If what I suspect is true about Jonah colluding with the insurance company and denying your claim, then when I get through with these bastards, no one's going to walk away without a limp."

Earl buckled. "You're going for big money, huh?"

"From what I've heard, Jonah Wolfe is worth millions, and he's going to part with some cash or be on crutches when I get through with him."

"Okay, partner, ride his ass."

"I'll stampede his cattle if I have to."

Earl examined his looseleaf scrapbook with scholarly thoroughness.

"Now you got all the names and addresses of who to contact? One of the key people is Mike Summers up in Fond du Lac. Last I heard, he was coaching a junior college basketball team."

"Why's he so important?"

"I'm not sure. But Jonah bought Mike a house."

"That's interesting. Go on."

"One night, Jonah and Mike had an argument on the phone. One of those 'I'll-burn-your-ass' humdingers. I could hear it through the walls of the motel. Jonah and I were wrecking a couple of gals. With more on the way.

. . . Jonah was so freaked out by his beef with Mike that he cleared out."

"How well do you know this Mike Summers?"

"I met him when I did a little unofficial scouting for Jonah. Something very serious went on between them. And Jonah, who's never scared, was in a panic."

"All right, Earl, I'll see this guy Mike and anyone else who can help the case."

Terry was not looking forward to parting with Allison and he wondered if he'd be wiser to go to the airport on his own. She insisted on driving him. They had agreed to keep their engagement confidential until he returned and they could plan an engagement party. He also needed to be around to shield her from Pat.

"I'll be a good girl and won't smoke grass. Fact is, since we've been together, I don't even like it."

"Does that mean I'm your new high?"

She brightened and her eyes rolled like a kid's. "You don't have to ask." He held her. He slipped his hand along her thigh. "I can't manage roving hands while I'm driving," she said with a smirk.

"Pretend it's a robbery—at a McDonald's."

A glint of a smile crossed her face. "People tell me everyone's too businesslike at a time like that to be going down on the driver."

They both began to laugh. His life with Allison was an open-ended game.

"I'll be staying at the Hotel Pfister in Milwaukee. Any problems, call me."

"Stop all this worrying. I'll charm Pat to death. It'll all be smooth sailing," she noted with the conviction of a poker player holding deuces.

"You okay for money?"

"Yes, Terry."

I can't help myself or bear to be without her, he thought.

"I am yours and you are mine," she said. "We are one with the Absolute."

*   *   *

While Allison kneaded dough in Milly's kitchen, Paul Cisco found himself in the midst of one of the most unpleasant meetings he'd had in his six years as the assistant D.A. He admired Terry Brett as a man whose legal talent bestowed upon him an unlimited horizon. Cisco's breakfast companion was Sergeant Barney Laver.

Laver was a vain man, with an iceberg pompadour and chickenpox holes on his forehead that had never refilled and he employed bits of pancake makeup from his wife's larder that hardened as the day waned. His prolonged nose was insulated with small spikes of hair. He was always well dressed in larcenous mismatching suit jackets and black flannel trousers. Standing or sitting, he leaned forward, like a greyhound wearing a tie. His smoky, protruding eyes zoomed around in search of the criminal activities of humanity. His world view was that if a felony was not actually in progress, one was at the planning stage.

As Laver sat with Cisco in the rear booth of Milly's Pantry, he was also unnerved. Cisco stoked his pancakes with butter, and Terry's future seemed to melt on his plate.

"Jesus Christ, Barney, I can't authorize another search warrant on the basis of a tip from Warren Paris. Last time that weasel came to me, the fucking Greek's case exploded in my face. I was humiliated. Walsh and the other sitting judges will knock us on our asses."

"This time it's different, Paul. We can't afford to ignore it. There's an LSD epidemic in this city. Kids are just flipping out on this acid. We're making arrests and busts day and night. And Warren Paris told me Allison's the one who's moving it."

"Terry Brett is my *friend*. I was a guest in his home on Christmas." Cisco failed to mention that he had given some consideration to resigning from office. To placate his wife, he intended to discuss some form of partnership with Terry when he returned to town. It galled him to see other lawyers making big fees while he and his wife scrounged on the salary of a public official. "We can't go into Terry's house and start ripping the place apart. And there's his father!"

"I know Pat real well. He did an addition to my place last summer—at cost plus ten percent. Now, I don't like it any more than you do," Barney said sullenly. "The fact remains the Bretts may be harboring a major drug connection."

"What the hell are you saying? That Terry and Pat might have knowledge and are co-conspirators? Jesus, Barney, I want to puke."

They looked at each other with deepening cynicism.

"I assume it would be in total innocence," Barney Laver said. "But she's as slick as they come."

Allison scurried out of the kitchen in her whites, carrying a tray of lemon meringue pies which she placed in the entry showcase.

"There goes hot pants," Cisco said. "I think I prefer her to the pie."

"What's going on with her and Terry? Is she really his client?"

"She had a beef with Judge Walsh. Let's say, Terry has *her* on retainer."

"I can understand why."

"I told Terry about your suspicions about Lady Allison's part in the McDonald's robbery."

"While he's basting her, he's not going to help us?" Barney said with a hint of yearning.

Paul Cisco was truly bugged and looked for a finesse. "Barney, just suppose, while Miss Allison's baking cakes here, you dropped by Pat's for a friendly chat about house extensions or had a drink, and felt him out. He might drive a nail through your heart or kiss your hand."

"I like it, Paul."

14

Now on his third day in Milwaukee, Terry's investigation of Jonah Wolfe foundered. He had talked to bartenders, vendors at Brewer Garden, a couple of sportswriters, and a dissolute madam who gave him the names of some of Jonah's fluff. Even with the help of a retired detective, Terry couldn't locate any of them. He grew frustrated by the fool's errand he had undertaken. His yearning for Allison heightened when they missed calls to each other.

He spent a morning at Marquette's law school library, where he had been treated as a visiting dignitary because of his law review credentials. He was surprised to learn that Jonah Wolfe had gone to night school there and graduated. He had practiced law briefly in Milwaukee but was no longer on the state bar rolls, and the firm he had worked for had folded.

Why had Jonah Wolfe bailed out on Earl? Terry was puzzled: Earl had a legitimate claim against Wolfe, and as a lawyer, practicing or not, Jonah would know this, as would the insurance company that had covered the team members for such liability. Some tantalizing element was missing. Terry was now lured by curiosity and a desire to bring back a trophy for his princess. He telephoned Mike Summers, the coach in Fond du Lac Earl had mentioned, and made an appointment with him.

Driving through the frozen Dells of Wisconsin, Terry entered Fond du Lac, which was adrift in titanic berms of snow. The streets barked with wind channeling from Lake Winnebago. As he walked to the college gym late in the afternoon, the fierce intemperate sound in his ears had the force of a bellows and almost knocked him down.

The Fond du Lac Community College locker room was rank with sweat and Oil of Wintergreen, but Terry was captivated by the young warriors in the icy, Neolithic gym. If only he could have been an athlete instead of some fastball lawyer with a good tennis serve, smooth ground strokes, but no mobility to back it up. He had switched to golf in his teens and taken out his aggression with a hammerhead five handicap that ate up competitors.

Smoke was coming out of Mike Summers's mouth as he gave a spirited strategy talk to his starting five. "We've got to clog the lane against Appleton because of their big man. Don't let them drive and pass off."

"Coach, we're freezing, can we put our coats on?" a lithe black kid asked.

"Endurance and pride is what this game is about. Man, we're building character."

Noticing Terry, the coach squinted in the distance. Although it was very cold, Summers wore only a T-shirt and sweatpants, which flaunted a barrel chest and thick arms. He was about Terry's height and he walked with an athlete's serene grace. His red hair was crewcut, framing a disarming, childlike face whose milky vellum skin was ribboned with bright freckles.

"Mr. Brett?"

"Yes." Terry extended his hand.

"You're not really some Big Ten scout, trying to steal my players?"

Terry handed Summers his business card. "No, I'm not scouting," he said. "I've checked into the Buttermilk Inn." Terry didn't like to interrupt a practice. "If you're free, I'd like to buy you dinner. I'm from the northwest, Port Rivers. Earl Raymond is one of our boosters." While the players went through some loosening-up exercises to keep them warm, Terry took Mike aside. "I was in Milwaukee on business and Earl insisted that I look you up. He said you're a brilliant coach."

"Did he? Earl, that's a name out of a scrapbook. Are you shopping for a coach, Mr. Brett?"

"No, this is purely social." Terry saw big ideas forming on Summers's face. "I came up to see you."

"I'm flattered. We can hook up after practice."

Terry stayed for a while, watching the team practice in this cold, pokey gym with its warped floor. The lean ebony stick of a boy called Whiz coasted with the grace of a ballet dancer on the floor. His vision was remarkable. He anticipated where everyone would be at any second, and his passes slinked rhythmically between defenders. He had a soft shot and a wonderful eye and could score at will, but took it easy on his teammates. Terry would pay the price of admission anywhere to see him play.

When Terry returned to the Buttermilk Inn, he tried to reach Allison at work but missed her. He dialed his home number and Pat answered. He was in a garrulous good humor and Terry was forced to listen to his father's legal entanglements.

"The lawyer you found for me turned out to be a genius. I'll come out with fifteen thousand on the River Cove house and the insurance company will cover all the plumbing defects. My bonding premiums aren't going to rise."

"We'll crack some champagne when I get home. Dad, are things all right with you and Allison?"

"So far so good. I don't see much of her. She leaves at the crack of dawn and I get home late."

"Where is she?"

"Have you tried her at Milly's?"

"Yes."

"I'll leave her a note. When are you coming back?"

"Maybe tomorrow."

"Terry, someone's at the door. I've got to run. I think it's my new client."

Armed with a bag of doughnuts and a thermos of coffee, snuffling and emitting Vicks VapoRub's hellish fumes, Sergeant Barney Laver, a man with a mission, strode into Pat's living room. He had conjured up the perfect fairy tale.

"Hi, Big Pat, I recalled you living in the neighborhood. We tracked a suspect near here."

"That a fact."

Pat was dismayed to have this visitor. The amorous contractor had expected an exceedingly attractive woman to come by to survey his kitchen catalogues. Afterwards, who knew? The signs were good. As Laver shuffled inside, the phone rang and his client upped the stakes by suggesting a cocktail-hour rendezvous at a motel celebrated for its pillow talk. Pat's geniality was restored, and he was fully prepared to do his part, combating the scourge of crime.

"Actually, I'm glad to see you, Barney."

"You are?"

"Yeah, maybe you can help me out. I've had a problem with some workmen on a house I built. They screwed me but royally, using cheap materials. If I catch them, I'd shoot them on the street. Can you help me track them down?"

Laver was taken aback but decided to jolly Pat along. "If you've got some pictures or descriptions, I'll have one of my men look into it."

"Great. Now, I don't mind hanging out with you. I haven't got anything important till later," Pat said exuberantly. "I could be an observer. Got .45s and hunting rifles, shotguns, if you need a hand." His face grew animated with the thrill of being with cops on a hot case—a stakeout. "Is this going to be dangerous? Can you tell me about it, or is it hush-hush?"

Barney Laver was distressed by Pat's honesty and his own shallow deception. "Pat, I'm sorry to have misled you."

Pat was mystified. "How've you done that?"

"I was going to ask your permission to use the house as an observation post."

"Fine, go to it."

"Thing is, the suspect is under your roof." Pat's face clouded with bewilderment and ire. "I'd like to spend some time here looking around. I have no search warrant or horseshit like that. I could get one," Laver added ominously. "I'd prefer it if you cooperated."

"What's this all about? Hey, I just got off the phone with Terry. Does this have something to do with one of his cases? He ought to know, ought to—" Laver raised a hand to cut him off. "Exactly who're you investigating?"

"Allison Desmond."

Pat's mouth went dry. "What? Why?"

"Is she legally residing here?"

"She's sort of . . . visiting, you could say, with Ter."

"Has she received any mail? Packages you know of?"

"Yeah. Books and art supplies."

"Art supplies, really?" Laver made a note on his pad. "Did you ever examine the content of these packages?"

"What do you mean? Why would I do that?"

"How long's Terry been away?"

"Almost a week."

"Pat, I'd like your consent to search Allison's room."

"God almighty, Barney, what the fuck's going on?" Alarm had crept into his voice. "This is my *home*."

"Naturally, you can come with me."

Pat's concentration wavered and he was seeing spots. "Jesus, well, she also uses the spare room to paint or something." Bile churned at the back of his throat. "The truth is, she and Terry have been shacked up and I don't like it one bit."

"Those things can be awkward. Look, I won't be pulling up the floorboards."

"This is outrageous. What's she suspected of, anyway?"

"Can't say."

"Well, one thing she stands guilty of"—Barney waited—"is ruining my relationship with Terry. Making a crazy man out of him. He can't concentrate on anything but this damned girl. You can bust her for that with my blessings."

Pat felt as if his lungs were collapsing as Barney sifted through drawers and suitcases, peered in corners, stood on the kitchen ladder shining a flashlight to view the back of her closet.

After two hours of watching Barney Laver methodically examine Allison's intimate life with his son, Pat went downstairs and poured himself a tumbler of scotch and belted it back neat. But it did not ease the foreboding that crept through his soul. Thwarted, Barney came into the den.

"Well, is she a witch or not?"

"Oh, she's a witch all right—I've thought so all along. But she's not practicing her crafts in your place."

A witch; the word floated crazily through Pat's mind. "How long've you known about her?"

"Since she floated into town, nothing's been the same. She's a suspect in the McDonald's robbery. Now please don't press me any more."

"What the hell do I tell Terry about this?" Pat roared, a bull elephant making a charge against the hunter.

"You two are real close."

"We were until she took over and spoiled things."

"I'm sorry to hear that. Now, I've been up against Terry in court. It hasn't been a pleasure. He is one very smart criminal lawyer. But lawyer or not, if he were my son, I'd sit him down and have a good heart-to-heart. Representing a criminal is one thing; having one live in your home is another. It wouldn't hurt to tactfully suggest that Terry improve the quality of his houseguests."

Pat responded in fury. "You can count on it."

15

In the Buttermilk Inn lounge, the local TV weatherman was attempting to console the residents about the impending snowstorm. As he pointed at charts, the bartender glumly turned away from the screen.

Terry smiled at him. "Your brochure says that your central heating is new."

"Don't let it fool you. That's why the rooms have fireplaces."

"Well, you make a helluva martini."

"Thirty years of practice. I hear cocktail shakers in my sleep."

When he was on a case, Terry had a talent for picking up gossip about the natives. The bartender generously shared his knowledge, giving him an earful. When Mike

Summers arrived, Terry was nursing a second martini beside the robust fireplace.

"I'm trying to stay on the wagon," Summers said, joining Terry on the sofa. Mike had promised his wife to quit drinking and he seemed to be relieved that she and his baby daughter were away.

Terry had heard all about Mike Summers's binges. "You don't mind me having a few pops, do you?"

" 'Course not. . . . Earl Raymond, I never saw a man work a bar like him. Women would be tearing his clothes off."

Terry leaned over confidentially and his mood took on a solemnity that drew Summers closer. "The past was a Mardi Gras for Earl. The present is a tragedy. He's crippled and in constant pain."

"I didn't know," Mike said sympathetically as one who had played the game. "His knee again?"

Terry nodded. "It won't ever go away. How long was Earl up here, scouting, was it?"

"Fair few times. He liked one of my kids," Mike said thoughtfully, then looked with interest at the cocktail glass Terry picked up.

"What're you drinking?"

"One of my father's concoctions. Beefeater's, a drop of dry vermouth, and some onion juice. I showed the bartender how I like it." In fact, Terry and the bartender had quite an informative chat about Mike Summers. "Want to try a short one?"

Mike pondered the question. "Maybe just one." Terry signaled the bartender and Mike's concentration focused on the alchemist's preparation. "I stopped drinking."

"I haven't. Coaches and lawyers, well, Mike, the only time they can be themselves is with some juice in them."

On his third drink, Mike Summers was liberating himself. Terry had that gregarious, mellow knack of questioning people in a public setting and getting them to relax.

"We're making a list of possible coaching assistants," he explained later, over steaks.

"Sort of whoever's traveling on your committee does

a little visiting?" Terry nodded. "I always enjoyed the northwest."

"The thing is, Earl likes you and we use him as an adviser, unofficially. So he put in a good word for you."

"That was damn nice of him."

"I wish someone would do the same thing for him. He really needs help. The owner of the Los Angeles Stars—Jonah Somebody—gave Earl a real going over."

Mike put down his knife and fork, jolted as though he'd seen his wife with another man. "Wolfe. Jonah Wolfe."

"Yeah, well, he cut Earl's disability and blew him out of his contract. If not for a few boosters, Earl'd be panhandling on the streets."

"Bastard."

"Earl?"

"Wolfe!"

When they were socializing over brandy back at the coach's rugged two-story house that might have been the residence of the town's leading stockbroker, Terry discovered his fifty-dollar tip to the bartender hadn't been in vain. His childlike face a red float, Summers was a triple threat with the bottle.

"Why do you think a man like Wolfe, with all that money, would bury a pathetic bust-out like Earl?"

"*Me,* he hates. But I don't know why he's got it in for Earl," Mike said.

"You *and* Earl?" Terry said, carefully measuring his sips. They were into a second bottle of keep-warm brandy. "Jonah cut his disability. It strikes me as unfair. Possibly illegal. I'd really like to stick it to Mr. Wolfe."

"Would you? Funny how people just fall into each other, Terry. You come out on some other business . . . possibly a coaching offer for me, and things from the past crop up."

"I'm really enjoying our visit, Mike." Sensing revelations hovering, Terry quickly changed the subject to avoid the appearance of probing. He'd let Mike make up his mind. Terry was going to hug Mike Summers to death. "So you really like this kid, Whiz. What's his real name?"

"Davis Wilson. We call him Whiz. He was a natural for a Big Ten scholarship. But he just can't handle the courses. His reading level is about fourth grade. He's All-American material," Mike said with conviction.

Terry was fascinated by the young magician. "Actually, he should be playing pro ball now," Terry said. "One serious knee injury and he'll be packing groceries for life. These kids need to grab their chances. College courses won't mean anything to him. Why have him go on failing when he has God-given talent and could be a star?"

"Could you do anything for him?"

"Maybe. I'd hire a tutor for him, have him skip college, and damn well try to get him a pro contract."

"I'll talk to him about it. At the end of the season."

It was almost four in the morning and the snowstorm had developed into a fierce blizzard.

"I better get a move on if I want to find the inn."

"I can't let you drive back in this weather, Terry."

"I don't like to impose."

"Please stay. If you're not sleepy, we can keep jawing."

"Sure." Terry grimaced. "This situation with Jonah Wolfe—whatever it is—is bugging me. Man, in Milwaukee, I saw billboards all over town advertising his hot dogs and sausages. I'm an advocate for the little guy who gets stamped on by moguls. And nothing gets me more pissed off than when somebody with big bucks gets away with murder."

Mike's face became taut with repressed fury and he strode around the living room with the agitation of a hyperactive child.

"Jonah just about did. But *I* let him off the hook."

Terry affected indifference. "You're a good guy, Mike, and when I get back home, I'm going to talk you up for a coaching job."

"I'd like to get out of the Midwest. Don't get me wrong. I love the kids and my job . . ."

"Say no more. It's a dead end. But you seem to be living well. In a lovely home. I'm very impressed."

Mike growled. "The memories are terrible. My conscience won't let me rest."

Like a bear raising its snout before prowling, Terry scented the movement of his quarry, the rustle of those unsilent leaves from within, the twig snapping.

"Conscience, damn, I know what you mean. Nothing worse. It's quiet sometimes. But like my leg from polio, it's always there." And now Terry took the reins, leading his witness. "Mike, when I saw those cold-assed kids in the locker room . . . well, Jesus, I thought it was a tribute to your abilities as a coach and an inspirational leader. I'll tell you, Mike, in my heart, I would throw up my legal practice just to be in one game with them and score twenty points. Funny thing is that not even my friends know how I really feel. I'm comfortable with you.

"It's been my experience, Mike, that once in awhile you meet a guy, a total stranger, and I don't know why, but you can open up, unburden yourself, reveal your innermost secrets. Then out of the blue, this kindly stranger says something or offers advice and you're grateful to him forever."

Mike agreed with the wisdom of this assertion and Terry watched him struggle before he was clasped in the bear trap. Several years earlier, Jonah Wolfe and Earl had come to town to see a young player. Mike had been a fan of Earl's and was thrilled to meet him as well as the owner of a professional team.

"This was before I was married, Terry. I was living in a trailer, doing okay. I had my sister, Karen, and a girlfriend of hers, staying with me. My folks couldn't handle Karen. She was into dope, running away. All of fourteen years old." He shook his head with resignation.

"Well, the folks pleaded with me to see if there was anything I could do to straighten her out. Me being a coach. Have her hang around with the campus kids. It was working out. Karen was back at school, actually going to classes, doing some homework, getting into the community.

"Earl and Jonah drove out to the trailer. We talked basketball, the future of the game." Mike smiled involuntarily. "Well, that Earl, he can't get enough."

Terry interrupted to make his host comfortable. Sharing confidences. "Tell me, I roomed with Earl at college for a year. He was on a scholarship and about to lose his eligibility because of his grades and I coached him."

Mike and Earl had left Jonah at the trailer as he was getting into his Caddy. Depending on the weather, Jonah was going to stay the night at a motel or drive back to Milwaukee.

"Have you ever seen Jonah Wolfe?"

"No."

"Good-looking man. He kinda of reminds me of a Robert Mitchum in his fifties. He's got those bedroom eyes. But, boy, he's a smoothie."

"I know the type," Terry said.

"Earl and I really took to each other. We decided to head into town and have a few pops together. Earl is a man who enjoys being hero-worshipped. And I was at his feet, was I ever. He got himself pissed. A waitress and him took to each other. She wrapped him up for the night at her place. I went back to the trailer feeling very up. I mean, what a night! *The* Earl Raymond all to myself for hours."

Jonah's Caddy was still parked there when Mike returned.

"And I thought, 'Shit, Wolfe's stuck and must've had to walk miles. He'll be sore as hell.' I found the trailer locked and the blinds were down. Just as I was going to bang on the door, there was a sound from inside. Once you've heard it, it's unforgettable: the groaning and whining of a woman having an orgasm. And screaming for more!" Mike continued like the snowfall.

Mike had gone around the side and peeked through a crack. He was shocked, immobilized.

Jonah Wolfe, Karen, and her girlfriend were naked in a daisy chain, whirling on the waterbed.

"I didn't know what to do, Terry; I was so rattled. Stunned. I just stood outside, pacing, talking to myself.

Then I remembered I had a key hidden. See, I never locked the place. I found the key and walked in.

"Terry, they didn't even hear me. Jonah was fucking Karen—and ramming his fist into her girlfriend and pushing her head down on Karen—Man, I thought I was going to pass out. My place reeked of grass. There were pills, coke on the table . . . and a batch of Polaroids of Jonah and the girls in all kinds of positions."

When they saw Mike, Jonah and the girls stopped abruptly, and covered themselves with the sheets.

" 'Everything can be fixed, worked out,' Jonah said to me. 'Just don't lose your head.' "

Rather than confront the surreal vision of the situation, Mike had picked up the photographs and was about to tear them up.

"Jonah jumped out of bed. He grabbed my arm. 'Don't tear them up. That's what this is all about. I collect them.' " By anyone's standards, Jonah Wolfe carried enormous sums of cash with him to relieve the distress of others. "He had bundles of hundred-dollar bills with bank bands still on in a satchel. He just started tossing them to me and got dressed."

"What about the girls?" Terry asked.

"They were laughing and refused to press charges. They dressed, got into his Caddy, and went to Vegas with him."

"What eventually happened to Karen?"

"No idea. She got swallowed up like pretty girls do. I haven't heard from her since."

"You never told Earl about this?"

"No one but you." Mike was sweating and tearful. "I was in such a quandary . . . so confused. I mean, how do you discuss something like that?"

Terry walked to the window. Bare tree limbs sagged, the wind was silent now, and daybreak carried gloom and more snow. He thought of the smells of Milly's kitchen—and Allison.

"Harboring something like this has been a helluva thing to live with, Mike. Some guys would've flipped out. You showed lots of courage and good judgment."

"Jonah gave me fifty thousand dollars that night. I used the money to buy this house afterwards. And I never thought of reporting him. It was all so ugly. Especially my part. But I was about to be engaged and I didn't want my future wife to move into a trailer. At least I've got a roof for her and our baby daughter. The property's appreciated, too."

"So Jonah walked away."

"Those kind of guys always do."

"I know that," Terry said angrily. "I suppose he took all the Polaroids with him?"

"No, I insisted on keeping them. Now and then, to prick my conscience, I open the envelope. But I can't bring myself to look at them." Mike cradled his head on the table. "Terry"—his voice was a low keen—"we're sitting in the house Karen's ass paid for, is what it is."

Terry put his arm around Mike, brothers in distress.

"I appreciate this confidence on your part"—Terry's voice was low, soothing. "What outrages me isn't the sex part, it's the offense to you—Karen's brother, her guardian."

"A girl that age needs special care. That's what galls me. I couldn't give it to her."

"Of course not, Mike. You did your best. Karen grew up too fast and was corrupted by forces beyond you. *You,* Mike, you're the injured party in all of this. Jonah Wolfe screws two fourteen-year-old girls and buys you out for peanuts! That adds injustice to injury," Terry bellowed. "One of those girls is your little sister! Your character saved you from murder. You've been cheated, Mike. It's a disgrace. An attack on your manhood!"

Terry gave the appearance of being so deeply wounded by the inequity that he barged out of the room and into the kitchen. He got himself a glass of water. With concern, Mike followed, cautiously watching.

"Earl, you don't want to know about. Down and out. He's been in the hospital . . . suicidal."

"I can't believe it. I mean, I believe you, Ter."

"A stumblebum. I gave him fifty bucks at Christmas." Terry picked up a photograph of Mike's wife and daughter. "Just imagine Jonah Wolfe alone with *your* wife."

"No! No!"

"If I were to file a lawsuit against Jonah, would you be prepared to testify against him?"

Mike Summers retreated as though from an armed assailant. Terry already knew that he would refuse, for Mike could not justify the bribe he had accepted from Jonah, and when Jonah's attorney demanded to see his income tax declaration, he'd be in serious trouble.

"I don't think so."

Terry had his man. "Mike, you have no annuity, no real security for your wife and child. You have to provide more for them. It's a moral obligation. I'd hate to think of baby Debbie being denied the opportunities that Jonah Wolfe's fortune buys for his children."

When the storm broke later that morning, and Mike was sleeping off the night of drinking, Terry telephoned his close friend Billy Klein, who was delighted to have him stay at his beach house and offered him the run of his law office. Terry drove back to Milwaukee and flew out to Los Angeles.

16

After two-thirty, business slowed at Milly's restaurant. Allison had been on her feet for hours. She more or less existed between the ovens and a little cubbyhole where she hung her raincoat and kept an eye on the roses Terry sent, which she had placed in a soup tureen on a shelf above the pot sink. The last time Terry called, she had left the oven and blown up the meringues. Cleaning it up was hell. Lips pursed, Milly informed her that she could only accept another call if the party at the other end were dying. Still, Allison loved every second of her new life.

Allison was saying her mantra, praying to Buddha to continue his good works and keep her in that changeless unalterable universe of total happiness. As part of her scattered education, she was reading Hesse's *Siddhartha* and sneaking in a Henry Miller novel to see if there were any new mating inventions that had not reached the provinces and would be of interest to Terry.

Allison picked up a stray blue plate from the counter and put it on the busboy tray. She filled a mug with coffee and spotted Georgie sitting with Milly in her booth by the register. Milly beckoned her to join them.

"Coffee refills anyone?" Allison asked before sitting down.

"No, thanks, honey," Milly said. She was pleased with her young recruit. Milly had told Georgie that she was diligent and had a flair for sauces.

"How's your leg?" Georgie asked.

"It's fine, but my feet are killing me."

Milly offered advice. "You've got to get these space shoes. They're expensive, but they're molded to the shape of your foot and give you extra arch support."

Allison laughed. Her Terry, Mr. Highboots, would really go for them. "I admit they look comfortable. But with all due respect, Milly, I'm hoping to build a relationship with Terry, not end it when he comes back. If my feet fall off, I couldn't wear them."

Milly really liked her around. They laughed and Allison was at ease with them and had a sense of belonging, residing in a cocoon. Allison kept quiet about Pat's activities. He was always phoning women to find out if their husbands were around. If not, he was handy.

"Have you heard from Terry?" Georgie asked with more than passing interest.

Earl had sent her scouting for a weather report on his attorney's progress. "A couple of days ago. It's frustrating, we keep missing each other with this time difference."

"Was he making out okay?"

"I don't know, Georgie. He doesn't talk business with me. He sounded rushed."

Georgie smiled optimistically. "If I know Terry, he'll

come home with something. Listen, you girls want to go to a movie tonight?"

Allison looked at Milly. They baked only half the morning on Thursdays, which was a slow day.

"You go, Allison. You can come in at eleven and work lunch on the line. What's on at the Rialto?"

"Earl's got basketball on TV and poker afterward, so I was thinking we'd catch this English film called *Darling*. There's this new actress, Julie Christie, and she looks like Allison," Georgie said. "You're welcome to join us, Milly."

"Get Pat into a movie? If it's not John Wayne shooting banditos with a six-gun, don't call him."

"I'd love to go, Georgie. I'll head back for a nap and see you at your place."

It was very dark and the rain slashing the windshield of Terry's Mustang blinded Allison when she pulled into the driveway. She put one of Terry's ski caps on her head and dashed inside. The front door was locked, which seemed odd. She wondered if Pat had a woman inside. But the lights were on and she saw him standing at the fireplace with a drink. She fumbled with the housekeys.

The moment she hit the hallway, she couldn't get her bearings. Her heart pounced into her throat and it felt like she was swallowing it raw and choking on it. Her old suitcase was beside the stairs and her duffel bag spilled out with her lingerie.

"Oh, this is terrific," Allison said, overcoming her initial panic, which surged into outrage. Her cheeks were purple and so were Pat's as they eyed each other.

"You packed up my underthings!"

"No respectable woman would buy stuff like that."

Withholding the name of the purchaser, Allison told herself, *I must be calm*. She had been schooled in the hypocrisy of philandering men.

"What's this all about? My underwear?"

"You're pulling Terry down with you! Into the gutter," Pat snarled and lurched to the bar. "You don't live here any longer, sister. And don't be taking Terry's car with you. I'll report it stolen and you'll wind up in the tank—where you belong."

Everything started to unravel so quickly that her mind went blank. She was frightened but not ready to cede her territory.

"You owe me an explanation."

He raised his hand, then thought better of it. "Shit's what I owe you."

"Pat, talk to me like a human being. What've I done?"

"Ask Sergeant Laver. Old Barney's wise to you. He was here investigating you."

"For what? Why didn't he come down to Milly's? You both knew where to find me!"

"He didn't want to create a scene there."

"That's not true. He saw me at work this morning."

"I could puke at the way you've wormed your way in everywhere."

Allison had spent enough time in saloons around spiteful, drunken, angry men with mean eyes whose repetitive outbursts made her think she was going crazy.

"You let Laver go through my things, didn't you?" she said with resignation. "There's a law against that."

Pat flailed his arms and spittle oozed out of the corners of his mouth.

"You're a regular jailhouse lawyer, huh? Guess you've been advising Terry on criminal codes and whatnot."

"I spent one night in the can on an assault charge. And it was justifiable. Self-defense. Since then the police have been rousting me. These clowns have nothing better to do than to hit on me." She pointed a finger at Pat and realized too late she was aggravating the situation. But she couldn't stop herself. "I'll tell you something, Pat. If I screwed that goddamn self-righteous Judge Barry Walsh, none of this would be going on. But I turned him down cold. He groped me in his chambers. And I whacked him across the face. Since then, they haven't let up on me."

"I'll bet."

Her throat was so dry, she thought she'd be sick and put her hand up protectively. The nausea was insidious.

She dropped to her knees, tearfully, supplicating.

"Pat, please, don't turn against me. Don't you know—I worship Terry. I love him more than the earth. I'll try to be good for him. Please give me a chance."

"Where do you come off to hook on to a man like my son? You're scum. A nobody from nowhere."

Allison lay prostrate on the cold floor. "Pat, I'm a person, I have feelings." She continued to plead. "Don't do this to me."

Someone knocked on the door. Allison saw Pat give a man a twenty-dollar bill. Pat returned and hovered over her. His thick, gnarled fingers and callused palm moved close to her face.

"Give me the keys to the house and the car." Allison pushed herself up from the floor and handed him the key ring. "Just get the hell out and don't leave a forwarding address."

The cabdriver took Allison back to town. She was growing desperate; something mechanical seemed to be going wrong with her mind. She didn't know where to go and he kept asking her for an address at every light.

"The movies? What time is it?"

"Seven-ten. Which movie house?"

"No, wait, I've got to meet a friend."

She'd been to Georgie's place several times but couldn't think of the name of the street. The cabby cruised the river around Astor Park. Allison finally pointed out a new building. She rushed to the intercom.

Georgie and Earl bolted downstairs and with the driver brought her things inside. Allison sat on the front steps outside. Gritty bits of hail snapped against her cheeks and into her eyes. She felt herself drifting into some hiding place of suspended consciousness.

Georgie's new condo was still stark: sheets on the windows, the emerald carpet shedding; a huge TV and coffee table were surrounded by a grotesque, modern sectional.

"We've got to talk to you." Mouth taut and her dark brown eyes apprehensive, Georgie eased Allison down on an armchair covered with brown wrapping. "Allison, Terry's in Los Angeles and he's been calling. I spoke to

Pat. He's going to pretend that nothing's wrong. Pat thinks Terry's there working on an important case with an old friend. So he's afraid to upset him. I caught Pat as he was leaving. He's decided to go to Seacliff so he doesn't have to talk to Terry right now and tell him what happened with Laver at the house."

Earl took over, yammering at her. "Pat doesn't know that Terry's working on my case."

They hammered at her like Gestapo agents. The light hurt her eyes and she wanted to sleep.

Georgie cautioned Earl. "I think she's in shock."

"Don't worry about Allison, she can handle it."

He handed Allison a glass of brandy, which she belted back.

"I don't understand any of this. What do you want me to do?"

Georgie sat on the armrest and said coaxingly, "Allison, we've worked out a story for you to give Terry. You explain that getting up so early and going into Milly's is too tough driving from his house, so I invited you to stay with me. Okay, honey?"

"What am I going to do about the police badgering me?"

Earl took Allison's hand tenderly and stroked it.

"Georgie will kick ass. They won't even have tails when she gets through with them. So don't worry."

"I can't help it, Earl. I mean, coming to the house and going through my clothes without a warrant. Pat wouldn't admit that Laver did that. He claims since it's his house, he could just pack me up and toss me out. But Laver searched."

"Be cool, Allison. Or else all this trouble is wasted— my pain—Terry's work."

Georgie was on her like a cat with a fish head. "Lives are involved. Terry's on a fast track and he's onto something. I don't know the details. But he's staying with a law school buddy and he's going to see Jonah Wolfe tomorrow morning."

Allison's eyes closed and her head drooped on her chest.

"Allison, baby, come back to us," Earl whined.

Georgie tightly gripped her hand. "Pull yourself together! Terry's going to call. If he senses anything's wrong with you, he'll dump Earl and run back here. Oh, I beg you! It's for me and Earl. Our future together." Georgie was bereft, in tears, pleading. "Please, Allison."

Allison shakily got up from the chair. "Excuse me a minute, I think I'm going to be sick."

The phone suddenly rang and Georgie answered, pointing to Allison as though she were a piece of scenery and had to be shifted.

"Oh, hi, Terry." She nattered on for a minute about the office. "I'll get Allison. Yes, she's here of course. It's ladies' night at the movies." Georgie cupped her hand over the receiver and shunted Allison into the chair. "Don't sound nervous," she hissed.

Allison trembled, becoming flustered. Terry's was a voice of celebration from another world. She gestured in frustration to Georgie, who gave her a sharp, reproving look.

"Hello, Terry." Georgie and Earl stood over her.

"Can't talk?" he asked.

"Uh-huh."

"You all right?"

"Just fine. I thought I'd stay at Georgie's till I get off this early shift at Milly's."

"That's a good idea. And it's a mean drive in this weather. . . . Important question, what's your bikini size?"

"What?" Allison lost her concentration and the thread of the conversation. He repeated the question twice.

"Depends on the cut. Eight, I guess. Terry, I don't need a bikini. I just want you back when you finish this case. Is it going well?"

Earl nodded with supervisory approval.

"Too soon to tell. I'll have a better fix on things after my meeting tomorrow. I should be back in a day or two."

"Where are you staying?"

"With an old friend. Billy Klein. You'll meet him. I want him to be my best man."

In a daze, she looked at Earl signaling for her to hang up. "What's his number?"

Terry was concerned that one of Billy Klein's doped, beach house trolls might pick up the phone and get cute with Allison.

"I'm not sure where I'll be," Terry said. "I'll call you."

"Okay, Terry, whatever you say."

When she hung up, Earl smiled and nodded cheerfully. "You did that very well, Allison. You lie like a pro."

Guilt never sleeps; it informed every muscle and bone in Allison's body and tainted her mind. Was Pat right? Was she bringing Terry down? Damaging his prospects? Wouldn't he be better off with a young woman who shared his social and educational background? A woman who brought something to the table. And yet, Allison knew there was something more, something deeper between them that could not be weighed on society's scale.

In torment, searching for a path, she shivered under the mothballed blankets in the camp bed she had been given in Georgie's second bedroom. Earl was hooting and cheering a basketball game on the TV and making calls for other scores. Every hour or so, Georgie poked her head in like a clucking hen to see if Allison needed anything. Then she dashed back to Earl.

She overheard Georgie say to him, "You put me in a bind with Allison. I don't know a thing about criminal law. I can't deal with Paul Cisco."

At dawn, Allison showered, located some clean clothes, and debated about going to work. Would Milly fire her? She dreaded another confrontation. Were Laver and his men going to be hounding her? Was Pat involved with them in a conspiracy? Before leaving, she counted her money. She had six hundred dollars and change. She took the bus to the restaurant and arrived a moment before Milly.

"I thought you were coming in late? How was the movie?"

"We didn't go."

So far, Milly's manner revealed no hostility. She was

the ever amiable military dictator in the kitchen. "Pat went up to Seacliff to visit my brother Harry last night." She seemed upset. "This is the last year he and Carol will be running my diner there. I'll miss them—both of them with arthritis. They're moving to Florida." She peered at Allison. "Something wrong?"

Allison shivered. "No."

"You're real pale. If you're coming down with some-thing, I don't want you in the kitchen."

"I do have a chill," Allison admitted.

"Then take off." Milly put her hand on Allison's fore-head. "You've got a fever. I'll get you some orange juice and beef barley soup. Allison, you can go to my house."

"Thanks, Milly. But I stayed over at Georgie's and it'd be easier to go back there."

"All right. Now call me later and let me know how you're feeling."

"Yes, Milly." *If I'm not in jail,* Allison thought, as she was about to collapse.

17

The O'Callahan & Klein building in downtown Los An-geles was across from Union Station and it housed a population of a hundred and fifty lawyers. Among its part-ners were a former assistant secretary of state, two U.S. senators, a lieutenant governor, several retired judges, an assortment of other political functionaries, scoundrels, a complete orchestra of tax fiddlers, and land real estate did-dlers rezoning the city. The firm specialized in arm bend-ing for corporations and insuring that rich people got exactly what they wanted without doing time or paying taxes.

The office also provided a perfect refuge for Terry's law school merrymaker Billy Klein, who had glided through on his guile, connections, and Terry's coaching. Billy had many theories, mostly about women: short, unattractive men like Billy Klein who possessed the nerve and good dope could always coax the pants off the prettiest girls because most men were afraid of being turned down. The enlightened sixties had found its prophet in him.

"I have a theory," Billy pronounced as he and Terry entered his suite at nine the following morning.

"You have one for everything."

"Since I'm always hungover, why look for a cure?" Recovering from his nocturnal prowl, Billy mixed himself a Bloody Mary, which he hit with beef bouillon and a bolt of Tabasco.

"Is there such a thing as coffee around here?" Terry inquired.

Billy buzzed his secretary on the speakerphone. "We need a black, two sugars, Harriet. Any calls for me?"

"Your uncle would like to see you with Mr. Brett."

"Are you in trouble?" Terry was puzzled.

"I billed six hundred thousand last year. How can I be in trouble? Working here, Ter, is a hobby with me."

They walked down the hall and entered an anteroom, its long wall embalmed with portraits of eminent jurists. The door to the suite was opened by a secretary. Behind an eighteenth-century partner's desk, Carl Klein sat as though posing for his own portrait. He was a thin, bearded, ascetic man, with a scythe of a nose, liver spots on his cheeks, and a flowing mane of white hair. He was a celebrated constitutional scholar. With the death of his partner the previous year, Carl was now the firm's chief scoundrel. Terry had met him several times during law school.

"Uncle Carl, you remember my friend, Terry Brett?"

"Indeed I do." Carl Klein extended a frail claw, which Terry shook. "In fact, I recall offering him a position here."

"You did. It's a pleasure to see you again, sir."

"Where're you practicing?"

"Up in Port Rivers."

"Doing all right?"

"I guess. It's mostly criminal work. I try to keep my

brutes out of jail. Lately my practice is sort of a grab bag. To pay the light bills."

"What brings you to Los Angeles, Terry? Something criminal or civil?"

"A little of both. I also wanted to see Billy."

"Our Billy is doing extremely well—he's become the office's genial master of ceremonies, as it were," Carl Klein observed with a captious note.

Coffee was brought in on a silver tray. The cups were delicate Sèvres and the coffee a rich Kona.

"I don't know if this is relevant or it actually pertains to your visit, Terry, but I had a call at home this morning from the managing partner of Wyler, Crosby, a sister firm," the old man informed him. "We're playing some chamber music together."

Terry raised his hand as though conducting. "Your little group sounds like Haydn and Mozart."

Through his hangover, Billy Klein was trying to get a fix on things and looked from his uncle Carl to Terry, then joined in. "Ter, what's going on? We're working on an SEC prospectus with Wyler, Crosby. There are substantial fees."

"Our stake's about eighteen million and they brought us in. Naturally, we reciprocate when the opportunity arises," Carl Klein explained. "This will be a significant public offering with Morgan as the lead underwriter," he continued.

Just a little nudge, Terry told himself, *and the old man will drop the beans.*

"If the company performs well, this could be worth many more millions to you in stock warrants and options," Terry said by way of speculation.

"Oh, I think our musicians will perform." The old man's creepy washed-out blue eyes focused on his nephew. "Billy, am I correct in assuming that you offered Terry the professional courtesy of our offices?"

"Naturally, we have no business together." Billy had a twinkle. "You may assume that if I were ever to find myself in Port Rivers, we could expect as much from Terry."

"Billy, did you call Wyler's office on Terry's behalf?" Carl asked, his manner now inquisitorial.

"Yes, I did. Terry wanted to see one of their clients."

Carl Klein rose to his feet. "Goddamn it, Billy. They're having fits over there."

The old bastard knows why I'm here, Terry thought.

"Is there some impropriety at issue?" Billy asked, now subdued. "I mean, Uncle Carl, what's so unusual about letting my friend use my office for a few calls? What the hell is this all about?"

"Jonah Wolfe," Terry said.

Billy was thoroughly perplexed. "What's Jonah got to do with this?"

"Wolfe Casualty is the public offering we're involved with," Carl Klein said in a tone of rebuke.

Billy was flustered. "I still don't understand the relevance. Frankly, I haven't discussed anything of a legal nature with Terry about Jonah Wolfe. His name never even came up. Terry and I have been too busy playing catch-up. I don't know anything about Wolfe or his company, except that we have a hunk of his business through Wyler, Crosby. And he owns the Los Angeles Stars."

"Maybe Terry can tell us why the underwriting team are so . . . so very distraught at Wyler."

"*That,* sir, would be an impropriety. And I hope you're not suggesting that we make some sort of arrangement."

Carl Klein flinched as though from a hornet sting. "You might seek prudent counsel, Terry," he snapped.

"I might, if I thought I needed it."

Billy was feeling the heat. "I think my uncle is suggesting that you present us with a hypothetical case."

Terry loved the cut and thrust of the law, especially with the complacent big boys who thought they could fix anybody. "As a courtesy to a personal friend—and an attorney as distinguished as yourself, sir—I will tell you that this is a matter which could be litigated," Terry advised the two lawyers. "Or it could be settled by Mr. Wolfe's attorneys and myself. It is not a case that I would relish bringing to court."

"Could it affect the underwriting situation?" Carl asked.

"Mr. Wolfe would be the best judge of that, sir."

Billy was chagrined. "Terry, come on now, we're very close friends and you're not being very responsive to a simple inquiry."

Regarding Terry sullenly, Carl Klein demanded, "Why the devil doesn't Wolfe want his attorneys present when he sees you?"

Billy was fully awake. "What? Is this matter so sensitive, Terry?"

"I wouldn't like to characterize it in any form."

Carl baited a trap. "You can certainly tell us if the litigation is civil? Are you going to file suit or depose him while we're about to take his company public?"

Terry rose and looked at the pellucid sky and the panoramic view of the city from Carl Klein's eagle's nest.

"Gentlemen, I have an appointment with Jonah Wolfe in an hour. I don't wish to appear rude to either him, yourselves, or his attorneys."

"Wyler, Crosby brought us in! We've worked together for years. You've just about compromised our position with a major law firm," Carl Klein said, his voice ringing with indignation.

"I'm sorry to hear you say that, sir, especially in view of my admiration for the lecture you gave at our commencement. It was an eloquent discourse about the McCarthy Hearings. 'Guilt by Association.' I hope that Jonah Wolfe and his attorneys will overlook the innocent circumstances of my visit to your office. Good morning."

Despite the onset of a high, viral fever, Allison was convinced she'd go mad if she didn't escape from Georgie's place. Earl had done one of his celebrated vanishing acts. After questioning Allison, Georgie canceled her appointments at the office. With a vengeance, she went out hunting for Earl. Allison had spoken earlier to Terry and he would be returning home that evening.

"How's it going at Georgie's?"

"Earl took off. Georgie may shoot him."

Terry was amused. "Earl must be spreading himself a little thin. Maybe there's enough of him for everyone to love, cherish, and deceive. Allison, your voice is a croak."

"It's just a bad cold."

"Do you want my doctor's name?"

"It's not serious. I love you so much and I miss you."

"You can't imagine how I feel." Terry was fertile with romantic plots. "Now listen, I've got an extra Diner's Club card in my desk drawer at the office. Pick it up and get us a suite at the River Barge."

"What? That'll cost a fortune."

"Please, we're going to celebrate. Hey, there's a Santa Ana heat wave in Los Angeles. That's why I asked you about bikinis. Everybody's out on the beach. I don't think people work here. And when they do, they bring the Coppertone along. I think I want to live here with you."

"Oh, darling. I don't care if it's back in my tent."

"No tents for us. Allison, I could be about to swallow a canary. By the way, is Pat back yet from Seacliff?"

"I haven't heard."

She dreaded another encounter with Pat that would elevate their conflict. She lost herself in Terry's plans. He said he wanted some time off so that they might pick a place for their wedding reception.

Allison phoned Milly at the restaurant, explaining that she was still running a temperature, then packed up. With Barney Laver bouncing around, nothing was secure or personal. When she left Georgie's, the day was clear, the river pointillistically etched with tugs steaming to port. The sharp saline air braced her. She was about to take a cab over to McCormick's, have herself a toddy and a bowl of soup. She dragged herself and her bags to the taxi rank. At the curb, Allison suddenly flinched.

Paul Cisco blocked her. "I heard you were staying here. I thought we might visit."

"I was going out to eat," she said. Her voice sounded disembodied and dreamlike. "I really have nothing to say, Mr. Cisco."

"I have a few things that've been troubling me."

"I'm not feeling well." Cisco peered at her eyes, searching for drug use or some legal reason to detain her. "And I'm really upset with Sergeant Laver."

"Allison, we're both upset with you. If you weren't involved with Terry, life wouldn't be quite such a picnic." Cisco's cheeks puffed out like a fish in a tank sucking for breath. "Now either we talk or I'll have you carted into my office. Pick a card."

18

Charles Wyler, the senior partner of the sister firm involved in the underwriting with the Kleins, had brought one of his cunning young lawyers to the meeting at Jonah Wolfe's house. Ned Mortimer had been a classmate of Terry's at law school. Ned was ready to do battle in his three-piece pinstripe suit. He stood like a Prussian mercenary, but behind his austere expression, he was terrified.

"Jonah, this is Ned Mortimer," Wyler said.

In a soft, mellifluous voice filled with surprise, Jonah said, "He's a boy, Charlie."

"One of our brightest."

Ned choked the handle of his briefcase and gazed longingly at the pitcher of iced tea, afraid that if he didn't wet his throat he might gag. Jonah noticed and poured him a glass.

"Sit down, Ned. My impression was that this Brett was older. I got a call from one of my people that someone was asking questions about me in Milwaukee. I guess I should've paid more attention. I thought it might be a reporter."

Charles Wyler was a burly drill sergeant with a truculent, confident manner. He'd been with the SEC, then worked the lobbyist track in Washington before moving in as managing partner in Los Angeles. He was also an expert at coddling.

"Well, Jonah, you've had a pretty full load lately. Running an NBA team is a full-time job. You dump an underwriting into the mix, and who the hell's got time?"

"You're right, Charlie. Now give me a rundown on this Brett character."

Wyler turned to Ned. "You called our connection in Washington and got Brett's last tax return?"

"Yes, Mr. Wyler. I have all the papers." Ned removed a thin folder from his briefcase. "Considering the legal market he's working in, Terry's doing extremely well. He made seventy-six thousand and change last year. From the people I spoke to up in Port Rivers and the Northwest, including your friend Judge Walsh, I heard that Terry has an excellent reputation. His practice is mostly cowboys and Indians. He has a junior partner who does domestic work. Her name is Georgina Conlan. She went to River State Law and had an undistinguished academic career. She's apparently competent but no ball of fire. Terry brings in the action."

"How old is Brett?" Jonah asked.

"Twenty-six and he's been in practice for five years."

"He graduated pretty young. One of the smart ones," Jonah observed without enthusiasm.

"Editor of the *Law Review,* Order of the Coif . . . He was valedictorian and finished first."

Wyler shook his head. "Jonah, we pitched him and he was heavily recruited by the big firms here and in New York. Roy Cohn, Edward Bennett Williams, Marvin Belli all wanted him to sign on. Percy Foreman even came up from Texas to interview him."

Jonah Wolfe's head was beginning to throb. "Like an All-American in the pro draft. Okay, he's a sharpie."

"Terry Brett was everybody's All-American, Mr. Wolfe," Ned said.

"Well, what kind of guy is he? A smug prick?"

"He's anything but. To tell the truth, we all liked him. He didn't have a big head or behave like a jerk. He gave the faculty fits in moot courts. The thing about Terry, besides being well prepared, is that he's very attractive and charming. My own experience is that if you make one mistake with him or put him in an adversarial position, he'll cut your throat."

"That's great. Then what the fuck was there to like about him?" Charles Wyler demanded.

"Well, sir, there is something very genuine and kind about Terry. There's a quality, I don't know how to quite put it . . . it's like a small-town neighborliness, which is why I guess he may have decided to go back to Port Rivers to practice. He's respectful but doesn't take orders.

"He helped Billy Klein, Carl Klein's nephew—and maybe a dozen other guys like Billy—through law school. In the Klein case, it was regarded as a miracle. You could go to Terry Brett any time and he'd work your brief over and raise the level."

Wyler and his client sat in stunned, horrified silence.

"I'd like to add that I was a fan of Terry's. When Billy put him on the phone to me the other day, I was delighted to talk to him and in fact invited him to dinner. But he demurred. He said he would only be here a short time and that it might cause a problem. It was all very enigmatic. I had no inkling that he had legal business with you, Mr. Wolfe." Ned Mortimer pulled out his yellow legal pad and showed it to Jonah and Wyler. "I made a short note when I realized the conversation wasn't entirely social. Here it is."

Terry Brett asked that I contact Jonah Wolfe re. Mike Summers.

"As you know, Mr. Wolfe, I'm very junior and I referred this to Mr. Wyler, who I gather called you."

Wyler studied the one-line note as though it would reveal the riddle of the Sphinx.

"I hope, gentlemen, that you consider that I've acted with due circumspection," Ned Mortimer said helplessly. "I feel that by delivering this cryptic message, my head is on the chopping block. If you'd like me to stay and see Terry with you, sir, I'll do whatever's necessary."

Jonah shook Ned's sweaty hand and he got up shakily.

"You can both go," Jonah said. "I appreciate your coming, but this is a personal matter. Charlie, I'm sorry I hit the roof when you called. I'll see if I can pitch this tent on my own."

Allison was growing disheartened by Paul Cisco's interrogation. Slumped in a back booth at the restaurant, she was confused and distant. He had killed her tastebuds. She couldn't swallow the clam chowder and she was dehydrated, drinking glass after glass of water until Cisco told the waiter to bring a pitcher to the table.

"The talk is that you're this town's acid queen. Now rumors just don't spring out of the blue. They're not some natural occurrence like raindrops."

"They get manufactured," she said, exhausted.

This informal interview Cisco had plotted was not working. He was utterly confounded, unable to follow her shifts and feints, and trying to keep her on track. Out of her handbag, she pulled a paperback edition of *Siddhartha* and Cisco found himself lost in a labyrinth of Eastern wisdom. She started to read:

" 'Why must he, the blameless one, wash away his sins and endeavor to cleanse himself anew each day?' "

His head was spinning. Terry had indeed met his archangel of deception.

"Accept destiny in all of its manifestations, Mr. Cisco. Listen to the music."

Almost by way of apology, Cisco heard himself saying, "I'm a Catholic. And I believe in body and soul."

"That's your problem. 'Your soul is the whole world.' There is no separation when we're striving for unity with Atman, the supreme universal self."

Giddy and about to shout for help, he slammed the table with his fist.

"Allison, none of this makes any sense. What *normal* people call logic has to be satisfied. Or else the mind can't rest. Why have you been singled out? Is there some grand cabal devised by Satan?"

"Cabal?" She made a note on her word list. Cisco was

lost in the scenery of folly. "Warren Paris wants to bury me."

"Paris? Why would he do that?" He protected his informer. "You just worked for him as a cocktail waitress for a while."

"He's a pervert. He wanted me to perform sex shows."

Cisco had a desperate urge to locate Terry and allow him to listen to the methods he had to employ in order to find a site for the space station in Allison's universe. She was taking him for a joyride through her intergalactic channels. Cisco put down his knife and fork and shoved his plate away.

"Now, let me get this right. You refused whatever request Warren made, so he decided to conduct a raid on your tent. I know Warren. He's a bookie and the Paradise is stacked wall-to-wall with pretty young girls."

"I agree. I don't know what it is with him."

"I wish you could say that you had a witness who was with you on Christmas Eve. Where was Terry?" The possibility of implicating Terry gave Allison the shakes. She squeezed her hands together under the table, staring at blurred faces at other tables.

"Terry must've been out somewhere with Pat."

"Okay. I can't imagine him at a joint like the Paradise."

"I didn't see Terry till Christmas Day."

"So you went alone to the Paradise to return a couple of cocktail outfits and get back your deposit for them?"

"Yes. I turned them in to Warren."

"And then as you walk out, you ask for a bottle, and in front of a couple of hundred people throw it against the bar mirror. And dance out alone." She nodded. "Why?"

Her energy vanished and the lights were whipping around like a gypsy carnival ride out of control.

"I told you."

"Warren allegedly kills your cat, makes an improper suggestion—and you wreck the place. I think there's another explanation. I believe you were dealing acid at the bar, and Warren didn't want to lose his liquor license and have his place closed down. He demanded that you get out. I'm convinced that you were out there in wonderland on LSD and didn't know what you were doing."

Allison pressed her palms against the edge of the table. "I have to go now, Mr. Cisco."

"Don't go too far, Allison. I'd like to know where you're staying."

Face flushed, she regained her strength for a furious salvo. "No *conspiracy* against me!" she bellowed. "You and Laver got me thrown out of Pat's house." Tears coursed down her cheeks. "I'm checking into the River Barge." She wiped her eyes with a napkin. "Terry'll be back tonight and you can discuss these so-called charges with my attorney."

"Rest assured that we're going to have another visit when Randy, the bartender, comes back from wherever he's hiding. Randy's girlfriend informed us that the account I've given you is what occurred on Christmas Eve."

Outraged, Allison levered up from the table, thrusting herself to her feet.

"Randy's 'girlfriend'! Tell me about her. Is she pretty?"

"Attractive, according to Sergeant Laver."

"You people are some detectives," she said. "You're all as useless as tits on a boar hog. I guess Laver and Randy go for the same type—swishing six-footers with Che Guevara mustaches."

"What do you mean by that?"

Allison sneered at him. "Laver must've met Randy's sister, but he was so intent on framing me as a drug dealer that he never bothered to ask her who she was. Randy's scene is guys! Mr. Cisco, I promise you that when Terry gets back, he's going to grind you into mincemeat."

Paul Cisco was extremely upset by her last remark. He watched Allison trudge out, lugging her suitcase.

19

Terry had left Billy Klein's beach house and checked into the Beverly Wilshire Hotel. He hadn't intended to compromise their friendship and hoped the breach was not irreparable. He picked up a rented Mercury Cougar and cruised through the slothful, laid-back village of Beverly Hills. He paused for a light at Carroll & Company, a very civilized haberdashery, and surveyed the English tweeds in the window. If he had time, he'd return and pick out a sports jacket. They might have a ladies' department and he could buy something for Allison.

He gunned the car up Tower Drive. After a series of hairpin turns, he located the entrance to the Wolfe estate. A man opened the gates and Terry wound up a driveway alongside an emerald lawn with acres of flowers, tended by Mexican gardeners. The road doglegged to the top of a hill where a colossal Spanish-style turreted castle stood in defiant grandeur, a bastion of defense against the barbarians. The house was the size of a resort hotel and Terry wondered if they offered postcards at the desk so that he could mail one back home to Allison. A fountain filigreed with mosaics of Aztec gods shot out fine plumes of water and provided a home for jumbo koi. Retainers were feeding the ducks and swans in the lake opposite the house.

Despite his self-confidence, Terry was momentarily intimidated. The feeling was purely material in character and caused him to reflect: No matter what he achieved in his lifetime, he would never be able to live on the scale of Jonah Wolfe and the knowledge pierced his armor. From somewhere within the walls, the sound of classical guitar music rippled through the air. It wouldn't have surprised him if the great Segovia himself was the court musician. Outside the garage were a pair of Rolls-Royces, a Ferrari, and an Aston Martin being washed and polished. Terry followed the houseman past a large, dark grotto pool with a Jacuzzi. Steaming water gurgled from a lava rockfall above. There were two tennis courts—one grass, the other clay—a putting green, and a manicured croquet lawn. Terry stopped dead in his tracks. On a flat pad was a regulation-sized basketball court with a view of the city to the east and the Pacific on the west side.

A man in white shorts and a sweatshirt imprinted with L.A. STARS was standing on the court practicing one-handed foul shots. He made four out of five and handled the ball gracefully. He might have been a stallion in his prime. He was probably in his early fifties and there was an insouciant splendor about him. He was deeply tanned, rangy, with rough good looks and as tensiled as a bolt of copper wire. His hair was long and thick, with some buds of gray, and his eyes were as dark as mahogany. Once seen, his was a face that anyone would remember.

"Thanks for coming, Terry, I'm Jonah Wolfe. Want to shoot a few hoops?"

He beckoned Terry onto the court. Terry put down his briefcase, picked up a ball, and took a shot from the keyhole. He was short, hitting the front rim, and Jonah fed him again. Terry swished one the third time.

"My eye's gone to hell."

"You've got to practice, work at it." Jonah's voice had an amused, midwestern, folksy twang that was not displeasing.

"Well, when my clients stop robbing banks and shooting their best friends, I'll have the time."

Terry tossed his blazer on the grass, slipped his rep tie into his shirt, and the men spent a congenial fifteen minutes on the court, shooting and talking basketball. Jonah Wolfe was foxing him, he knew, and he allowed himself to be led on. Terry was winded and faded. He had not run himself ragged and left Allison so that he could shoot hoops with the enemy, and yet he found he could not actively dislike Jonah Wolfe. The man was certainly not the cigar-champing slob with a belligerent manner he had expected, but rather a self-possessed aristocrat with worldly eyes.

They walked to the house like buddies after a one-on-one. A houseman took their drink orders and both men decided on beers. Terry looked around the baronial living room, which had a large atrium and a courtyard running around it. Overhead, a tinted domed skylight created a sense of two environments.

"Well, Terry, let's go to work. Are you here to make representations for Mike Summers of all people?"

"No."

"No? Now you've really got me curious."

"Mike's got nothing to do with it, except in a contingent way."

"Is that a fact? Then what have you got?"

"Some Polaroids of you and his kid sister, Karen. Remember her? I don't think they'd make *Sports Illustrated*. But with a public offering of stock for your insurance company, the *Wall Street Journal* might be interested."

"Polaroids?"

Terry handed his host one of the photographs of himself and the girls, all of them naked, linked, like dogs. Jonah blinked and the veins bulged in his neck. He flicked some sweat out of his eyes and threw the photo on the coffee table.

"Oh, boy . . ." He was less affable now. "Who exactly are you representing?"

"I'll let you know when I'm ready. By the way, whatever happened to Karen and her girlfriend?"

"We split up in Vegas after a few days. I was glad to get rid of them. Booze and grass. And those Quaaludes. Well, I was in a haze. I sobered up and tried to get myself back to normal."

Terry appeared to consider the circumstances sympathetically and act like he was one of the guys. But notwithstanding the drugs, Jonah had managed to set up his camera on automatic for the shots, bribe Mike, and drive the girls to an airport. It was, however, too soon to spring Earl Raymond on him.

"My wife and I had an acrimonious divorce. A real

bloodletting. She died the week before I went up to Fond du Lac. On top of this, her family took me to court on her behalf. I even had to have my daughter deposed and treated as a hostile witness. I was so angry that I didn't go to my ex-wife's funeral. There was a time when I'd loved her very much. And to lose my daughter as well. We'd had a fabulous life. Until it went sour."

Terry offered commiseration. "You were in pain."

"Serious pain."

Terry wondered how someone with Jonah Wolfe's resources could have gotten himself involved in a situation like this. It wasn't as though he was shocked that an older man had seduced two young girls. It was Wolfe's capricious nonchalance, his sloppiness, the absence of cover.

"Well, Terry, as these things go, I got caught up with the team I'd bought. I hung out with the guys, chased. Half the time I didn't know what the hell I was doing. I drove up to see one of Mike Summers's prospects with a player I used to pal around with."

Terry nodded. At least this part of the account had been confirmed.

"Jonah, I don't understand. How does such a smart guy like you compromise himself this way?"

"It was an accident. Impulse, call it what you like. I was leaving to go back home after the game, and as I was getting into my car, Karen asked me if I'd drive her to the liquor store and buy her and her girlfriend a bottle. I always traveled with a full bar of good stuff. So I gave them a bottle of Black Label and had a drink with them. I was curious and . . . a little turned on. No matter what age they are, the sad thing about women is they're like the Indians. All they ever learned was to trade beaver for firewater."

Jonah Wolfe's attitude repelled Terry. His cynicism was so absolute that it almost belonged to another period in history. During the slave trade when ivory, women, children, and gold were pursued by desperate, conscienceless marauders, Jonah Wolfe would have been a chieftain, the pirate captain who dropped anchor and went ashore on those isles of innocence and mercilessly pillaged them.

"Let me tell you something. Karen and her friend may have been young, but believe me, they were experienced. They'd been around. They weren't children by any stretch. Karen Summers was a wild animal. They had lots of drugs and pills.

"Terry, *I* was the one seduced . . . not the other way around. When they got me high, frankly, I admit I lost control. We all were out of it. Look, Terry, I'm no expert on the psychology of this, but, you know, there are young girls who like getting it on with an older man." He smiled and winked. "It's sort of why people prefer mature doctors, the gray locks, the wisdom of experience."

Terry supposed that Jonah's hollow pretense of remorse was so imbued in his character that it would be useless to probe. He pecked lightly on these flimsy justifications.

"I'm with you," he said cordially. "What I can't figure out is why you'd take pictures."

Jonah ruefully shook his head. "Karen started doing her girlfriend. She . . . she pressured me. I always had a bunch of cameras with me for professional reasons. To take shots of players. Karen was tripping and insisted that I take the pictures. This could've happened to any man."

It was time to do a skin test to see if this impresario of teenage girls would bleed. "Good thing you don't run your business like this. You'd be eating that stuff you peddle to the cheap markets."

Jonah vigorously took issue with Terry.

"My hot dog and deli stuff is no better or worse than the brand names. Put mustard, mayo, ketchup, onions on dog-shit patties or stick it in a casing and the American public will eat it if you make it cheap enough. I found what gamblers call a 'middle' in the business when I was working myself to death as a kid. Prisons, bughouses, hospitals, and the good old American Army, they buy price—not quality. I developed a sales force who made friends with these institutional purchasing agents.

"The same thing's true about my insurance company. The mooches go for our freebies and the uninsurable buy it," Jonah said, rising and pacing the throne room. "Terry, unscrupulous people are the salt of the American earth, the fabric of our society. Without their deceptions, there would be no commerce. Nothing would ever sell. I create capital."

Terry took a pull from the beer bottle. "I'm afraid we're not in total accord."

"Are you kidding, being a lawyer's dirtier than anything."

"Then why'd you become one?"

Jonah Wolfe was taken off guard, then he smiled. His teeth were perfect, chiseled and without a blush of stain.

"For occasions like this." He paused and had a sly look. "You certainly came with loaded dice. But Terry, I still don't know what you actually want or why you're here."

"If you'd done the right thing, I wouldn't have had to leave my sweet nest at home and dig into all this."

For Jonah, the enigma deepened. "Who then are you representing?"

"Earl Raymond for compensation due him."

"What? You're here, sweating me for Earl?" For a moment Jonah Wolfe lost his scrupulous composure, the glibness vanished. "That lowlife!"

"I don't think Earl's character is the issue. He was seriously injured and is now handicapped. The fact is, you cheated him. Why, as the owner of an insurance company, did you dismiss a bona fide claim? It's a mystery to me. It would have been peanuts to you. Nothing more than a simple accounting procedure. The team pays premiums to Wolfe Casualty, so it's a tax write-off. And with your kind of money, you could've easily absorbed it. It wasn't as though millions were involved from some disaster. You pension the bum off and forget it."

Jonah went to his bar, a copper-inlaid extravaganza that featured the liquors of the world. "Shall I get you a real drink? I'm ready for one."

"I'm not much of a drinker. This beer's going to my head."

Jonah poured himself a large Stoli in a bucket glass and loaded it with ice. "Do you know much about Earl Raymond?"

"Just the usual fables a client spins his attorney. I felt that he had a righteous cause."

"I wouldn't give that bastard the right time. In fact, I hoped he'd take me to court."

Terry was now confounded. "Really? Earl could've sandbagged you with expert witnesses, doctors, the works. You had no chance to win a civil suit if it was properly filed."

Wolfe took a long pull on his drink. "Not at all, Terry. We all have a basket of snakes under the bed. The fact is, Earl didn't want to go to jail. That's why he didn't take me to court."

"Well, according to Mike Summers, Earl wasn't part of your sexual tag team match. The two of them went into town in Mike's car. They got drunk and Earl went off with some waitress."

"That's correct."

Terry waited for Jonah to load his cannon.

"I had my reasons for blowing Earl off."

"Please share them with me since this isn't sub judice."

"Okay. I found out that while Earl was on *my* team, he was involved with some bookmaker named Warren Paris at home. And there's a clause in every professional basketball contract that relieves the owner of responsibility of all financial obligations if a player dumps games, shaves points, or tries to influence others to do something like that. I would've had Earl Raymond's ass in jail if he came near me. When Earl tore up his knee, it was a godsend to me and the team. The worst part is that I liked the bastard."

"That's an intriguing moral position, Jonah. But apparently you bend the rules just a bit when fourteen-year-old girls are on the table."

"Let's separate things, please. Earl was a fixer for a bookie. That's why I let him go to hell. And I paid Mike off. He's a small-town coach with a fine roof over his head, thanks to me."

"I think you shortchanged Mike."

Jonah raised the mainsail and tacked in the wind. "It's clear to me that you've got sports in your blood. I'd like to make you an offer, Terry. Don't bother pursuing this. Leave your muskrat town and come down to Los Angeles. Be my house counsel and get very, very rich."

"Oh, you'll get me a job running errands for Charlie Wyler."

"No, I'll fire his ass and set up an office for you."

Jonah's proposition was attractive and Terry thought about it for almost ten seconds. He would have liked to have had this case prosecuted by the district attorney. But there were thorny problems: Mike Summers would be in jeopardy; Earl might in fact be charged with a federal statute felony; and Jonah would be charged with raping two minors and go to prison. The underwriting of Wolfe Casualty that Carl Klein prized to the tune of eighteen million dollars would be doomed. As the whistle-blower, Terry himself would find himself giving endless depositions and his own practice would suffer. But more importantly, his wedding plans with Allison might have to be postponed. At every juncture, Terry found himself stymied.

"I appreciate your offer. But I have my own life." He smiled. "I actually specialize in murder cases. And I'm afraid you might call me in the middle of the night and tell me you've had some unfortunate accident and there's a dismembered body in your bed."

Jonah sank down on the sofa, a saturnine expression on his face.

"I've had a number of contemptible clients, Jonah. Earl Raymond ranks close to the top."

"How many pictures of me with the girls have you got?"

"Eight, and that includes the one on the table."

"What about copies?"

"There are none." Terry reflected for a few moments as Jonah waited anxiously. "The only solution I can come up with is abhorrent and dishonest as far as I'm personally concerned. But I don't see a way out. I guess it's a *middle* of sorts. *We* have to come to a reasonable settlement. I'll give you the photos, vanish out of the smoggy sunshine . . . and head back to my angel in the rain forest to plan my wedding."

"Does Earl know about what went on with me and the girls—the pictures?"

"No."

"You'll never tell him?"

"Of course not."

"Don't ever trust him." Jonah sucked on an ice cube. "How much is reasonable?"

"Half a million dollars."

He might have stuck a branding iron on Jonah's stomach. "That's insanity!"

"If I don't have a cashier's check for that amount, you'll discover just how crazy I really am. Consider it an underwriting fee." Terry pointed to the old masters on the walls. "My God, look what you own. My demand is chump change to a man of your means."

"What guarantee have I got that you'll sign off and that this won't be ongoing?"

"I've prepared a quit claim to the effect that you've settled with Earl. I have power of attorney to execute it. You can bring in someone from Wyler, Crosby to witness if you like."

"That's hardly insurance."

"It would be extremely difficult for me to go any further. I said there are no copies of the pictures. And I'm going to see that Mike gets himself an annuity out of this money. The other thing is, I've loved basketball since I was a kid. I don't like players who shave points and dump games any more than you do. I'd give anything to own an NBA team, and I understand how you feel about Earl."

"How do I reach you?"

"I'm at the Beverly Wilshire."

"Give me a couple of hours," Wolfe said, then became hesitant. "I have to shift money from an account."

"Sure. I hope we have a deal."

Jonah Wolfe nodded before standing up and formally shaking Terry's hand.

"You've got a nice touch on the court, Jonah ... especially from the foul line."

"It's nothing compared to Earl's. You'll see ..."

20

Jonah Wolfe was alone when he met Terry at the Bank of America in Beverly Hills. Jonah's manner was brusque and dismissive as they went to a private room set aside by the manager in the safe deposit area.

"How's the money going to be disbursed? Does Earl get the lion's share?"

"I'm Solon, the lawgiver, in this, so please don't concern yourself with these details," Terry fired back. He took out an envelope and placed it on the table. "Here are your snapshots."

Jonah hesitated, then opened his attaché case. On top was a cashier's check for five hundred thousand dollars made out to Terence S. Brett Client's Trust Account. As they signed the agreement, Jonah's distraught eyes roved the empty room. "You're sure there are no copies."

"I told you there were none."

"And this matter will never be discussed with that scum, Earl? I need to be reassured."

"I gave you my *word*. And my word means everything to me."

"Okay, Terry, you've done your good deed. Morality triumphs. Have a safe ride home. And do us both a favor, don't come back!"

"I have no intention of returning. In the meantime, Jonah, try to conduct yourself like a real gentleman. It may mean nothing to you. But maybe there's a payoff."

"To who?"

"Try yourself."

Jonah Wolfe's laugh had a Doberman bite.

"I'd like to do everything you suggest. If only the little hippie girls in this town would stop flashing their tits in my face and dropping their pants. It's a waste of time talking to women. They're only here to serve us."

As a man who considered himself sensitive, Terry was insulted. As a lawyer, he was bleak-faced and walked away from a conversation that was nothing more than a wasteland with a man like Jonah Wolfe.

Terry was buoyant after he had the bank make a wire transfer of the funds to his account in Port Rivers. And now Miss Allison would have her turn. Smiling at everyone in the street, he had a delightful stroll over to the hallowed Tiffany & Company. It took about fifteen minutes before he settled on an elegant two-carat solitaire for fifteen thousand dollars. Then he raced into the Beverly Wilshire's El Padriño room for a champagne lunch he was giving Billy Klein, who had been deeply offended by his flight from the beach house.

Billy was already at the bar, gabbing with Ned Mortimer and some other familiar faces from school. The place had become an unofficial clubroom for Hollywood lawyers like them who had gasped through law school. He was greeted by some reverential classmates he'd coached for the bar exam.

"You're still batting cleanup, Ter," someone's voice cut through the circle of attorneys and Terry bought the coven a bottle of Krug champagne.

"Get your hand out of your pocket," Billy said. "This is my hometown and it's an expense account lunch. I'll let you send me some of Miss Allison's brownies. Tell her to put some hash in them."

"I have to remind her to keep it out."

When Terry broke off with the usual perfunctory exchange of cards and home addresses, they were seated at Mr. Klein's booth away from the piano.

"Now first of all, I'm truly pissed off at you for thinking that our friendship could be compromised by this business, Terry."

"One never knows."

"By now, you should." Billy's face was florid. "Uncle Carl wanted to join us, but I suggested that it would be better if you and I did this alone. The point being, he wishes to offer an apology for his undignified behavior. He was extremely embarrassed and you handled yourself like Justice Frankfurter. You did it with grace and great style."

"Tell Uncle Carl his behavior was dignified. It's just that I refuse to take a dive for him or anyone. I'm curious, how'd he wind up with elegant trash like Jonah?"

"Now wait a minute, Terry. It's not entirely despicable to court a client like him. Jonah's diversified financial interests fit in with our own expertise. Los Angeles is a dirt pit. When you practice law here, it's walking through shit."

"Carl would stop kissing his ass if he knew about the man."

"Vice is universal, if that's what you're alluding to. And frankly it's somewhat more interesting than innocence."

They ordered steaks, and Billy guided them to a fine bottle of Nuits St. Georges.

"Right or not, I'm sorry for the trouble I caused between your uncle and Wyler." Terry clasped his hand. "Our friendship means a lot to me as well, Billy."

Billy was uncharacteristically contemplative during lunch. Finally, over coffee, he made his pitch.

"I would like you to trust me and carefully consider what I'm about to say. At the firm, we've got this rich slag heap of advocates led by Tommy the Tuxedo, running the litigation department. He's a former assistant attorney general and he doesn't know shit, except how to make a butterfly bowtie. By the time you're thirty, you could be a senior partner."

"I'm—"

"Please hear me out. You scared the life out of the two largest law firms in Los Angeles. That calls for some sort of respect." Billy refilled Terry's glass. "Carl wants you to come work for us. You can be top gun in litigation. Tommy will remain titular head so we have a body to send to the black-tie functions. We'll keep you in court. You bill five hundred an hour, take two months off a year. You get an expense account, a Mercedes. Call the tune, maestro."

Terry did not function well in groups, preferring to be serf and lord in his own barony. "Thanks for the kind words. But I'm going back home to my honey and my unglamorous practice of defending knaves."

"Look, the knaves here are richer, grander. What'll it take, Ter?" Billy was on a riff. "Set up housekeeping with Allison. I'll get you a beach house near me. All the repressive shit we grew up with is out the window. We're living in the sixties and we're successful. Terry, look at me. I'm a fat, prematurely balding, Jewish lawyer and I live like King Farouk. Let's be young together. I love you, man."

"I think Allison would do best bottled up. Los Angeles has too many distractions."

"What exactly has you so hooked on her?"

Fingering the velvet box holding the engagement ring he had purchased for Allison, Terry said, "Allison is . . . I don't know how to quite put this . . ."

"Try it without slurrring, Ter."

"It's madness. She's eighteen, very raw and . . . somehow a collector of experiences. She's had a ballbreaker of a life." Terry paused and tried to analyze the nature of the attachment. "Allison has touched something in me so deeply, some part of myself that I never knew existed—" He mused and was conquered by the waves of brandy that soaked his brain. "I have found rapture . . ."

"Huh, what the fuck is that? Jesus, it's four-thirty already. Go get packed and I'll run you to the airport."

"First have a look at Allison's engagement ring," Terry said, thrusting the blue box on Billy.

"Ah, Terry, you're such a *goy*. I could've gotten you a walnut for what you must have paid at Tiffany. You people who get suckered in by boxes and labels."

"I don't think Allison ever heard of Tiffany." Terry rose with much steadiness of purpose and little of foot. "But I have. I want to give her everything she never had."

He staggered. "Hang on to it for me, Billy. I'm so loaded, I may give it to someone in the lobby."

Terry took the elevator to the fourth floor. Bleary-eyed, he tried to determine east from west to locate his room. In his expansive sloshed condition, he started to sing aloud, when he spotted two bellhops. One was crouched over a trunk, the other was in the entryway of a room. Terry whipped ten dollars out of his pocket.

"My lucky day. Just the guys I want to see. Would you gentlemen like to help me pack?"

The bellhops wheeled around with warning.

They wore stocking masks. The first blow was so sudden and startling Terry couldn't react. Fists from every angle slammed into his face, smashing his nose. As he corkscrewed to the floor, he was hit on the temple with a metal bar. He writhed, flopped on his back, and they began wildly kicking him. In the ribs . . . the belly. Terry puked up something bilious and felt himself choking.

The men were hacking him with metal scourges that split through his head, and then they stomped on his face.

A woman in a slip, hearing the commotion, peeked out of a nearby room and walked into the hallway, calling softly for maid service. When she saw the violence of the scene, she shrieked.

The men standing over Terry stopped abruptly and threw their weapons toward the woman. She continued to scream. Out of his unclosed eye, Terry saw blurred figures running past the frightened woman.

Terry's last vision was of the marine welders in the secret darkness of their Port Rivers shop, the discharge of their flame torches branding him, plunging him into abandoned space. A pitch of blackness descended over him and he was engorged in the quicksand of a sinkhole.

21

For five days, Allison haunted the Port Rivers airport waiting and searching for Terry. Reservation clerks, bartenders, and waiters on different shifts nodded at her. Dark cups lined her eyes and she took on the haggard aspect of a hospital visitor waiting in suspense, praying for good news from the doctor about a loved one.

On the sixth evening, the pressure had become intolerable. Allison checked out of the suite at the River Barge, leaving Terry's Diner's card at the desk. Terry had disappeared. In the grip of an inexorable despondency, Allison made a final pilgrimage to the airport with Georgie.

The experience of loss, coupled with a sense of her own worthlessness, overpowered her. Georgie took her arm and guided her away from the arrival gate. Perhaps it was the sternness and the tightening of her friend's mouth which made Allison believe that she had news of Terry or had withheld information. Allison's mind was skittering from miraculous hope to the abyss of paranoia.

"Shall we discuss this, woman-to-woman?"

"I'm ready," Allison replied. "Not knowing where I stand is the killer."

Georgie was also concerned about Terry's disappearance, but as an authority on domestic relations and the behavior of men who had made promises to girlfriends and wives that they were reluctant to keep, she concluded that she must put Allison out of her misery.

"I've got to be cruel to be kind." Georgie scowled. "Men—you probably know this better than I do. They get hot and promise you the world. I see them cringing in court every day." She took Allison's hand. "The lies these bastards tell about their wives."

"I guess I believed Terry was different."

"Well, he is. He's special. No question. He'll stand up to anyone. But maybe not you."

"What do you mean, Georgie?"

"I like you very much, Allison. And I can't bear to watch you suffer this way. My gut feeling is that Terry's met someone else in L.A. And he can't face you."

Allison had already resigned herself to this eventuality and maintained a stoic attitude.

"Look, in a way you're luckier than most. They're women who've given men their youth, women with kids, women stuck with mortgages they can't pay when the guy takes a powder." Allison cast her eyes on the floor and shook her head. "There are the problems with Pat. And this thing with Paul Cisco and the police won't go away. It's on your plate—yours and *Terry's*."

Allison's confidence was shaken and she timidly asked, "Have you spoken to Terry?"

"No, I haven't heard a word."

"Has Earl?"

"Not that I know of."

"You would tell me?"

"Of course. Allison, I'm trying to protect you. All men want is to have a woman spread her legs . . . tell them they're wonderful and no harm will come. They're all small boys. And so is Terry."

Determined not to cry, Allison turned away. "You're right. Pat and he had to have spoken." Her red-rimmed eyes had a disturbing fixity. " 'I am become death, the destroyer of worlds.' "

The vacant look on her face worried Georgie. Suddenly, Allison took off, tearing wildly through the terminal.

Head slunk low in her stained baggy raincoat, Allison stood outside on the observation deck, gripping the rails. On the tarmac, lights flickered and the runway resembled one of the dance platforms in the clubs she had once worked, scrounging long enough to endure the trip to the landlady with rent money.

"Oh, Terry, how have I lost you?" She looked to the heavens. "God, tell me . . . tell me, will you?"

The logic of Terry's behavior became clear to her slowly. How could a man like him give up everything for *her*? It had been another affair for him, one that got out of hand. His impulsive proposal had no reality. Men were always telling women they loved them. It had been madness to believe that Terry would actually marry her. She had let down her guard and she was devastated by the outcome.

But what did Terry want from her and why had he led her on? Was this simply a sport whose sole object was sexual plunder? She had given in to him. But what obscure purpose lay behind the mirage he had contrived? His cruelty exceeded anything she'd ever experienced at the hands of a man. Like other women carried along by optimism, the man would never explain the rules. In Terry's case, the craft of the lie depended on his skill, and its shape and form had been specifically tailored to fit her circumstances. The malice behind his role was breathtaking; but then again, he was a lawyer by trade, and men like Terry Brett hid behind imaginary codes of ethics that relieved them of responsibility.

Allison watched the planes sprinkling the sky until dawn, knowing once again she must find her own way.

22

Two weeks later, on the flight home from Los Angeles, Terry couldn't help but notice how people turned away at the sight of his bandaged face. He made his way down the aisle to the restroom; kids were pointing at him, and mothers hushed and growled at them. He locked the door and unavoidably saw his face in the mirror.

Terry Brett was no longer pretty.

He had been unconscious for six days. His nose had been broken, the left cheekbone fractured. The stitches inside his mouth constantly irritated him. But that was the least of it. He had three broken ribs which had punctured his lung; to repair the injury, a tube had been inserted through his chest wall. His ribs had been strapped, but the pain was agonizing whenever he breathed. He still had dizzy spells, a buzzing in his ears, and headaches, but the skull fracture he had suffered was not as serious as the doctors had first thought. All Terry could remember was the vague outline of Billy Klein's worried face at his bedside.

Terry's mind was still sluggish, pulling things out of the wrong compartments. His thought process was as discontinuous as a home movie. He was assured that this was a temporary condition. There was, however, no such optimistic guarantee for his recurring nightmares, which starred a smiling Jonah Wolfe passing a basketball to him. The thought of Jonah brought him out in a cold sweat.

Apart from Terry's absolute conviction that Jonah had arranged this farewell, there was a conspicuous lack of evidence. Billy had insisted that they could get the police to question Jonah, but according to Jonah's office, he was out of the country. Terry knew that his own actions in settling Earl's claim could not bear scrutiny. It had been a dirty case and he was paying the price.

Terry had a sense that something was also wrong at home. On his last day at the hospital, he had been on the phone most of the day, leaving messages for Allison. Georgie was in court. Earl was out of town. Apparently, his father was still on a hunting trip. And Milly could not leave her ovens. Terry couldn't figure out why he was unable to get hold of anyone. The River Barge had nailed him for a six-day stay and the manager had no idea why Allison had checked out.

None of this might have been significant or lodged with the intensity of an aneurysm in his brain if Allison hadn't been missing. The thought of seeing her made him almost tearful. The doctors had said this was the labile affect, a direct result of the ferocious attack on him.

As the plane approached Port Rivers, he found himself in terrible pain from his injuries. He listed to the bathroom again at the end of the cabin. Once inside, he cupped his hand under the water tap and swallowed a Demerol. He had a few left and after they were gone, he would switch to codeine. In a few moments, he was in a relaxed daze. A red light came on and an announcement blotted by static about landing shortly came over the speaker. He peered at the message.

" 'Please return to your seat,' " he said aloud. "I can still read."

Assisted by a flight attendant, he wove his way back through the cabin. She fastened his seat belt. "Are you all right, Mr. Brett? We can radio ahead for medical assistance."

The drug kicked in. "No, that's all right. I'm feeling better."

"Are you sure? Mr. Klein insisted that I keep an eye on you, so I hope you don't mind."

At the Port Rivers airport, he was paged when he got to the baggage claim and as he moved to the phone, a chauffeur intercepted him.

"Mr. Brett, Mr. Klein arranged for me to take you home, sir."

After the dusky Santa Ana winds in Los Angeles, Terry embraced the clean rain sprinkle outside and began to feel revived. Holding the limo door handle to steady himself, he raised his face up to the sky. He was alive and had to put this disaster behind him. Driving through Port Rivers, he decided to stop by his office.

He was not surprised to find a new woman typing. Georgie could not keep a secretary or paralegals no matter how much they were prepared to pay. His own secretary was on maternity leave. Temps wandered in and out. He introduced himself to the new lady and learned Georgie was due back shortly. She handed him a stack of messages.

He drifted into his office to his desk and sat down in his high green leather chair. He tried his home number, then called Seacliff on the off chance that Allison had gone down there to join Pat. Maybe they were together. Allison's charms would work their magic. He closed his eyes and listened to the rhythm of the rain striking the window and the car tires below sweetly squishing. The sounds brought with it a memory of Allison and himself drenched and rolling over the muddy riverbank beside her tent.

"Oh, God, Terry!" Georgie's desolate scream plunged into the room. "What happened? A car crash? And we thought . . ." She was at his feet sobbing.

His bandages stretched when he forced himself to smile. "I was really out of town."

"That isn't funny."

"I know. I really don't know what happened. I bought an engagement ring for Allison, and two guys may've followed me from Tiffany's. Or there could be another reason. I'm not sure. I was mugged in the hotel."

Georgie pushed herself up and spread out on the stack of files covering his desk. He was listless and wanted a drink. The pills weren't agreeing with him. He found himself fighting the cloudy befuddlement.

"Are you going to be all right, Terry?"

"Oh, Christ, yes. Please, tell me where Allison is?"

Georgie eased off the desk and her manner became more formal. Terry observed the mournful, litigious expression with which she welcomed her clients to the death of their marriages.

"I don't know."

He poured himself a shot of a client's Christmas malt scotch. His mind slowly began to function. "Do I have a jittery witness?" he asked.

"No, an unhappy one. The last time I saw Allison was at the airport. She was going there every day looking for you." Georgie paused to swallow and Terry suspected that she was holding out. "That was about a week ago or more."

"Did anyone try the Stradivarius coffeehouse?"

"No, was I expected to?" Masking her culpability, Georgie became evasive. "Allison's in a lot of trouble. I mean, Paul Cisco's been talking to her . . . and Laver's after her. They were going to arrest her on drug charges. Terry, I'm not a *criminal* lawyer. Allison needed one. What could I do? And my caseload has been heavy . . ."

Terry's eyes fluttered. He was convinced she was lying. In court, he would have laced into her. Now exhaustion and the drink he'd unwisely mixed with the painkiller had smothered him, dulling his senses. He listened to her rattle off a list of circumstances to exculpate herself.

"Cisco called and you never got back to him?" Terry asked.

"I did. But either he was in court or I was. Terry, I'm exhausted. And Barney Laver was on my back. Have a heart. I had the Arnold case to close with the state, and a dozen divorce filings."

"Hasn't Allison been working at Milly's?"

"I haven't spoken to Milly for a while."

"Don't you eat there any more?"

"I'm still on the diet Earl put me on before Christmas."

Georgie was anxious to discuss Earl's business, but the time was wrong; she reluctantly did not mention it. She consulted her diary, and Terry wanted to weep as her equivocations became more distressing.

"The only thing I'm asking, Georgie, is do you know where Allison is? Did you have an argument?"

"No, not even a cross word."

"What about Earl? Did he have a beef with Allison?"

"Absolutely not. He adores Allison. Earl's been moving around, doing some scouting for some pro teams. He's in and out of town."

"Are you and Earl still together?"

"Yes. And he treats me like a queen."

"I'm glad to hear that. Try to think: Can you give me any idea where Allison might be?" he begged.

"If I knew, I'd tell you." A snivel crept into her tone. "Please stop treating me like a hostile witness. I have to get back to court to file a motion." As she was about to leave, her avid need for information about Earl's situation overcame any notion of tact. "Should I ask how you made out in *Earl Raymond* v. *Jonah Wolfe*?"

Terry gave her a vague look. "I'll save that for my client," he said, depleted by the effort.

When Terry arrived home, he searched for Allison. Her clothes, books, and drawings were gone. There was no trace of her. Nothing made any sense. He crept into his bed with foreboding. He fought to stay awake, but a dull lassitude crept over his aching body and he fell asleep.

The following morning, he was awakened by Pat's voice outside his room. The drug hangover was devastating. He was still disoriented, then realized he was out of the hospital.

"Terry, welcome back."

Bursting with paternal bonhomie, unshaven and still wearing his waterproof hunting jacket and high boots, Pat stood at the threshold, staring at his son's bandaged face. Terry reached out his hand.

"I'm still woozy, Dad. Can you help me to the bathroom?"

Pat rushed to his son and cradled him in his arms. "My God! What happened to you, boy?"

"The truth is I don't know. I don't know. Now please don't ask me anything more."

At breakfast, Pat stood over him with the solicitude of a nursing mother. But he was shifty when Terry persisted with questions about Allison.

"Please, Pat, give it to me straight. I'm too whipped to play games."

Pat poured himself another mug of steaming black coffee, then dosed it with some brandy, Terry noticed. He'd seldom seen his father drink in the morning.

"About two to three weeks ago or thereabouts, Barney Laver came by. He gave me some story about needing to use the house for a command post because they were staking out a suspect nearby."

"Are you serious? With no warrant?"

"Hey, I was being a good citizen and I was curious. I had a few appointments, estimates and what-have-you. But nothing burning. Indoor work. So I asked Barney if I could hang in with him and watch them work the case. Sort of like the FBI TV series."

Terry listened with dead-eyed incredulity to the disjointed account of the devious search. His head throbbed, but he forced himself to remain calm.

"I didn't want Barney to get a court order and come back with a whole squad of people and rip the place apart. We live here and that sort of thing isn't exactly positive advertising."

"Oh, Pat, he suckered you. If Barney thought he could get a court order, he would have been here with the troops." Terry sighed. "So you gave your permission."

"Terry, don't glare at me at that way. I'm law-abiding and I didn't want trouble. Man, if I knew where in hell you were, I would've called."

"Laver and Cisco waited for me to leave town."

"Look, Allison was involved in drugs, damnit. It's an epidemic, sweeping the country. These kids on communes—running naked, screwing in front of TV cameras, rioting, the protest marches. Black Power—it's destroying everything I fought for in the war. Christ, I didn't see you or your mother for three years. I was in fucking foxholes, eating K rations and shitting in trenches. For what? Do you think millions of Americans suffered for Allison and her kind to tear the country apart?"

"I see. Allison is personally leading a revolution to dismantle society." Terry paused to collect his scattered thoughts. "But in the meantime this revolutionary menace is sweating it out in your girlfriend's kitchen, trying to learn a skill. She's extremely dangerous. I suppose once she learns the secret of peach cobbler, she could spread this information and an armed insurrection would be the result. Have you had a two-by-four drop on you lately?"

Pat was still babbling. "Her kind . . ."

"But the point is, Laver found nothing. Nothing!"

"Nothing," Pat admitted, crestfallen. His temper flared again. "Well, when Allison got home, we had an argument."

Terry was overpowered by the wariness enveloping his

father as he continued to lie. Reluctantly and with distaste for the trap he laid, he allowed Pat to sink into the morass of inconsistency characteristic of someone attempting to justify his behavior.

Pat continued, "What a mouth on her. She was offensive and abusive."

"About you or Laver?"

"Both of us." Pat took some deep breaths and his hand trembled as he lighted a Camel. "I mean, it's my house—ours—so why do I have to take this guff from a . . . ?"

"That's why Allison went to stay at Georgie's, isn't it?"

"I suppose."

"Do you recall suggesting that she leave?" Terry asked in a friendly, cajoling tone.

"I suggested it would be a good idea."

"I'll bet you did. You had a nice heart-to-heart with Allison."

Terry got up from the table, rubbed his palm on the smooth marine-varnished surface and the beveled edges that he had worked on with his father many years ago. It had been an amazing experience from start to finish. They had gone up to the logger's camp and sawed down a Douglas fir tree together, milled it in the workshop, then built the table. Terry had never felt so bonded to his father.

"You know something, Pat, even you and I have a moment when the relationship we have stops being important. Whether it's jealousy or good intentions, we look to save our asses.

"Now, I'm going to tell you something. Allison and I are going to be married in May. I asked her up in Timberline—the way you did Mom. I find it hard to accept that she would have spoken to you in an offensive way because she had nothing to hide, except that we were engaged. I asked her to keep it a secret."

His father recoiled as though from a shotgun kick. Shaking his head in confusion, he opened his palms in a gesture of entreaty, peering to the wall for an invisible witness to spring out as a third party and settle this dispute.

"Engaged? You barely knew her."

"How long did it take you to propose to Mom?" Terry waited, then flew at Pat. "Three weeks, Mom said. I never heard you contradict her, either!"

Pat regressed before Terry's eyes. The small boy and the blameless contractor—who pleaded innocence when something went wrong during construction—joined forces. He was oblivious of the fact that if he tossed out the girl his son loved, there might be cause for trouble.

"Dad, look at me and please put the brandy down. This might seem like slush to you, but Allison cared about you. She had hopes that you'd be like a father to her. For Chrissake, she was an abused girl. I can imagine Allison getting sore and throwing things and saying the most outrageous things. But *never* to you, Pat! She wouldn't have jeopardized her future in an argument with *you* of all people."

Terry slipped on his jacket, pausing for a moment, staring at Pat's eyes, retreating, confused, in peril.

"As for drugs, she was clean! Because that would've been the end for us. And she knew it."

Pat sank down on the living-room coffee table. He suddenly picked up the antique ivory elephant and flung it at the wall.

"Everyone—but you—knows this girl isn't worthy of you," he hawked acidulously.

"I'll tell that to my heart."

23

It took several days before Terry could schedule a meeting with the very busy, very important assistant D.A. Paul Cisco was hiding behind the authority of his office. He had successfully ducked Terry and had gone so far as to change his breakfast habits, which the regulars at

Milly's noticed. He called his order in and had it delivered. As for Sergeant Laver, Port Rivers's esteemed criminal expert, an extradition case in California had removed him from the state. Terry's anger relentlessly fed on itself and grew malignant.

He dropped into the Stradivarius coffeehouse countless times. The clientele were invariably stoned and no one had heard from Allison. As his desperation grew, he took out boldface full-page ads in newspapers in the underground journals Allison read:

ALLISON DESMOND
WHEREVER YOU ARE, CALL TERRY BRETT

As the days passed, Terry began having rapid pulse beats and panic attacks, which increased in severity at night when he was alone in the house with Pat. They nodded when they ran into each other, but Pat backed off and simply couldn't face him. One afternoon, Pat packed up some clothes and moved in with Milly to have his misery soothed.

The family doctor removed the stitches inside Terry's cheek and pronounced good healing of the zygomatic arch, which meant his cheekbone was re-forming. With a flat Band-Aid across the bridge of his nose, and a purple-brown mouse under his eye, Terry might have been playing the role of some middleweight club fighter with a local following who had stepped up in class and run into Sugar Ray Robinson on a good night.

On Friday, Terry's fears threw him into a free fall. He discussed his problems with a former cop he had defended and now sometimes employed as an investigator. In the hope of locating Allison, Terry agreed on a thousand-dollar retainer for Stanley Hoffman to begin searching for her.

"It would help, Terry, if I had a picture of Allison."

Terry handed him an envelope with glossy eight-by-tens. He remembered Allison's self-consciousness when they had posed for a hotel photographer at the Timberline. She had nestled her head on his shoulder. In Stanley's narrow, vulpine face, the eager, close-set eyes, Terry scented the detective's appetite for easy money.

"She's a knockout. If there was a betting line, I'd make her an eight-point favorite on the road," Stanley said. "These sopranos like to play hide-and-seek."

"Not her!" In a fury, he seized hold of Stanley. "Now listen. I'm not some fucking mark you can bullshit and waltz around at a prom. You check the communes, ashrams, the coffee bars in Eugene, Corvallis. I don't give a damn where you have to go or what it costs. Stanley, I want her found!"

"Terry," the detective said, from his depleted reservoir of human sympathy, "don't go to see Cisco in this condition. You're real vulnerable, man."

Terry frantically brushed past him and left for the courthouse. Several attorneys with sullen clients and a few cops were waiting in the stuffy reception area outside Paul Cisco's office. Cisco was buzzed by his secretary and came to the door to welcome and console him.

"I assure you, Terry, if this mugging had happened to you here, we'd have the bastards the same day. In L.A., they don't give two shits."

Terry was brusque. "Doesn't matter, Paul."

"That's an awfully cavalier attitude after the injuries you've suffered."

"I know who was behind it, and believe me, I'll fry his onions."

"Terry, be sensible. I'll call the D.A.'s office in Beverly Hills. I'll kick some of those fat-asses I've met at our conventions."

"This one's my exclusive property. Believe me, he's going to have a less than happy life."

Terry tried to relax in the familiar domain. Paul Cisco's only weakness as a prosecutor was that he was too aggressive and never let a case unfold.

"Ter"—Cisco opened his arms in a comradely embrace—"the important thing is you're alive." Cisco put on his glasses and shuffled his files. "My calendar doesn't indicate that we have anything pending. And I'm on overload. Why don't you come over for dinner? Any night, pick one, and I can hear the whole story. I'll call Margo right now and tell her to do the duck and wild rice you like."

With resolute intensity, Terry's eyes fixed on Cisco's chubby face, his soft figure. Terry's spacey gaze made him fidget.

"We have Miss Allison Desmond pending, Paul. We have illegal search and seizure. We have harassment by you and Barney Laver. We will have state bar hearings, a judicial inquiry, and a police internal affairs investigation. Miss Desmond won't be pending very much longer. Your calendar, Paul, is going to be a very heavy one. You might consider seeking the advice of counsel."

Cisco's pudgy neck seemed to vanish like a turtle's into its shell. He knew that Terry's remarks were not merely rhetorical threats.

"What? I'm outraged by these slurs."

"You rockhead, you haven't been accused yet. These are allegations. See the movie first, before you comment. As far as I'm concerned—as a brother attorney—your tendentious behavior toward Allison is a form of fanatical witch-hunting that ill serves your office." Terry could not restrain his fury. "I'm going to put you out on the street."

"Listen to me. I had information from a bartender about what Allison did at the Paradise. . . . She was peddling acid there and just about destroyed the place."

"Destroyed the place? Where's the police report? Warren Paris surely called them and had her arrested."

"For some reason, he did not," Cisco replied with growing frustration.

"I wonder why?" Terry asked icily.

Cisco had not been able to answer that question either.

"Look, the town has flipped out. Laver's had dozens of drug cases since she was at that joint on Christmas Eve. Wacko acid heads breaking and entering, car accidents, robberies!"

Terry listened patiently to Cisco's tirade. He removed his wallet and looked through it, then found a phone number.

"Christmas Eve, Paul, I was with Allison at the Paradise Inn."

Cisco slammed his fist on the desk. "Stop this bullshit, you'd say anything to protect her. You were out celebrating with Pat in Seacliff."

Terry picked up Cisco's phone, dialed the number on the Diner's Club card, and asked for his charges on December 24. When the billing supervisor came on, he handed the receiver to Cisco, who listened. ". . . December twenty-fourth . . . Those were the charges, signed by Terence Brett? Yes, okay, thank you."

"I suppose Diner's Club would also lie to protect Allison, wouldn't they? The fact is, we were together. The reason she asked me to go with her was that she was afraid Warren might become violent. She was bringing back her cocktail outfits. And Warren was very nasty and foul-mouthed, so she lobbed a bottle at him and it happened to hit the bar mirror.

"On top of it, Mr. Cisco, I gave that bartender a five-buck tip. Randy, I think his name was. He'll have an opportunity to identify me in court and refute my statement. Or perhaps to deny I was there. It would be a good idea for you to advise Randy that our very square judges deplore perjury and hand out punitive sentences. In the meantime, I've got my receipt and the monthly bill from Diner's at my office. Shall I have a messenger bring it over before I file charges against you?"

Cisco's liquid brown eyes blurred and roved around the office. "Jesus F. Christ, Terry. Why didn't Allison tell me you were with her? I gave her ample opportunity. She claimed you and Pat were together. If she had just indicated that you were with her, it would have been over."

Terry was aghast that Cisco himself had pursued her.

"After Laver illegally searched my house and didn't find any evidence, you brought Allison in and questioned her?"

"The house is owned by your father and he gave Barney his authorization to carry out certain investigations."

"Okay, Paul. You're on solid ground there." Terry's

thoughts galloped wildly and he tried to bridle his emotions. "On what basis did you determine Allison was worthy of an interrogation?"

"Interrogation, my ass. She's your girl. And I invited her to McCormick's. We had a very cordial luncheon."

"I assume, of course, you were still in your official persona as district attorney during this very cordial lunch." Terry's mind began to function with clarity. "May I also assume that in view of the Supreme Court's pending decision on *Miranda* v. *Arizona,* you advised Miss Desmond of her legal right to an attorney?"

Cisco poked his head out the door and saw the lineup of attorneys and fearful clients. He took his time coming back.

"Terry, could we discuss this in an unofficial capacity and in a less bellicose fashion? Say over a drink."

"I'm afraid that's not possible. It's a legal matter, Mr. Cisco, and anything you say outside this interview might not be helpful when I subpoena you for a deposition. Please bring the cordial lunch receipt, which is relevant. If you paid out of your pocket and didn't bill the city, then it can be argued that it was social. If you put it through as expenses, then it was official."

Cisco was screaming: "Stop, stop! Terry, stop!" Veins protruded from his temples, his body stretched as though he were bound on a medieval torture wheel. "There is no case against Allison Desmond. This office has no interest in her! Past or present. Now will you leave me in peace."

Terry picked up his briefcase, but his triumph was joyless.

"My client is missing. When I find her, you'll be the first to know if she intends to seek any legal redress against you. In the meantime, I'll try to stop hating you for wrecking my life."

Terry returned to his office and was not surprised to find Earl there, legs draped over his leather sofa. Easing up to his feet with delicacy, he offered Terry a drink from his own bar. His client had a new look, a King Arthur haircut with bangs.

"Hey, amigo, you've been through the wars."

"Looks like your hair has, too."

"What can I do, Georgie likes it. Now forget me, will you please?"

Earl had been warned by Georgie to give Terry room, and to avoid probing about the outcome of his meeting with Jonah Wolfe. She was convinced that Terry had freaked out. She also suspected that there was an element of chicanery in Terry's conduct.

"Ter, if you want to get loaded like the old days, let's do it. This shoulder was big enough to belt Elgin Baylor in the mouth when he tried to drive down the lane on me. So use it, you've got a friend."

They wandered over to the Surf Rider bar and Terry started to loosen up amid the familiar faces, the horseshoe bar, wet sawdust on the tile floor. Their table was ready and they sat down with their drinks.

"Allison was terrified she'd be busted and vamoosed. Chicks get paranoid when their old man doesn't report in. It might've crossed her mind that you were shacked up with some L.A. belle."

"What? It's impossible for me to believe that Allison thought this was my way of breaking up with her."

"Terry, you were gone for ages and no one had heard from you. What was *anyone* going to think? Come on, man to man. It was obvious that you wanted Allison to fade out. Hey, I knew that Rich Billy Klein would be laying girls on you day and night."

Terry slugged down a tequila shooter. "Did you imply it?"

Earl became huffy. "I have ethics about that sort of thing. I never even saw Allison. I was in Vegas with Warren to check out some sports lines."

"*You* have ethics? I'll try to forget what they are." Terry choked on this precarious censure, for he had also scorned his own moral principles. "Shit, Earl, I'm sorry. I can't even get drunk. I'm so worried about Allison."

"She'll flit around for a while and show up when you least expect it. I know she's hooked on you." Earl had enough of love-life conversation, called the waiter over, and ordered three dozen oysters for them. "And Jimmie, don't bring us the Dumbo ears. I want the small sweet Olympia valentines. With the scallops, bring extra tartar sauce for Mr. Brett here."

Old Jimmie had been serving the Bretts for years. He looked at Terry. "I wish you'd bring in a better class of client, Terry. See if you can get Earl up in a Sputnik over to 'Nam and let the Viet Cong kids eat him with extra tartar sauce."

When they were at the bar after dinner with Irish coffees, Terry marveled at Earl's discipline. Never once had he mentioned the disposition of his case with Jonah Wolfe. It must have been all those training camps and practices when he had avoided asking the coach if he'd been cut from the team. If there was bad news, Earl preferred having it travel slowly. Discussing the results of the settlement made Terry queasy.

Finally, Earl could no longer endure Terry's silence. "You get to see Jonah?" he asked timorously.

"Yes."

Earl massaged his knee and rested it on a vacant wooden stool. Then he swung it off and stood towering over Terry like some referee who had called a charging foul on him and he was out of the game. His Adam's apple bulged.

"Did Jonah pitch a shutout?"

Terry handed Earl his trust account check for two hundred thousand dollars. "You're going to be a very comfortable man if you watch yourself, Earl."

Earl's eyes leaped out, he clutched the check to his heart; the check itself and Earl seemed to be combining in a Jekyll-Hyde union, some new life form.

"Amen. The Lord is my Shepherd! I shall not want. I'll buy the Paradise Inn."

"What? Why?"

"It'll be a money pump. Guys chasing women at bars and watching topless shows is never going out of style. And Warren Paris is in the shithouse. The basketball season killed him. Every bettor in the county royally beat his ass." Earl paused and his voice became ominous.

"Your old client Aristedes and his Greek friends are coming after Warren. They're sore about him setting them up with that phony clothing case with the D.A. They want their money. Warren is looking to disappear."

Through his narrowed, drunk eyes, the memory of Allison's enemy stung Terry. He'd hang Warren alongside Jonah Wolfe on the yardarm of a tall ship.

"Earl, be careful with Warren."

"I'll have Georgie negotiate. Nobody can fuck her over."

"What's going on with you and her? Earl, I'd hate to have her hurt."

"Let it unfold. That's what Allison used to say."

"Allison." Terry signaled for more Irish coffees. "Let the world beware, you're Rich Earl now."

Earl's loon cackle filled the room, disturbing everyone. "Ter-rrr-ee-eeey, this is—I don't know . . ."

"It's your score, and there probably won't be another one like it. Look after it. Invest it in something better than that joint."

"I have heard the word." He slurred. "Warren has some operation." Earl was churning with antic wiles. "Terry, take half my money or whatever's fair."

"I have already taken my percentage. We were paid half a million dollars."

Earl was quick as a mongoose. "What? You can't do that!"

"But I did."

"That can't be! What kind of fucking Chinese arithmetic is this?"

"I don't think it would be advisable or morally profitable for you to pursue this any further."

"Talk about a beat count . . ." Earl's arm swept over the bar, accidentally knocking down the drinks. "I intend to take this to the limit! I better have a righteous accounting!"

"I split the three hundred thousand between Mike Summers and myself. That brought my percentage from forty percent to thirty. Mike actually deserved it all. He's a good guy—true blue—and I had to lie and con him for your benefit. Without Mike's help we wouldn't have gotten a penny and you'd still be mooching for beers."

Earl was flabbergasted. "Mike? What's he got to do with me destroying my knee?"

"He made the case."

"You fucking jayhawked me! This is unbelievable, Terry. I'll sue your ass forever if I have to."

Terry's eyes dropped in lament, resignation. "If you try it, you'll go to jail. I'll never understand human nature, no matter how cynical I become. Earl, do what you have to. But you'll have to deal with me and Jonah. Our publicity-crazy district attorney, Mr. Cisco, for sure. In the way that these things go, I suppose the U.S. Attorney will be filing felony charges and taking you to trial as well."

"For what? You're skunked."

"Asking players to go into the tank for a game is a federal offense."

Earl's nose flared, a bull confused by the flutter of the cape, and he retreated. "I guess that would be a problem for me. I didn't know you felt so deeply about point spreads."

"I don't give a damn about them. I understand though that whatever Jonah might be guilty of, you're no lamb being held by an angel and ascending to heaven. For God's sake, Earl, you were a player! How would you have felt the year you were All-American and someone propositioned you to dump?"

For a long moment, Earl considered the question, then gave a whinnying laugh.

"They did. And one thing I knew even then is that you don't get anywhere by turning people down. The truth is, no one cares. The night I scored fifty-six points at Salem, I was in the tank, hogging the ball. I knew we'd lose. We were just four-point underdogs. We lost by nine. Did it matter—really? I got a thousand bucks from Warren Paris for it." Earl stretched while rising. "Still, I thank you for what you did for me."

"I did it for Allison!"

"Doesn't matter, pal. You did what *I* wanted."

On that note, Earl turned away and set the bar up with

drinks, sending shock waves through the Surf Rider. As everyone was drinking his health, he decided to make a dramatic exit.

"Drink up, gentlemen. It's the last drink Earl Raymond will ever buy anyone." He raised his glass to Terry. "Screw you and Allison. You deserve each other."

24

The hangover Terry had was so wretched and painful, he took the phone off the hook, then quickly put it back. Just his luck, Allison would respond to his ad in the *Trotsky Newsletter* and the line would be busy. Nothing he could think of would make him feel better. He decided to shower, take a long walk along the river, clear his head, have lunch at the University Club, and see what springtime larcenies the big wheels in town were orchestrating for the hibernating populace.

On his third cup of coffee, which tasted like poison, he somehow dressed, laced his shoes, and went out. The day was sharply crisp with sun spokes wheeling through bleak cloud banks. He passed the mailbox and flipped the lid down, scanning the envelopes. His hand trembled when he spotted one with franked stamps, honoring Gandhi. He immediately recognized Allison's brazen calligraphy. He walked down to the river's edge and stood at the point remembering how much she had enjoyed the view with him on Christmas morning. With a burst of anticipation and optimism, Terry opened the envelope and touched the slippery onionskin sheets.

Calcutta, India

Terry,

I gave away my dictionary to some kids learning English, so my spelling might not be perfect. But you'll get the message.

Before moving off on my pilgrimage, I'm spending a few days here in the city named for Kali, the goddess of death and destruction. Her idol is black, smeared with blood. She has red eyes, four arms, large fangs, and a tongue sticking out, also dripping with blood.

I feel very much like her because I am now dead. I hope at the end of my pilgrimage, I will feel differently. I will be studying religion so I can learn how to deal with lies and deceivers. I trusted you. I stopped thinking because I believed you. I was off guard. I should have known better.

Terry, I wish you'd had the guts to face me instead of having Georgie do your dirty work for you. You're a coward, Terry. You had Laver and Cisco hound and humiliate me so that I would have to run for my life. Cisco said there was a cabal (a secret group) against me.

I hate you for making me love you so desperately and also making me believe I wasn't worthless. I'm trying to find a way of getting over my rejection. You led me on, filling my head with fantasies of a life together and that there was something to me. Why did you lead me on? What did I do to you? Will I ever find a reason for this?

Couldn't you have had the decency to tell me you acted too quick and you were sorry but you couldn't go through with the wedding? I probably would have killed myself but at least I'd've understood.

Instead, you sicced Pat on me. He was like a mad dog with rabies, saying the most vile things to me. If he wasn't *Your Father,* I surely would have killed him.

Pat had packed up my clothes and threw me on the street in the rain after I came home from Milly's. Then he called a cab to hustle me out. Pat took your car back. I didn't know what hit me. I'd been up for fourteen hours and working in the kitchen since three A.M. And I was sick with what turned into pneumonia.

Wow. I'm in awe of you. The way you planned this. I guess that's why you're such a good lawyer. When you fuck someone, you really do, and they don't get up. Pretending to go out of town on this case for Earl and then having me attacked by everyone. How could you?

Now I'll tell you what happened before we met and how I really broke my leg. You and your pals, the great guardians of the public—Cisco and Laver—will enjoy this.

I was living at a rooming house at the edge of the woods and trying to be happy. I was supporting myself, standing on BOTH FEET. I worked at the Paradise Inn as a cocktail waitress four nights a week and was making good money. Nights I was free, I'd read and work on my word lists. Or go over to the commune nearby, listen to music, and smoke some grass with the people and socialize and talk about organizing some protests to stop the war and getting this country together.

The day of the McDonald's robbery I saw these two guys from the commune get into their van to head for town. I'd saved money for wheels and was going to see a Dodge Dart I saw advertised. The car lot was on the way. The guys said they'd drop me.

Well, I checked out the car and a few others on the lot across from the McDonald's. I was there maybe five minutes. This salesman tried to get me in a car for a "test drive." I told him I wouldn't screw him for a brand-new yellow Thunderbird and a trip to the Rose Bowl.

After I dusted him off, I walked over to Mac's to eat and check if anyone was heading back my way. I spotted the van, so I hung around waiting to see if I could hitch back with the guys. This thing at Mac's was bad timing and seems always to happen to the losers of this world.

The two dudes who'd dropped me off suddenly stormed out and before I could say anything, they jumped into the van, backed out, and ran me down.

Then everyone dashed outside and started screaming they were robbed and I was laying on the ground with my leg broken.

An ambulance took me away. I got questioned, did I! The drug chemists used their money to feed people on the commune. I couldn't betray them.

Somehow Warren Paris got the idea I was *in* with those dope dealers and Warren does many things for the public. He thought I would collect acid for him.

I told Warren the people who make the stuff are not reliable. They have an acid-and-speed business and it's like moonshine and sometimes the still doesn't work. Warren then changes the subject while I'm waiting for my uniform deposit back. $67.

He says he and some very fine customers love live shows with girls and groups. I could make good money. These freaks like girls crippled. . . . I was on one leg and I thought I better get away from Warren before I shoved a crutch in his eye. I told him I'd think about it.

Warren went to see these people on the commune and they trusted me, said I was to deliver acid. Nobody asked me if I was all right with being the delivery girl for the acid. I was told that I would get $750 for it and not to ask questions.

When the delivery was late because they made a bad batch, Warren got the idea that I had all the acid and was holding out, or that he could beat the guys who produced it, get the acid, not pay, and leave yours truly in the middle. Which is why Warren raided my tent and murdered my cat.

That's when you entered my life.

You picked me up outside the hospital that first night and my pussy was so wet, I thought to myself, Dear God, I have to have this man. I must. If nothing good happens to me and I wind up with some beer belly in a trailer park, I'll know I can fall back on the night I spent with this beautiful, educated man. I would remember this gentleman in his blue

Mustang who stood in the rain FOR ME and excited me and was kind.

But when we got to my camp and everything was destroyed, I lost it and we tangled. You see, I got angry because I wanted to be with you, Terry. It got worse after you offered me a royal Chinese dinner with egg rolls. We could heat it up at your house. I was afraid you'd think I was a lowlife tramp, which I'm not. I was so confused and desperate that I pushed away the first decent man I ever met.

Next morning when you came back, I was sick to my soul about my beloved cat Johnny being murdered. He was a lost Himalayan I'd found starving in the woods. Your kindness and interest perked me up. I was in heaven, having you drive me to the Y and then taking me to breakfast at Milly's.

Terry, Terry, I gave you everything. You could've had my life. There was nothing I wouldn't do for you. If you wanted other women, I swear I would have looked away. I prayed at the orphanage that one day I would meet someone like you and give him all the love that was inside my soul. The love of a child for the parents I didn't have, the love of a woman which my heart bequeathed to you, the love of a mother, *and* I was your friend.

I *thought* you loved me. After we truly got to know each other and we were in Timberline and you proposed, my spirit split and became one with a rainbow. I felt like I was with a god. Terry, in the deepest way I hate myself now for not being on guard and baring my teeth. Yes, I'm very guilty of rotten judgment and loving you more than a normal person should love anyone.

Oh, never mind. Why am I explaining?

I guess Pat was right. I have no right to a man like you. I only wish you could have had the kindness of letting me hear it from you and not him. I never want to see you again.

Kali

Clipped to the back of the letter was the grimy, torn title page of the Maugham novel she had been reading:

The sharp edge of a razor is difficult to pass over; thus the wise say the path to Salvation is hard.

Terry was beside himself with grief. He crashed to his knees on the muddy point. For hours, he lay on the bank clawing at the ground, peering at blurred barges on the river until it was dark and he was hoarse, wailing her name into the night wind.

"Allison . . . Allison . . ."

25

Hollow-eyed from insomnia, Terry's face took on a gauntness, and he gave off the sour air of defeat. Night after night, he was torn by indecision. Should he try to follow Allison to India? Would she still be in Calcutta? Could he track her down and explain what had happened? Ultimately, resignation brought forth inertia. Something within him had been shattered. It was as though a shell fragment had lodged in his brain and he couldn't concentrate on anything. He hadn't told anyone about Allison's letter or where she had gone. In his mind, he tried to kill the very image of her, but phantasmagoric demons began to insinuate her into the wasteland of his dreams. When he awoke, he was left with a taste of ashes.

He had let his practice slide and wouldn't return phone calls. He was driving around aimlessly during the day and missing court appearances. He couldn't physically drag himself to the office. Something hard and mistrustful flourished in the dark interior region within him. Allison was gone, but he clung to her memory like a mourner.

Stanley Hoffman, the investigator he'd hired, was receiving reports of Allison sightings at truck stops and in college libraries. Terry wondered what Stanley was smoking. Terry finally contacted him at Allison's orphanage in Tillamook. Stanley returned and proudly handed him a manila envelope with all of Allison's records.

"I've been to a bunch of these homes, but this one was the roughest I've ever seen." Hoffman shook Terry's arm. "You've been on some bender, huh?"

"Thanks for your trouble, Stanley."

"I'll go on searching if you want, Terry. You know me, I never quit."

"No, she's gone," Terry said, writing a check for three thousand dollars.

Milly and Pat were alarmed by Terry's behavior. Privately, they agreed that he ought to see someone. The word "psychiatrist" was not used. Neither of them could muster up the courage. Lost, Pat started hanging around the restaurant until closing.

"We're all guilty, Pat," Milly said solemnly. "I wish I hadn't been so tough on Allison from the start. But it's my way to test apprentices to see if they're serious. And Allison was tireless. She was a good kid, Pat."

"Yeah," he replied with sullen guilt. "What're we going to do about Terry?"

"Right now, I think the thing is, is to leave him alone."

It took another week before Terry came around and found his bearings.

"I didn't know it would all hit you this hard," Pat said one evening when Terry was staring blankly at a basketball game on TV and drinking his dinner. Although Terry was no longer belligerent, their camaraderie had vanished with Allison. It was his son's apathy that disturbed Pat more than anything. He made a variety of suggestions.

"What about a fishing trip down in Baja, or we could get us a golf package in Hawaii? What do you say, Terry?"

Escaping from a dark place Terry replied, "I'm going to hit the road."

"What? Where you headed?"

"I'm not sure. I can't live here any longer."

Pat found solace in at last penetrating Terry's fortress. "Maybe it's time for you to be on your own. How about if I see if I can get you into the new waterfront complex downtown?" Pat's manner was obeisant, subdued. "I did the framing." When Terry did not respond, he broke down. "Terry, please don't hold this against me. It's tearing me apart. I'm just sick about my part in this."

"It wasn't only you but a combination of things. They all hit Allison at once. I've been doing some thinking. I've spoken to Paul Cisco. He wants to leave the D.A.'s office. He's interested in taking over my practice. I've agreed."

Pat was stupefied and his beefy face froze. "You're going to *leave* Port Rivers, give up your practice?"

"I have to do this. I want to drop out, lose myself."

"But you've got all your contacts and friends here. Terry, don't be so rash."

Terry rose and his father opened his arms to embrace him, but Terry shook his head, and Pat moved away at the staircase to let him pass.

"Everything reminds me of Allison—"

"What about us, our friendship, the love we have for each other? Someone else will come along. Plenty of them. You're a prize and you can't even see it."

The following morning, Terry packed his clothes and left the house where he had lived since childhood. When he drove through Buccaneer Square, he didn't bother to look up at his office. It belonged to another time. He knew he would never return to this place.

Book II

HOW LIKE A WINTER

26

April gusted out of nowhere, accompanied by the whine and crackle of thrashing Santa Ana winds, which hacked off the fronds of palm trees. The condition created unexpected ocean swells that brought out gaggles of drugged surfers who flipped over and were sucked under cresting waves and rescued by exhausted lifeguards. On the beach, the stupefied audience applauded, then took another hit on their joints and made plans for orgies. In a stunned daze, Terry spent his days sitting on the deck of Billy Klein's beach house in Santa Monica, observing the lunacy.

Even as he lived through the period, he despised the sixties, and Allison represented the herald of the era, its siren, proclaiming shallow freedoms, the idolization of the ego and defiant self-indulgence. Perhaps if he had stood his ground and remained isolated, he might have saved himself from her. But she had drawn him out into deep water, then left him alone in the riptide.

For a man who had considered himself a hard-nosed realist, Terry unearthed a new part of himself, the delicate membrane beneath the protective coating of maleness. Allison had dominated him, brought out a degree of tenderness that he might have once scorned. She had seized the feminine territory of his inner self and implanted her sensibility within him. He now hated her with a passion, but even beyond that, he was trapped by self-immolation and disgraced by a feeling of hollowness. He grappled with this polarity every day, but her thorns were everywhere, embedded in his flesh. No matter how he attempted to spurn and discard her influence, she occupied a permanent place in his heart. He would never love again.

His grasp of real time had become unreliable. He would watch the waves for hours and the movement re-

laxed him. He drifted along the beach on walks or took
bicycle rides down to the pier. His skin had a bronze
sheen, but the life within him was still scattered and he
was unable to find his center. This no longer troubled
him. To alter his mood, all he had to do was peer at the
sky and he was dazzled by the sun vision; the fantasy of
California; the illusion of separation from home—from
Allison.

Sometimes, a young woman in the distance caught his
eye—speckled by the tangent of the sun littoral and an
ocean wave, and he would stop in his tracks, afraid to
advance or retreat. It might be *her* returning to reclaim
him, like a spirit from a dark world. She could only
wound him.

Billy's large, gray-shingled beach house was below the
Palisades and set back from the Pacific Coast Highway.
Three bedrooms and bathrooms were furnished in an expensive, motley Hawaiian style with cane chairs and
florid print sofas. A wide teak bar with hanging baskets
and a dozen swivel stools gave onto a mirrored wall
whose shelves brimmed with exotic rums, arcane brands
of tequila, liquor for every whim. Cases of champagne
were stacked like cargo at the hatchway.

The deck overlooking the beach was deep and could
accommodate forty people at Billy's mostly naked bar-
becues. Bachelor paradise had arrived in Santa Monica.
Entire closets were given over to linen and large towels.
An industrial washer-dryer hummed constantly but never
drowned out the rock music emerging from speakers
everywhere. Along with peyote, acid, and mushrooms,
many women whirled through Billy's chambers. Terry
avoided them all.

"Billy, the place is very comfortable, but it looks like
a whorehouse."

"That's exactly what I told my 'inferior drekherator' I
wanted. It's called the groupie, slut style."

"And you spent a fortune on it."

"What else should a man with inherited wealth do with
his money? Do you think my father worked himself to
death so that I should suffer and count pennies? Terry,

I'm not exactly Steve McQueen. But I've made the best of it. I'm one of the happy few, a slob who can get ladies by providing resort amenities. The full American Plan. I've reinvented myself. For the first time in this nation's history, the ill-favored men among us are being pursued by the most beautiful women in the world."

Billy was patting his cheeks with Canöe aftershave. He wore white trousers and an orange psychedelic Day-Glo shirt imprinted with the word LIVE. He powdered his feet and slipped into his hand-crafted loafers.

"By the way, Terry, what're you going to do about that face of yours?" he demanded while preparing himself for his evening adventures. "The scar on your cheek can be cleaned up by plastic surgery."

"It's healed and I don't give a fuck."

"That's idiotic, you should care."

Then Terry thought of the actuality: it didn't remind him of the old Terry. All was right with the world, he reflected, sipping a beer. The maid had vacuumed, straightened the cushions on the rattan sofas, and mopped the tile floor. Billy had directed her through the linen-changing in his bedroom and created a Jackson Pollock riot of black satin sheets splashed with madras pillows. And just about everywhere the human hand could reach, champagne was cooling in ice buckets. However, the pipe cleaners in the ashtray were mute testimony to the single task the master of the house performed himself. He had reamed out the bowls, screens, washers, and lips of his Haight-Ashbury custom-designed bongs and loaded them with ZAP hash. Its soft, oily, blackish, salmonlike skin was lined with white veins of pure opium.

"Terry, do yourself a favor and see my doctor for a checkup and a referral to a shrink. You need a tuneup. I don't think your heart's pumping."

Terry turned on him furiously. "Fuck it, now lay off, I'm okay."

"You're acting like a yellow dog, so lay down and die!" Billy exclaimed.

The early-bird honor guards of Billy's collection arrived for sundown cocktails. A depraved mother-daughter combo were voluptuous red-headed dopers who alleged that Billy was working on an important case for them. While Billy was preparing his special narcotic guacamole dip in the kitchen, they sized Terry up like housewives at the butcher's. They gabbled about the war, the Beatles, orgasms, and strange practices in Pasadena.

It was one of those typically manic, discontinuous conversations that Terry constantly encountered since his arrival in Los Angeles. They were hard to follow, and rather than make an effort, he walked out on the party. Billy chased after him.

"What's wrong with you? We'll do them both. This is the cocktail hour, man, and it's followed by the dinner show. Then the late show. I have movie studio starlets coming in vans."

Terry grabbed a bike off the deck and rode down the sunlit shoulder of the beach, staring into the orange sun heading toward Hawaii with the sailboats. He stopped off at the basketball court near Muscle Beach in Venice and shot hoops with a couple of kids until there were enough men for an easy half-court game. Only when he was playing did he find a degree of tranquility within himself. He burned out, trying to keep up with the darting moves of college freshmen who hung around down there and bitched about how they were shortchanged after they were recruited and given phony scholarships.

Terry listened sympathetically to the boys, most of whom were black and could not do college work. Some of them could hardly read. After the game, Terry joined them for a beer, and a spirit of kinship slowly developed when he told them he had formerly been an attorney. He blithely agreed to look at letters of intent sent by coaches and advise a few of the players who were in danger of being booted out of school.

When he rode back on the bike path, he felt useful and more comfortable with himself. It had been a good idea to leave the hothouse of Port Rivers with its memories of Allison.

*   *   *

Led Zeppelin erupted through the beach house when Terry rolled in at midnight. Through the fumes of hash mist, the svelte, greasy bodies of tanned girls with stark white streaks under their breasts and men with beige asses were busily pulverizing the sofas. In the scented, flickering candlelight, a young woman's hand reached out and seized Terry. It was the young Pasadena belle he had dodged earlier. Her curved mouth dripped with red wine.

"It's getting real dirty, Terry. My old lady's getting it on." She pulled Terry against her bare sticky belly. "I want to do threesomes. I've got a gorgeous freak waiting for us. What a figure she's got. We'll really give you a workout."

He jerked away from her. "Where's Billy?"

"Who cares? Come on, sugar, let's get it on."

"Forget it!"

She was surly. "Where'd you leave your balls?"

Terry wasn't certain if it was the timbre of her voice, her threatening demeanor, or some distant reflection of Allison when they had first met. In an instant the woman assumed Allison's face, her naked figure, and the room was filled with dozens of Allisons all offering themselves in a monstrous, daisy chain of distorted orgiastic frenzy.

He wanted to strike her but caught himself. His heart was thundering and a silky cold sweat dripped down his back. He began to shake uncontrollably, bolted into his bedroom, and discovered a couple making love. For a moment, he couldn't move and slumped to the floor. His left side was becoming numb and there was no sensation in his fingers. The room started to spin in crazy angles. An eerie panic overwhelmed him. His pulse raced and he couldn't catch his breath. He was convinced he was having a heart attack.

"Billy, Billy!" he shouted.

Several people came over and tried to rouse him, then got spooked. They shouted for the host.

Clutching a sheet, Billy rushed in. "What's wrong, Terry?"

"I don't know. I can't move."

Billy switched on the light and shooed out the lovers. He grimly examined Terry and helped him onto the bed. Terry's eyes fluttered. His breath rasped as he was trapped in the terror of hyperventilating. His skin was washed out and ridges of sweat ran from his forehead into his eyes.

Billy flung on a pair of trousers and dashed out. "Terry, stay calm. I'm going for a doctor."

Terry knew something fearful was happening. The fingers of his right hand trembled. He was dizzy and more frightened as the minutes passed. He couldn't get a grip on reality. It began to fade and he sank into a stupor.

He was losing the energy and drive that were keeping him alive.

A cold object touched his chest. It gleamed like a silver dollar.

A voice said: "I want you to take a deep breath and try to relax."

A pen flashlight shone into his eyes and roved over his pupils. A cool hand pressed his carotid artery. He saw a brown bag rolled up with a cuff.

"Breathe normally into the bag. Easy, easy. You're just scared. I don't think you've had a heart attack. Have you taken any drugs?" Terry shook his head. "Are you telling the truth? I'm not going to judge you or report anything to the police—"

"He doesn't use drugs!" Billy snapped.

There was a hushed whispering, which Terry made no effort to understand.

"Are you sure, Billy?"

"Of course I am. Should I call for an ambulance?"

"I don't think it's necessary. His signs are good and the color's coming back. Something set off an anxiety attack. I'm going to give him a shot."

In a few moments Terry felt himself drifting. He imagined he was holding Allison, dancing with her on the sand as he slipped into a weightless sun vision sleep.

27

Terry awoke in a drugged haze and blearily peered out at the beach where a young couple were making fresh footprints on the smooth sand. A tremor went through him. He had only a vague recollection of what had occurred. Dozing in a chair, Billy was startled when he heard him stir. He leaped to his feet as Terry swayed.

"You all right?"

Terry realized he had had yet another emotional collision. "A little groggy, that's all."

"You scared the life out of me, Terry." Billy backed away. "What do you think happened?"

Terry rubbed his eyes, attempting to visualize the scene. "I . . . I don't know. I came back to the house, feeling good, and this girl grabbed me. It was so strange, Billy. Something started to flood inside me. My chest was heaving. . . . I had these palpitations. I felt like I was choking on my own blood."

Billy scratched his stubbled chin; despite his inclination to fob off everything as a gag, his mood turned grave. He was deeply concerned about the transformation in Terry. He put a consoling arm around his friend. Tears trickled down Terry's cheeks but he seemed unaware of it.

"Come on, buddy. You have to accept this thing with Allison." Billy touched him lovingly. "You know you can't bring her back. So stop being despondent. We've got to get you on your feet."

"Do me a favor and never, never mention her name again!"

As Terry was shaving, Billy sat on a stool and gave him directions to the office of the doctor who had treated him the previous night.

"You up for this?" Billy clucked like a mother hen.

"Now you know where to turn on Montana Avenue."

"Sure. Shit, yeah."

Terry hadn't been able to listen to him, and lost his way riding his bike up from the beach in Santa Monica. Eventually he found a two-story wood and brick-faced office and looked around the small neighborhood shops. He parked his bike and reluctantly went inside.

Stepping over dolls, skates, and an assortment of toys, a smiling, very attractive, lissome blond young woman came toward him. Her inky fingers clutched a batch of folders, on top of which was a box of lollipops.

"Hello, I'm Jane Ashley, Dr. Holland's assistant. I'm so thrilled to be working with such a brilliant doctor. Let me help you fill out the medical history, sir."

Terry retreated from this exuberant woman. "I think I'll wait for the doctor."

Jane sat beside him. She was pleasant, talkative, and concerned. "Are you scheduled?"

"Probably not."

Jane smiled and said, "That's a relief. We've had six emergencies today."

"I won't stay long. I just want to thank Dr. Holland."

Terry waded through a stack of magazines, health rags, searching in vain for a sports magazine, and wound up reading property ads in the local giveaway. It was close to five on the office clock and he was about to leave. Heading for the door, he felt disoriented.

"Hang on, you're next," said a woman in a white coat, with intense dark brown eyes, coming out of an office. A stethoscope dangled from her neck. She was with a young mother and her small boy, who waved a toy fire engine at Terry. She accompanied them to the door, holding their hands and reassuring them. When she returned, she checked her appointment book with Jane and wearily looked through the messages on the spindle. She turned to Terry, scrutinizing him professionally.

"I don't have an appointment," he said.

"I don't think you need one," the doctor said. "And you're a little too tall for my practice."

"I'm confused. I thought *you* were Billy's doctor."

"I'm his neighbor and that's more than enough," she said.

She was slender, with short, boyishly cut, sunny chestnut hair. Her nose was freckled, her skin tanned, and she gave off an aura of athletic good health. Terry was puzzled. There was something familiar about her features that tantalized him. His memory seemed to be playing tricks. Who did she remind him of? Yes, of course, hers was the last face he had seen before losing consciousness.

"You look just fine today, Mr. Brett. But the thing is, I only treat *little* boys."

"Maybe that's why I'm here, doctor."

She had an ironic half-moon smile on her face which broadened her mouth, giving her face a girlish gentleness. Terry called out after her, "Can I hang out?"

"I've got some paperwork. Could be awhile."

"That's all right, doc." He picked up a tin soldier from the floor. "I'll play until you're ready for me."

Out of the office and the white coat, she appeared younger. Her face was delicate and there was a certain fragility about her. They cycled over to the Santa Monica Pier and found a table outside a fish fry joint. She had changed into jeans and a sweatshirt with a Johns Hopkins insignia. She rarely socialized with patients, but as her specialty was pediatrics, she would refer him to another doctor. He was very comfortable with her as she related the daily grind of her practice.

"You don't have to keep calling me doc. My name is Valerie Holland."

He shook her hand and was surprised by the strength of her fingers. "Hello, Valerie."

"Hello, Terry."

He ordered beers from the kitchen hatch while she commandeered a wobbly table beside the rail. He sucked in the crisp ocean air and tried to rid himself of his depression by confronting it.

"I'm embarrassed about last night; mortified, in fact," he said. "I don't normally behave this way."

"I'm sure you don't." She was sympathetic. "Have you had these episodes before?"

"A few times."

"When you're working an orgy I guess these things happen."

"Ah, if only."

"You were an innocent bystander? I'll believe anything." She had a worldly, husky laugh that set off an elusive echo in his mind that he couldn't quite grasp. "You just happened to be passing Billy's place and he recruited you."

"He's a very old friend and I'm staying with him." Valerie studied him for a moment. "We were at law school together."

"You're a lawyer, too," she said with unconcealed disdain. "Let the world take heed."

"An unemployed one."

"I wish there were more of you."

"You had a bad experience."

"The worst."

"Malpractice?"

"No, just a slam-bang ugly family squabble."

"They're very painful." He smiled and knew the problem at once. "Families get very emotional about money."

She nodded. They continued fencing over a basket of delicious greasy jumbo shrimp and fried clams, slopping them with globs of hot sauce.

"What did you shoot me up with last night, Val?"

"Twenty milligrams of our friendly cure-all, Valium."

"I don't like drugs."

"I didn't have much of an option. It helped. You know, you might need a prescription for pills. You really ought to go on some medication until these episodes stop. It beats winding up in the ER, or getting me out of bed and in the middle of another of Billy's friendly gatherings. I can refer you to someone." She was curious. "Do *all* these people arrive naked?"

"They were when I walked in. I think it's Billy's dress code."

Val regarded the livid scar on his cheek, the puffy

bridge of his nose, and observed how edgy he became. She had a compulsion to touch him. He seemed so profoundly troubled and wounded.

"You don't fight in bars, do you?" she asked sardonically. "Car accident?"

"I wish; at least I would've had a case."

She pushed up from the bench seat. "Let me buy the beers this time."

"No, I'll do it."

"My round."

While she waited on line, she wondered why she was intrigued, and couldn't find a satisfactory explanation. Last night, she had held him in her arms. Her fingers had been on his body and she remembered how much she savored the feel of his damp skin, the blond hair on his chest, the leverage of his shoulders.

She handed him a bottle of beer. "May I ask what happened to you?"

"I came down to L.A. to work on a case I never should have taken . . . and . . . oh, never mind."

She watched him squirm and changed the subject. "Where're you from?"

"Port Rivers, it's north of Portland. Population around a hundred thousand souls." He peered at the last light, the vanishing sun, waiting for the mysterious green projection. "It was a peaceful, quiet place some months ago. Then some bad things happened, Valerie."

She reached for his hand and he clasped it without thinking. After a moment, she said, "I know a lot about that. At times I think I'm a historian of bad times. Not only what happens to other people and their kids."

He was conscious of holding her hand and guiltily released it, trying to seem natural. The wind picked up and bales of dense ocean fog rolled in. Valerie and he were wraithlike in the mist as they walked their bikes back on the verge of the beach.

Virtually against her will, Valerie found herself concerned about him. She hadn't been this attracted to a man in years and she wanted to get to know him, share his sorrow. Terry was skittish when they reached her beach house.

"Hey, come on in for a drink, Terry," she said with a warm-hearted air. "We'll light a fire and tell each other what's made us so miserable."

He glared at her, unable to control his moodiness, which had rambled through depression and succumbed to anger.

"Thanks, doc, but I'm not into instant confessions. What is it with California? People meet and in fifteen minutes, they're either taking off their clothes or discussing their souls."

Val was unprepared for this hostility and she was incensed. "What a brave little soldier—I didn't think you needed some jelly beans, pal. Who the hell do you think you are, scolding me that way?"

In an instant, the mannerly Terry returned. "Hang on, Jesus, I didn't mean to be rude."

Val had already wheeled her bike inside and Terry wasn't sure she could hear him through the high tide of crashing waves. He watched her turning on the lights. She stared through him, standing on the deck, then did something no one who lived at the beach would ever imagine. She closed the shutters and killed her view of the moonlit waves, locking out the sight of him.

28

Valerie had no contact with Terry for weeks. She was surprised by the impact his abrasiveness had made. It had wounded her, and she often found herself thinking about him during the day and after office hours. She'd sit on her deck, nursing a beer, and when she glimpsed him coming out of Billy's house and heading down to the water's edge, she'd duck inside. She recognized that her behavior was becoming childish, unseemly, especially for a doctor. But she was human, and something about Terry Brett's anguish, the way he had cast her off, had hurt and offended her dignity. His emotional turmoil was threatening to her. She hadn't handled his rejection with the serene obliviousness she expected of herself. It nagged at her. He was so strange and uncontrollable.

One Saturday evening she ran into him at a neighbor's birthday party on the beach. She was wearing a hot pink jumpsuit, had been in the sun most of the day, and felt healthy and attractive. She stood within a cluster of bronzed men, including the host, a producer, and one of the courtiers who had been pitching her for months with invitations to screenings, discos, and adventures in Mexico.

It would be lovely to whack Terry on the head with her sandal, but even after an endless supply of slushy Margaritas, Valerie still made a point of avoiding him, waiting for him to notice her. He infuriated her, shucking and jiving with some of the black athletes who seemed to be around him all the time.

For Terry's part, he enjoyed himself with these players, whose easy, uncomplicated company made no emotional demands. With a hundred and fifty thousand dollars as his share of Earl's settlement, Mike Summers could explore his options and try to find another coaching position in California. Terry had persuaded Mike to come down from Fond du Lac for a visit and bring his star forward Whiz Davis with him. The young player was a friendly, affable kid, who accepted Terry's recommendation and agreed to forego college for a professional career. In the scrimmages with college players who had formed a summer league, Whiz had outplayed boys who were predicted to be future All-Americans.

When the guests were on line for the Mexican buffet, Valerie half-listened to Gary, the hotshot producer who was fawning over her. "Val, the reason I want to marry you is so my mother would believe that I made something of myself by bringing home a doctor."

"That's a magical proposal. It's too Freudian to resist. Oh, Gary," she said with a taunt, "I can't tell you how long I've been waiting to hear about good old mom."

Valerie's fingers made their way through the thicket of medallions, chains, Aztec gods roped around his neck like offerings waiting to enter the temple of his heart. "You're a walking El Dorado. I could lose an eye in bed."

Terry was nearby and she hoped he'd overheard. He gave her an indifferent nod, which intensified the slight. The sharp-eyed producer noticed the subtle interplay.

"Have you met him?"

"Uh-huh . . . briefly."

"Poor bastard's Billy Klein's basket case. It's a tragedy." Valerie was suddenly attentive. "Terry's an exceptional guy. He did me a helluva favor. I'd negotiated a deal with the William Morris Agency. They gave me a screwing and I didn't realize it. I asked Billy to look at the contract. Well, he gave it to this Terry and he made changes and changes. He said the contract was really weighted on my side but they had somehow buried my profit percentage into something called 'recoupment.'

"I marched back to them with all of Terry's notes and a contract *he* drafted. He made me . . . I don't know how much money. When I asked him for a bill, he refused. He told me the fee was to let him bring these black guys to my birthday bash. He hangs out with them at Venice Beach, playing basketball. It's really bizarre."

Valerie loaded her tortilla with carnitas and beans, then bashed it with fiery hot salsa while the mariachi band went from table to table playing requests. Terry and his horde ate as though this was Christmas at the Salvation Army.

"What made Terry so uptight?"

"Billy told me he got beaten up. Then when he got out of the hospital and went home, he found out his fiancée had died. Something horrible like that."

Dancing with Gary made Val dizzy and she wiggled away. She leaned over his shoulder and watched Terry leaving. After a moment, she broke away and followed him out to the street. He was saying good night to his boys, who were piling into a battered convertible. He was giving orders to a red-headed man at the wheel of the car.

"Mike, don't let Whiz out of your sight. We might have a deal with Chicago if he passes the physical." Terry then turned his attention to the other athletes. "I'll see the chancellor about those scholarships, or I'll try to get you a deal with a pro team. No bars and no grass, guys, you hear me?"

Grateful sounds of "Thanks, Terry," were followed by waves and salvos of "See you."

Terry was about to walk back to Billy's house when Valerie rustled beside him. He was warily silent but his manner had no sparks of bitterness.

She hesitated awkwardly. "I owe you an apology, Terry."

"I think it's the other way around."

"I'm afraid to ask if you want to come over to my house . . . or shall we talk on the street?" she asked, pulsating with nerves.

"Whatever you like."

He was in beach uniform, barefoot, white linen trousers and a blue boatneck sweater. His skin had a deep tan and his sun-streaked blond hair was longer, reaching below his collar like a rough-hewn beachboy.

"Any more problems?" she asked.

"No, I think they're finally over."

"Maybe all you needed to do was to relax."

Despite her warmth, he was wary and realized he was frightened of her. He followed her inside with the caution of a cop investigating a crime scene for clues. Her house was orderly without being meticulously neat: whitewashed adobe walls; tile floors; and paintings of Mexican peasants in marketplaces. Valerie's beach hacienda revealed that she was a woman with taste who cared about her nest. The place had clean lines, comfortable furniture to lounge on, with batik pillows on the floor. She put on Ravel's String Quartet, and the poignant sounds sweetened the room. Her abiding interest was poetry. On a glass table were volumes of Blake, Christina Rossetti, Swinburne, Eliot, and Auden. He picked up a leatherbound edition of Swinburne's *Poems and Ballads* and noticed that it was old.

"I collect Pre-Raphaelite first editions, and paintings, which are in storage. The salt air is a killer."

"Why that period?" he asked.

"It was my mother's favorite and she used to read to me when I was a girl. Swinburne cures broken hearts." In an effort to loosen him up, she said, "Now I don't have to work tomorrow. Are you into tequila?"

"Be serious, I'm Billy's houseguest."

"I've got some really good Herradura."

"Let's do it."

Valerie sat in an armchair opposite him afraid that she might be crowding him. In the dim light, he was a war-like young Viking god.

"Do you remember the boy with the fire engine when you came to my office?" Terry leaned forward, detecting something troubling her. "When we went out to the pier, I was very upset. It's hard to show that sort of thing in the office. I have to be a model of insensitivity and confidence. I suppose I grew more troubled as the evening went on with you. I thought I could talk to you as a stranger." She belted down her shooter and poured herself another one. "The boy's tests came back and it was as I suspected. Leukemia. I had to tell his mother."

Terry touched her hand. "Valerie. I'm very sorry. I missed the signals."

"And I misunderstood you, Terry. I didn't realize that you'd just lost someone . . . and were in mourning."

He walked to the window, staring out at the black water and lovers illuminated by campfires. Music drifted in from the beach. He thought about what Valerie had said for a few moments. *He* hadn't lost Allison. She had been savaged by his father; attacked by Paul Cisco and the police; betrayed by Georgie. Earl must have played some role, as well as the vindictive Warren Paris. Allison had coalesced these disparate components into a grand conspiracy. This pack of wolves had hunted her down like prey, torn her apart, and killed her. He was now able to share Allison's persecution complex. He mirrored her paranoia, and the answer came to him in the flow of a remarkable rationalization.

"She was murdered."

"Murdered! Oh, good God, no. I'm so sorry. What a tragedy."

"If I'd been home, it wouldn't have happened. I could have saved her." He sighed and his lips pursed in a wounded smile. "I guess it was one of those vengeful acts of fate. The cosmos was never very kind to her, nor were the people around her."

"That's horrible." Valerie had lost him again. "Terry, we all have our time. We can't bargain for more. You can't blame yourself."

Valerie's tranquillity and commiseration enabled him to fuse the fable of Allison's death into some form he could tolerate, for the truth was unendurable. He reached out cautiously, a man in a dark room trying to locate the light switch. Valerie kicked off her shoes and moved beside him.

"What was her name?"

Terry re-created the moment of his proposal in Timberline. "Maia . . . Maia. She was named for a Roman goddess who became one of the stars and the wife of Zeus." The invention allowed him to gain some distance from the existent Allison, who in this otherworldly guise could no longer torment him.

"Listen to me, will you? I want to help."

"Can I hold you, Valerie?"

"Yes . . . yes. Do I remind you of her?"

"No, not at all."

"I'm glad. I don't want to. . . . I'm someone else."

Terry embraced her and kissed her hair, her forehead, her eyes, her cheeks, and blindly explored the contours of her face. His touch was delicate and she discovered the inner voice that told her she could care very deeply for him. The prospect terrified her, but he was irresistible.

I'm alive, and she's dead, Valerie told herself. *I must act.*

"Can I be your consolation, Terry?"

"Is that all you'd like?"

"No, I think I want more. I know what you're going through. I also lost someone. It's been hell and taken me years to put my life together."

Terry held up her face. She was trembling. He kissed her with compassion for them both, which stilled the flailing wings of their grief.

"Will you stay with me?" she whispered.

29

They held each other tightly under the blanket, like frightened children seeking refuge. A half-empty bottle of Herradura stood on Valerie's wicker night table. It was two in the morning and they had eased into that companionable intimacy of lost souls and were drinking from the same glass. At the same time he could not ignore the fact that he had rediscovered his sexual interest. They both pretended not to notice and there was some confusion about what to do. She waited for him to make a move, and when he didn't, she resisted the temptation to force things. They were both at ease in this transitory alliance.

"When did you get married, Val?"

"Second year of med school. Kenny Holland was so needy and I had to help him through his courses or he would have been booted out. He was one of those marginal students. Sad and good-looking. We were together all the time. And I thought, what the hell? So I married Kenny. My father hit the roof. He despised Kenny for being weak."

"Maybe that's why you married him."

"You could be right. I've stopped analyzing it. I found us a little furnished apartment in downtown Baltimore near the harbor. It was very romantic. I liked playing house. I shopped, cooked, coached him through exams, and just about took courses for both of us.

"After finals we hung around for ages, sweating for

our grades. Kenny was a wreck, taking speed, and he started to use heroin. I know he was stealing Demerol, Seconal. Any barbiturates he could from the hospital pharmacy. I couldn't control him. He denied he was hooked.

"When my grades came and his didn't, Kenny was very shook up. I didn't give it any thought. They're slow as hell at medical school because most of the professors give precedence to their own practice and they're out hustling lectures or consulting on cases."

Valerie laid her head on Terry's chest, then turned, and their eyes were fixed on each other in a dead reckoning.

"Kenny was called in by the dean. Three of his professors were waiting for him. They had hard evidence that he cheated on the finals."

Valerie sank her head on Terry's knees, then gave a quirky laugh.

"I was at the bank at the time. . . . My checks had started to bounce. I couldn't understand why. Kenny had cleaned out my account. I had to call my uncle to bail me out."

Terry felt her despair and reached out and held her tightly. Her slender body and lovely firm breasts rested on him.

"I'd already made up my mind that our marriage would never work. I didn't respect Kenny. It must sound antiquated and maybe senseless, since we're living through the crazy sixties, but to me trust and friendship are my foundation, the rockbed.

"When I got back from the bank to our apartment, I was so pissed with him. He was stealing from *me*! I was going to tell him I'd be filing for divorce. I'd rehearsed all that bitter stuff I'd held back. Like, 'I want to have children, but not with you. You don't make me happy. I despise drug addicts, especially when they're supposed to be doctors.' "

She clasped Terry's neck and curled into him, entwining her long legs around him. "Kenny was waiting for me in bed—" Valerie was crying so softly, almost as though she were afraid he'd notice.

"Oh, Val, come on, get it out," Terry said.

"The wall behind our bed was spattered with his brains. I felt so guilty for not loving him. He had a .45 locked in his hand.

"Terry, I don't want to spend my life with this weight, this regret." He kissed her tears. "It's maddening. I've thought such a lot about you and I'm so insecure now. I don't even know why you came to the house tonight. Or if you even like me."

He felt a kinship with her vulnerability. "Of course I do."

"Terry, can I make you feel again?"

And she did.

Valerie made perfect soft-boiled eggs and they companionably shared the newspaper. She read the main section and Terry the sports. The Brandenberg No. 3 was playing on her professional quad stereo system and the sun flooded in from the open French doors. After they'd finished, he watched her water her plants on the deck. He liked the curve of her body, her legs, the shape of her breasts as they beamed through her T-shirt, the way she moved in a glide in the faded cutoffs she wore. There was a natural rhythm to her, as well as an intellectual clarity that appealed to what had once been his logical mind.

With her office calls and chores completed, she asked, "Do you surf?"

"I never have. I'd like to learn."

"It'll be good for your leg."

"I didn't think you could still tell."

"That you had childhood polio? 'Course I can, but how you overcame the limp must've been hell."

"Years of therapy. But it was worth it."

"I'd say." Val tried to gauge his mood. Terry seemed relaxed, but she remained tentative. "I'm off this weekend. Want to hang out and have a good time?"

He was not prepared for Valerie's transport north up to Zuma Beach. He had only seen photos of the gun metal gull-winged Mercedes. Shifting gears resolutely and with sharp reflexes, Valerie drove the car with ass-kicking confidence, shifting with the precision of a Grand Prix driver. He assumed she had put her life savings into the car.

At the beach, he proved an apt pupil while they bellied on their surfboards with anticipation, waiting for a good wave to ride. He was enjoying the alteration of their moods—one moment serious, the next needling each other.

"Valerie, you'd make a fortune running an abortion clinic for Billy."

"I could work mornings and be a beach bum all day. I'd need a house lawyer of course to bail me out." She urged him onto his surfboard. He was about to be swallowed up. "Ter, we've got one!"

It was a good six-footer, but he bailed out. He'd have to get accustomed to the wall and not give it up. Low tide came in and they changed out of their wet suits, wiggling under towels on the parking lot.

"You have any dinner plans?" he asked.

"Yes, as a matter of fact." He seemed disappointed. "With you. There's a place in Santa Barbara I think you'd like. The drive's pretty up the coast," she said, handing him the keys. "You drive a shift?"

He held the passenger door open for her and gestured grandiloquently. "Doctor, I am the son of contractor. My first car was made in Peoria, a very gentle earth mover."

The power of the car astonished him and the drive had a magical never-never-land dreaminess that allowed Terry gradually to escape from himself. The sleepy small Mexican village atmosphere of Santa Barbara entranced him. But on the beach and back in the hills, he saw the lighted pillars of wealth, mansions perched on points. Valerie directed him to a hotel with a circular drive and a large sheltered terrace across from the ocean.

"I thought we could have drinks and dinner here."

"Beats the pier. While we're at it, tell me where we are. When I was in college, I never got up here."

"You were too busy swotting, huh? This is the Biltmore."

Over their third Margarita, Valerie became giddy. "Terry, do me one favor: If you ever have the fucking nerve to drop me, don't bring any of Billy's tarts here."

He smiled at her through bloodshot eyes, leaned forward, and amiably kissed her. She leaned into his arms.

"Val, I'd never pack a tuna sandwich to a wedding."

"Good. I'd like to change and get cleaned up for dinner," she said.

"Fine. I'll spring for a room. You've got a lawyer loaded with dirty, filthy, scarred contingency money."

"Bigshot, just follow me."

She led him through the clubby English lobby. The staff treated Valerie with cordiality. She knew their names, and when she stopped at the desk, the manager greeted her and handed her a key. High on tequila, Terry carried a kit bag with their wet towels and followed her through the grounds to a bungalow.

"Now I get it. You bring all your guys here."

"Is that what you think?"

"The witness may give a discretionary answer. It's your car, your towels, your beach locker. I have no further questions."

"My mother's family uses the hotel as a winter retreat. They're from the Midwest and they come year-round. So I keep some stuff here."

"Oh, really. Anything in my size and color? I'm fussy."

Val opened a clothes closet filled with men's garments. "Sure," she said with winning casualness, "grab a sweater, trousers, anything you like."

"I may need to protect myself if any of your strays drop in. Do you have a gun . . . any weapons?"

"That's why I brought you, Mr. Brett. Come on, this isn't the time for discovery proceedings. I've got sand in ticklish places. Let's hit the showers. We'll have a talk later."

He entered a sitting room with a fire already blazing. Fresh baskets of potpourri were scattered around and massive vases of flowers. Two tapestried wing chairs were separated by a table with a bottle of champagne in an ice bucket. Valerie pointed him to a bedroom. He discovered the bathroom and a robe with "B" stitched on it. Everything was there: shampoo, shaving cream, and Colgate.

He was feeling like himself, the old Terry, ready for Pat's gibes, Paul Cisco's courtroom antics, and Georgie's latest domestic civil war.

Before Allison . . . What a life of innocence he'd led—despite his defense of murderers, he thought. The ugly vision of Allison fermented flurries of homicidal anger, sending the attorney into legal strategies and eloquent advocacy. In the shower, he addressed the court:

"The accusations in Allison's letter are beyond libel and defamation. My defense will reveal the truth of the events that actually occurred."

As in court, he knew the truth would prove useless.

Valerie was checking messages with her service and trying to towel-dry her hair at the same time. She pointed Terry to the dresser and gestured for her comb. He brought it to her and she dismissed him.

"Amy's allergic to penicillin. Give her sulfur diozine." While Valerie combed and talked, he opened the bottle of Taittinger and poured. After she finally hung up, she had difficulty switching into his mood. She asked for a few minutes alone. He heard her swearing about the doctor who was on call covering her cases.

He handed her a glass of champagne.

"I wanted one weekend without all this."

"I know how it feels."

"You do?"

"Sure, when someone's arrested for murder or a jury's out deliberating on a case."

"Just like us."

At dinner, Valerie was dressed in a dazzling red silk pants suit, a blouse with a cowled neck, and an intricately embroidered white vest. Apart from an antique signet ring, she wore no jewelry. She had on a perfume he had never smelled before. It had a strange, alluring scent of lemon verbena, which she admitted to having brewed herself. She hated commercial scents, particularly Chanel. He looked at the menu and she asked if he could eat shellfish. He nodded and she ordered a pair of three-pound Maine lobsters and a bottle of Bâtard Montrachet '59.

He was astonished. Valerie Holland was beyond sophistication. She combined familiarity and the breathtaking aristocratic poise of a woman whose personality had been shaped by dynastic rule.

When he was drifting away from her, she was prescient. "Terry, Terry. . . . I wouldn't want to mess up what's left of your life by letting you enjoy it. I'd hate to be unkind and force something like that on you."

"Give it a try."

They wove back drunkenly to the cottage and he carried her to bed. After they kissed, he looked at her for a long time, but remained passive. Her mind cleared for an instant. Terry did not want her to initiate the advance. He kissed her shoulder and became indecisive. She responded to his divided mood and turned away without anger.

"It was a lovely evening."

"For me, too. Good night, Val."

As Terry drifted off, the screen of his mind was impregnated by Allison. He visualized a photo of the Taj Mahal that he had cut from a magazine. In his dream he found himself at the entrance. Allison was in a white votive sari. Terry heard himself say, "I'll buy you a Chinese dinner—" As he reached out for Allison, a blind fakir with a mendacious smile bolted out and thrust himself between them. He tore off the sari, stripping Allison, forcing her to her knees. Terry fought with the beggar. But the man's fingers were powerful and horned with webbed gristly bone. They were around Terry's throat, strangling him. In an instant, Allison was gone, sucked into the beggar's filmy eyeless sockets.

Valerie was rocking him. "It's all right, okay, Terry—"

He bolted to a sitting position in bed. "What, what happened?"

"You had a nightmare." She did not tell him he had been screaming and raving incoherently.

He swung his legs over the side of the bed. A sweat stream ran down his back. "I'll sleep in the other room."

"No, no, stay . . . stay with me." Valerie went to the bathroom, brought back a glass of water, and handed it to him. "Do you need something to get you through this? I've got some sleeping pills."

"No, I'll work it out."

"Terry, don't be afraid. I'm here for you. But you have to want to heal, to go on with life."

An hour later, he was still wrestling with insomnia and she heard him leave. In the hotel lobby, Terry spotted a Mexican woman with a mesh net lifting butts out of the sanded ashtrays. A desk clerk at the switchboard was eating ham and eggs. The tired bellhop unpacked newspapers. Terry walked across the street, climbed over a rocky wall, and reached the beach. The black outcast shadows of fishing boats mounted, rose, surged over the vanishing littoral of islands.

He grappled with the vision, bellowing in the wind:

"Allison, Allison! Let me go!"

And . . . suddenly it was daybreak and he was back in the cottage, watching Valerie sleep. Her face had a serene loveliness. She stirred, reaching out for him. Then her eyes fluttered open. His desire for a woman returned. She smiled lazily, hugged him, alert to his appetites.

"You look like you might want to . . . get down to business with me?"

"Possibly."

"Well, I think I'm on call." She pressed her warm, naked body against him. "I wouldn't want you to have an anxiety attack."

"You'll be sorry for that remark, Valerie."

She stroked him. "Have you been carrying this evil-looking thing around for *me*?"

"For a while."

"I'll see if there's a cure for it."

Valerie leaned forward, dropped her head, and grasped his cock. It grew harder in her mouth. Her tongue slipped down over the head, and for a moment she was afraid he was ready too soon. She hungered for him to be inside her, tearing into her. She guided him into her and she raised her belly and in a slow circular rhythm forced him deeper and deeper into her and they were joined in a dance that became more punishing as he became wrathful and fierce. She felt him, girding his thighs, tightening, holding back.

I will make you forget her, she thought. *I will never, never let you go.*

She was coming again, and Terry relentlessly forced himself into her harder and harder. She was screaming with gratification until he erupted and their gasps matured into a chorus of release. She took his face in her hands and kissed him. His smile of gratitude was so genuine that she began to cry.

"Am I the first one since her?" she asked.

"Yes."

"I will heal you and make you happy. Just let me."

"Can I make you happy, Val?"

"As long as I have a part of you."

His eyes were filled with suspicion. "I want her to go away more than you do. But I can't seem to shake this."

"You loved Maia very much. You'll give her up in time, Terry. She'll fade. I know I can make your life wonderful. I need you to fulfill mine. I want your babies, Ter. Nothing matters to me as long as we're together. Let go, stop torturing yourself, she's dead."

Valerie sensed that she was making him apprehensive, and she clashed with her dead foe, desperate to keep him from sliding away. But it was too late. The mood was broken and Terry had fallen back into the abyss of the past.

"We're not going to make it," she said, giving in to her frustration.

"Yes, I know."

"You won't release her."

"Maybe I'm afraid of you, Val—and commitments."

"I'm glad you used that word. Because from my point of view, that's your problem. You had a career and you dumped it. You have nothing to hang on to, Terry, and it's a pity. You're a young man and you're shutting the door on yourself."

She sat beside him on the window ledge. "You see, I'm the kind of woman who can accept a time of mourning when it's for someone else. But what's happened to you is that you're mourning what you once were and how you felt. You can't move on. Terry, have you ever seen a trompe-l'oeil painting?"

"Yes, of course. It looks like the object is in a third dimension."

"Exactly—and that's what you've done with your own situation. You've trapped yourself in a cell that isn't real. I won't and can't be another woman's double. Grief is a mood, and then it develops into a poisonous environment, and you keep exploring it until you're lost in the maze. You've been indulging yourself and you don't want to find your way out. So how can I have any reality as a human being?"

30

Slowly patching himself up, Terry found a degree of stability. The cracks within him were shored up through Val's invisible psychological invisible mending. In a modest way, he could function. Working with Mike Summers, Terry had arranged tryouts for Whiz Davis with several professional basketball teams he had contacted. In August, he secured a forty-thousand-dollar contract for the young basketball star from Fond du Lac with the Chicago Bulls, the new western expansion team in the NBA.

He and Valerie were inseparable, but he wouldn't move into her beach house. They had discovered a profound friendship and enjoyed each other's company, whether it was going to a Dodgers game or a pop concert. When they were together, they seemed to be sending off those flares of people rebounding, remaking their lives in the flimsy hope of a resurrection.

Valerie was responsible for the even keel of his days and she provided a different dimension to the companionship he had lost. The playfulness of Allison's scatty world was replaced but not completely displaced by a woman bound by professional conduct and a brutal schedule of office hours, hospital rounds, and midnight emergencies.

Valerie handled everything with admirable coolness and imposed a degree of order on Terry that he accepted. Not long ago, he had also been a professional with a clear path. Valerie was a woman worthy of respect and his admiration for her grew by the day.

With an ironic smile, he told Billy, "With Val, it's all very controlled and adult."

"I hope it doesn't happen to me. I never want to grow up."

Terry considered this option. "Val's given me something priceless."

Billy continued to forage through his address book for recent acquisitions to his party list. "I'm all ears."

"My peace of mind. I never thought about it, until I lost it."

Terry's new life had no fixed pattern; it was completely different from Port Rivers's courtrooms and its rain. Some of the manic, magical fun was missing and Terry sometimes wondered, while killing time on the beach with his covey of ball players, if this new stage of maturity was what real life ought to be about. In Valerie, he had found the healing earth mother, and an undemanding lover who pleased him.

And yet . . . despite Allison's letter, she continued to live and flourish within him. He realized that she'd had no recourse but to escape. He clung to the honeyed memory, the wild scent of her. No matter what he did, she would remain the girl of his dreams, embedded in his soul, and he felt fortunate to have experienced those incandescent moments of enchantment given few men.

But with every passing night, Allison's ghost receded into the myth of the Roman goddess. Terry accepted the equivocal situation and suspected that perhaps his destiny was to covertly love both women. If this was the balance that could keep him from cracking up again, he would face up to the schism within his soul.

The day before Valerie's birthday, on a Friday afternoon in September, she had escaped early from the office. They took out her thirty-six-foot Swan sloop, tacking in the Marina del Rey channel. Terry loved the classic old boat with its thickly varnished teak planks and oak beams, gleaming brightwork and handmade marlinspike. Even with sea spray in her face, the very tanned, modish, slender Dr. Holland at the wheel possessed an unruffled elegance that he marveled at. They reached her slip and the churlish old salt who looked after her boat helped her dock. She handed him the wicker hamper, which was filled with caviar and truffled pâté, cheeses, and whatever else was left over from their picnic.

"Keep it, Charlie. There's also a bottle of champagne. Have some fun with your old lady."

Lowering the stentorian hawk he used for the other amateur boaters, he smiled and said gently, "Thanks, doc, you're a treat. I hope this beach bum appreciates you."

Mistress of largesse and the unpredictable grand gesture, wherever Valerie went there were always minions swarming, trying to please her. They were crazy about her. There was a natural and extraordinary generosity about her, and Terry had no idea how she managed it. She was very specific about her medical practice and shadowy about herself. She worked with several other doctors and had been in private practice for five years. At times he wondered how much Val had to earn to support her extravagance.

Back at her house with a couple of beers and dressing to go out for a casual dinner, he was stunned when he found next to the solitary pair of jeans he had left in one of her closets piles of cashmere sweaters, linen jackets, trousers, polo shirts, sneakers, white bucks, Docksiders, a flock of ties. He walked out to the deck to clear his head. What was she trying to do? Then he saw a brand-new Colnago bike in silver that matched hers. On it was a card with his name and he shouted with the surprised enthusiasm of a kid:

"Val, get your sweet ass out here!"

She had a sly smile. He liked her hair longer. He'd asked her to grow it. He was a man whose moorings were fixed to the flowing deltas of voluptuous, Rubens women, and Dr. Holland had been too cautious about taking advantage of the flow of her extraordinary femininity. She had given him back his fire and he was going to return the favor by drawing out the girl in Valerie, which she was at pains to conceal most of the time.

"We have to talk, young lady. I'm pretty well fixed—comfortable, in fact—and I like to live well, spend a buck. But you're outrageous. Where do you get this kind of dough?"

She put her hand between his legs. "I've got a couple of old guys on the side with special tastes and I do a little very fancy hooking. We don't talk price."

"I'm thrilled to know that I have a certified degenerate on my hands. But Val, I really do want to talk."

"Sailing with you makes me horny. In fact, Ter, I'm always hot with you."

"I'm deeply flattered. The feeling is mutual. I'm still waiting. . . . I think it's time to take your deposition. I've been out of practice for a while and I like to keep my hand in."

"Why? Are you reconsidering the job as a litigator with Billy's firm?" she asked.

"Hell, no."

"You'll be my house counsel."

"If that's the case, this is the time for full disclosure."

Terry sat down on the hammock and she wiggled him over and nestled her head on his chest. She narrowed her eyes at the parade of lazy beach walkers, sweaters tied around their waists, strolling up to the Santa Monica Pier. She and Terry had spent many evenings alone, quietly rocking on the hammock, casting out his demon, the attachment which Valerie hoped was atrophying as she held fast.

Nevertheless, she felt stalled with him. As he recovered, a curious, self-reliant detachment revived in his personality, which to her alarm had the effect of drawing them apart. He listened to her advice too readily now—and ignored it. He was cutting loose, and it gnawed at her. His face was stronger, the scar poised on his cheek took on the emblem of an honorable war wound, which added another dimension to his virility. He still made love to her almost every night. She had never known a man who could arouse her so quickly. She was enthralled by him and their lovemaking. Pure magic how he had her number.

"How can you afford to live this way?" He waited for her to respond and noticed her reluctance and the clues an evasive witness gives off. "I know pediatricians do pretty well."

"Off the record, counselor?"

"Naturally. But the truth, please, or at least a version I can live with."

"You're being bad . . . and mean. I want you to kiss me first."

He took a slug of beer. "Dr. Holland, lay it on the line."

"The truth is in your hand."

He was baffled by her obscurity. "I'm touching your breast."

"And what're you holding in your other hand?"

"What, I don't understand. A bottle of beer?"

"That's the secret."

Terry jerked up suddenly and they almost fell off the hammock.

"Bach Beer?" She nodded lazily. "What's the connection?"

"My mother was Elisabeth Bach. She was the daughter of Jason Bach, whose father started the brewery. My grandfather Jason had a daughter and two sons who eventually inherited the company."

He read from the label: *"Bach Imperial Lager, the Beer that made Milwaukee Famous."* It was a slogan that he and the rest of America had heard or seen on billboards for half a century. Bach Beer was a part of the language.

Terry was disconcerted and had to pin all this down. "She was one of the owners?"

"Yes, with her two brothers."

"You mean it's still a private company?"

Val deflected him sharply; the disclosure was vexatious.

"Enough family history, please. Can we go to dinner now?"

They biked over to their dinner local, Chez Jay. The insouciant dark speakeasy atmosphere, sawdust on the floor, the good shots at the bar, the walls implanted with nautical artifacts, and the gabby, congenial owner appealed to them. Terry's eyes went up inadvertently to a gold-flecked sign above the cash register:

BACH IMPERIAL LAGER

31

The shock of Val's enormous wealth had dissolved from awe to suspicion. Over his charred New York steak, Terry tried to come to terms with her penchant for secrecy.

"Now I understand how you can afford two-grand Colnago bikes. Keep suites at the Biltmore . . . and cruise around in a Mercedes. Valerie, were you ever going to tell me about this?"

"Terry, it's not very interesting. I don't like to discuss money."

He was growing irritated. "I don't mean to probe. But I think you should lay it all out in a spirit of frankness.

I have a lawyer's brain and it makes me suspicious when I think you're holding out."

Val knew she was treading on dangerous ground. She had restored his ego, but she recognized that it was still fragile. He had lost his great love and treated his fiancée's death as though he himself had been the victim. She realized that her money would be a major hurdle for him to overcome. More than anything she loved his sensitivity, but it was a deadly prize for a woman. She had to be very careful or he might bolt.

"I don't mean to be furtive. But people get intimidated when they find out about my connection. You see, Terry, there's so much pain involved for me with my mother. She died in a sanitarium while I was in medical school—just before Kenny blew his brains out. I'm an only child, like you. I inherited her share of the business. My two uncles run the breweries and I never question their decisions." Her face was pinched with conspiracy. "Terry, no one knows about my connection to Bach. I like being a very private person."

"Well, Valerie, I'm not going to start advertising it."

"You see, that colors people's perceptions of me."

"I would imagine it does."

"Are you suggesting it's going to affect us?"

"I don't think so," he said, amused, taunting her. "I mean, how much free beer and sex can a man tolerate?"

But he was unable to put her at her ease. She proceeded to construct a logical argument and he found her becoming defensive.

"The thing is, I've found it's easier if people just think I'm a successful doctor who spends a little too much. When we formed our group practice, I bought the building. Young doctors starting out are always in debt and have to grab anything so they can pay back bank loans or their families. And I wanted to work with these people who were wonderful physicians I knew from med school and from my residency at UCLA.

"Well, when I spoke to the guys, they jumped at the chance of us all being together. And one of the considerations was the low rent and the space in the building to expand. It would be very awkward for me if they knew I engineered it all. That I am in fact the owner. Terry, try to understand me. I enjoy giving. I bought you the bike because you can't keep up with me on Billy's old Schwinn."

"As long as you don't try to buy me. It wouldn't work."

"I know. The only thing bigger than your cock is your ego. But darling, never forget who gave you your balls back."

He laughed. "I really admire your scientific approach to life."

"I know you're very competitive, Terry. It's one of the things I treasure about you. I love a man with drive." She faltered and stared at him grimly. "Tell me the truth: Does the fact that I have money upset you?"

"I'm not going to let it change anything." He leaned over and kissed her.

"Oh, thank God, Terry. I was so worried about how you'd feel."

"Val, I'm really impressed with the way you've handled yourself."

"I wanted to do something useful with my life. I have a calling. And I love kids. When parents bring in a child and I can help, it's magic. Terry, the greatest high in the world is to cure a sick child."

Pat and Milly would be coming down from Port Rivers to meet Valerie. His father would no doubt approve of an heiress who worked for a living. The prospect of being reunited with his father pleased Terry. The last months had been a difficult period for them both.

Valerie, he noticed, was reticent about her father, observing only that she had not seen him for some years and the breakup of the family had been ugly. She was indecisive about reconciling with him.

"I wish I knew what to do. He called me this morning. I guess I'm still his baby and my thirtieth birthday is a milestone for both of us." Val's eyes clouded. "He was in tears, pleading with me to make up. I don't know what to do. Maybe it's time to mend fences."

"I think it's a damn good idea. I'm all for family unity. Whatever went on in the past, you're big enough to forgive him. I'm sure he had his reasons."

"Oh, honey, you're right. You see, I sided with my mother when they got divorced."

"That's not unusual."

"He was brutal."

Terry thought of Georgie and her discourses about divorce horrors. "She's dead, he's alive. Don't have this on your conscience."

Terry ordered brandies with their coffee. Val's birthday conveniently fell on a Saturday and she wouldn't have to be up at five-thirty. He told her that he and Billy, the major domo, had arranged a dinner party at Chasen's for her. Uncharacteristically, Valerie sank into an odd, withdrawn mood. He reached across the table but she resisted him.

"Now what's the matter?"

She was distant and averted her eyes. "I don't know, Ter. I'm so afraid to talk about this. I don't want you to start thinking I'm trying to corner you."

He was ruffled. "Hey, Val, tell me what's on your mind?" He wondered if he'd offended her. Flustered, he asked, "Are you pregnant?"

"What do you take me for? Do you think for a moment I'd trap you with something like that? That's not my style." She was becoming very emotional. "My biological clock is ticking and at times it sounds like a time bomb to me." She turned her face into the corner of the wooden booth and was crying. "Oh, Jesus, I'm sorry. I hate scenes."

She rushed out of the booth and flew out the front door. He threw some money on the table and chased her out to the street. She was unlocking her bike. He took hold of her.

"What . . . what is it, Val?"

"Don't you understand how much I love you? I feel so humiliated. It's as though I'm begging." He held her rigid body tightly against his and kissed her. "You're better now. I'm just drifting along in your life and it's driving me crazy. I'm going to be thirty tomorrow and what am I? Your girlfriend, a piece of ass?"

He was shocked. "Is that the way I've been treating you? I can't believe you'd think that."

"I'm sorry. I didn't mean to. . . . Even I can get confused and sometimes I need you to reassure that all this isn't going to blow up in my face. If you leave me, Terry, I'll *never* get over it. One day I'm afraid I'll wake up and you'll say you're going back to Port Rivers and try to pick up your life there. It's like you're at an airport waiting for a connection and passing the time with me."

He ran his fingers through her hair and she shivered in his arms.

"I love you, Valerie."

"Not like *her*!" she said bitterly.

"Okay! Goddamnit, it is different," he admitted. "Is that what you wanted to hear?"

"I can't go on living with that bitch Maia. She comes in and out my bedroom like a whore. Then vanishes inside you." Valerie was weeping inconsolably. "When we're making love, you're with *her*, not me!"

His pained expression caught her off guard.

"Oh, Terry, I didn't mean it. I don't know what I'm saying. It's like you've been promiscuous and that ices it with me. When I feel you coming, it's like I'm not there and you're with her. I feel so helpless and temporary and all I want to do is have us find our own way."

"I wish you'd waited with this, Valerie."

She had gone too far, totally sacrificing what self-possession remained. Her distress was now woven with the toxic rivalry she knew existed and was embedded in Terry's heart. "How'd you get so good in bed? Screwing her to death. I'll bet she was an expert."

Valerie's waspishness brought out his fire. "Not just her, Val. I had plenty of other clients for my talent. Lots of them rich."

"You bastard! I'm going wake up thirty years old with a pair of fucking earrings from you and in a dead end street."

"What have I done to make you so desperate?" Terry

touched her hair, but she pulled away violently. "Honey, I wouldn't hurt you—not after the way you've treated me."

Valerie was not persuaded and knew it was over. She had relinquished herself to his needs. She hadn't intended to fall in love. She had hoped to fill a void within Terry, but now realized that all he had needed was a bridge to his future.

"I guess maybe you wouldn't . . . intentionally," she said ruefully, wiping her eyes with her sleeve. "But I have to be strong. And do what what's best for me."

"And what's that?"

The challenge he saw on her face was not of a woman posturing.

"Let's not see each other any more, Terry. It's too tough on me. I have to give this up . . . to save myself."

Hard legs pumping on her bike through the traffic, she glided out of sight as he watched with disbelief.

Arriving at her house, Val was clear-eyed and stoical. She'd been a fool. Terry was irretrievably damaged by the murder of his fiancée and the effort of resuscitating him while battling a dead woman had proved to be beyond her. Lost and disillusioned, she picked up the phone and called Chasen's. The maitre d' put the owner on.

"This is Dave Chasen, Dr. Holland. I've just been told you're canceling the party. I'm terribly sorry for you and Mr. Brett. But I know these things happen."

Thoughts jumbled, Valerie was becoming unhinged. "Well, it's just another damn birthday."

"Now, you've got me confused," the owner said. "Billy Klein arranged your engagement party with Mr. Brett."

Valerie's pulse raced, spurted, and she was covered by a slick, vellum sweat that started to dribble down her forehead. She heard Terry's disembodied voice echo:

"I wish you'd waited . . . waited . . . waited . . ."

Hysteria surged through her. "No, please, don't cancel anything. I'm just having a nervous breakdown."

"It's okay," he said affably, "I guess it's another case

of bride's temperament and groom's remorse. We have them all the time here. I look forward to meeting you."

Valerie put down the phone and raced outside over the cold, wet sand.

"Oh, please be there, Terry," she cried.

She leaped over Billy's deck rail and burst through the open sliders. Billy raised his hand for silence and pointed to the sofa. Don Drysdale was working on a no-hitter. Terry, lynx-eyed, came out of the kitchen with a bottle of tequila.

He ignored Valerie. "How's Double D doing?"

"Pete Rose fouled off three straight pitches."

"Terry—" she began.

"Val, this is no time for a lover's quarrel," Billy interjected. "There are more important things in my cosmic view than your problems with the squire."

Drysdale wound up and threw a baffling curve ball, which nicked the outside corner. There was a momentary hesitation by the umpire before he yanked his thumb.

Billy squealed, "He got Pete!" His tension eased, he winked at her. "Now, Terry, please kiss and make up and you two get the hell out of here and let me watch the ninth inning in peace."

Terry was silent, his face a mask of hard angles. He headed with Valerie to the beach. Retreating into his impenetrable shell, he nursed a drink and walked down to the water while she straggled after him.

"Ter, don't do this to me," she pleaded. "I made a mistake. I called Chasen's . . . Darling. I had no idea . . . I apologize for loving you too much."

"Well, what the hell upset you?"

"I'm jealous of your past with this girl. It's killing me." He cuddled her in his arms. "You do love me, Terry, I know you do."

"Yes, of course."

He heard an eerie reverberation of his voice. He was vowing his love to Allison in Timberline. But there was nothing cynical about the compromise. The women represented two sides of the coin in his emotional realm. In fact, it was a relief to have made a decision to marry

Valerie before he had learned of her fortune.

"They told me it was an engagement party, Terry. Why didn't you mention it?"

"So much for surprises. That's why I was asking all those questions about your family. I thought if I could get in touch with them. Oh, well . . . in any case you'll meet *my* father and his lady love. They're coming down to L. A."

Valerie put her arms around him and their bodies locked. "Terry, I've never been so happy. Please come inside . . . to bed." *Valerie Brett,* how she loved the melody of it. "I want to make love to you forever."

32

Terry could not restrain his father's ebullience. Pat was cackling and dancing from room to room in the large bungalow at the Beverly Hills Hotel. Valerie had booked it as her gift to her future in-laws.

"Bach Beer! Goddamn, Milly, can you believe this boy!"

Milly, Pat's lady-in-waiting, paid no attention to him. She was hanging up their clothes, daring each article of clothing to be creased. She had packed with the same nursing care she gave to a pie.

Pat had been to Los Angeles only once before, staying overnight for Terry's law school graduation, and had seen little more than the college campus. For Milly, it was all a voyage through interplanetary space. In her fantasies she had never conceived of a pink hotel with matching bougainvillea growing outside her window.

"Wait till they hear about this at home. Man, you bagged a Triple Crown winner."

Milly made the call at the turn. "I hope the hell you don't talk that way around Valerie, Pat. She's not some horse."

Terry recognized that his father had always possessed

the not entirely innocent skill of ruffling him. It was one of those magical powers born of spending too much time raising roofs in saloons with his nail-pounders.

"No one's going to hear about it, Pat. That part of my life's over. I'm not planning to have anything to do with the people I knew in Port Rivers."

"Enough said," Milly interjected. "Terry, you're right about those rats."

Knocking back everyone's Bloody Marys, Pat's feverish mind was rife with byzantine plots. "Suppose we see if I can get me a Bach distributorship for the Northwest Territory."

Terry finally laughed, but Pat's enthusiasm was not yet tethered. "You always think on a grand scale. Why not build them a brewery? That's your line of work," Terry said.

"Now you're talking like a Brett. I'll bet one of those suckers can run forty–fifty million."

Milly piped in, "And while you're at it, Terry, I'll take the cafeteria concession. We can do championship bratwursts and kraut."

"Now stop kidding, Milly. This is business. Families have to stick together. We've got to sit Valerie down and roll this over. Naturally, Terry can't keep taking on lowlife cases like Earl's, and thieves, if he's going to be the Bach company lawyer."

Essentially withdrawn without a menu in her hand or making change at a register, Milly put her arm around Terry and kissed him. "We're thrilled you're happy, and back on your feet."

With the adroitness of a car salesman switching a customer to the top-of-the-line model, Pat grandiloquently extended his arms like an after-dinner speaker. "I envision a big church wedding. I want to get myself a set of tails. Now think about this. . . . Suppose we ride to church in the Bach carriage. Pulled by those glorious Percherons." He scooped Milly in his arms. "Honey, I'll bet this makes TV. Even David Brinkley's sick of talking about Vietnam and the acidheads marching."

"I'm going to see if there are any stars in the Polo Lounge while your crazy father carries on."

It was strange to be back in the loving fold of his eccentric father and his loyal paramour, Terry thought while waiting for Valerie to finish dressing at her house. Billy Klein had rented a limo for them, and the driver knocked at the door to tell Terry that he was ready.

The excitement of the occasion rippled through him as he fixed his bowtie and slipped on a white dinner jacket. He was fit, tanned, and his strong, clear hazel eyes had regained the lustrous focus of an earlier day. In some ways, his life had improved in Allison's absence. Only months ago, he had believed everything was over—a glorious destiny had forsaken him—but now he relished this unpredictable turn. His future with Valerie took on a regal glamour, filled with promise. The nagging ache that encapsulated his passion for Allison had almost vanished.

So much for rapture, he reflected.

In a primrose tulle off-the-shoulder Dior gown, Valerie had a gaiety and the radiant wholeness of a woman dancing to the music of the spheres.

"You look magnificent."

"Thank you, darling. It's all because of you. Terry, I took your advice and spoke to my father and asked him to come."

"Terrific. There's no point in holding grudges at a time like this."

"He's a man's man; maybe you'll understand him better than I do."

Valerie had a small velvet box in her hand, which she asked Terry to open. "It was my grandmother's ring. And if you don't mind, I'd like it to be my engagement ring."

In a Victorian setting, the diamond was emerald cut, clear as a sliver of ice and besieged with chips. The ring he had bought for Allison at Tiffany's still resided in Pat's safe at home, a pathetic talisman. He slipped the crown jewel on Valerie's finger.

"Until I get you one, this'll have to do."

"Darling, I don't need a thing. I have you."

"I'll be able to afford something the size of an iceberg on my salary at O'Callahan & Klein."

"You took the job, Terry!"

"While you were at the hairdresser, I made my deal with old Carl Klein. And I get to pick my clients. I'm not going to be a hired gun they can hand to any bigshot who can buy his way out." Valerie embraced him, then backed away, for something severe and aloof clouded his face. "Valerie, we're going to live on what I earn. And not your money. So please don't start looking for some mansion." He was bursting with self-esteem and she welcomed his return to good health. "The beach suits us fine. When I go on salary, I'll hack the mortgage."

"Is there such a thing as fun money? Like the boat?"

"Sure. And the picnics that go with it. Shit, yes. I'm not asking you to take a vow of poverty. But, Val, I'll buy my own clothes, so get a credit on that stuff you bought me."

"You're the boss, Terry, always," she said with such sweet contrition that he was almost convinced she meant it. It would be uncivilized and boorish to take aim at her insidiousness. Valerie was so adept. He had watched Pat bribe officials and building inspectors since he'd been a kid. Valerie was a good deal smoother. He decided to take the bounce. He'd string her along for the time being to ascertain how hard she pressed when she wanted someone to buckle to her will.

"You won't accept a gift?"

"On Christmas and my birthday."

All kittenish, and purring, she retreated into his arms for an appeal.

"Honey? Come on, don't be so tough. It gives me so much pleasure to shop for you, Ter. When I was picking out those cashmere sweaters and knowing you'd wear them, I just about had an orgasm. The salesman at Carroll's thought I had a funny look on my face." She smirked and kissed his ear. "Actually, I think I did."

She had redeemed him and he kissed her ardently. "It's a deal."

*　　*　　*

On the ride to Chasen's they passed through the Santa Monica Hills, which arched over the undulating coastline. Valerie knew Terry enjoyed the view, and frequently he would spend hours up there before meeting her at the office. She had inherited a good deal of property from her mother. Most of this hillside now belonged to her. The area wasn't as damp and foggy as living on the beach and they could bike down in five minutes. It would also be closer to her office. In the summer, the Pacific Coast Highway traffic choked her. She'd talk to an architect, commission drawings and renderings. Then she'd stroke Terry while sitting on his lap.

She would present it as a bolt out of the blue from her trustees. They had informed her that for tax reasons she would be forced to sell the land she owned there or build a house herself. She imagined evenings entertaining her colleagues and Terry's from the firm and the social life they would create. The innocent wonder of this man. It was still startling to have found someone with no interest in her money. In spite of some poor and questionable investments made by her trustees, her estate was approaching thirty million dollars.

Terry would have a fit if he found out it was throwing off almost two hundred thousand dollars a month! There was no way she could conceive of spending that much in a year. She lived on what she earned as a doctor. Occasionally, she would take a flyer and buy something expensive—the Colnago bike for Terry, a Chanel suit. But in her heart, she deplored the ostentatious trappings of the rich with their platoons of servants, the reckless vulgarity of parvenus who flaunted their new money in public. She and Terry would be the modest rich, blending into the landscape, frogs croaking through the high grass around the lily pond in summer.

Photographers framed the entrance of Chasen's, which was studded with Rolls-Royces, Bentleys, and Ferraris. The red-vested valets dashed through cars like a bucket brigade. As Terry and Valerie moved past them, Dave Chasen handed them champagne and they glided past the red leather booths and were immediately engulfed by an island of friends and admirers in the elegant Chestnut Room. A dozen tables for eight were set with bowers of roses and peonies. Four bartenders had been employed so that no one had to wait for a drink during the cocktail hour. The illustrious Pepé was preparing his fire dance martini with a flambéed skin of orange peel for an audience cheering on the matador. Buffets were laden with industrial-sized bowls of caviar, giant Gulf shrimp, and oysters.

In the crowd were Val's partners in the pediatric clinic, their wives, along with Val's beautiful assistant Jane Ashley. Billy Klein was in deep conversation with his uncle Carl and several lawyer friends of Terry's. Billy had taken control of the guest list and had invited the cream of Los Angeles socialites, their bank accounts, and lawsuits.

Terry had learned that morning that O'Callahan & Klein, his new firm, had decided against his protests to pay for the party. Although it was Valerie's birthday celebration, which had evolved into an engagement, Billy informed Terry to "Just lay back and enjoy it. It's your coming-out party, babe."

Moving in on Valerie was Terry's father, all big hands and weaving shoulders, beaming, rough-hewn in a dark blue suit. His girlfriend wore an elegant gown. Pat kissed her, then took Terry aside. "Encourage Valerie to make it up with her old man. I've been talking to him. He's one helluva guy. You'll love him."

Valerie spotted her father surrounded by a large group. He wore a white Palm Beach suit that set off his glowing suntan. When she was eight and admired a similar suit, he had taken her to his tailor on Worth Avenue and measured her for the same one. They had surprised her mother by wearing matching clothes one night at the Alligator Club.

She and her father spent their time on the beach or sailing in Palm Beach while Elisabeth with her blond hair and silky Garbo-like skin sat on a chaise in the shaded loggia reading. When her parents dressed for an evening

out, journeying to her room through the phalanx of servants to say good night, her father always left last and
would sit on the bed stroking her hair. Her mother would
be in the marble hallway, heels clattering, heading downstairs, calling after him, "Honey, we're running late." But
he ignored her. Arms around his neck, trying to prolong
the moment, Valerie would be thrilled by his animal mas-
culinity and feel the absolute glory of being her father's
true love. It was their secret.

With her mother dead, abhorrent facts emerged. Her
uncles claimed he had raided her share of the Bach estate.
He had borrowed money from Elisabeth and refused to
repay it. He argued that it was a gift, contested the case,
and took endless depositions from them and Valerie. He
forced continuances and intensified her marital problems
with Kenny, who blamed her father for their quarrels.
Since then, Valerie had despised lawyers and it had taken
some time before she was able to tolerate Terry's profession.

Out of the corner of her eye, Val glanced at her father's face, with its fine lines of late nights and good
times. She was imprisoned by ambivalence: Should she
go to him or wait? She remained rooted beside Terry and
her doctor friends. When Terry drifted away to meet
some of his new colleagues, her father stood before his
daughter with head bowed like a knight waiting for the
queen to decide his fate.

"I know how you feel about last-minute invitations,
Dad," Val said.

Her father was uncharacteristically tentative and reticent.

"I make exceptions. Hello, Angel. Happy Birthday."
Valerie touched his face and kissed him, "I wanted to see
you very badly, Dad. I don't know how many times I
thought about calling you."

"You're a little headstrong like your mother. Baby, can
we forget all this ugly, old family business and see if we
can start again?" His voice broke. "Val, it's so important
for me to have you back. You're all I've got."

"Yes, let's try," she said, embracing him.

Finally, Terry reached through hugs and shaking hands and arrived beside Valerie. Shimmering with excitement, and gauging every nuance of emotion, she said:

"Terry, this is my father. Jonah Wolfe, meet Terry Brett."

33

Jonah Wolfe did not miss a beat and with a gracious smile extended his hand. "Mr. Brett, I've heard remarkable tales about your astuteness as an attorney from Carl Klein himself. He says you're going to be the firm's star lawyer."

Jonah might be playing make-believe or possibly feigning amnesia, but Terry imagined he heard the sound of granite smashed by a pickax, chips flying, then pulverized with the cataclysmic frenzy of a Kansas twister, whirling him through the darkness. Returning unbidden, Terry felt again the hideous sensation of choking on his own blood in the hotel corridor as the men beat him.

Still stunned, Terry now knew that during his healing process, Valerie had unconsciously awakened visions of this dark force, the avatar of his nightmares. Jonah was the eyeless beggar of his desolation, swallowing, consuming Allison, a python simulating human features. In restaurants when Valerie wanted a particular table, her index finger stabbed the air like a dagger, and her mouth pursed in the same supercilious manner as Jonah's. At some tonality, her husky voice replicated Jonah Wolfe's:

"Have a safe ride home. And do us both a favor, don't come back!"

Terry could visualize Jonah's cloying smile during his meeting in the bank. Terry had actually believed he had effected a bloodless escape with his swag for Earl.

Terry involuntarily pulled away from Valerie. The man and his daughter shared an aristocratic greyhound demeanor. Terry forced himself to control his explosive anger when confronted by the sweet con Valerie had perpetrated. And yet, had she? Was he suffering from some requiem of paranoia? Val couldn't be privy to the range of Jonah's perversions. They hadn't been in contact for years and she shared Terry's rancor toward her father. Jonah was *their* demon.

Once over his initial shock, Terry realized that in this wonderland, the possibilities for revenge were endless, an infinite progression in the long night of Jonah's days. Valerie had inherited Jonah's coloring and his dark-hollowed, penetrating eyes. Terry stared incredulously at Valerie and discerned previously unnoticed congruencies in their faces and gestures.

Valerie stood puzzled, looking from Terry to her father. "Come on, shake hands, you guys. I want us all to be friends forever."

The sly flesh of their palms met, and frozen smiles pleased Valerie as she pressed her hands on their shoulders to bring them closer.

"Can I assume I'll get season tickets to the Stars games, Mr. Wolfe?"

"Please call me Jonah. Pat and I had a fine chat before you got here. I really like your father. We'll all sit in the owner's box any time you want," Jonah said, reaching out.

"Do I bring my own hot dogs?"

Jonah Wolfe winked conspiratorially. "No, I'll have my specials sent in from Milwaukee. Val used to love them. At least she did before she became a doctor."

"I still do, Dad."

Flushed with excitement and already wired from many glasses of champagne, Pat thrust between them to claim his future daughter-in-law. He gave Terry his he-man nod as though this were a subcontractor's bash at the Surf Rider.

"May I have this dance, Valerie?"

"Of course, Pat."

In the flesh again, Jonah was hardly the rapacious, spectral figure treading through Terry's dreams. There was a boyishness beneath his rigorously carved features.

Terry remembered the heavily muscled torso, toned like a bull's. But now Jonah had the charming enthusiastic friendliness of an orchestra leader taking requests.

All smiles, he said: "This is terrific, Terry. I'm really pleased. Inordinately pleased that Val hooked up with a sharpie. I prefer a man like you to some mooch who'd try to take her to the cleaners like that bust-out Kenny she married."

"I heard he committed suicide."

"I'm only sorry I didn't load the gun for him. Cheating in medical school. Imagine that prick with a license, treating somebody's kid."

They moved to the bar and Billy Klein helplessly threw his arms up in innocence, then abruptly turned away from Terry's incisive glare.

"How long is this charade supposed to go on, Jonah?"

"I'm prepared to pretend we've only just met. No one's going to say anything"—he indicated the group of lawyers edging away—"*unless* you do."

"Did they know?"

"To the best of my knowledge, they couldn't have. I had no idea Valerie was seeing you and things had gone this far." Jonah handed Terry some champagne and was tempted to tap glasses, then thought better of it. "But the fact is, Terry, you and Valerie will do really well. You go together. She needed a shark to pilot her through dangerous waters. My only concern relates to your future strategy."

"Oh, I see. My strategy? Regarding what?"

Jonah averted his eyes and shook his head. "Are you going to be unbelievably reckless and use me to hurt Valerie?"

"I love Val and we're friends."

"I'm glad to hear that. Because, Terry, I'd hate to think that your legal practice is confined to investigating me."

"Frankly, I have no further interest in your affairs."

"That's good. All men have their vices. Valerie is my solitary virtue and I wouldn't want my flaws to be her cross. She's a good human being with a shining soul. I don't mean to offend you by being poetic about my daughter, but she represents the true capital of my fortune. Do you understand that?"

"Perfectly. If I'd known the two of you were connected, I don't know what would have happened."

"Well, a few minutes ago, when I learned *you* were her fiancé, I really wondered if this was some elaborately malicious and devious game on your part. When we'd parted company, you were friskily cantering back home with *my* money to marry your rain forest princess."

"That was my plan." Terry reflected. Only in death could he contend with the tragedy of Allison's flight. "A McDonald's was robbed while my girl was there. She stopped a bullet."

"I'm sorry you had a rough passage."

Terry signaled the bartender for a tequila shooter, belted it back, and told him to leave the bottle.

"I would like to clear up our last bit of business."

"Like what? Not Earl again. Fact is that jack-off called me a few months ago and this time I did speak to him. He claims *you* ripped *him* off."

"Earl has many claims, none of them with any merit, as you know. I just want the names of the two guys you sent after me."

"I beg your pardon," Jonah Wolfe exclaimed in frustration. "I have no idea what the hell you're talking about. Come on now, Terry."

"These guys were kicking field goals with my head. I was checking out of the hotel when they grabbed me. No one calls me pretty any more."

"You think I'm responsible?" When Terry's jaw tightened, Jonah laughed in stupefied embarrassment. "You've got me down as the Antichrist." Jonah turned his hands over, exposing his palms. "No cloven hoof, Terry. But, let's get this straight: When I go after someone, I'm like you. I do it myself. Two things I don't need help with—kicking somebody's ass or my sex life.

"Man-oh-man, I let you off scot-free even after I explained the circumstances of my craziness in a spirit of candor. Shit, I thought you'd go for a walk or at least be reasonable. But you wanted to chuck one in at the buzzer from half court and score. Well, you did. I paid what I regarded as a hefty fine, and that's it. There's no vendetta or bad feeling on my side, especially now that you and Valerie are going to be married. Actually, I'm a fan of yours, Mr. Brett. You skinned my ass, so I know that my darling is in good hands—the hands of a man and not some fucking pussy."

Jonah could not be underestimated. His labyrinth was inviting, with its implicit promise of favors, favors based on ability. What could be more flattering than the praise and eloquent defense of a multimillionaire who was smart enough to rip off the Bach Beer heiress?

"I'm surprised you didn't hang around to see what I looked like after I had the shit kicked out of me. Where'd you disappear to?"

Jonah waved at a few guests. "For your information, I attended the Cannes Film Festival."

"I didn't know about your interest in the arts."

"I'm actually more interested in the young ladies who perform in films than the films themselves. You know, I own a basketball team. It's entertainment and I'm making a study of the opportunities in the entertainment business."

"Of course, and you get to take some pictures."

"I hope we can terminate this discussion."

"By the way, how do I address you in future? Do I call you Pop or just plain Dad?"

"Don't bait me. Can't we forget this for good? Terry, I expect you and Valerie to have kids. I want to be part of your life."

"In spite of tonight's hugging and pledges of love, Val will never forgive you for the way you treated her mother." Jonah raised his glass for the bartender, who scooted over.

"Hey, Terry, guys do things in anger. The truth is, Elisabeth Bach did a number on me."

"What did Valerie do to make you take her to court and threaten to sue her?"

"It was a mistake and one I won't make again. I needed some more capital for my meatpacking business.

My wife gave me some money. It was a gift and not a loan. Val knew the truth. She was there when it happened. After my wife died, her uncles sued me to recoup the money. They claimed I owed it to the estate. I was so angry at them that I decided to grind the Bachs into dogmeat. The reason Val stopped talking to me is that I countersued her uncles. I got a few million from the beer barons. Like you, they settled out of court."

Out of the corner of his eye, Terry saw Val's assistant, flushed with drink, smiling at Jonah. Jonah raised his glass to her.

"She works for your daughter. She's Val's protégée."

"I'm very good with protégées," Jonah said, beckoning Jane with his index finger. "She's already drawn a bead on me. What a wicked body she's got. These honeys just keep coming." Jane, a bit high, serpentined through rapacious bands of lawyers who turned to stare at her lithe, long-limbed figure, her flowing blond hair, which she tossed as she headed for them. Jonah snorted with amusement. "Try looking at it from a woman's point of view, Terry. Here comes Jane, a honey in her early twenties, probably scrounging for rent with three other girls in a Hollywood apartment and she gets the lowdown on me— Val's rich father. I'm a good-looking man with millions, a mansion, a pair of Rolls-Royces, and I can screw till the dogs stop barking."

"You're a fucking pig, Jonah."

"Tell me something I don't know." Val was also approaching through the throngs of well-wishers and Jonah was diverted. "Please treat Valerie well and with kindness, Terry. I don't know if she's told you, but Kenny Holland used to beat the shit out of her. Do what you like, but don't hit her."

"Drop dead, you lowlife prick."

Jane waited on the perimeter of the group and signaled to Jonah while Valerie slipped between the two men.

"I'm thrilled to see you basketball groupies hanging out." Val hugged them both. "My boys."

Jonah gave Terry a courtly bow, then put a proprietary

arm around his daughter. "Your assistant Jane looks lonely," he said.

"Well, dance with her, Dad."

"Maybe later. I like to play hard to get. If it's okay with Terry, can I have this one with you, Angel?"

Under duress, Terry forced himself to get through the rest of the evening, but a white-hot poker of madness was thrust into his consciousness. Even after the party was over and he and Valerie were in bed, he wondered if she had been part of some conspiracy to seduce him. He could rely on nothing, least of all his own judgment.

Magical thoughts of Allison drifted into a hellish image. Had the Kali of Allison's letter made a pact with the ancient gods of vengeance and through some mysterious curse clouded his future with Valerie? Naked and very aroused, Valerie slithered close to him.

"Why didn't you ever mention Jonah Wolfe was your father?"

Terry had slipped into the role of inquisitor and she was disconcerted.

"Does it matter? It never occurred to me. Apparently, you know who he is."

Mr. Wolfe is also a well-known philanthropist of teenage girls, whose pictures he takes in a daisy chain.

"Sure I've heard of him. By reputation. We have hot dogs and basketball in Port Rivers, too."

"This is all very sordid, Terry. I had divided loyalties. I preferred my father but . . . I defended my mother."

"It may surprise you to know that I've heard a few evasive tales of folly before I became your patient and stud."

"What's going on with you? I don't understand. It's been the happiest evening of my life."

He pushed Val away. "Don't ever hold out on me again. If I'd been suspicious of you—or your motives— when I fell under the hypnotic swaying of your magical stethoscope, honey, I would have found out the goddamn day you had your first period, the time, the place, and if there were witnesses. What the hell do you think I did for a living before I met you?" Terry's tone was so acidulous that Valerie became tearful. "Valerie! I took you on trust!"

"Why are you blaming me? Please, please, I haven't done anything. I love my father. And I've paid a horrible price for being his daughter."

Terry relented. He had her by the throat and hated to bully her. Still, his attitude was filled with reproach. He saw that she was frightened and vulnerable, and he reached out to comfort her. The deep friendship he felt for Valerie had become a comfortable habit. She had cared for him, suckling him like a mother, assuming his pain. His love for another woman had been intolerable and humiliating for this intelligent, patrician woman.

"I implore you, don't let our engagement party end like this."

The bad taste in his mouth came and went like seasickness, bringing with it a wave of sad confusion and ambivalence toward her. Valerie was someone who could sail a man out of a storm, but she could not resolve his emotional impasse.

"All I want to do is please you." She kneeled worshipfully on the floor, resting her head on his lap.

He looked down at her distressed face and cupped his hands around her temples, soothing her, as she had comforted him when he had been distraught. They had become sentries, guardians of the anguish of their former lives.

"Are you having second thoughts?" Val asked in a tone that offered forgiveness, a way out.

"No, don't even think such things. We'll be fine, darling."

"Will we, Terry? Please let's try to find our own way. I can't live without you."

He thought for a moment of Allison and knew that he had to uproot her presence from this room, this place. Slighting the elision of seasons, the silent glide, the leaves trammeled, the days uncounted, he banished Allison to eternal winter.

Book III

SIN WITHOUT SHAPE

34

Val's Italian was fluent and melodic, honed in Swiss boarding schools. She had spent many summers with her mother in Venice while Jonah had remained at home with his roaring meatpacking plants and proliferating mistresses. Terry welcomed the suggestion of a honeymoon in Venice and now as he sat on the terrace of the Gritti smoking a Havana with his espresso, he relished his newfound happiness and admitted to her that the socialite life had been agreeable even in the backwater country clubs of Port Rivers. But in the heart of the European mainstream, among the contessas who sent invitations to dinner parties at their palazzi and the legion of millionaire industrialists carrying gold champagne swizzle sticks in their handkerchief pockets, Terry revealed an adroitness that surprised and enchanted Valerie. She had defined his station; when they returned to Los Angeles, he would be welcomed by O'Callahan & Klein as their principal criminal litigator.

She looked up from her book, invariably a volume of Ruskin's *Stones of Venice,* and was pleased with her accomplishment. The emotional investment she had made in Terry had paid inconceivable dividends. They had met in April and now with fall creeping over Venice and the tides of the Grand Canal rising perilously, she knew that he was the prize of her life. Her fortune was a matter of indifference by contrast with her soul mate. She had never loved anyone with this intensity; this yearning to inhabit him never left her. On the surface, her demeanor might be cool and professional, but inside she was ablaze with desire for him.

"Terry, I have to read this to you from Ruskin: 'Remember that the most beautiful things in the world are the most useless; peacocks and lilies for instance.' "

"It's true. I'd be a bum if we lived in Venice. I don't

know how anyone works here," he said, observing gondolas spiraling and pirouetting as they approached the hotel terrace from the direction of the Santa Maria della Salute. They seemed to rise from the church domes like multicolored soap bubbles.

Val leaned her head on his shoulder. "That's why we came."

The previous night they had attended a madrigal concert at La Salute. The rich and resounding Monteverdi harmonies were uplifted by multiple choirs. Terry listened to the music with reverence, surrounded by a feast of Titians and Tintorettos. The grace of Venice and its meandering walks, its worlds within worlds, during which he invariably lost his way and Val set him back on course, had a profound effect on his stability. He let himself go, absorbed by the captivating history of the city and his fresh life with Val. She no longer fussed over him and he vanquished the phantom of Allison. But somehow or other, no matter what he contrived to do, Allison responded to the provocation.

When he woke up that morning at dawn, he imagined he had seen Allison's face among the guests in Tintoretto's painting *The Marriage at Cana*.

"We dressing for dinner?" he asked, casting off gloomy thoughts.

"Just a dark suit," Val replied, checking the time. "Wear one of your new Brionis . . . the navy pinstripe. You'll look gorgeous."

He nodded. "Si, signora."

"I can't wait for you to put it on and then let me take it off when we get back."

Val's beau monde profligacy outlived their last duel. A few days ago, while he browsed at the Fantoni art bookstore and wondered about buying her marbelized notepaper, she vanished and acquired six suits for him and a collection of silk ties from Rovoletto behind San Marco. Armed with his size, she acquired shirts remorselessly. Munificence was inbred in her. All of this additional clothing naturally led Val to a six-piece set of crocodile luggage from Vogni, which, prefixed with his initials, arrived that afternoon. "Honeymoon remembrances," she called them. Her unwavering desire to please him was unnerving and he asked himself what he'd done to deserve such a woman. Rather than revert to his cool protests, he yielded placidly but was wary whenever he had to answer the door of their suite. He was tired of tipping smiling bellmen and tailors who looked like philosophy professors.

"Are you up for cocktails and another magical garden?"

"Sure," he said, holding her hand. "We haven't had a Bellini at Harry's since yesterday and I haven't changed clothes for almost three hours. Oh, and I can only read the *Trib*'s sport section so many times." She began to laugh. "Whose garden this evening?"

"My old schoolmate's mother, Pia. Her chef makes the best gnocchi in Venice and she asked if she could give us a farewell dinner."

"That would be the Contessa di Taranto."

"You amaze me Terry. How do you remember?"

"I'm a lawyer—hungry for clients. Who knows? I might have to call her to the stand," he said with a flourish. "It's all in the details."

Terry Brett was an original. His courtly manners dazzled the women, and Val realized that as the son of a contractor, Terry must have applied himself to develop them. On the other hand, there were men who were natural aristocrats and she counted him among them. He had something interesting, an enigmatic feature, recessed in his personality that drew people to him but she could not analyze it. She would have liked to have tapped into his past, but decided it might be unsafe. The death of an obscure woman had been her regeneration.

Red flags emblazoned with imperial gold lions furled on the contessa's private motor launch, which arrived at five. Terry held Val's hand over the swaying dock. Tonight she was resplendent in a deftly cut, long black Chanel dress, cinched at the waist and with a hint of red piping that was picked up by her black and red velvet cape.

Terry had occasionally wondered if their marriage had been too hasty. Was it all a random mood inflection? People getting caught up in the consolation of company, disposing of uncertainty and settling for familiar habits. The fatality of living time on this level still mystified him. In less than a year, as he was closing in on the idea of bachelorhood as a permanent condition, two women had sprung forth. The previous accounting of months and years vanished by comparison. He had known Val longer than Allison, but the impact that they had made on him could not be gauged.

Val leaned into him and he held her close. Her necklace was of black pearls and her diamonds refracted the sunlight in dazzling rainbow flashes.

"You're positively beautiful, darling."

Val's smile was luminous. "Beats my long white office coats. Terry, it's all your doing."

"You've got the big rocks out tonight, huh. They sure like the fresh air."

"Diamonds weren't cut to fit in safes, and doges ruled kings in Venice."

"Ruskin?"

"No, Valerie *Brett*."

"What a smart lady you are."

"You bring out the best in me, Terry."

The steward offered them delicate Murano flutes of champagne as they cruised through the Dorsoduro *sestiere,* a snail-shaped hump of land opposite San Marco. In the late afternoon sun the water turned choppy and assumed the marbled palette of a blackish viridian. Under the Accademia Bridge, lingering tourists leaned over the rail to watch them pass. Val continued to point out the opulent bastions of the rich: Baroque palaces, sinuous Renaissance towers, secret gardens, all of them harboring a delicious, poisonous treachery that encapsulated the history of Venice. Here were the enduring scandals of centuries—mistresses and money, illegitimate children, dying heiresses, bankers who pillaged, lawyers who invented wills. This was the earthly paradise of the unscrupulous and the estranged, for in Venice the history of corruption was linear, its topography, waterways of deceit. Casanova may have entered the language as the great lover, but here he was alive and still plotting.

The boat crept around the point to the Dogana di Mar where the palazzi inhabitants were in session, drinking in the *piano nobile,* lounging on terraces, playing their Puccini arias. Terry heard the giggle of money. Gracefulness itself evolved into a morbid pursuit.

The captain of the craft eased into an electrified boathouse whose mossy grille rose laboriously. They were escorted over a small bridge and into a series of sharp turns before finding themselves facing the boat again through a stockade of doors. A family of gypsies leaped at them, waving ferns and stalks of long grass in their faces, and the steward bellowed, "Zingari infernale!" but they stood their ground hissing and spitting out a babble of Romany.

"Fortuna, fortuna, maledetto . . ." they shouted in chorus.

Terry reached into his pocket for some bills and was suddenly embraced by a young girl with a large basket. Out sprang three cats dressed in smiling *carnavale* masks and wearing toddler clothes made from old fabric and ribbons. She opened a fishbox whose sides were decorated with the demonic arcana of Tarot cards. The box contained packets of rolled slips.

"Lira, lira," the girl cried. "Bene fortuna."

"Here, take this," Terry said.

"No, give to *il gaddo.*"

"Don't, Terry! There are masses of feral cats," Valerie protested.

He ignored her. Suddenly fascinated, he placed the money in the cat's outstretched paw. The cat funneled the bills into a pocket and the gypsy family struck up a charivari with a scratchy fiddle, concertina, and piccolo. The cat selected a scroll and presented it to Terry, who clapped his hands and bowed. After a series of guttural curses from the steward, who had been forced to stand by, the gypsies dispersed.

Terry and Val reached the villa entrance and were escorted into the garden by a liveried butler. Terry unrolled the piece of paper and showed it to Val.

"After all this drama, tell me what it says."

"Oh, it's just some stupid horoscope." As she was about to tear it up, he saw the image of naked twin women, floating, ethereal, the symbol for Gemini, and took the scroll from her. "Terry, listen to me. Sometimes these cats carry viruses that can kill—even from a scratch."

"I'll remember next time. Meanwhile, as proof of my bravery, I'd like to keep it."

In a moment they were embraced by Pia. She was a very tall, large-boned, splendid woman in her late sixties, with an aquiline nose, sparrow eyes, gray hair piled high and held fast by a silver comb. Her musical voice seemed midway between a chortle and outright laughter. She struck Terry as a woman who had never had a bad day and he found the scent of her perfume, lemony and lavender, intoxicating.

"Ahh, my darlings, I'm so glad you were able to come before the others." Her English was forged by one of her late husbands, a London barrister. "This is the perfect time for the garden—just before sunset." She took both their hands like a governess, then paused and looked at Val. "Something upset you, *cara*?"

"The gypsies outside. They scared me. It was silly."

"Them," she said gravely. "I've reported them to the police. They steal everything, especially cats, and try to train them. If they fail, they drown them. Sometimes at night from my bedroom, I hear the cats shriek when they're stuffed in bags and thrown into the canal."

The image of Allison's cat floated through Terry's consciousness. He had watched her digging a hole in the loamy silt above her tent by the river. She had kneeled and chanted incomprehensible words—an Eastern prayer for the dead, she later told him—and he watched her body heave with grief-stricken cries. After she completed the ceremony, she wiped her cheeks with the sleeve of her parka, came up beside him, and said:

"What will the future hold?"

"You can count on breakfast. I'm sorry about your cat."

"Thank you for being so gentle with me. I don't deserve it after last night."

And now he was following Pia, the Contessa di Taranto, through a labyrinthine garden originally planted in the sixteenth century. The impression was overwhelming to his senses: statue-adorned fountains; Turkish sundials with rusting hands; pergolas thick with wisteria vines; walls of faded ochre Istrian stone. He came upon an S-curved nymph triumphantly leaning against a lion. Above the naked goddess, a majestic cedar of Lebanon formed a parasol. A rush of leaves in the wind swept across his field of vision, then he froze. The face and body of the statue were Allison's. He darted away.

". . . these were trysting places centuries ago. After dinner while the husbands talked business in the *salotto*, every form of scandal had its birthplace in gardens like this. Cabals, plots, even murder emerged from these serene settings," Pia was saying.

Terry sat for a moment on an ivy-covered stone bench, peering at a swarm of crows churning in the sky, then descending to the cypresses, the water lapping furiously from the blustering wind, the magnolia bushes shuddering. He stared at the nymph. Val called out:

"Terry, look at the sunset, it's like a peach. Our peach sunset."

He guiltily examined the gypsy fortune, then folded it into squares until it was the size of a postage stamp and put it into his wallet. As he rose, he gave up on the idea of dispelling these visions of Allison. She was alive, within him, here in the garden, outside his horizon, spying on his every move.

"The gnocchi and the Branzino were wonderful," Terry said, as he and Val shared a glass of Sambuca and sipped their espressos at the Café Florian later that evening.

San Marco was filled with merrymakers relishing the dueling orchestras playing outside Florian's and at Quadri across the piazza. This rivalry between the establishments had gone on for years until a temporary armistice had been achieved. The opposing musicians would take turns and not drown each other out, but tonight the clash had resumed. Verdi versus Rossini in musical combat, and each café had its claquers.

"I'm glad you enjoyed it." Val took his hand. "You were so distant at dinner. Is something bothering you?"

"No. Well, maybe . . . the story about the gypsies drowning the cats. Funny how things affect you. I've been in cells with murderers and never thought twice about it."

"Oh, well, it'll pass," she said with reassurance. "I never knew you liked cats. Let's get one when we're home."

"I'd rather have a dog."

"Okay, but please not some fancy Westminster Show breed."

"We agree. My old collie died when I was away in law school and Pat decided to fly solo after that." He leaned over and kissed her. "I love you, Val."

"I know you do."

They were passing time while hotel valets and maids packed their clothes for the flight back to Los Angeles. Their two weeks together had buttressed their alliance. Moments of passion merged into days of respect and friendship. Terry found himself on solid ground and, thinking like a lawyer, settled his own case.

"Can we keep coming back to Europe when we've got a stretch of time?" she asked.

"Absolutely. How about Paris and Antibes next trip?"

"Terry, you're wonderful."

"No, I'm not. I'm your creation."

"I don't think so. I didn't mold your character, you did that yourself."

35

After their honeymoon, Terry took up his position in criminal litigation at O'Callahan & Klein downtown in Los Angeles. His office was a prime corner with panoramic views that occasionally helped his villainous clientele focus on something besides their indictments and court appearances. He hired an expert to give some of them Keeler polygraphs, but he knew the pack of them were guilty of embezzling, insurance fraud, and other mayhem. One wealthy client had shot his wife accidentally while cleaning his .45 in bed. Terry categorically refused to take rape cases, which irritated the partners. He found himself constantly in and out of court, filing motions to keep Carl Klein's high-profile cronies out of jail. Terry hardly thought about Allison as he labored to get a handle on the firm's caseload.

He and Valerie danced to the frenetic pace of a young married couple without enough hours in the day to burn. Valerie was a capable planner. With colds and flu going around, her practice was busier than ever. But she made certain that nothing interfered with her marriage. She wanted a perfect life with Terry, immediately.

She hired an architect to begin plans for the house she intended to build on her hilltop property in Santa Monica. Terry insisted on putting down fifty thousand dollars for the house. But Valerie was the one determined to shape their lives. It was a smooth working partnership of two mature people devoid of the maddening highs and lows he had experienced with Allison.

He was also devoting a good part of his time to advising the young ball players he had met in the spring with Mike Summers and Whiz Davis. He had become Whiz Davis's financial adviser and was arranging tryouts for other players with professional teams. Jonah had called him several times about his clients, but Terry turned a deaf ear to his requests. He resolved to avoid Jonah at all costs.

One evening in mid-December when he was about to dash to a meeting with a client, his secretary Martha caught him at the elevator.

"Your father's on the line, Mr. Brett."

"Tell him I'll have to phone him back later tonight."

"He sounded extremely upset. It might be important."

Terry returned to his office. Always hustling and determined to expand his contracting business, Pat had been involved in another shady land swap with a developer.

Terry picked up the phone. "What's up, where's the fire?"

"In our backyard."

"Don't tell me you're being sued again."

"No. I haven't called because of that." Pat took a deep breath. "Terry, Allison's back from India." A sledgehammer seemed to have pounded against Terry's head again. The stifled, soundless wind within him was no longer baffled, and he was overcome by the sweet sickness of her emotional pull. For a moment he was speechless.

"Is she all right?"

"No. I saw her in Aristedes's restaurant. I was in there having lunch. She brought something back with her. I think she's sick." Terry's immediate thought was that Allison had contracted some plague. "You better get up here."

"That's impossible. I've got too many cases, and Val and I are going skiing next week in Sun Valley."

"Terry. Listen, Allison's carrying an infant around with her. Stuffed in a bag like a papoose. It's a boy."

"Oh, no." Terry's mind went blank. Anger surged through him. She had destroyed part of him and he was unforgiving. "Have you spoken to her?"

"I tried. I even offered her money."

"And did she take it?"

"No, she just stared straight through me. She never said a word. She's like a zombie. I hung around. She's working in the kitchen for your old Greek client. The life's gone out of her. She's so very thin and distressed. Shit, I feel terrible, Terry."

"It's a little late for compassion, isn't it?"

"Okay, Terry. Whip my ass. Maybe I deserve it. The point is that baby is *my* grandson. Will you come back and see if you can do something to help her and the child?"

"Did you tell her I was married?"

"No, of course not. I couldn't bring myself to do that. Ter, I feel responsible for what happened. She's breaking my heart."

"Okay, okay. I'll try to fly up tomorrow."

With a sense of desolation, Terry wondered how he could get through the evening.

"How long will you be in Port Rivers?" Valerie asked while they were decorating the Christmas tree. Hundreds of ornaments dazzled in silver and gold, held fast by red and green cascades of ribbons on the twelve-foot Oregon fir tree. She hung rare miniature casks of Bach beer, sleighs with Percherons, and other memorabilia she had inherited from her family. They were placed to the front. At the turn of the century, Alfred Bach, her great-grandfather, the company founder, had designed these as giveaways to taverns in Milwaukee. They were appended to fragile angels, Teddy bears, and Santas Val had collected on her world travels. At the base, the brightly wrapped bounties of Saks, Neiman-Marcus, and half a dozen other stores lay at their feet.

She came down from the ladder and nestled her head on Terry's shoulder. A thwarted, uneasy expression crossed her face. She could not bear to have Terry out of her sight.

"I don't know for sure. I'll have to file some motions and see if I can get a hearing, or better yet settle this."

"Exactly what is the problem?"

"Pat's been indicted as a co-conspirator in a fraud."

"Oh, Jesus. If he needs money, can't we pay a fine or something? And get rid of it. I don't want you to go, honey. There's so much happening here with the new house and everything. We've got to approve the architect's plans. I really want you to decide on the layout and the style."

"Val, I trust your taste and judgment."

She cuddled him. "Terry, I'm so excited. We've got lots of trees and I love the neo-Georgian renderings. There are six acres. Old oaks and maples. Views of the ocean, but it's sheltered from the wind. There's a flat pad, and we can have a grass tennis court."

He was distracted and inattentive. When she pressed against him, he turned away.

Allison has my son.

"Terry, this is going to be our first real home. I need you to be involved. Please, put your trip off for a couple of days."

"I can't!" Terry shouted, and she shrank away, hurt and dispirited. Before he fathomed the transformation, he became convinced of his lie and emerged as an indignant attorney. "Don't you realize, my father could go to prison!"

"Why does he get into trouble?"

"Why the hell does yours?"

"What you mean by that?"

"Don't you know why Jane quit working for you?"

Val shook her head uncomprehendingly. "She went back to Omaha because her mother had a car accident. She was devastated about having to quit UCLA."

Terry brushed some pine needles from Val's hair; he took her hand.

"Val . . . honey, you don't get suntans in Omaha in December." Her dark eyes roved over his face. "I saw her with Jonah slunk in a back booth at Perino's last week. I was with a client and a few guys from the office."

Val shook her head in despair and walked outside to the deck. The ocean roiled angrily and the air was rank with old seaweed. "How could Jane do this? I was going to support her through medical school."

"Jonah made her a better offer."

"No, Terry."

"I thought you knew."

As the realization gained substance, Val's bewilderment increased. "I spoke to my father two weeks ago. He was in Palm Beach in my mother's house. He was going off to dinner at the Alligator Club. It's the most exclusive private club in Palm Beach. My mother got him into it. I remember how badly he wanted to be a member. They said he was just a sausage salesman from Milwaukee and she went crazy. She started calling everyone: Gus Busch, the Pabsts, and all the beer barons, to see if they could help. Jane and my dad? They were in Palm Beach together? It's obscene, and such a waste. Am I stupid, Terry?"

"No, Val, that you're not. You're looking after sick children, some of them dying"—he pointed to the medical charts stacked on the dining-room table—"and gossip isn't something you rate highly. I'm sorry I told you."

In bed together that night, Val lay staring into space, then turned to him. "Don't leave now, Terry."

"I have no choice."

"I never complain about all these ball players hanging around you. You spend nights with them." Valerie could not retreat. "Between your obsession with sports and the law, where do I fit in?"

"This is a *family* emergency and I have to accept my responsibility. I'm the one who got my father involved in this situation in the first place. Blame me."

"Oh, Ter, I can't blame you for anything. You'll be back for our dinner party?"

"What dinner party?"

"Oh, the office staff and friends. Didn't I tell you about it? This time *I* called Chasen's to cater it. I know you love their chili . . . turkey and all the fixings."

He faltered, confused and torn. "Count on it."

It was five in the morning when Terry slipped out of the bedroom, but not before leaving a note of apology on his pillow.

At the sound of the car driving out of the garage, Val awoke deeply upset. She read the note and smiled, but she was incensed, although not by Terry's departure. She had been dreaming of her father.

36

Violent winds raked the streets of Port Rivers, driving the snow into Terry's face as he dodged through the stalled parade of trucks and cars across Jacob Astor Circle. The statue of the fur trader, covered with icicles, still held his pelts of beaver. He smiled smugly at the people cupping their hands below their hat brims. Winter havoc was familiar to Terry, but not the prosperity that had made a belated landing at the Piraeus restaurant.

A golden Greek galley with oars now hung above the restaurant with King Priam of Troy manning the ship. Through the window, Terry discerned new lacquered pine chairs and tables, which had replaced the splintery wooden benches and refectory tables. Laminated posters of the Greek Islands and the fledgling Piraeus Travel Services offered another fiddle for the Aristedes clan of thieves.

Terry stood outside with Pat, who was looking at the glossy menu stationed in the hand of a recently acquired Diogenes in this newly hatched temple of truthseekers.

"Do you want me to come with you?"

"No, Dad, I'll see you later."

"Okay, but don't take forever. I'll be back. Now, Terry, you've got something damn good with Valerie. Don't mess it up. Let's do what's proper for Allison and the baby, but not have a scandal."

"Thanks for the advice, Pat."

"Meesta Terry Brett's here! I'm so happy to see you. We have more cases for you!" Aristedes bellowed when he caught sight of his former attorney. Terry's unexpected arrival and regal welcome at Piraeus was about to devolve into an interminable discussion of the family's legal woes. A squadron of stogie-smoking relatives were at the counter, debating horse bets and when to torch another of their businesses that wasn't paying off.

Aristedes whispered, "That bestid Warren Paris. We feex his wagon."

"Stole his car," the Greek chorus joined in, chanting, "Caddylack."

"In Montreal, he is, but we'll catch heem."

Terry dismissed them. "Is Allison here?"

"In back of kitchen. . . . Terry Brett, you'll take cases?"

Terry pushed through the kitchen. Every surface was pocked with grease, but the smells of olives and feta had a pleasing fragrance. A butcher was cleaving lamb into cubes and stabbing metal kebab skewers into them. Terry asked around for Allison, and a dishwasher pointed him outside.

He burst open a screen door in the alley and found himself in a windowless storeroom. In the rear, facing a blank wall, beyond crates of fruit and canned goods, he caught sight of Allison. She sat hunched on a cot with a raw mattress. He shunted through cartons of food blocking the aisle.

Allison's eyes were closed in a waking sleep. She was nursing a baby whose fingers clamped on her breast. His son's eyes were also dreamily closed. Allison's long, luxurious hair had been chopped off. Apart from her milk-laden breast, she appeared a ghost of herself; the rich endowment of her beauty had hardened. She might have been a victim of famine and drought. She had a gradual awareness of someone standing over her and awoke startled.

"You!"

"When'd you get back?"

"I have nothing to say to you. Clear out."

"You're not running the show, Allison. You've made one mistake after another. If you'd only waited, we'd be married."

Surprise, dismay, uncertainty. "You never, never would have married me! I've been wronged, so don't think you can forgive yourself." Her breath came in heavy rushes. "I don't know why you bothered to lead me on—you were already screwing me. Was it a game, some turn-on? What else did you want?" She screamed and the baby howled with her. "I gave you my soul, goddamn you!"

She soothed the baby and wrapped him in a cheap blanket. Then she placed him in a wooden box, stamped DOLMADAKIA IMPORTED FROM GREECE, which served as his crib.

"Why'd you do this to me? I never hurt you," she pleaded.

He put his arms around her and she shivered, then cast him off.

"Allison, I never hurt you. And I don't intend to now."

Again he tried to hold her, but she ducked away. He leaned over and kissed his son, tasting her sweet milk on his lips.

"What's his name?"

"Sean."

"Sean? That's my middle name."

He detected a chink in Allison's armor and persuaded her to come out with him. One of Aristedes's daughters offered to baby-sit until dinner. Over a drink at the Surf Rider she expanded on his son's name.

"He was delivered by a *harijan* woman, an untouchable, who befriended me while I was living in a village near Fatehpur. When I was in labor, I lost consciousness and I kept dreaming about 'Jack and the Beanstalk.' How he brought his mother the hen that lays the golden eggs. I thought maybe one day, my baby boy will do that for me."

"So you called him Sean?"

"My book of names said it means John or Jack."

Terry looked at Allison's callused hands, the uneven nails, her sickly pallor, and he was unable to control his desire to touch her. He reached out for her, yearning for what they had lost. His passion for her had never ceased and he felt gripped by her powerlessness and the futility of his attempts to release her. In her presence, his defenses were stripped away. She had captured the core of everything within him. He thought back to their weekend in Timberline, when he'd proposed. She must have gotten pregnant then.

"Did you know you were pregnant when you went to India?"

"I had no idea. After a few weeks in Calcutta, I was feeling a little funny at times and thought it was the water or the food, the heat. And then I went to a clinic when I was late, and they told me I was going to have a baby."

He was afraid to press her, afraid that she would disappear again.

"What are you going to do? You and Sean living like this, so rough."

"Aristedes is temporary. Just shelter. He was kind enough to take us in. Crooked as these people are, *they* believe in family. I'm working there in the evenings and doing short-order lunches on the line at Milly's. She asked me to move in with her. I don't know. It's like I haven't taken a step forward.

"Carol and Harry retired to Florida. Milly offered to let me run the diner in Seacliff until she can find a buyer. oSo I'm going to head down the coast. I'll try to make a go of it. Port Rivers has been my undoing. It'll be good for Sean, the sea air. He hasn't been well. Eczema, and he's got the colic. That's why I came back from India. The conditions in the village were unspeakable. I couldn't stay there with him."

Terry covered his face with his hands.

"You don't look very well either, Terry," she said with concern. "Tell me what happened to you . . . your face?"

He described the lunch with Billy Klein and how he had been so badly beaten that he lay in a coma for days.

"When I got back home after the hospital, I looked everywhere for you. I put ads in the papers you used to read. I even hired a private detective. Then your letter came from India." Her hand brushed his face. "I couldn't stay in Port Rivers any longer. I gave it up. I hated everyone, even my father. I handed over my practice to Paul Cisco."

"He was a true friend of mine," she snapped at the mention of his name.

"I know. He was hungry for a buck and I know he can't cut it in personal practice. My feeble attempt at revenge for you. Then I drifted down to L.A. Anything to get lost.

"I was staying with Billy Klein. He was supposed to be our best man. I was sick about us." His chest tightened, but now he was able to control his angst. "The fact of the matter is, I had a nervous breakdown. I can't explain how it happened, even now. All my life, I'd been so tough and smart. I never imagined anything emotional like this could've happened to me. The truth is, Allison, you broke me."

She was frozen by the bleak admission. "I didn't do very well either."

Against his will he continued. "I met a very kind woman. She's also a doctor, and she patched me back together."

"Is she a psychiatrist?"

"No, she's a pediatrician."

"What happened to her? Where is she now?"

"At home." He vacillated. "I had to rebound or sink after you left me and she gave me hope. In the state I was in . . . she fell in love with me. I just couldn't bring myself to hurt her. I . . . I married her. It was the right thing to do."

Allison's eyes grew large, haunted by disbelief. She fought to control her sobbing. Her head keeled onto the table and he lifted her face and wiped her tears.

"Oh, Terry—my darling, how could this have happened to us?"

"Allison, Allison, I never would have given you up—ever!—don't you know that?"

He took from his pocket the blue velvet box from Tiffany's and put it in her palm. She shook her head and made a move to get up and run, but he held her fast.

"Open it, Allison, it's for you."

She looked at the sparkling engagement ring. Tears trickled down her cheeks and seeped onto the scratched wooden table.

"There's no fixing it now."

"I'll take care of you and Sean. I want to. I need to."

"No, Terry, my darling, we're not going to see each other again."

There was a new maturity and inner serenity in Allison's face. Her eyes were knowing. He was distraught by the prospect of life without her—again.

"This is a clean break. I love the baby, especially since he's yours, Ter . . . I have a chance for a fresh start."

"I can't let you go, Allison."

"You don't have much choice. Your wife, what's her name?"

"Valerie."

"She's a doctor, you're a lawyer. It's a different world from mine. And that's where you belong. With Valerie—not someone like me."

"I want to be Sean's father. I can't let this end. He's my son, too. This is real life."

A glimmer of the old Allison, full of fight, engaged him.

"From the moment I started breathing, I have lived *real* life, every second of it . . . in ways that are beyond you." She closed the box with the ring and slid it across the scarred table. "Good-bye, my love."

Waiting for the last customer to leave the bar of the Piraeus, both of them brawling drunk with accusations, he and Pat quarreled bitterly.

"No, they're not staying at your house! I've got them a place at the River Barge," Terry barked.

Fists clenched, Pat heaved himself up from the table. "I will not permit my grandson to go on living in this hellhole. If I have to call the authorities and take the boy from her, I will!"

"You'll do nothing of the kind, you goddamn phony."

"Phony? You're the phony," Pat raged. "Sean's my blood. He has to be cared for—provided for."

"None of this should have happened. And you know that."

With that, Pat listed from table to table like a marionette and lurched into the dark street.

* * *

It was ten o'clock and Allison was still in the kitchen, washing up in the large, chipped sink. Terry cornered her.

"I've taken a suite downtown for you and Sean."

"Please, don't start. I'm too beat."

"I went down to Meir's and bought a lot of baby stuff. Crib, carriage, clothes, the works. Tomorrow, we'll look for a place for you to live."

"Oh, Terry, please, please, stop this pressure. Go home to your wife." Allison roughly pushed him away and he leaped at her, pinned her arms against the wall, and grappled with her. The cooks left the range to intercede, but when Allison collapsed on Terry, they retreated.

"You and Sean are never going to leave me again."

Exhaustion conquered Allison and like a captive she accompanied him to the River Barge Hotel, the town's brush with elegance. Terry had taken the largest suite. It provided a kitchen and two bedrooms. He'd also made arrangements with housekeeping to provide a baby-sitter.

Terry waited for Allison, who was taking her time in the shower. Virtually sleepwalking, she finally appeared, huddled in his plaid robe. She fingered the glossy mahogany rail on the new crib, and leaned over to check that Sean was clean. She noticed some mobile wire birds Terry had put up.

"I diapered him. The rash is awful. It's all over him."

"Yeah. I'll take him back to the hospital to see the skin doctor."

"Will you try to get some sleep now?" he asked.

Allison shook her head furiously. "When I was in the shower, was that Valerie you were talking to on the phone?"

"Yes."

"Blissfully ignorant, still, huh?" She glowered at him. "Terry, I'd like to kill you."

"I feel the same way about you."

"You're something, Terry."

"I don't want to fight. I've had enough for the day."

Catlike, skittish, suspicious, she pawed the blanket. "I'll sleep on the sofa by the baby."

"Come here, I want to hold you."

"Call your wife back if you're lonely." Allison carried a pillow and the bedspread from the other bedroom, then she suddenly seemed to have a change of heart. "The beating you took ... oh, God, Terry. I'm horrified. It must've been gruesome."

"Well, at least your friend Earl's sitting pretty. You did your good deed. He bought Warren's bar with the money I leeched out of Jonah Wolfe. Georgie negotiated the sale of the Paradise Inn for Earl."

"Earl will meet his destiny in hell. What a treacherous, rotten bunch they all are, Georgie included. She said you must have found yourself a gal in L.A. and you were too cowardly to face me."

"Georgie—I thought as much when I got back."

Sean woke at four, wailing. Terry persuaded Allison to bring the baby to bed with him when she finished nursing. He put Sean on a pillow and studied his features, the shape of his hands and feet. He knew he could not relinquish him.

I am the bequeather of his fate.

"How about driving to Seacliff and we'll have a look at Milly's place together?" he said.

"Why would you want to do that?"

"Allison, stop questioning everything I say. There's no motive, and never has been, so stop looking for one. That's all there is to it."

"I wish you hadn't come back to Port Rivers, Terry. I guess I've got Pat to thank for it, along with all the other kind things he's done for me."

37

They stopped off at Milly's restaurant, picked up the keys, dropped Sean off with Milly, and drove along the tortuous road beside the raging white waters of the Rogue River. Terry was pulled apart by his affection for

Valerie and the desire Allison infected him with. His life without her had been filled with an unending hunger for her. He loved her beyond redemption, beyond dignity, beyond his aspirations.

For a time, Valerie had delivered him from the sweep of this monstrous desire and the humiliation he had felt so deeply. He was fragmented by guilt and regret for the wife he had left behind who believed in him and was striving to build a future for them.

Allison was silent, austere, detached, and only became spirited when they reached Seacliff. A filament of sunshine trickled through the purple-blue sky, illuminating the wide sandy beaches, the ocean-washed nineteenth-century lighthouse guarding the breakwater. Below it stood commemorative statues of Lewis and Clark. Allison's enthusiasm and curiosity were roused by fishermen beside their brightly painted boats, auctioning their catches at the customhouse dock.

"My God, there're sea otters here," she said with delight. "You know they're the only animals who actually use their feet as a tool. They search for a rock, put their catch on their chest, and bang open the shells of the abalone to get at the flesh."

"How do you know that?"

"I worked a fish fry shack once and went back there before coming to Port Rivers. I couldn't get a job anywhere." She lifted her callused palms. "I wasn't cooking either but pounding abalone and shucking oysters. My nails turned yellow from the saline and gutting. They were like a bat's claws and I was afraid to touch Sean. Terry, what a place. It's heaven here."

"I used to come here summers and visit the Canfields. Milly and my dad would roll in for weekends. It was quiet and remote. But there was an air of history that hung over the place. I first read *Moby-Dick* here after I went to the whaling museum. I'd spend hours at the old Astor Fort and the log cabin."

She became less vigilant, lapsing into a softer mood. "Your magical childhood."

Terry turned to look her, assuming her comment had been intended to be acrimonious, but it was one of reverence.

He drove up Fool's Hill, which meandered to a craggy bluff where purple ling heather and laurel danced in the wind. Below, a cleft of rock formed a natural island in the ocean and blowholes spouted in the rough tide. Milly's diner was situated across the road; its front faced the sea, and the rear opened onto the snow-dotted Cascade peaks.

"In the summer, Carol and Harry would have trestle tables outside and people would eat family-style," Terry said, unlocking the door of the diner. There was a ten-seat counter with six wooden booths in the back and marine-varnished pine tables. "There's an apartment upstairs. Harry used to rent it out to the cooks. They have a cottage with some acreage down the road."

Allison roamed around the kitchen in bliss, and he followed her to the upstairs rooms, which had a sweeping view of the harbor and the cluster of fishing boats.

"It's going to take a lot of hard work to get this place operating."

"What doesn't take hard work?" she said with a hopeful smile, extending her arms to embrace the sea.

They walked up the pebbled road to a weathered wood-shingled house, surrounded by towers of spruce. A FOR SALE sign listed three bedrooms and three acres with Milly's address in Port Rivers. The price was twelve thousand dollars, furnished.

"Can we go in?" she asked shyly, the permanent outsider. "I just want a peek, do you mind?"

"It's not a palace but it has good memories for me. There was so much laughter in this house. Last Christmas Eve was the first one I'd missed with them in years. When I was ten, Harry got me drunk on something he'd brewed. He said it was mead. Jesus, what a hangover I had."

The living room had a collection of shells, a galley-hatch table, nautical artifacts, pride of place assumed by a whaling harpoon over the broad-bellied fireplace. She peeped into the beamed bedrooms, which had high ceilings and varnished moldings. Allison was enchanted.

"Maybe if Milly doesn't sell it, I can rent it." She was ablaze with optimism. "Well, no, I guess Sean and me would be better off living over the diner. Save on the heating bills. And I can cook all night."

Terry sat on the four-poster, staring at the cold fireplace. At the bay window, Allison lost herself in new possibilities. Small houses on crooked cobbled streets leaned toward the harbor, which was veiled in a light rain. Fishermen in slick yellow waterproofs wrenched the hawsers of their boats and cleaned their decks.

"What a chance this is for me."

"Allison, please come over here."

She ignored him, yearning to hold him, but hostility made her irresolute. She wanted to keep connected to Terry, yet she dared not. He belonged to another woman, and her insecurity and jealousy crushed her passion.

"What do I have to do to prove I still love you?" he asked. No response. "I'm going to buy this house for you and Sean. I'll work something out with Milly so that you can take over her diner."

She stood before him, even-tempered and solemn.

"*My* son and I are not for sale."

"Allison, I didn't mean it that way. What can I do?"

She folded her arms as a debate roiled within her.

"Keep your promise."

"What does that mean?"

"Keep your word, your sacred promise. Give Sean the history I never had. Parents, family, a name! That would mean everything to me, Terry," she said softly and with defeat. "Jesus, he'll grow up fatherless, a bastard. Illegitimate like me." Wrenched by indecision, she leaned against the wall, finding a corner. "The history of a human being begins with bearing a name. What's he going to be called? My last name came from a dead matron at the orphanage. You can't ever be whole unless you have a history. Something's always missing.

"Terry, listen to me and try to sense what it's like. When Sean starts school, what's he going to say about his father? People aren't going to be sympathetic. They mouth all this good-Christian crap, but they don't care. They blame the child. I know all about that." She shuddered. "They look at you as though there's something wrong with you. We're the ones who broke the rules. But it goes on *his* record. *Born out of wedlock.*

"Sean and I are unwanted people. We're outlaws. We have no family tree. We don't exist. We're the eyeless creatures who've burrowed up from the underground and the good folk don't want any part of us. Because we are sin!"

He was disturbed by the logic of her reasoning.

"Allison, stop persecuting me. I can't apologize for what happened. Neither of us is to blame."

"Do you love this woman?"

"Yes. She healed me. Try to see my point of view."

She kneeled in front of him and rested her head on his knees.

"I love you, Terry, to the point of obsession and madness. I missed you so badly, my insides used to shriek out with pain and grief. . . . And now we're together, here, alone finally, and I'm beside myself with the senseless injustice of it."

"I know."

"What do you feel, Terry?"

"Terrible rage. Immoral. Like a criminal for loving you so much."

He had withheld something from Valerie, something vital and primal, the real heart of himself, which belonged to Allison. No matter how he tried to escape from her, she had been the phantom, dislodging any pleasure he might feel. Without Allison, something would always be missing. Her absence had mangled him. He struggled with the predicament. Whatever he did would not be right.

He lifted her to her feet, clamping her in his arms. He caressed her hair, stroked her face, and kissed her, wild with anger and the ache of her loss.

*   *   *

Holding Allison's sleeping body in the hollow of his shoulder, Terry shuddered through the night, speculating on their hopeless situation. At every turn he hit a concrete wall. Nothing of a rational character presented itself to him. Sudden, stabbing dreams came and went until four in the morning, but still the prospect of sacrificing her was unendurable. The concealed torments of the day were friendless at night.

He smoked a stale old Camel cigarette he found under the bed, roved out on the deck, dropped down on a grimy canvas lounge, listened to the clash of waves throbbing against the rocks. Allison came up from behind and wrapped her arms around his neck. He felt her warm skin, still smelling of pine bath oil and bed, and knew that he would do anything to be with her and Sean. Every notion of justice he had mastered was sucked out by the tide, swallowed by the sea.

Book IV

THE GHOST OF A GARDEN

38

Jonah Wolfe's bedroom was a happy, high-density playground: carved French bombés held Lalique vases with seasonal flowers; stylish antique mirrors were on the walls and above the elevated bed; a bar trolley filled with iced Dom Pérignon could be reached by the connoisseur; three TVs mounted in the wall provided news, sports, and information; at the touch of a switch, he could record his erotic escapades on a brand-new TV recording device which Ampex had developed for more public network viewing. But the room itself seemed to be swallowed by a gargantuan stone fireplace, its blackened roasting spit still intact, which Jonah had liberated from a French castle.

The marble bathroom had been modeled after the Spa in Palm Springs and contained a special needle shower, barber chair, massage table, Jacuzzi for two, sauna, and wet steam rooms accommodating a dozen when Jonah presided over his weekend saturnalias. His open high French doors revealed an English rock garden and a heated Olympic-sized swimming pool where Jane Ashley, his naked Primavera, tirelessly swam laps.

She had been a delicious companion since he poached her at Val's engagement party. But Jonah was a ceaseless explorer of beautiful young women. Although his interest in Jane hadn't quite waned, it was scattering. He had met several new young ladies. Jane, the current infanta, had also met them the previous evening and ensured that the encounter was hospitably perverse. Jane Ashley had worn out everyone at the party. She was the kind of woman whom the English deferentially referred to as a saddlebreaker.

Jonah's butler buzzed to tell him that his visitor had arrived, and Jonah asked that he be delivered to the bedroom. Jonah was still sprawled naked on the bed, for this was the way he usually disarmed underlings.

Davis Wilson, six feet four and black as an ebony walking stick, was about to retreat when he caught sight of Jonah splayed bare above the red satin coverlet. Jonah watched the nineteen-year-old boy nervously tap his shoe.

"How are you, Whiz?"

"I'm more than a little confused, sir."

"I'll clear everything up. And please stop with the 'sir,' " Jonah said, "you're not spit-shining my shoes. It's Jonah. All my players call me by my first name."

Whiz shook his head. "Well, Jonah, I'm supposed to be playing against the Stars tomorrow night."

"There's been a change of plan. You'll be starting for me and the Stars instead of sitting on the Bulls' bench. I bought your contract this morning. Chicago needed a big forward and I wanted a sparkplug—a playmaker."

"What? Nobody said a word to me. Not even Terry."

"Terry is out of town. I'll deliver the good news myself when he gets back."

"My salary the same?"

"It's higher."

"Higher?"

"I'll stud it with bonuses based on performance. In a couple of years they'll be saying you're better than Dr. J."

"I got a ways to go before I'm in Julius Erving's company." The room expanded when Whiz smiled and enveloped the world with such innocent pleasure that Jonah was stirred by his luminous charm. "You really think that much of me?"

"Yes, Whiz. Believe in yourself as much as I do."

"I'm floored, man. Wait'll Terry finds out."

"Did you know that Terry was married to my daughter Valerie?"

"Yes. I peeped in at the wedding."

"I wanted to meet you then."

"I left early with some of the other guys. We kinda didn't really fit in with that crowd."

"You'll fit in with my crowd—perfectly."

"I am truly honored to be a part of this predicament."

Jonah laughed and found he couldn't stop. "Predicament. You're wonderful. Whiz, have you got any plans for this evening?"

"I was going to pick up my mom at the airport."

"What time is she arriving?"

"Midnight. She's down in Milwaukee and catching a flight from there."

"You pick her up in style in my limo."

"You're kidding. She'll die. She's never been in a limo."

"We want to give her a real Los Angeles welcome."

"Oh, dear sweet Lord, my dreams are coming true. Terry told me they would."

Jonah concealed his aversion to Terry. "What are you doing for dinner?"

"Dinner? I was going to grab me some of that good spaghetti at Frascati's with the guys and maybe a gal's number." With a shy smirk, Whiz Davis shook his head. "Really pretty ones out here in L.A."

Jonah beckoned him closer to the bed and Whiz approached cautiously as though he might have been looking for potholes on the road.

"The champagne is for you. We have to celebrate."

"I don't drink before a game. Only Cokes."

"The game is tomorrow. You can have a couple of glasses. I'll keep score."

"I'll go out and get us some pizza."

"How about a sandwich for dinner?"

Whiz accepted a glass of champagne and studied the dazzling bubbles in the fragile glass. He was afraid of dropping it or crushing it. He had never touched anything so fine. "Like a ham sandwich?"

"How about ham and cheese?"

"Sure. American cheese, please. I hate that stuff with the holes in it. You'd think they'd give people a whole slice for their money and a sweet taste."

Jonah studied the wiry black swan who, for this meeting, had dressed in a team blazer, a red-and-white striped tie, the colors of the Chicago Bulls, and a white button-down Oxford shirt.

"This is going to be the sandwich of your life."

"Like a Dagwood with all that deli meat? My mother's been buying the Wolfe brand all my life. When I used to shop for her, I didn't buy the store specials, but your own brand with the little black kid at the stream. I love that label: 'Fishin' for a bite.' "

"What did your father do?"

Whiz acted as if he was fouled driving for the hoop. "Never met the gentleman, and my mother said he was one."

"Is your mother religious?"

"I'm a Bible child. Never sang, but I played ball for the church."

Jonah was entranced. He had achieved his goal. He had improved his team at Terry's expense. Miracles deserved adoration and the faith of rewards.

"Do you know the Bible story of the Garden of Eden?"

"I think so."

"You know what the true story is?"

"True story?"

"Yes. It goes like this. Eve had her legs in a scissors around Adam's neck and Adam looked down at the patch between Eve's thighs. He looked up to the sky and asked the Lord what it was.

"And the Lord spoke: 'It's a pussy, Adam, what else could it be?' "

Dropping her beach towel, Jane, naked and tanned, skirted into the room. "You called my name."

She dropped to her knees beside Whiz. The young man was too surprised to speak and fell backward. Jane straddled over his face and Jonah dove from his high place and joined in. Jane yanked Whiz's trousers down and he said breathlessly:

"Oh, yes, Jonah, I want to live in your ark."

Throughout the day at the free clinic Val had secretly funded, she found her concentration wandering during examinations. It was dangerous to her young patients.

She called the resident she was training to administer smallpox vaccinations and to continue later under supervision with one of the doctors from her practice.

"I'm absolutely useless today," Val told one of her partners. "I've got a family thing going on that I have to settle."

She had called Jonah's office and been told that her father was at home in meetings. As she drove through the estate, passing the gardens, the marble statues, walking swiftly over glassed-in lighted fish ponds, she knew that her father was a man who possessed elegant tastes. She was embarrassed about interrupting his team meeting, but he might be able to spare her a few minutes and explain what his intentions were regarding Jane Ashley. Val had a right to know.

She entered the house through a side door and saw the staff in the kitchen lined up at the butcher block where the chef was carving rare cuts of prime ribs. She decided not to intrude on them. It was lovely to be at home. Maybe she'd bring home a roast beef sandwich for herself and an end cut for Terry, who might be catching a late flight home. She'd wait up for him and fix a salad and a cold beef plate or sandwiches, which she would lather with Coleman's English mustard and horseradish, just the way Terry had told her that Milly had done for him and Pat when they were going out on the river to fish.

As Val walked through her father's den, passing photographs of her childhood, with Lake Michigan and their sailboat behind her, she thought of the good times, the new Bach lager she had drunk from the keg when it was young to test if it was a good batch, joining in the dancing that followed in the brewery garden.

She knocked on her father's bedroom door and heard perilous sounds—squeals of pain that her training enabled her to recognize—the cry of a stroke, the pitch of a massive heart attack. Without thinking, she had carried in her medical bag, and she rushed into the room.

At first, Val felt faint and stood paralyzed, undetected, staring at the wild gyrations of flesh. The sweaty fetor of animals in the field was overpowering and she thought she was about to vomit. Amid the tangle of bodies, Jane had been mounted by a black man, and her father now screeched in orgasm.

Suddenly Jonah caught sight of Val. Breathing heavily, he emitted a growl.

Val tried to regain her balance, then teetered forward when the spume of the naked black man exploded on Jane's face. In a fury, Val picked up a poker from the fireplace and lashed out at her father, but the black man, in fear of his life, struggled with her and disarmed her.

He gasped in terror. "Lord no, no, no, no, Missus Brett."

"You fucking pigs!" Val screamed. She pushed Whiz aside, then slammed her father's face with the back of her hand. On all fours, Jane crawled along the floor, reached her beach towel, and wiped her face.

"They're not pigs to me, Val," Jane said with a derisive smile. "I call them conquests."

"Then you have a death wish, Jane."

39

Bigamy was a felony according to the criminal statute that Terry read while waiting in Georgie's office, one that carried a prison term. Paul Cisco was in court and Terry was relieved not to have to go through the ceremony of greeting the former assistant D.A. Their friendship had floated into the ether along with other illusions of gracious behavior.

After many failed diets, Georgie was back to Milky Way sugar rushes in the morning. She was awkward and embarrassed. She acted as though Terry were a school principal about to expel her for cheating. She tried to forget how she had betrayed him and Allison.

"It's been awful since you left the practice, Terry. It wasn't a good idea putting me together with Paul. His wife pushed him into it. But he's not you. He can't hack it. He hates criminals and they hate him. I don't know how long we're going to last. I've got a sixty–forty split with him on the billing. Problem is, I'm bringing in twice as much business and he's taking home the lion's share. I'm his Wonder Woman and grunt."

"Sit Paul down and tell him what you want."

"He avoids any discussion. He starts ranting that he was an assistant district attorney and was going to be mayor one day. Hey, Ter, you know how I hate confrontations outside of court. A man raises his voice, I turn to jelly."

Georgie poured them coffee and selected a cinnamon bun from her briefcase larder, which he declined. She had heard that he had married a doctor in Los Angeles.

"I was really surprised. Frankly, I've never seen a man more in love with anyone than you were with Allison. But I guess you never know." He glared at her and she averted her eyes. "Maybe I should have done more for Allison."

"Oh, does it bother you still?"

"Yes, of course it does. But I try not to dwell on unpleasantness. I have enough of that with Earl. He's stalling me. I'm 'engaged' to wait. He's been using me for his legal problems with the Paradise. Warren took off up to Canada with Earl's money.

"Warren had the liquor license under the name of a third party. It's not transferrable and the Alcohol Beverage Control board aren't thrilled with Earl's track record. There were a few bookmaking offenses." Georgie reached for some aspirin. "Earl's still very sore at you for splitting up the money Wolfe paid you to settle his claim."

"I'll do my best to live with Earl's ill will."

Terry had been up all night, pondering his decision. He had serious reservations about trusting Georgie, but ultimately came to the conclusion that he had no alternative.

"I'm not here on a social visit or to play catch-up on the local gossip," he said sourly. "I don't care about anything that happens in Port Rivers. I'm here as a client and what I'm about to tell you is confidential. You remember that sort of thing from the bar and your oath."

Georgie was bewildered. "You, a client? What do you want, a divorce?"

"Not exactly." He handed her an envelope with five thousand dollars inside it. "Paul can't know. And certainly never tell Earl. The money's for you."

"Terry, stop this. It's unnecessary. I'll get you an annulment free and kill whoever you married—prenuptial or not."

He shook her off and watched her nervously gnaw at a Hershey bar she had hidden in her desk.

"You bailed out on Allison and changed my life. It can't ever be put right. I was your friend, Georgie. From scrambling for ten grand a year, and mooching around the courthouse, you started to make twenty-five, then forty the last year. You were respectable. I built your practice."

She was defensive and flustered. "I'm aware of that."

"I did it because I liked you. And I wanted you to succeed. I was proud of you. I respect and admire women like you. You were like a sister. I entrusted you with the well-being of the woman I loved, and you turned tail and dumped her."

"Terry, Allison was about to be busted. I did what I thought was right. I couldn't help it," she wailed.

"You can now. Did you know Allison was going to India?"

"She never said a word about it. She took off into the night with her mule, drug money. Earl said Warren Paris had to pay her for delivering the LSD to the Paradise Inn the night you were with her."

"I know all about that. Allison's back in town. With my son!"

"Oh, sweet Jesus, I'm so sorry." She shook her head. "Sorry for everyone."

He allowed Georgie to immerse herself in guilt.

"Before I got hammered and wound up half dead in the hospital, Allison and I were going to get married."

Georgie was red-faced and sweating. "She didn't confide in me about that."

"Georgie, I am going to marry Allison. And I am *not* about to divorce my wife."

"What?" She was flabbergasted. "Whaaat?"

"You heard me."

"But, that's bigamy."

"I read the statute before you came in."

"Why, Terry? This could be . . . , prison. Why put yourself in such terrible jeopardy?"

"Because I love Allison and our son more than myself. My wife Val pulled me together. I also happen to love and respect her. I can't destroy her. Just pick myself up and tell her that my former fiancée came back from the dead with my bastard son who wouldn't have been illegitimate if things had worked out as I intended."

"This is totally insane."

"You don't understand anything about Allison's background. She was like one of these refugees from a death camp. She was a displaced person until she met me. She probably would have wound up in jail. I can give her a chance to have some kind of life. To be respectable. And my son's not going to be a bastard with 'Father Unknown' on his record, dogging him forever.

"I can't have Allison and my baby boy on my conscience. Two losers wandering through life with no future. I'm going to take a dangerous chance and do something that may be criminal but that is morally right. It sits well in my gut. Do you understand what I'm talking about?"

With a long sigh, Georgie digested the argument.

"I think I'm going to faint. You are the most gallant man I've ever met."

"I don't feel that way at all, Georgie. Now legally you're not going to be compromised."

"What do you want me to do?"

"Around the time Earl first came to see me—I can't recall the time frame—you had a client, a seaman or some other client who died."

She looked at him blankly. "Let's see, that would be—?" She burst up from her desk and rooted in her disorganized file cabinet. "Christopher James Arnold. He was in the Merchant Marines. The captain's report says he needed emergency surgery. He had appendicitis and died of peritonitis off the coast of South America. He wanted to be buried at sea and his wish was fulfilled. I have the death certificate." She looked at her notes. "Oh yes, on your advice I kept his retainer."

"How'd you come to meet him?"

"He found me at the courthouse when I was hustling for business. His ship was docked in Port Rivers."

"Was there a will?"

"Yes, prior to the divorce proceedings, his wife was to get everything. And since he died before the dissolution, she of course inherited his estate and a small pension."

"Any children or family?"

"No. It was a clean and simple parting of the ways."

"What happened to the wife?"

Georgie flipped through the file and found some correspondence. "There's a letter from her about the estate. She was Dutch and she married a KLM airline pilot and is living in Amsterdam."

Terry eagerly took possession of the Arnold file. Georgie, still demurring, suggested a trust fund for Allison and implored him not to go through with the marriage.

"Three people will know about this—my father, Milly, and you. I'm going to set Allison up in Seacliff and marry her there. I've already spoken to Milly about it."

"And your father?"

"I haven't told him yet. As for the future, if Mrs. Christopher Arnold has any problems, I'll ask her to contact you. You'll have to go there. We've agreed that her showing her face again in Port Rivers would be unwise. Here's my number in Los Angeles. Call me only in an emergency."

She was overwhelmed by Terry's grand gesture and clung to him. People—men—didn't act like this. Still feeling something of his old protectiveness toward her,

Terry hugged her. "My advice to you is, get rid of Earl. Sooner or later, he'll carve you up."

"I know, Terry. Believe me, I do."

Terry dropped by the Easy Acres Bowling Lanes. The bar was filled with a rabble of bookies, their shylocks, and a crew of asbestos siding closers. Stanley Hoffman was waiting for him in a corner, nursing a Bloody Mary and a two-day stubble. His baggy suit might never have been pressed and a jam stain gilded his black wool tie.

"If you're still looking for that gal, she never showed and I have no new information." He had no idea why Terry called, but was pleased to see his former client. "Sorry I let you down, Terry."

"You did your best, Stanley. It's a dead issue."

"Terry, if you want me to work for you, I have to inform you that my license as a P.I. has been suspended again."

"I don't want you to do anything honest."

"In that case, I'm for hire."

"What does a really well-bred pair of phony papers run these days? Birth certificate, marriage license."

"Soup to nuts, a thousand. The passport, another grand will see you through." Stanley smirked. "Oh and a finder's fee for me. Two g's . . . and we'll all be smiling."

"I'll want a Rembrandt for these documents."

"I have a *legendmaker*," Stanley said with veneration. "He worked for the CIA creating counterfeit papers for their secret agents in Berlin. He's not Rembrandt, he's Leonardo da Vinci."

Terry peeled out a roll of hundred-dollar bills. "The woman's name is Allison Desmond Arnold, the father is Christopher James Arnold. The boy's name is Sean Patrick Arnold. Let it read that he was born at Good Samaritan. Date it from now."

40

Milly had been sympathetic about the situation but remained perplexed. Terry forcefully argued his case, and finally persuaded her to accept terms on the house in Seacliff and an option purchase of the diner. Terry had paid cash, but the bill of sale was to be made out to Allison Arnold. Letters to establish credit were written to Dun & Bradstreet and the Better Business Bureau by Milly, and Georgina Conlan, Allison's attorney. A straight checking account was set up at the Bank of Seacliff where Milly had a long-standing relationship with the president and an appointment was made to introduce the new owner.

Returning to the house he had shared for so many years with his father, which he knew so well, Terry had a sense of living in a dream. The river with its haze of steel clouds drifting over their fishing spot on the point, the basketball hoop over the garage where he had spent days and nights honing his eye, the cords of wood stacked on the porch, all possessed a foreign quality. Everything seemed cramped and yet the same. What had changed so vividly were not the familiar surroundings but his perspective. He had distanced himself from memories and bricks.

Pat was outside, surly, pacing with his cashmere overcoat draped over his arm. Milly nervously stood beside him, a mink stole on her shoulders. She looked beautiful, regal, and Terry kissed her.

"I've left three building sites. Jobs I need. Now for Crissake, tell me why am I wearing my best suit at noon and Milly's in a cocktail dress? What the hell's going on?" Pat demanded.

"Let's go."

"Man, you better phone your wife before we go anywhere. She's goddamn hysterical. Valerie thought I was in jail. What in God's name've you told her?"

"I spoke to her before I got here. I said you were going to trial. I lie, you swear for me."

"Oh, okay. I got it. Just stop getting pissed off at me."

"Get in the car and don't ask questions."

It was an hour's drive to the coast but it might have been another planet, measured in light-years. Pat sucked at his flask of scotch and listened as the intrigue unfolded. When Milly took Terry's side, the men clashed like bears.

"I won't be a part of this!" He lashed out at Terry. "Never thought when I called, you'd do something so unbalanced. Marry Allison, commit bigamy! It's demented."

"I love Allison."

"And what about Valerie? She's a fine person. Even though she's dripping millions, she acts like a *real* human being!"

"I love her . . . too."

"Stop the car at that gas station. I'm getting out."

Fearing they would come to blows, Milly interceded.

"Pat, I had to swallow hard when Terry told me his plans. But I've gone along. Illegal it may be, but somehow I know that their marrying is proper." She twined her arm around Terry's neck. "His heart's in the right place. I love Allison and Terry. And if you don't come and be a witness as he's asked, you won't see me, him, or your grandson again."

In defeat Pat was apoplectic, consoling himself with the flask. Raising his fist to the sky, he stumbled out of the car half drunk at the cottage in Seacliff. Milly gave him a sharp, warning look. Terry went ahead, lugging a case of iced champagne.

In the house, the furniture gleamed with fresh polish and a crackling fire brightened the living room. The dining table was set for five, with white linen and a centerpiece of peonies. Allison came out of the kitchen, carrying a baguette fresh from the oven. She had her hair cut evenly in a pageboy and wore a blue velvet dress with a white sash. She toyed nervously with her diamond engagement ring and smiled shyly at Terry.

"Welcome home, sailor." Allison said with incredulity. "I can't believe that you're really going to marry me. I'm an absolute wreck. I can't catch my breath. It's insane."

He looked into her lambent cornflower eyes and kissed her softly, with reverence. "You have that effect on me. And frankly, your reasoning about Sean's future is my feeble defense."

"Great. I'm relieved that you're not about to commit bigamy because of any personal attachment or fondness toward his mother."

"Will you ever give me a break?" Terry said sputtering with laughter. "You are gorgeous, darling."

"Thank you, my lord. This place is a treasure-house. The books in the attic. Oh, how I love my life. You are the most wonderful man."

"How's our little guy?"

"I was up most of the night with him. He's got a hacking cough and the colic won't go away. I stopped nursing and tried some honey in his milk and he's sleeping now."

"Any problems with the house?"

"No, it's fine. I'm just waiting on the phone company to hook us up." She was fidgeting with excitement. "My American dream's come true. A couple of years ago, I was packing cheese in Tillamook. Today, I'm marrying a man without a tattoo and not living in a trailer park."

No matter what the circumstances, she had the capacity to make him laugh.

"Don't ever get too serious or too respectable."

"I don't think I have to promise you that."

Her mercurial humor altered and she shuddered reflexively.

"What is it, Allison?"

"Oh, Terry, I'm terrified. Are you sure you won't be caught? The locals might know who you really are."

"I never socialized with them. I'm just a face that sometimes stopped for gas."

"No one knows you as Terry Brett?" she asked under her breath.

"No. Only Milly's family, and they won't be back."

She couldn't control her nerves. "What about someone showing up from Port Rivers to fish or stay at a guest-house? And you're recognized?"

He had to reassure her. "They don't come here."

"It's not classy enough for them?"

"Something like that."

"I should fit in perfectly," she said.

"Cut it out, Allison. Seacliff is isolated and it's a very inbred community. The way you go on. This isn't another McDonald's."

"This time I won't be an innocent bystander." She held on to him tensely and labored to regain her composure. "Are you sure you want to go through with this . . . or do you want to call it off?"

"Why, do you?"

In that moment of hesitation, Allison realized that she had become the passage to Terry and Sean's future, and the responsibility daunted her. Whatever answer she gave would be the wrong one.

"No, I don't want to call it off," she replied finally. "I'll put Seacliff under a magic spell and make it Arcadia for us."

"I know you will."

Milly had found a retired ship's captain who abhorred sobriety and was empowered to perform marriage cere-monies on land. After awhile he and Pat came through the door rocking on their heels. Terry shook hands and produced the marriage license in the names of Christo-pher James Arnold and Allison Desmond. Rounds of drinks were served and it was clear that Allison had a definite flair for cooking. She had prepared shrimp re-moulade, curried lobster mousse, and a terrine stuffed with pistachios. She excitedly showed Milly the shelves of cookbooks she had discovered in the attic and organ-ized in a bookcase she had moved into the kitchen.

"My sister-in-law Carol collected them, but she stuck to plain cooking in the diner."

"Well, I'll fix the usual stuff and see if I can start a dinner house with some French dishes."

"I admire your ambition. But it's going to be uphill, Allison."

The captain called them to attention, had the documents signed, and began the ceremony by reading from a weatherbeaten Bible. Allison cried when he said: "Do you, Christopher James Arnold, take this woman, Allison Desmond, to be your lawful wedded wife?"

Terry took out a crescent-shaped gold wedding band engraved "C to A," which he placed on her finger. They kissed as though in a trance.

Pat, who had finally signed on as a witness, grumbled to little effect and awkwardly pecked Allison's cheek.

"I will do anything to gain your respect and friendship," she said to him, holding his rough hands.

"Promise me that no matter what happens, you won't let Terry down or betray him."

"The secret's safe with me. I swear on Sean's life, no one will ever know."

The atmosphere took on a more convivial tone when they dined on lamb noisettes in a Madeira wine sauce, garnished with duchess potatoes filled with a hint of pâté de foie gras and asparagus tips in lemon butter. Pat and the captain unfurled compliments to Allison. She anxiously waited for her husband to approve. Terry raised his glass to her.

"I found this book by Escoffier. I don't know if I'm pronouncing his name right. Well, he invented these dishes. And I'm his student."

When the Cherries Jubilee were lighted, Sean woke with a cry, and Pat picked him up cautiously, soothed him tenderly, and beamed when his grandson settled down.

He leaned over to Allison. "I have a personal favor to ask. Can I have Sean for the night? You might not trust me, but you know how reliable Milly is." He waited for her response. "It'll give you and *Chris* over there some time alone."

Terry was gratified to see that his father had warmed to Allison. She and Sean would not be cut off. It would be a fragile bridge, but they'd have his family.

Milly said, "It'll be a treat having our grandson."

"Okay," Terry reluctantly agreed. "We'll pick him up in the morning. I'm due to fly back to L.A. at eleven." He thought aloud. "That'll get me in at one."

Allison packed a bag for the baby while Pat reloaded his flask with Courvoisier. "I'll prove myself to you, Pat," Allison said, handing him the baby. "I'll make this work."

"I hope to God you will."

With a crisp hundred-dollar bill and bottle of champagne under his arm, the captain departed. Outside in a fog-shrouded pelting rain, Terry took his father's arm. "I want you to know how much I appreciate this. I love you, Dad."

Pat embraced him and struggled to ward off his tears.

"It's a fearful choice you've made. I so want you to have a good life."

When they were alone, Allison handed Terry a glass of champagne and they flopped onto a large club chair by the fire.

"Do you think of *her* when you're with me?"

"No, I think of you all the time." He curved his arm under her back. "We should make it a rule and not talk about her because it hurts me. I'm not some two-faced cheat. This has taken a toll on me. I'm not having my cake and eating it too."

He had a dismal insight. If he hadn't married Allison, he might eventually have found a quarrel with Valerie, which would have culminated in divorce. It would have been a cheap and unscrupulous way out. She placed on his finger a gold band with a worn engraving.

"I found it in a little antique store in the village. Will you wear this when we're together?"

The ring fitted and he peered at the inscription. "What is this word? I can barely read it."

"*Mizpah* . . . it's from Genesis . . . 'The Lord watch between me and thee, when we are absent one from another.' "

"I love you, Allison. But sooner or later you'll despise me for using you."

"I won't complain about that just now, Ter."

Her eyes beckoned him. Flushed from the fire, she opened three buttons of her dress so that the tender flesh of her voluptuous cleavage was exposed. She wove his hand under her dress along her smooth thighs, unlocking his fantasies.

"What are you thinking?" he asked.

"Only of this moment and our rapture."

41

Pat was in a philosophical mood as he drove with Milly and his grandson back to Port Rivers. "Allison is pure sexual attraction."

"I think you're dead wrong about that, Pat. They have a love that's special, unique." Milly took a sip of brandy again. "Keep your eyes on the road, Pat. We'll settle Sean down and then I'll be your victim. Take you to a wedding and you go home with a rocket. I love you, though. Cheating on me and all. Now get us back in one piece."

"Thing I adore about you, Milly, is you're a wild animal and nobody knows but me."

"You'll be having your favorite grief from me tonight."

Juices roiling, Pat turned into his serene dark lane. Suddenly, he was forced to slam on the brakes, spinning into his own driveway and almost rear-ending the car blocking the garage. The brandy dripped off Milly's lips, and Sean gave a rasping cry.

Hollering, Pat jumped out of his car, brandishing a fist at the driver. The car in his driveway gave off nasty alcohol fumes from its heater, and the windows were fogged. He yanked open the car door. A haggard woman came out into the air.

"I'm very cold."

"Valerie? What are you doing here?"

She was extremely pale, careworn, and underneath her

sodden raincoat, she wore only a thin gray dress.

"I had to see Terry. I've been calling all day and there's never any answer."

Pat snaked away, huddled indecisively with Milly, and assisted her into the house with the baby. It was that rare occasion when words wouldn't come and his mind refused to respond. He rushed to the sideboard for whiskey, spilling it on the carpet in his eagerness.

"Terry mentioned something about interviewing witnesses, Milly. Where are they?"

Milly set the baby on a sofa pillow. "Oh, I'm not sure."

Pat fell back on the contractor's razzle-dazzle patter he had perfected over a lifetime. "They're all over the county," he finally rasped. "There's a plot against me, Val—the realtors and the banks have joined forces to put me out of business. On most of the jobs, I'm the low bidder. That's set off a four-alarm fire!"

"They're trying to box Pat in. Terry's fighting to save him."

"See, Valerie, I don't pay anyone off, and in the building trade, they all expect bribes."

Pat's garrulousness aside, Valerie was bewildered by the way they avoided specifics about Terry's role. She asked for brandy, and Pat set down a brimming glass, sloshing it on the coffee table. The baby squirmed, crying. Pat remembered the diapers were in the car. He rushed out like a madman.

Milly thought quickly, hoping to pacify Val. "His name's Sean. He's my niece Allison's baby boy," she said, taking control and calming the suspicious wife.

"Put him on a towel, Milly. Let me have a look at him."

Pat dashed back with enough supplies for a Turkish bath. He bulled the furnace up to eighty, lit a fire, busied himself with Johnson & Johnson Baby Powder.

Valerie put her ear to the infant's chest, undid his diaper, took his pulse, felt his head. She cleaned him up, and called for a thermometer. The baby was short of breath, trying to cough up phlegm. She saw rose spots on his chest and stomach and started to ask questions when the mercury registered 104 degrees. He had diarrhea, streaked with green mucus, and his pulse was weak.

"We're going to have to get him to a hospital. Can you call your niece?"

Milly was aghast. "She's away for the night. She'll be back in the morning."

"This is an emergency. We can't wait that long. You'll have to sign him in and be the responsible party. How old is he?"

Pat crumpled into his armchair, squeezing his glass.

"I wasn't around when he was born. I guess he's a few weeks old," Milly replied.

Valerie regarded the two faces and knew that they had things to hide. "Was he born locally?"

"No, in India."

"India?" Valerie echoed.

"Allison was seeing the sights, shrines. She's a religious girl. She took one of these journeys of the soul."

"Is she a hippie?" Milly nodded. "Has she been nursing him?"

"Oh, yes."

"That's probably how he contracted it. I think he has Salmonella gastroenteritis. I hope there's no typhoid."

At ten the following morning, Terry and Allison found a note from Pat stuck in the door of the house:

EMERGENCY, SEAN SERIOUSLY ILL.
VALERIE ARRIVED! DON'T KNOW WHY.
WE'RE AT GOOD SAMARITAN.

When they rushed into the hospital, Sean was in a glass isolation room on a respirator. Two intravenous drips were plunged into his twiglike arms. In surgical masks, Valerie and several other doctors were around him, monitoring his vital functions.

Pat dragged Terry and Allison into a corner and explained the situation to the alarmed parents.

"She's trying to save his life."

Terry felt needles of anxiety puncturing his skin, then

gouging into his flesh when Valerie came toward them. Her eyes had an angry stillness when they rested on him, but moved off him and focused sympathetically on Allison. Terry stood a few feet away while Valerie questioned Allison. Standing frozen, he had no idea how to greet Valerie or what was going through her mind. Did she suspect? How could he explain anything?

"He doesn't have typhoid. I'm sure of that and so are the other doctors. But you might. It's Allison Arnold, isn't it?"

"Yes, doctor," Allison replied, looking wanly through the glass at her baby.

"People can carry the bacteria for months without knowing it, so it'd be a good idea to have yourself checked out. Especially your milk. You may have drunk contaminated water when you were in India."

Allison choked on her words and explained that she had no chills or fever and that her health was normal.

"Well, from what you're telling me, Mrs. Arnold, Sean wasn't delivered in ideal circumstances. Maybe the midwife was the carrier. There's no way of tracing this. People can be asymptomatic or even develop an immunity and still infect other people. Newborn infants are extremely susceptible once they're not protected by the mother's immune system."

Allison pleaded with Valerie. "Is he going to live?"

Valerie grimaced with fatigue, but her mood gave way to optimism. She reached out and took hold of Allison's hand, sensitive to this young mother's fears.

"I think so. The drug we're treating him with seems to be working. Sean's responding well to chloramphenicol. We've brought the fever down to a hundred. The other IV is a glucose and water solution." She put her arm around the mother's shoulder. "Don't be frightened, he was dehydrated and still is."

"I'll always be in your debt, Dr. Brett. I thank God you came up for a visit."

Valerie shot a glance at Terry. "It was a spur-of-the-moment thing. I got fed up waiting for my husband. But

I'm glad I was here for your baby. We want this boy to grow up and be somebody special."

Allison studied Valerie while she conferred with the other doctors. In spite of being exhausted, Valerie was extremely attractive, with a calm dignity, an assured voice. Allison could not help but extol the accomplishment and qualities of Terry's wife. She now fully grasped the reasons for his marriage to her. There was nothing despicable or contemptible about marrying someone like Valerie on the rebound. Dr. Valerie Brett had been Terry's healer and now she was hers.

Terry and Allison contritely listened to the local doctors praise Valerie. Valerie handed her white coat to a nurse, shivered in her flimsy dress, and finally nodded at Terry.

"I'm glad to see your father's not in jail. Are you ready to come home?" she asked Terry.

"Yes."

Val stopped at the nurses' station to sign some forms and the infant's chart. "I'll be out in a minute."

Despair consumed Allison's soul when Terry looked at her at the entrance of the hospital. She walked outside to the bus stop shelter where on a rainy night she had taken her first ride with Terry. Pat rolled down his window and furiously signaled that Valerie was coming through the doors.

"I'll be back when I can," Terry whispered.

"Are you sure?"

"You don't have to ask. I've got to leave now."

Valerie came beside her. "Thanks again, Dr. Brett," Allison said, gratefully embracing Terry's wife.

As they drove off, Allison limply waved and sat on the bench under the shelter. Her life had stopped once again.

Terry knew that the efficacy and the seductive impact of deception came directly from the person for whom it was designed, and its credibility depended on the conviction of the perjurer. After Pat dropped them off at the airport, Terry was on the verge of revealing the truth to Valerie;

but when she told him why she had come up, the intention was stillborn. She curled into the hollow of his shoulder.

"This wasn't something I wanted to discuss on the phone." She would wait until they were home before recounting the nightmarish spectacle she had witnessed at Jonah's house. Nothing must spoil this moment with Terry. "When you were gone for five days, I couldn't bear being without you a moment longer. The reason I didn't want you to leave for Port Rivers had nothing to do with the architect's plans. I was waiting for the results from my doctor. I got them the day after you left."

"What results?" he asked.

"I'm going to have a baby, Terry," she exclaimed with a burst of exuberance. "Our baby. You know how much I love children. Now we'll have our own."

Every nerve fiber within him wailed. He stroked her trusting face.

"I love you, Valerie, and I always will."

42

Terry was only vaguely aware of the fact that another year had passed. It was already the spring of 1967 and he often felt that he was being twisted and charred to a cinder on a spit. He was either making guilt-ridden excuses to Val about having to go out of town to see a client or passing a frenetic weekend with Allison and Sean.

During these furtive visits to Seacliff, he played with his firstborn son and occasionally ventured into the diner kitchen, scraped plates, and observed Allison working at the range with an old woman she had rehabilitated from the local mission. Two waitresses, wives of fishermen, handled the counter and tables. Business was brisk from 5:00 A.M. to 11:00, then there was a short lull of casual coffee drinkers. By noon, the place was jammed with customers who had pre-ordered Allison's meatloaf with a sherry mushroom sauce or the pot roast cooked in thickly textured wine gravy. The food that Allison turned out was now beyond anything produced by Milly.

"How do you do it?" Terry asked, after saying good night to one of the high school baby-sitters.

"Passion," she said, regaining her glow.

"How many hours a night do you sleep?"

"About five. Sean's an important sleeper now that he's recovered. He hasn't been sick a day since I brought him home from the hospital."

"Is five hours enough?"

She smiled. "When you're here, I can do with even less. Oh, Terry, I live for these days. I save up my good times and they see me through. I'm so lucky to have you, a business that's throwing off money, and our Sean."

He lovingly held her face in his palms and kissed her ears, her nose, her throat. Her excitement mounted.

"Your touch makes my blood boil. Terry, darling, take me to bed . . ."

She left their warm sheets at four in the morning, used the downstairs bathroom to shower and dress, and drew hearts with her lipstick on the mirror. At eight, Terry would wheel Sean to the diner in the new English pram he had bought, wipe the sweat off Allison's brow, steal a kiss and deliver French toast to a table on his way out, then floor his Ford pick-up to Port Rivers to make his plane back to Los Angeles.

The leisured days and nights he had complacently accepted as his due when he was a bachelor had been transformed into a diabolical race with time. When he was not in court defending one of Carl Klein's millionaire freebooters, he raced back to the house on the hill to be with Val and *their* newly born son, Aaron.

During that year, he managed to travel to three fictional business conferences and one imaginary seminar out of town in order to be with Allison and Sean. Another aspect of this Faustian pact became evident to Terry. It had nothing to do with the women. He had discovered the horrors of working in the large legal factory at

O'Callahan & Klein. He could not be master of his time or assimilate into the firm. He was jaded by criminal litigation and the endless days in court, defending clients he knew to be guilty. He was unhappy and stretched to the limit.

He was deeply embittered by the tactics Jonah Wolfe had employed to seduce Whiz Davis. And as for Jonah's treatment of Jane, Terry fell back on his legal training to subdue the murderous rage he felt. Although he and Whiz had never had a formal contract, Terry decided to waive the commission he was entitled to for having worked out terms with the Chicago Bulls. The fallout from Jonah's behavior worked in Terry's favor. Val now saw her father with his eyes, and without his urging, she vowed never to see him again or allow him to visit Aaron. With all pretence of a detente between Terry and Jonah buried, Terry had the hollow satisfaction of not having to tolerate his father-in-law in their new home. At the same time, Jonah's exile acted as a lever to Terry's professional life, for out of it the resolution of his counterfeit existence emerged. It was typically quirky and fortuitous.

Throughout his youth, Terry had admired athletes. The single reflex of their lives assumed a holiness, the air they breathed was rarefied. What they did had the mysterious significance of mountain climbing and the dedication of the priesthood. Terry's natural attraction to athletes kept him enthralled by these magicians. He observed in their rhythms a mystical gravity that defied Newton's law. It was his mission to safeguard their talent.

Val was confounded by his decision to quit and tried to persuade him to reconsider it. But Terry needed the freedom to travel in order to spend time in Seacliff without arousing Valerie's suspicions. Not even Billy Klein, his closest friend, could be trusted with his veiled other life.

While watching the NCAA finals on TV in the kitchen and feeding his infant son Aaron, Terry took the leap into the future.

"Val, I know what I'm doing. I've decided to represent professional athletes and market them."

Val looked up from her sprawling files. She brought her work home, determined to keep her patients' charts current.

"What kind of profession is that, Terry? Are you going to become some kind of agent?" she asked.

"Something like that. But I think it has a future."

"Oh, Jesus, Terry, what a waste! Is this some Hollywood trash that Billy Klein got you involved in?"

He had expected her support and was confronted by scorn.

"No. What makes you think Billy could influence me?"

"I don't know. It's just the sort of hustle he'd go for." Terry put Aaron on his shoulder and patted his back, but stared into space, and Val was afraid that she'd gone too far. Lost him. "Terry, living and working in L.A. and having a family is a tremendous adjustment for you. It's all happened so fast for both of us."

He measured her coldly. "Yeah, very fast. Val, you don't know anything about practicing law, except that you despise lawyers. If I were to sign you up to do abortions at UCLA instead of pediatrics, how would you like it?" She remained silent. "No? Not for you? Working for Carl Klein is the same as doing abortions for me."

Val slipped off her smeared glasses and made her way over stacks of *Sports Illustrated* magazines to nestle up against him.

"Oh, Terry, we're both burned out and I've been neglecting you!"

"No, babe, never."

"You want to leave the firm?"

"I'm in charge of their pervert collection and I can't go on with it. Carl's firm is packed with rich grifters, stock market insiders, and double dealers who'd steal the pennies off a dead man's eyes." There would be no more social amenities to observe or parties to dodge. "So do me a favor, Val: worry about your practice and I'll do what I want in mine. Believe me, we won't starve, and I won't live off your money."

"I never thought you would." She tried to fathom his

mood, which seemed less about changing his practice than something unspoken, enigmatic. "Are you having anxiety attacks again?"

"Only when I go to work and have to feed Gerber's Baby Food to criminals who want to pay Carl fifty thousand in cash—off the books—and I get a lecture about the law from him. I don't give a shit about the law any longer. There is none. We're living in a society of feral predators and *green* is the color of innocence."

They had never had such a rancorous discussion, and Val now perceived the level of Terry's depression, the hideousness of his professional life.

"You have such character, Terry."

"Oh, really? That's news from the front."

"Well, for me, it's not just a question of loving you to distraction, it's a case of idolizing a human being."

"That's a fundamental mistake and an evasion of the laws of rationality. I am fertile with deception."

"Not to me, Terry."

The newly incorporated firm of Sports Associates began its existence in a one-room ground-floor office on South Beverly Drive. Martha, Terry's secretary, signed aboard and supervised the purchase of two used IBM typewriters and the installation of a TV and four phones.

For Terry, it was a painless transition. He was happy to be on his own. He had already seen the possibilities. Professional athletes were little more than indentured servants. Team owners like Jonah and their partners made all the big money. General managers sent out contracts and the players either signed them or were put on suspension. If these uneducated college graduates—dumb kids is what they were—haggled with the front office, they were hammered, classified as troublemakers, not team players, and eventually traded or dropped.

Terry had done a few favors for some athletes he knew, run through their contracts, gotten them properly insured, and suggested some business investments. Word spread about this new lawyer, and young players gravitated to his office. Before anyone fully understood what was actually happening, including Terry, he had accumulated thirty clients who gladly paid him fifty dollars an hour. After a time, he set a percentage fee, brought in an accountant to do their taxes, and bookkeepers to see that their bills were paid. All the athlete had to worry about was playing ball.

At the same time, Billy Klein found himself in serious trouble. Impervious to discipline, he had been discharged by his uncle in disgrace after he was arrested with a client's wife and a stash of cocaine. Terry had talked the judge into a suspended sentence and saved Billy from disbarment. Terry took him into the firm. Gregarious to a fault, and adored by the press for his excesses and generosity, Billy provided the perfect front man for Terry.

The final member of the triumvirate was Mike Summers. Resigned to a life of frustration and obscurity, coaching JC basketball in Fond du Lac, Summers welcomed the opportunity to bring his family to Los Angeles, where he became a twenty-five percent partner of Sports Associates. It was a gamble, but the three men developed a powerful alliance and friendship. Each of them was fulfilling a dream.

Book V

SHADOWS IN THE DARK

43

By 1978, the business that Terry had stumbled into by expediency had made him and his partners all millionaires. No one questioned his frequent trips throughout the country to recruit players. With Terry traveling so much of the year, Valerie and their eleven-year-old son Aaron became a couple. Aaron was a frail, solitary, withdrawn boy, much like Valerie had been as a child. Aaron had her interest in science, and much to Terry's chagrin, found the ball games and sporting events that so excited his father to be uninteresting. Sharing Aaron's loneliness, Valerie decided to give up private practice and took a position as an assistant professor of pediatrics at UCLA medical school. She had more time for her son and lately she and Terry quarreled about his absences.

The Brett house was nestled in the Santa Monica Hills, a sprawling English estate of guesthouses, staff quarters, a grass tennis court, croquet lawn, vistas of the ocean, the undulations of the coastline as pleasing as a woman's smile. With Terry gone, it took on a wearied look, not of actual neglect, but rather like a gloomy station waiting for a train to arrive.

Terry faced another one of those crazed Christmas holidays. He awoke before daybreak. He didn't know who he was that morning or where he had slept. Through the years, these questions of identity and location had arisen countless times, always alarming him. The mystery would be resolved when he heard the voice of one of the women he loved. Only then would he feel safe. His credentials established, he could navigate through the dangerous shoals of the day. He had not lightly chosen these roles. A man possessed, he was always in flight.

He was adored by his two families and held in high esteem by his colleagues. But as far as he was concerned, he was a coward, a liar, a grand deceiver, gutless, and a backstabber. It hacked at him, splitting him apart, because the real Terry Brett was none of these things. He was honorable, a man of spirit, thoroughly trustworthy. Balancing this mercurial equation had become his life's work.

Eyes still tightly closed, he waited for his identity to be disclosed: Terry Brett or Chris Arnold.

"Terry, you up yet?"

It was Valerie curled up beside him, reaching out, smiling, stretching. He kissed her.

"Is this Christmas Day?"

"No, Christmas was yesterday. Today's the twenty-sixth."

He peered at the suitcases in the sitting area. Were they traveling? Where were they going?

"Terry, are you all right, honey?"

"Oh, sure."

Behind the placid exterior, he was frequently baffled. He could hardly keep up with himself or track his movements.

"Aren't you going to Chicago?"

She was puzzled. "No, Terry, I was there two weeks ago."

He was certain that Valerie had told him she'd be leaving for a medical convention in Chicago while he would be en route to one of those holiday basketball tournaments for small colleges. Actually, he was heading up to Seacliff and planned to return for New Year's Eve to be with Val. He stood in the middle of the bedroom, disoriented. Where was Aaron? He had misplaced his son.

"What's Aaron doing?"

"He's in Aspen at the ski school." Valerie sputtered through her toothpaste. "I don't mean to sound like a doctor. But, Terry, I'm glad we're taking this break. You really need it."

"We'll do it."

"Sweetheart, we are! We're meeting Aaron in Aspen."

"No, that can't be possible!"

"What are you talking about? You're the one who insisted Aaron go there to learn to ski. He went to please you. Don't you remember?"

Terry opened his attaché case and pulled out his appointment book.

"I apologize. This is a royal screw-up. I'm absolutely certain I mentioned the basketball tournament in Oregon. I'm arriving in Aspen on the thirty-first."

"Why can't Mike or Billy go?"

"They do. But I'm the *signer,* the one the families trust."

Valerie was furious. They had two sets of airline tickets for different places. Valerie checked her book, then studied his appointments when he was dressing. Terry gulped his coffee, grabbed his bag, and hugged her.

"Sorry about this, Val. It can't be helped. If I don't sign this kid, the firm's whole strategy for the year is up the creek. Everyone's counting on me. I'll see you for New Year's Eve, darling. And we'll stay a few extra days."

"I'm so pissed at you, Terry. You don't have to bother coming at all."

"Give me a break."

"Aaron's counting on you and so am I."

But Terry was out the door. He had his houseman Antonio speed him to the airport. At the last minute, he remembered he had Christmas presents in the trunk. By the time·he settled in his seat on the airplane, he was sweating and even more confused. He changed planes in Portland and flew in a single-prop puddle-jumper to Seacliff.

On the flight he was thrust back to the second year of their spurious marriage: Even though it was May, and Allison's birthday, they treated the occasion as a wedding anniversary.

There must have been some French-Dutch among the rogue genes in Allison's shadowy ancestry, for she had developed into the ultimate housewife—everything dusted, linen fresh, floors polished, cedar cubes in the drawers, potpourri in the bathrooms. Sartre and Camus topped her advanced reading list and existentialism had edged out mysticism in her literary canon.

"I live by the sea," Allison said gaily, "so I'm pretending it's Normandy. Ter, will I ever go to Europe with you? Couldn't we take a trip? I want to go to museums, buy lace panties in Paris, and sit on a bench with you in the Bois de Boulogne. Have you all to myself."

The very depth of his deception was exposed and he felt crushed by Allison's desire and Valerie's amiable trust. Never once had she questioned Terry about his long trips.

"I wish we could."

Bright-eyed with enthusiasm, Allison drifted into the latitude of forlornness. "One day, I'll have to take a step beyond dreams. . . . In *Summer in Algiers,* Camus said: 'If there is a sin against life, it consists perhaps not so much in despairing of life as in hoping for another one.' "

To get his attention, Sean in his playpen had bopped his rattle like a boxer on the speed bag. Terry stooped to play with his infant son and watched Allison in her kitchen, fragrant with pungent smells of rosemary, shallots, and garlic from her herb garden, and sweet 100s tomatoes in a pottery bowl that they would eat like grapes. She had become a magician.

Although his visits were infrequent, he gained ten pounds that year feasting on her rich boeuf Bourguignon, the legs of lamb. She cooked at night, using the kitchen as a laboratory, then brought the food into the diner he had bought for her from Milly. Allison was transforming it into a small bistro, cooking her way through the bible of some long-dead famous French chef whose name he now forgot. She experimented with curried oysters and explored the French language with Berlitz tapes. With the babble of French in the background, baguettes baking in the oven, dodine de canard with confit for dinner, Sean sucking on an end of croissant, he might have been in a farmhouse along the coast of France.

But it was during those clinging nights when her hands were glued around his waist, the two of them cleaving to each other, that he knew he would always be her prisoner. She had bought an old Provençal mirror, placing it at the foot of the bed so that they could watch themselves.

"*Ma glace d'amour.* When you're away, you'll imagine you see us."

He had never met anyone for whom he was so perfectly suited. There wasn't a bad day with Allison. Her sense of adventure, and the way she struggled to educate herself, were a source of deep pride to him. She was recreating herself.

44

It was a cloudy afternoon in Seacliff, with snow squalls biding time, the small airport deserted. Terry waited for a cab to turn up. He hadn't been sure that he could catch the flight and told Allison not to meet him. He had been delayed repeatedly on other trips and she and Sean might wait hours—sometimes all night—when he missed a connection or had been on a recruiting mission in another part of the country and socked in at the airport.

These journeys to Seacliff were seldom planned, making his appearances as inexplicable as those of Merlin. In his life with Allison, he was Chris Arnold. To Sean his son and admirer, Chris worked for the CIA, leading secret missions, the nemesis of Communists in East Berlin. All very hush-hush. Like aces, lies ran in pairs, and Terry channeled this fable into Sean's mind to account for his absences and sporadic letters. When Terry wrote to Sean, it was on CIA stationery with the agency's letterhead produced by his legendmaker. If someone Terry knew was going abroad, he ensured that a letter with foreign stamps would be posted to Sean Patrick Arnold. He explained that he had a young friend who collected foreign stamps.

Terry's throat was tight and he was short of breath as he hurtled up the driveway of the Seacliff cottage. He found Sean in the back garden with a stack of firewood in his arms. The logs flew through the air, clumped to the ground, and Sean sprinted to him.

"Oh, Dad, Dad, Dad! You came. I knew you would!" Sean looked at his face. A piece of tissue had stuck to Terry's neck. "Were you wounded?"

"No, no, I must've cut myself shaving."

"You look tired. Was it a long flight?"

"We had a layover."

"Where?"

Terry thought quickly. "Greenland."

Sean's mouth widened. "Greenland," he said in wonderment. "Did you see any Eskimos on dogsleds?"

"Yeah, they were picking up provisions at the airport."

"We're studying about them in school." With enthusiasm and faulty intelligence, Sean tracked his father's fabled journeys as well as possible. "The weather report in the paper said it was snowing in Berlin."

"Yes, Ace, it was very cold there."

Terry had devised a system of nicknames, which worked for his two sons. Dreading a mistake, whenever he was frazzled, he fell back on Ace for both Sean and Aaron. To the boys he, too, was Ace.

"How did your mission go?"

"It was a tricky one."

"What about the spy—the double agent—you were worried about last time you were here?"

"We caught him," Terry said obligingly.

Sean beamed proudly at the hero, but he could not suppress the apprehension that attended his father's absences.

"Last week, I read about the Commie border guards shooting some people going over the wall. I pray to God every night that you'll be safe. Oh, Daddy . . . Daddy."

"Ace, you have to stop worrying." The boy's anxiety and fearfulness upset him. "I'm not really in danger."

"Dad, I've missed you so much. I dream about you every night."

"I've missed you too, Ace. I'm really fine now."

"When you didn't get leave for Thanksgiving, we

weren't sure you'd make it this year. Mom's still at the bistro, finishing the lunch buffet."

Terry picked up the apple-cheeked, solid thirteen-year-old boy who bounced loud kisses off his cheek. Terry crept inside with his son, always circumspect about intruders, like a burglar casing a job. The Christmas tree lights sparkled in the entryway and several packages were underneath. Allison had become acquisitive, always out hunting for antiques for the house and the diner, which had been renamed "Allison's Bistro." He noticed a Victorian grandfather clock at the end of the hall; a seaman's steamer trunk pressed into service as an occasional table; a Chinese urn holding potpourri. Apart from the Sony TV and a stereo, Allison regarded anything new as junk. She had in the course of time completely redone the house.

Everywhere there were books: on cooking, needlepoint, European history and philosophy, and the novels of the masters. Flaubert, Stendhal, Balzac, and Proust had given way to Tolstoy and Dostoyevsky.

"I made halfback on the freshman football team. I've got practice in a little while. Please come and watch, Dad."

"Let's see what your mother wants to do."

"I don't care if she comes. I want you there."

A flood of sadness burst through Terry's soul for this sweet, good-natured, lonely boy he loved.

" 'Course I'll come."

He handed Sean his Christmas present and waited with childlike anticipation for him to open it. Through the commissioner's office at the NFL, Terry had secured a prize that would thrill his son. Sean wildly tore open the paper and dug into the box. A look of consternation muddled his eyes.

"The Young Scientist's Gilbert Chemistry Set, huh?" Another box exposed "a microscope? Isn't this what the doctor listens to your heart with? A stethoscope?"

No, no, no—these gifts were intended for Aaron. Sean was to receive a signed Raider's football and a helmet celebrating their victory in last year's Super Bowl.

"I don't get it, Dad."

"You . . . uh, can do experiments at home."

"I'm not that interested in science."

Terry was in turmoil, furious with himself. "Well, I thought . . . look, the truth is, there's been a mix-up. I guess I left your other presents on the plane. I'll buy you something else."

"Don't worry, Dad. You don't have to. Having you home is the best present of all."

Sean helped him unpack, folding his sweaters and putting them in the dresser. Allison now had a maple four-poster in the bedroom with a Persian tapestry bedspread. A china pitcher was filled with mums. The lace curtains were freshly laundered and the love mirror focused with a camera's directness on the bed. The sun bit through a seam of clouds and Terry tingled with the thrill of soon being alone with her. In a silver chalice on his bedside table was his gold wedding band and he slipped it on his finger. The odor of wine directed him to the kitchen, where a broad copper pot held a simmering coq au vin.

"I put it on to cook an hour ago," Sean said. "When I asked Mom when it'll be ready, she said when you get home."

They laughed at the absurdity, relaxed by the fire, and drank Cokes while Sean drew him into his own world, vastly different from Aaron's. One lived in a fortress, the other outside the walls. Should Sean smoke like some of the other boys? What did you actually do with girls when they let you put your hand between their legs? Did you use a rubber for such an occasion or were you safe without one? Aaron already knew the answers, and unlike Sean, he could clinically describe the reproduction process.

Sitting on his father's lap on the leather club chair, Sean tightly locked his fingers around Terry's wrist.

"I gotcha. You're never going to leave again. Promise me."

"Wish I could, Ace."

In a little while, flushed and bouncy, Allison danced in, carrying a magnum of champagne. Her hair was long and wild again and she smelled of brandy and pine needles. She would be thirty-two in May and her beauty had ripened into an otherworldly pre-Raphaelite sensuality. Terry was reminded of Allison even when he was at home with Valerie, who had inherited Rossetti's *Roman de la Rose* from her mother's estate. It hung over the fireplace in the house in Santa Monica, an imminent encapsulation of their plight. When Terry couldn't sleep, he would sit in front of the painting, nursing a brandy and captive to its bewitchment. In the Rossetti painting a knightly couple were seen kissing as an angel of darkness shadowed them with its black wing.

She embraced Terry. "Welcome home, squire."

"Good to be here."

The split second after they kissed, Sean barreled in between them.

"We've got to go. Dad's going to football scrimmage with me."

Allison winked wickedly at Terry and whispered, "Anticipation makes the heart grow fonder." Then to Sean, "Get your gear and give me a minute with your father—alone, please."

Terry pressed his lips against her cold cheeks. "I missed you."

"Did you? Keeping you pretty busy in L.A., huh?"

"Unfortunately. Allison, I'm losing it. There's been a terrible mix-up. I'm supposed to be in Aspen."

Allison's fragile gaiety vanished and she succumbed to panic, never far below the surface. She shrank back.

"Are you here just for the night—a few hours?"

"We've got five days." She collapsed in his arms as though he'd granted her a reprieve. "How long does Sean's football practice last?"

"Oh, around five-thirty." She pouted. "Maybe you can slip away."

"What about the social niceties?"

"Save them for civilization. You're in the wild now."

"What've you got in mind?"

Her mouth broadened in a lush smile. "You and me."

"Oh, really? Well, Allison, you're going to have to ask very nicely. Coax me."

"What about begging, will that do?"

He started to laugh. "Like a dog?"

"Drooling with a wet tongue." .

"Sounds good."

"We're wild animals up here in the provinces."

Sean was between them hugging them both, then full of energy, yanking his father away. Terry was barely able to kiss Allison. .

45

After an hour at the school field, Terry was exasperated to find that lights had been installed and that football practice was no longer called because of darkness. He sat behind the Seacliff bench, nodding to a stray father, and took pleasure in observing Sean's powerful moves. However, the expert on athletic prowess soon determined that his son was too slow and blocked more naturally than he ran. Maybe he'd be a linebacker in high school. He could forget basketball; the gliders and acrobats had taken over the game. During a break for coach instruction, Terry crept away.

A pot of caviar with toast points, champagne and flutes icing in a bucket were outside the bedroom. Allison stood smiling inscrutably at herself, adoring the return of her cycle with Terry. She glanced at herself in the mirror, bikini white silk panties, her nipples tense, her sumptuous breasts heaving, an invitation to a feast. The moist scent of her new Vitabath invaded the air, thickening it like humidity. Gracefully turning, the princess extended a hand to her frog.

Terry closed the door and undressed.

Everything about Allison suggested something untamed, a woman living in a world he had yet to fully explore. Would he ever really know her? He was always captivated by their erotic rites.

They drank a glass of champagne and enjoyed the solitude. Allison studied their naked images in the mirror as though their reality existed only in reflections. He cradled her on his chest and moved his hand along her breasts.

"I didn't think it was possible, but I love you more all the time, Allison."

"You are everything to me. The giver of my life. I wish I didn't have to say this. I can't help it"—she was tearful—"I worry about you so much. You fly all the time. There are plane crashes. I watch them on the news."

"You and Sean are provided for. Allison, I've made millions doing something I love. I can't tell you how much satisfaction I get from helping these young athletes. They were being ripped off by the team owners since sports began. They've got homes and security now."

"That's not what I mean. You're stretched out so far. You can't ever make a mistake. People need some leeway. How do you keep it all straight?"

"I don't know. Maybe it's a habit now."

"Oh, Terry. There're so many times when I feel like our love is destroying you and you'll snap."

He constantly seemed to be fighting against a permanent state of fatigue. He refused to admit to himself and certainly never to her that the burden was becoming unendurable. In Valerie's arms, he closed his eyes and pursued Allison. When he was with Allison, he imagined he saw the sensitive, troubled, perplexed face of Valerie. There was no mistaking it, beneath the surface, Valerie was suffering. He vanquished these thoughts, yielding to the murmurs of Allison's breath and the shadows of desire that mocked him when he was with Valerie.

"My darling, I'm going to hold you all night long," she said, "and crawl into your skin."

"Maybe we'll never have to get up again and face the world."

He had changed into comfortable, baggy old gray cords, a plaid shirt and sweater, all from the JC Penney catalogue. At the door Allison stood naked. She took the pea jacket she had bought for him off the rack at an Army-Navy store and helped him on with it, kissing his neck.

"You're back and *we're* alive. It's a miracle."

He was mesmerized by Allison. "I'll *always* come back to you. I'm going to pick up our guy."

Terry found a muddied, bruised Sean waiting for him outside the football field in the empty parking lot. A film of snow thrashed in the wind as they walked home along the cliffside. Like seamen on a heaving deck, they linked arms. Below them foam flowers raced to the beach, entangled by rocks in the churning sea. They settled into tranquil companionship.

"Uncle Pat and Aunt Milly stayed over for Thanksgiving."

"You have a good time?"

"Great. I love him. He's so good to me. I finally got to use the .22 you bought me last year."

"What did you do?"

"Went hunting for deer."

"You get one?" Sean was abashed and hesitated. "Come on."

"I learned how to shoot and I had my first taste of brandy."

Terry began to laugh. "Sounds like Pat. How many did you have?"

"A couple. But the next day, I had the cavalry firing cannons in my head."

In the new family configuration, Milly was Allison's aunt and Pat Brett her husband. The lies they had devised now had the weight of a biography of their own, solidified through time. These hardy seeds, nurtured by the four conspirators, had sprouted into a towering family tree. As the inventor of this history, Terry became convinced that he had helped achieve an ideal childhood for Sean.

When they arrived at the cottage, he accompanied Sean to his room, which was a treasure trove of sports memorabilia Terry had sent up to him. On the dresser was an album with his letters, sent from the CIA.

"Aches and pains?" Terry asked.

"I've got some lulus."

"Maybe you should take up tennis or golf," he said, and Sean laughed. Terry took out a small jar and opened it. "Come on, Ace, strip off, I'm going to rub you down, like the pros."

"What is this stuff?"

"It's Tiger Balm, comes from Hong Kong. Athletes call it 'red hot.' "

Terry worked on the boy's arms and legs, then kneaded his shoulders and back, delighting in the well-formed muscles and power of Sean's physique, which he had inherited from his sturdy mother, along with her coloring and eggshell blue eyes. He was an amazing replication of Allison.

"Catch forty and then shower for dinner," he said to his dozing son.

He and Allison had a quiet drink by the fire while Sean showered, and then in new pajamas with the tag still on, Sean lay on the rug, resting his head on Terry's slippers. Occasionally, he would look up with wonder at the figure of his father, the dauntless warrior shielding not merely his family—but the nation. Terry ran a hand through Sean's thick hair. His son was doing well in school and Allison told him that Sean could skip a grade, but she didn't want to rush his education. Terry agreed.

I belong here with them.

Another part of him violently resisted the break with Valerie and the terrible loss of his dazzling, brilliant Aaron. Even in these sweet moments, Terry felt the spur of guilt, the ordeal of perpetual deception. All through dinner he was distracted, looking at Allison, with desire humming, wanting her again.

"Ski lesson tomorrow, Sean. Then we'll hotdog down the slopes," Terry said. Then it dawned on him. He had sent the wrong son for ski lessons. Poor frightened Aaron was in Aspen alone. The boy had cried and pleaded not to go. He hated snow. Aaron had been planning a chemical experiment, which Valerie was to supervise. He would be without the master Gilbert Chemistry Set.

Sean rose, stretched, and smiled. "A family day skiing sounds great. For being such a wonderful dad, I'm going to go to bed quietly this time and leave you and Mom."

"Don't be smirking at us, mister," Allison said.

Terry kissed his broad forehead and watched Allison's swaying walk to the kitchen. She brought in coffee.

"I also made Napoleons for you."

"Do I get to eat the cream off your belly?"

"Oh, well, if you're good. You're really insatiable. Maybe we'll have to call these events something like 'Occasional evenings at Allison's,' and I'll bake a pan of Alice B. Toklas's hash brownies."

"You wouldn't."

"Shit, no, I gave up good smoke for you."

"Allison—"

"Yes."

"Nothing."

"Nothing with you is usually serious stuff."

Terry enticed her on his lap and she slipped his hand under her bright yellow cashmere sweater. The sensation of her flesh always tantalized him. Even more satisfying was the erotic boldness of her compliance. She lifted up her turtleneck and he kissed her warm shoulders. He realized that his love for Allison transcended any risk. She finally wriggled away and faced a sink of dishes.

"Don't clean up right now. We can eat everything tomorrow. You always liked food a day old, didn't you?"

"Oh, Terry, you're so evil. Back then, I didn't know anything." She kissed him. "I was living in a tent when I met you."

"An air-conditioned tent, Mrs. Arnold."

In the bedroom, he had a copy of *Howard's End* in paperback on his night table. He couldn't remember where his place was. On Allison's side was Turgenev's *Fathers and Sons,* along with the omnipresent dictionary. Carrying a bottle of brandy under her arm and Napoleons on a tray, Allison nearly lost her balance. He leaped out of bed like a rocket and took the bottle. As though on a picnic, she carefully arranged the tray, glasses, napkins, plates, and forks over a linen cloth.

Allison climbed into bed and served. She seldom had an opportunity to discuss her daily obligations and asked his advice about plans for building a roof garden above the diner. She also wanted to purchase a new spit roast to use outdoors during the summer.

"Maybe it's frivolous, but what I'm aiming for is the ambiance of a French country inn. Business is picking up." She was concerned about the money involved. "Is it a problem?"

"That's the last thing to worry about. Spend whatever you need. I've become a millionaire because of you."

"You always cared about athletes. I adore you, Terry."

"I love you more than ever, Allison. The way you've raised Sean makes me so proud. I only wish—"

"It's fine, Terry. Don't get down on yourself."

"The last few times I've been here, Sean seems nervous." She hesitated and Terry stared at her. "Is he okay?"

"It's nothing to worry about. But he has a sense that something's out of whack. He gets hyperactive and then he starts to panic."

"Have you taken him to the doctor?"

"When he had his last checkup, I asked the doctor about it."

Terry was disturbed. "What did he say, Allison? Is there a diagnosis?"

"Oh, he feels it's just a phase, the onset of puberty. That sort of thing. Nothing to worry about."

"What do you think?"

"Sean's high-strung and he gets unsettled. It's not a big deal."

Allison snuggled in his arms and they started to get comfortable when the doorbell rang. "It's just Nancy with the dinner receipts. We don't use the night deposit when the weather's this bad," she explained.

"Kiss her good night, fast as you can."

"Will do."

Allison slipped on a new scarlet silk robe with a gold initial "A" that she had saved for Terry's visit. She had bought it during one of her rare outings to Port Rivers. Terry switched on the TV to the local news and dimmed the lights. The grizzled weatherman pointed to a chart, indicating a low pressure system. Suddenly, Allison burst in.

"You better come quickly!"

She dashed out and Terry heard her voice quiver. She was saying something about Sean. Terry grabbed his old sheepskin bathrobe.

Valerie was standing by the dying embers of the fire in the living room.

She heard him come in and without turning, said, "Are you dressed or have I interrupted you?"

The invasion made him feel tainted and somehow dirty.

"I'm dressed—and, yes, you have interrupted something."

"I see your magical Roman goddess is back from the dead." Valerie sighed wearily. "But her name is Allison Arnold and not Maia, isn't it? I'll believe anything you tell me, so why don't you try?"

Allison shuddered, clutching her arms tightly around her shoulders.

"Please, Dr. Brett, let's not have a scene. My son's asleep in the other room."

"Didn't Terry, or whatever his name is, tell you I don't scream? Not even when I have an orgasm. I've been house-trained into submission."

Valerie lost her trend of thought when her eyes fell on the wedding band on Terry's finger. She wanted to strike him, stick his hand in the fire. Her anger swelled, reaching a peak. The chemistry set and microscope which *she,* not Terry, had specially ordered for Aaron lay on the floor under a side table. She had put it in the trunk of his car the night before. When she discovered it was missing at the airport, every aspect of Terry's behavior converged into unassailable suspicion.

In the confusion of the morning, Valerie, ever credulous, had looked in Terry's appointment book and found a ticket to Seacliff. It was made out in the name of "Chris Arnold."

After Terry left for the airport, she had called Aspen and spoken to Billy Klein. He had agreed to pick up Aaron at the ski camp. Without thinking, or premeditation, she innocently asked if Chris Arnold was the player Terry had gone to scout. Billy did not recall a player by that name, nor did Terry's other partner, Mike Summers. The entire party was awaiting their arrival in Aspen.

The Seacliff operator was very obliging. Although there was no Chris Arnold listed locally or in Port Rivers, there was an Allison Arnold. The name "Allison" struck a chord from the past.

"Terry, you were in such a hurry to leave that you got careless." Val's eyes roved over the two of them, their faces flushed and penitent. "It's another example of your contempt for me."

"Valerie, listen to me," Terry said, approaching her. She glared at him, raised her hand, and shoved him away.

"I didn't come here to listen to anything you have to say." She scowled at Allison, who waited cautiously for her to resume. "Does integrity—oh, forget that. How about common decency—does that mean anything to either of you? And what about Aaron?" She pointed accusingly at Allison. "*My* son's father sees him once in a blue moon. Terry never has time for him. My Aaron has been put on a shelf." Her eyes roved over Allison's cowering face. "And what about your son? *I* saved his life. Does he know who his father really is?"

Valerie lowered her face and shook her head; the pain of it was unbearable.

"Terry, I save lives, I don't trash them. If you want to trash me and Aaron, let's trash everyone while we're at it. I'm not prepared to be your martyr or have Aaron tossed into limbo."

"What do you want us to do, Valerie?"

"It's what you want. I have no idea if that marriage band you're wearing is real or for show." Valerie was wobbly and he implored her to sit down, but she shook him off. "You lie to this woman and lie to me and what good does it do? Whatever the hell your reasons might have been for this twisted double life, well, they don't make up for the humiliation. Nobody's important. Not her or me." She stabbed the air at Allison. "You as a mother know how cherished and precious your son is. I mean, when you were at the hospital and thought he was dying—When was it? I can't remember how many years ago—I can't forget the love and concern on your face. You couldn't have been faking it. What's this going to do to your boy for the rest of his life? Have you ever thought of that, Allison?"

With her robe sleeve, Allison wiped the tears from her eyes.

"*I* am also Terry's wife."

Valerie had forced herself to remain dignified and calm, but this disclosure stunned her and she flared up. "If that's true and it comes out, it could mean prison, Terry. You're the sharp lawyer. Can you get out of that one?"

"Val, we never wanted to hurt you," Terry said, looking at her with sympathy and tenderness. He wanted to console her, but she rose above it to save what was left of herself.

"Did Terry ever mention what he was like when you dumped him? He was an emotional cripple. He crashed and had a nervous breakdown. *I* put him back on his feet. *I* gave him a reason to face life and to make something of himself. And Allison, I assure you, I'm not deluded when I tell you he was happy. That *I* made him happy! Or I thought I did . . ."

Valerie lost control of herself and began banging her head against the wall. Allison pulled her back, but Valerie wrested away from her touch. She was wailing inconsolably.

"Milly and your father. My God, what a joke they must think I am. All of you were in this vicious plot against Aaron and me! Why, why? Terry, how did we harm you? If you didn't want us, then you should have been man enough to ask for a divorce."

At first Terry was too shaken to respond. "The truth is, I didn't want to lose you."

"But you've lost everything now. Terry, I'm not going to go on paying for your misery. Or be a victim so you can whitewash your conscience. This is the real world and you've played a murderous game with people's lives. Your way isn't the right one. It never was and never could be."

Valerie hurried out, stumbling down the twisting path, falling headlong in the fresh snow. She staggered to a waiting taxi. The driver came out and warmly greeted Terry and Allison. Valerie was staying at the Wayfarers Arms. Terry knew its chilled, narrow rooms, the drunken fishermen at the bar with their itinerant whores.

"Don't worry," Valerie said. "I'll be gone tomorrow. I'm not important, Allison, none of us are. But the children are sacred to me. And this has to end."

46

Allison dreaded the consequences, the exposure. The dead Chris Arnold would be unearthed at a trial. Terry's career would be over. She would lose the history, the respectability that she had aspired to, won, and which had sheltered her confidence. She and Sean could move to another town after Terry came out of prison, change their names, but the stigma would follow them. Sean would not only be their hostage but also the fugitive of their love.

In her heart, she had no grievance with Valerie *Brett*. She had wronged a remarkable, generous woman. It was obvious to Allison that she would always loiter as the outsider, the poacher, who had snaked her way into another woman's garden in order to steal the fruit in the orchard. Gloomily, drinking brandy with Terry by the fireplace, Allison searched for a way out. Valerie's doom-laden words reverberated: "And this has to end."

I must rescue Terry before he destroys himself and all of us with him. If this came out, it would devastate Sean. I have to keep him innocent.

"Terry, please go to her. Don't leave it this way. She might do . . . do anything."

"If I have to go jail, then I will."

In this mood he was intractable. Allison was numb. "You can't. You'll lose everything—your good name, your business. What and who you are. I can't let you go through this."

"Maybe I deserve it. Once I was a criminal lawyer, and now I can see that punishment has a purpose. There was a covenant between us which I broke."

"Stop it. That's self-pity."

"I'm not looking for any self-serving excuses either. I've cheated, lied, been dishonorable."

A solution slowly dawned on Allison. In anguish, she knew that she had no choice but to set him free.

"You think you have. What you did was nothing compared to me. When I look back, I realize how easily I trapped you."

He was astounded by the remark. "What the hell're you talking about?"

"Come on, I was Earl Raymond's girl all along. He needed a lawyer to defend him and you were his last hope. We planned it. Earl said I was your type. A needy case you could play God with and reform."

Terry's mouth quivered, for he had detected the old Allison, the outlaw who could effortlessly rationalize her actions. This was a side of her that had lain dormant like a malevolent virus and sprang forth when it detected weakness.

"No," he protested. "You and Earl? I don't believe this. You never slept with him, did you?"

"I set you up, so you'd take Earl's case against Jonah Wolfe."

Terry's throat constricted and his thought processes went haywire. Something deep within him was being crushed.

"You forgot to mention that in the letter you wrote

from India," he said caustically. "You were on a religious pilgrimage, purifying your soul. I loved you so much, I was fighting every day for my sanity and not to commit suicide." He dropped to his knees. "I believed in you. I trusted you."

Allison relentlessly slashed at his defenses. "What was I supposed to do? I was broke and homeless, with a busted leg. Terry, I did fall in love with you. I wanted to tell you about Earl the first night you gave me a ride outside the hospital. Get it out of the way. See if we had anything going. Instead, I gave you a hard time. If I hadn't, you would have treated me like garbage. Terry, you were my dream, don't you grasp that yet? I was nobody, going nowhere."

Everything had collapsed for him. He had torn Valerie and himself apart. He stared at Allison with rage:

"I jeopardized everything for you. I've destroyed everyone. And I thought, no, what I've done wasn't really wrong. After awhile, I convinced myself that we'd made something together. Part of a life with a son we love. No, it's not perfect."

Allison strode into the bedroom, put on jeans and a sweater, and she looked like the tough, hardened street girl he had met years ago.

"I lied to Valerie and deceived our son so you could have a fucking meal ticket."

Through the accusations, Allison caught fire. "Ever wonder about me? The thousands of nights alone. I force myself not to think of you with Valerie. Making love to her. Going to sleep together, waking up together, laughing together. Having a complete life *together*." She snarled at him. "And goddamn it, I can't hate the woman because she saved Sean's life. But I'm jealous of every breath she takes beside you. Ask yourself, Terry, who was cheated most in this?"

Allison stared at the bed she had made earlier with such exhilaration. On it were the crisp linen sheets and the lace pillows she had ordered from Ireland months ago. She had done everything imaginable to please Terry and make him feel that she offered whatever comforts he might have with Valerie.

"I hear you and Earl laughing at me."

"Earl was too serious and motivated to laugh much. Funny, why you never asked me if he and I were making it? I wonder why. Weren't you curious?" she added, taunting him. "Oh, but you were doing murder cases then, and defense lawyers aren't supposed to question their clients about whether they chopped their kid's head off."

The turmoil within him built and he fought to hold on to his lucidity. "You're right about that. I never confronted a client with a question I didn't know the answer to. In my business, which you don't know shit about, Allison, I still do. If I had any suspicions about Earl, they were consumed by you. I was overwhelmed by your tragic life. I wanted to make it all new and good."

"Come on, Terry, admit that you wanted to get out of this phony bullshit life with me for years. You've got your chance, amigo. Take it. This running back and forth is burning you out. Me, I'll do just fine. *I* really can look after myself."

The sight of Allison now repelled him. Terry dressed in the cold, lifeless bedroom with its rank, spilled brandy and curdled cream. He conquered their collective deceptions, once more transcended his emotions, and evolved into what he was—a lawyer.

"We have a final decision to make. I want to be able to see Sean. I'll send him to Pat for the time being and visit him there. Then I'm taking him home with me, where he can have a decent life without a fucking whore for a mother. If you want to go to court, I'll look forward to it. Even if I have to go to prison, I'll fight you for Sean!"

Allison called upon all of her resources and saw through this legal armor. She struck with suddenness.

"I'll look forward to it, too, Counselor."

Her defiance disconcerted him and her shifty smile magnified his suspicions. "I'm leaving now." The grotesqueness of Allison's confession was shunted aside by his concern for Sean. "I'll be back with Val in the morning. You might tell Sean the truth, because I sure as hell will. I'll never leave my son again!"

The harshness of Allison's laughter mystified him and once again he detected the cunning, vicious streak that she had taken pains to hide from him.

"Oh, spare Sean this one, will you?"

"He'll adapt, kids do."

"Terry, when I found out I was pregnant, Earl wouldn't fess up. But he gave me the money to get an abortion, or, preferably, lost." Allison took the bottle of Yukon Jack off the mantelpiece. It had been a token, their joke, of her evening at the Paradise Inn.

She took a slug from the bottle and the liquor splashed like grease on her lips.

"Your old partner Georgie was a money pump and Earl wasn't about to tell that load that *we,* me and him were *the* couple. Whatever, he didn't give a fuck. Terry, don't you see, you were the ideal father? Earl wouldn't have given a shit about Sean or me."

Terry's face lost its color, and he trembled. "What?"

"Sean isn't *yours.* For Crissake, he's Earl's!"

Terry's cry of anguish filled the room. Allison's confession no longer had any meaning to him. It was merely a baffled sound in a death chamber and Terry bowed with insane grace to her.

He moved to the fireplace and stood between Allison and the fire poker. In an instant, the resolution became evident—a flash—to him. He didn't have to listen to any more of this slut's ridicule. He stampeded through the house and reached the hall closet. On the top shelf was his loaded .45. He'd kill Allison then himself. He reached up.

She sensed the danger at once and was on top of him like a wild animal. They struggled, and when he turned to strike her, she butted him hard. The automatic fell and, like a top, slithered on the floor she had polished on her knees. It was spinning under the space beneath the grandfather clock.

Terry leaped at her and seized her ferociously by the

throat. She kicked at him; her head bashed against the mirror, and she pulled free as the fragments of glass flew through the room. She seized a razor sliver, and with a weaving hand thrust it under his eye.

"Don't go near the gun. Just get the fuck out."

In a daze, he ripped off the wedding band she had given him and flung it in her face.

"Tell Sean that *you* murdered his father."

"Oh, fuck you and your rich wife. I've had enough cold dinners and Sunday TV."

"I'll never give Sean up! I'll find a way."

"Maybe you shouldn't," she said with derisive calculation. "If you honestly gave a damn about him or anyone but yourself, you'd grant him a pardon. Be a hero, Terry, let him go."

Terry stumbled and fell constantly down the snow-driven walk he had taken earlier with Sean. His hands were frozen and the scent of the Tiger Balm he had massaged into his child's flesh clung to him. All he could think about was his son. The fury of the snowstorm began to subside and he made his way to the Wayfarers Arms, a local tavern and general store with a pair of frozen gas pumps. The place was about to be closed and he peered through the window, slamming his raw, chillblained fist on the frosted glass.

The owner opened the door. Valerie was sitting alone with a drink. Terry strode toward her, and he was blinded by a vision of the happy, high-spirited woman he had once known. He had a flash of the two of them years ago when they had met and she had taken him sailing. He was flooded with tender feelings. The bartender, changing to leave, came over.

Valerie was stultified as she watched the bartender put his apron back on and shake Terry's hand. He and the last of the regulars waved to Terry, welcoming "Chris Arnold" home from the sea, asking the mysterious seaman if he'd had a good voyage. The bartender served Terry a tequila shooter. Terry took the stool next to Valerie in a corner of the bar.

"There are no flights out till morning and I can't rent a car," she said. "Anyway, I'm not up to driving."

"Do you want a divorce?"

"I don't know what I want. I need a way out." She pulled away from this intruder wearing a pea coat who smelled of sour liquor. "I hate myself for failing to understand what was going on with us. *You loved her* all along," she cried bitterly, pierced by humiliation.

"Yes." He grappled for his sanity and to find the words to express the hopelessness of their situation. "Val, it's been a nightmare for all of us. I committed a crime and I don't care about legal implications, breaking the law, but I care about how I broke your heart and destroyed us because of this. The crime was against you. Of all the people I love, you're the last one this should have happened to."

She shivered and her face trembled. "Terry, I believed in you so completely. I thought nothing could ever harm us. You're everything to me." She could not control her sobbing. "You're the center of my soul."

"Can we ever put this behind us? Val, I want to come home for good."

Valerie was confounded by the idea. It seemed remote and bizarre.

"Please stop. You don't have to be kind to me, Terry." She shook her head ruefully. "Go your own way. Look, I'd never tell your boy about me. It's just not in me to wound him that way."

"I know that," he said, reassured by her grace. She took his hand and noticed the wedding band was gone. "Val, can you forgive me?"

With her head bowed, she said, "No, Terry, I don't believe I can. Let me explain something that you couldn't understand unless you were a doctor. I've seen so much death. The death of children. *I* can bury this. But I don't think you can ever do that. If you were to come back, do it for Aaron. You two are strangers. Don't do it for me. He needs his father."

The invitation twisted within him. It would take time, but it was possible. He would assume the identity of the

real Terry Brett, a man no longer bearing the lesions of
a divided heart.

"Yes, I want to, Val."

"Terry, you'd have to *bury* Allison. Can you bear it,
endure it?"

He reached out for Val and pressed his lips on her
clasped hands. "Yes, I can, Val." Terry signaled for the
bottle of tequila and spattered the bar with it when he
poured his drink. "I'll spend my life trying to find Aaron
and what's left of us."

She clutched his head, holding it in her palms. His
body leaned against her breast, with its strange, foreign
scents of another woman, who had invaded the realm she
had once thought was secure against the treachery of in-
vaders.

She was shaking again. "Terry, I want you to see the
boy you had with Allison and provide for him. Don't
ever forget that child. Don't exclude him from your life.
When Aaron's older, we'll be straight and tell him he has
a brother."

"Val, Sean—the boy—he *isn't* mine! But I love him.
Allison had someone else besides me. She finally admitted who the *real* father was."

"Are you sure?" He nodded in a bar fury. "What're
you going to do?" Val asked, frightened by his demeanor.

"We can't ever talk about this again. It would be poison. I'll fix it so he thinks I'm dead." Val placed her
arms around Terry and pressed his face against her neck.
She began to cry, quietly, discreetly. "Val, stop, I have
to let Sean think that I'm gone."

"You can't do that to him."

"I have to free him. Give him a life without me."

The bartender was about to leave and made a note of
Terry's tab on the chalkboard. "I can trust Allison to keep
score. Mrs. Arnold is true blue," he said, casting a dis-
approving eye on Valerie. "But Chris, you worry me,"
he added with a smile.

Val touched Terry's face smiled and scoffed, "You
have a solid reputation . . . *Chris*. Here and everywhere."

Terry walked to the bar pool table in the cozy corner

where he had shot eight ball with all comers. He picked up a cue stick from the rack and chalked the tip—the former Chris Arnold, house hustler.

Valerie had never seen this man before but thought he was familiar through the grazing damage of dreams, and time. She was drawn to him—the power and loving charm she had been starved for in her days and nights. She wanted him, simply, basically, but without the snarl of confusion.

She pressed her fingers through his wet jacket and touched his chest. "Could you really love only me, Ter?"

"I always have, but I didn't know it until now."

47

Valerie was not petulant or calling the shots from a position of power and he appreciated this quality of tact while they drove to Port Rivers. The following day she agreed to wait at the airport and try to arrange their flight to Aspen.

"I have to see Pat."

The name acted like a cattle prod on Valerie. "I have Jonah for a father and a man like Pat for a father-in-law. God, that's two men nobody deserves." She had found an outlet for venom. "Tell your father he won't ever see Aaron or me again. We are mortal enemies." Valerie shook her head in consternation. "Milly must have been buffaloed into this scheme by your father. A blind lamb in a snowstorm."

She waited for Terry to bring something beyond sorrow to her. He kissed her, and for the first time since she had met him, she had a sense of something releasing in him. Whatever he was holding on to was now hers.

Pat would eventually assume the responsibility and hang for Terry's bigamy. A defense of his father's actions would have added fuel to the incendiary circumstances and hurt Valerie. Terry hoped he could contact his father before Allison chimed in. Terry eventually tracked him to a construction site in the center of town. No one had ever trusted Pat with a job like this. An office building. Terry marveled at his slippery ascent to gentleman contractor.

Machinery meshed, forklifts angled below a tangle of steel girders being welded. Webs of blue sparks rained down. Wearing a yellow hard-hat, his father stood with a group of foremen outside a trailer. Above them, flapping in the breeze, were banners in the colors of the Irish flag, bordered with four-leaf clovers. PATRICK BRETT, CONTRACTOR was imprinted on each.

Pat was pointing to a blueprint and hollering. His father had an expensive filigreed flask in his tool pouch, and Terry said, "The union'll bust you for drinking on the job."

"That's the only way they get a day's work out of me."

Pat had longed for the pleasure of seeing his son at this monumental job. He shooed off the group with his typical instructions, "Build quality, and build it quick."

Pat's trailer had an entertainment bar, tomato red Stratoloungers, and a built-in sound system; even an icemaker.

"Well, Terry, how do you like this? I finally got a job downtown. My bid wasn't the lowest. I got it because the developer said *I* had a good reputation. That's what eventually happens when you stuff people's pockets long enough. You wind up with a hole nobody wants to fill. I crammed ten big ones into your pal Cisco's kick for reelection as D.A. You should see the endorsement letter he wrote for me. You'd think I built the fucking Panama Canal."

"At long last, everyone appreciates you."

"I always thought big. I've also got the inside track for the new bus depot at the wharf."

"You'll be filling the sinkholes."

"They pay the light bills." He poured hefty glasses of Chivas Regal and beamed at Terry. "I had no idea you'd be around. The man of mystery. What a beautiful surprise." With a drink nervously wavering in his hand, Pat embraced him. "It was such a miserable Christmas without you. Allison prepared a banquet for us. She can cook better than anyone in Port Rivers. Pity she's stuck in Seacliff.

"Sean made her hang on till seven at night before serving, on the offchance that you could make it. Then I got snoggered and sentimental and upset her. What a prize you got yourself there. Listen, I'll call Milly and we'll all party!"

"I have to talk to you, Dad."

"Sure." He hugged Terry. "I'm thrilled to see you."

It was still early at the Surf Rider with the milk and scotch drinkers at the bar. Pat sidled into what had become his booth. The shucker at the wet bar brought them a giant platter of oysters.

"Three years, is it, since we've seen each other?" His father's face puffed up with sad rebuke, then collapsed. "Can you believe it?" A bottle of Mersault appeared and was poured. Pat proudly informed him that he had his own section in the restaurant cellar now. "Allison's introduced me to French wines.

"How about I give you and her some time to yourselves and grab Sean for a few days? Take him hunting. Sean's a dead shot now. How's that sound? Him and me go to the Trail Blazers games. I want to thank you for those seats on the floor. I'm a bigshot in these parts nowadays. A million friends. The bankers kiss my ass."

Then Pat's head slunk down on the table. "Three years, Terry, I haven't seen you. That's too long for me."

"I know. Dad, I'm bleeding to death. It's over with Allison and me. I won't be coming back again."

Pat's eyes were distended and he gasped. "No! I never stopped having nightmares about something like this." When Terry tried to interrupt, Pat stuck his palm in his face. "I don't get it! The last time you called me, you said you and Allison were never happier.

"Speaking for myself, I was never more wrong about anybody than I was about Allison. She's about the nicest, finest human being I've met. Terry, I beg you, please work things out with her."

"It's too late. We're finished." Pat sank into a stupor. "Valerie found out about everything. She followed me to Seacliff last night."

"Oh, dear God, no. Poor woman!" He lowered his head. "Valerie didn't deserve this. I guess we're all cooked now."

"I think so. Other things came out. That case I took for Earl. He was making it with Allison. She was his bait. I can't live with it."

"Earl? I mean, this was a long time ago. Allison was a hippie queen with the drugs and that Buddha bullshit. It was the sixties, everyone was sleeping with everyone."

"They worked out a plan. Allison does me and I represent Earl on the case."

Pat fell back in the booth. "What a horrible, shitty lunch I'm having with my son. What happens with Sean and you? He worships you and needs you."

Terry found himself sinking into the morass of this catastrophic family tragedy.

"Sean . . . Sean's not mine. Earl is his real father."

"Earl!" Pat grimaced as though from a hook in the gut. "Awww, no, Terry, no," he cried, slumping in the booth. "How could this be?"

"I was sandbagged. Allison admitted it last night when Val came. I never want to see Allison again."

Pat pleaded. He and Milly were covert grandparents, and weren't prepared to resign their rights or compromise their affection.

"Look, you took a terrible risk marrying Allison. I didn't understand it. I fought you. You were right. You gave Allison an identity and she was off to the races. She's made something of herself and she's a marvelous mother."

Terry had built a wall and the prospect of not being with Allison again justified everything.

"You had to hear from me how things stood. Pat, it was all a house of lies. And I'm not pleading innocent. I'm the guilty party and I'm choking to death on it."

Pat rose roughly, slamming the table, and the drinks spattered.

"Can't you forgive Allison? She was desperate. That scumbag Earl. If I ever see that motherfucker, I'll blow a hole through his head!"

They sullenly walked out onto the restaurant deck, which was deserted in the winter. Terry leaned over the rail and stared at the shrouded boats making their way down the Columbia in the ripening wintry fog.

"We can't change the past. But, Terry, you can't turn me against Allison. I'd walk into a buzz saw before I'd give up Sean and her. They're *my* family!" His father howled like a child and tears coursed down his rough, leathery skin. "I know I've lost you, Terry. I can't die for you."

"I've already died for them. Good-bye, Dad."

48

The passage of time had not healed Terry nor vanquished the loss of the boy he still regarded as his son. He was at the mercy of events that had lain fallow, below the surface, and now rose up again to obsess him. These harrowing moments attacked without warning and were sometimes precipitated by dreams and, this morning, a nightmare. When he left his house, he began jogging down the hill. A November cloud cover, with mists hovering, summoned him back into the landscape of night. He remembered why he had awakened so upset.

It was 1993 and Sean's birthday; he hadn't seen the boy for fifteen years. Despite Allison's revelations, he could never relinquish his love for Sean, whom she had hacked out of his life but not his heart. He could never disavow Sean. Time and again, he had thought about getting in touch with him. Ultimately, he concluded it would be to no avail. He hoped that Allison might have had the decency to tell him the truth, but he doubted it, and there the matter rested in the cold grave of distorted fictions and equivocation.

My God, Sean must be twenty-seven—no, twenty-eight. What've I done? Terry asked himself.

Other questions about Sean besieged him. Was he alive, dead; did he have a job, a wife? Building up speed on the deserted beach, Terry ran hard for some minutes. Then he pulled up short and dropped to his knees. A shimmering vision of Allison, the dream mermaid, glimmered over the waves. She vaulted toward him. In this flurry of intoxication, Terry craved for her touch. Even after so long, this apparition yielded to his unfulfilled desire. But the sensation, like everything about her, struck him as disreputable, which he recognized had been the very grain of the attraction. He wondered what had become of the squandered family.

Sean would be celebrating with Allison. There would probably be some kind of drunken bash with Pat shelling out from the big roll of hundreds he packed. Terry felt a morbid chill. All of them were blurs, black holes in the dead universe of his former world.

He sat down at the water's edge and mindlessly let the wet sand drizzle through his fingers. He knew that Allison had wronged him in the truest, deepest sense.

"Allison, how could you, we, have done this?"

He left the beach in a bleak mood, knowing he'd give up everything if she called. Through the years, he had battled with the demons, but he could not release her. He could no longer assign blame, point a finger at anyone but himself. The choice had been his and he had broken his own heart.

Chris Arnold a.k.a. Terry Brett was gone forever.

At the house, mature after a quarter of a century, his houseman Antonio was drying his British racing green Bentley, rubbing a chamois over the hood. They exchanged good mornings and Terry picked up a mug of black coffee.

Still bewildered by this morning's unhappy, unplanned descent into the past, Terry stood in the entryway of the house, fumbling with the newspaper. Through the archway at the breakfast table in the large, airy French country kitchen, he observed Valerie and his son Aaron.

Have I done anything wrong, keeping them happy?

Aaron had also chosen to become a doctor. He had recently begun his first-year residency in psychiatry at the UCLA Neuropsychiatric Institute and Terry was happy to see him, for he deflected the ghost of Sean.

Valerie was once again on a tear about Aaron's fiancée.

"If you want to throw your life away on someone like Kit and live with thrift shop furniture, do it," Dr. Valerie Brett informed Dr. Aaron Brett.

Terry's cloud lifted and vanished.

"I didn't know you were here. Welcome home, doc," he said to Aaron, rangy and slim as his mother. He rubbed a hand on his son's shoulder. "The crazies give you some time off?"

"Oh, I'm never off. I thought I'd stop by to see how America's most normal couple are doing."

"Actually, Aaron came to borrow a dress for Kit for some event madam will be attending."

Kit Palmer, a lush Southern smoothie, was a theatrical agent who dashed to screenings, galas, charity bashes, and was photographed more often than her clients.

Terry bent down and kissed Valerie on the forehead while scooping out the sports section.

"I hope it wasn't your wedding dress."

"Believe me, she'd have the nerve to ask. Nothing about Kit would surprise me," Val said.

Terry touched Valerie's hand. She was deeply upset. Aaron had been her constant companion, her date, a bulwark against loneliness, the object of her adoration when Terry had been out of town, recruiting, dissembling, weaving the other fabric of his existence together and hoping it wouldn't unravel as it had.

"The drama goes on. How are you, Dad?"

Terry thumbed through to the professional basketball scores. The basketball season was only beginning, but Jonah's woeful team, the Los Angeles Stars, were in last place.

Terry smiled. "I'll call somebody for an appointment for you and your mother, and then I'll find out." Mother and son smiled reluctantly in return.

"Kit can have the dress. I don't give a damn about it. I don't give a damn about anything," Valerie said captiously. Appealing to Terry, "If she'd called, I would've given it to her. But she gets Aaron to do her skulking."

Aaron adopted a professional manner as though the patient was waiting outside his office for her fate to be decided.

"Dad, we don't need tests. Here's my diagnosis: We have a strong, self-willed woman accustomed to controlling people. Even though she's a doctor, she's behaving childishly. Her attachment to her son is being severed by his fiancée. This threat and imaginary rejection anxiety exists only in her mind."

Terry agreed with Aaron, but his loyalty was pledged to Valerie.

"Oh, cut it out," Valerie said. "That sounds like an analysis you prepared for your faculty adviser."

Lately, they were always at each other's throats and Terry intervened. "I think there's a simpler explanation. Your mother just plain doesn't like Kit."

"That's a pity"—Aaron scowled at his mother—"since Kit admires you. She's idealized our family life and the closeness we have, and she wants to be a part of it." When Valerie did not respond, Aaron looked to his father for support. "Mothers don't like to let go," Aaron informed him as though this svelte professor of pediatrics were some breast-beating matriarch.

"Give me a break and don't patronize me, Aaron. I'm entitled to have reservations," Valerie said.

Terry listened to the debate. Usually understanding and forgiving, Terry saw a grim woman with fiery brown eyes, slender, with a freckled nose, short hair bob, who now gave off the aura of a field commander astonished by a soldier questioning the high command's strategy.

Her mouth twisted scornfully. "Kit's found a handsome, rich doctor destined to have a brilliant career.

What's not to love?" Their skirmishes, invariably blood-less, had recently sunk into acrimony.

"I know she's not one of us."

"Aaron, tell me exactly what Kit's bringing to the ta-ble?"

They glared at each other, stalking each other ner-vously, neither about to surrender.

"Mother, I'm not going to tear out my heart and give up the woman I love for you. You don't have to live with Kit, I do." He icily measured her. "And with all due respect, Mother, what you think about my future wife isn't relevant. In fact, I don't give a shit about it any more."

The undercurrents of his son's defense resonated within Terry. Aaron was neither robust nor gifted with athletic prowess, but he behaved as though he was invin-cible. His determination and forcefulness had always come as something of a surprise to Terry. Valerie's com-pelling sweetness was lost in the exchange. Her broad mouth tightened like a clamp.

"And you're about to be a psychiatrist?" Terry asked.

"I'm beginning to wonder about that myself," Val in-terjected. "The issue, Aaron, isn't what I like or don't like. I know she isn't right for you."

Containing his indignation, Aaron rose from the table and adopted a genial but peremptory attitude, terminating a patient session, aloof, unharmed, making another ap-pointment.

Terry put down the newspaper. "Guys, let's try to act like family, shall we? And talk this out."

As Aaron was about to flee, Terry gripped him hard.

"Didn't you forget something, Ace?"

Aaron shook his head. "Like what?"

"Like kissing your mother good-bye, damnit. Is that out of style? Or doesn't Freud allow expressions of af-fection in families once you get your license to practice?"

Shrink or not, trained to be neutral, Dr. Aaron Brett was abashed and realized that he had been properly chas-tised by his father, the person he admired more than any man. He dutifully kissed Valerie on the cheek.

"Let's be friends, Mother."

"Coming from you, Aaron, that's an astounding request. I've never been anything else."

From his dressing room, getting ready for the office, Terry glanced over at Val at her makeup table. She was staring in the mirror at some void rather than her face. Hand suspended in midair, poised with a lipliner, she had frozen.

Terry slipped on his tweed jacket and stuffed a tie in his pocket. Coming up behind, he sat beside her on the bench and smiled at her in the mirror.

"God, Terry, you look sensational." She rubbed the tanned sun lines on the corners of his eyes, then ran her hand along the graying sideburns and his luxuriant head of sandy blond hair. "Don't men ever age?"

"Shit, Val, I'm fifty-four."

"And still the most magnificent hunk."

"Ahh, I work out with my boys."

"I love you madly."

"It's reciprocal, my darling."

They seemed like youngsters at a party, ready to play a duet. He took her hand and kissed it and her attractive features fell back into their rightful places. She had never been a shrew, or dictatorial.

"I've done everything to keep this family together and to lose Aaron to someone like Kit is humiliating. There I go. I sound like a goddamn scold. See if you can patch it up with us, please, Terry."

"Look, the fact is, I do like Kit very much. They're engaged, so accept it."

"If only Kit wasn't such a tramp. I mean to say, she lived with some crappy actor. She's in this theatrical agency business, always hustling. She must've slept with every guy in town."

The irony amused him. "Well, people pay top dollar for experienced players these days."

"Can't he see through her? We know there's more to

a marriage than sex. Aaron has to have some brains."

"Since when does intelligence matter, when you're in love? It's a cold, sinister transaction in life—good guys fall for bad girls."

49

Even now, so many years later, remorse for having deceived Valérie hurtled along with the wicked November Santa Ana unseasonably cruising through Los Angeles. The blistering current of desert air with its fiery grains of sand lashed at the drought-burnt landscape. Along with the infernal wind and some cases of early flu coasting in from Hong Kong, there was the pulsing of a rumor, something unformed and intangible, making select rounds. Faint whispers intimated that Jonah Wolfe was going to be murdered.

This threnody had become more than a murmur in the back room of the Pacific Dining Car downtown; it whirled through the glades of the country clubs and squalled into cocktail parties at the beach. Terry had heard it murmured around the dining room at the Bel Air Country Club. In fact, the developing mordent seemed composed so that he would hear it. He decided to do something about it. At the very least, he would have it confirmed.

Terry's management firm, Sports Associates, was now located in a sinuous gray Century City tower that he had acquired for Valerie in the late sixties when the area had been a morgue of unrented office structures. Terry whipped past computer workstations in the office, the glass cubicles of his young Turks who were tracking their clients' schedules, arranging public appearances and advertising promotions, ensuring that bills were paid, keeping the tax accounts and insurance premiums up to date. They listened to the players' complaints against the ruthless magnates who paid them millions to swing a baseball bat, catch a pass, or dribble a basketball, and who flew into rages when these prima donnas didn't show up for practice because they were hungover or high on drugs.

Outside Terry's office there was a commotion. The booming voice of Terry's newest young basketball star echoed. Benny La Salle, the power forward he had signed with Atlanta, was dancing past his secretary Martha.

"Partners' meeting in five minutes," she reminded Terry.

Terry regarded the gangly young man with his ponytail, Apache sides, and crewcut on top. Three hairstyles on one human head. Benny's long jaw sagged and his eyes were puffy.

He brandished a legal paper. "I have to see you, Terry."

"Martha, tell Billy and Mike I'll be a few minutes."

Terry's office was comfortable, with soft leather chairs and sofas, English hunting prints; a collection of dueling pistols, reputed to have belonged to Wellington, were mounted on the wall behind a long Victorian writing table. He skimmed through the court document. It was an attachment of Benny's salary signed by a judge in Palm Springs on behalf of an outfit called Pearl Investments.

"How do you owe these people a million dollars, Benny? You don't even live in the Springs. Who the fuck are they?"

"I'm not really sure. See, Ter, before we met," Benny began in a sheepish manner, "I hooked up with these guys at a charity weekend. They had this huge condo project and said all I had to do was put in a hundred thousand and I'd make a fortune. Double my money in a year on California property. Jonah Wolfe was involved with these investors. I figured, how could I go wrong?"

"Why didn't you mention this when you signed with me? Our contract has a provision for the firm making your investments. It's structured so that you don't get whacked by the IRS or get your eyes ripped out by con men."

"I was embarrassed. Look, I thought it was all cool."

"They left you holding a nasty piece of paper, Benny. You co-signed a promissory note for a million dollars, according to this. There's an old saying about a co-signer. I guess you hadn't heard it." Benny looked mystified. "He's a schmuck with a fountain pen."

The young man conceded. "I never saw the development."

"I'm sure you didn't. It hasn't been built. Did you think it was?"

Benny tearfully paced the office. "They told me it was built. I saw pictures."

Terry put a paternal arm around him. "You saw artist's renderings."

"Whatever. Terry, don't let me go down the tubes. I'm just starting. Will I go bankrupt?"

"Not if I can help it."

"What're you going to do?"

"I'll file a countersuit, charging fraud, racketeering, breach of fiduciary contract. And we'll seek punitive damages as well on lost investment opportunities while your money was in their hands. In the meantime, concentrate on tonight's game against the Lakers."

With reassurances, he escorted the young man out. "Any time someone asks you to sign something, tell them the truth. You can't read or write—and to talk to me."

In the conference room, a temple filled with awards and plaques their players had won, Mike Summers was standing at the blackboard writing the names of companies and opposite them the athletes he intended to match with them for product endorsements.

Mike still had an undaunted Jack Armstrong attitude and incomparable judgment when it came to spotting players who, with a little maturity, would develop into solid professionals. He also had a sense of which ones wouldn't be able to withstand the pressure of big bucks and would bust out. No matter how much Terry or Billy Klein liked a player who wanted to sign up with them, they would defer to Mike's opinion.

"He won't be a team player. He has personality problems. He hates authority. He'll freeze when an important game's on the line. It's all a question of character."

These were important considerations for Sports Associates and they had turned down a variety of All-Americans in all sports because of these factors. They had been wrong occasionally, but by and large, Mike's intuition had saved them from some ugly scandals and lawsuits.

"Morning, Ter. How do you like the lineups?"

"They look fine. But I'd scratch Nike. Unless Michael Jordan has a bad season, gets hurt or whatever, they won't make a move for any of our guys. From what I've heard, they're scouting around for a woman . . . a movie or TV star with young crossover fans. They want to widen their appeal outside the black community."

There had been a remarkable physical transformation in Billy Klein. He worked out like a demon and was now muscular and fit. He had a thick mustache, and a successful hair implant provided curly steel gray hair that he fluffed up over his receding hairline. Billy had become the embodiment of good health and wore a permanent feel-good smile. He had on a red and white warm-up suit and advertised his conversion to conditioning. He carried in a bowl of oat bran with low-fat milk and a fistful of vitamins. His third wife had recently given birth to his first child and he was taking parenting, survival, and his diet seriously. He had done several stints at the Betty Ford Clinic and had run out of long-suffering friends.

It had been a merry ship. The three men had worked together comfortably for many years now. Mike spotted the talent; Billy was the PR specialist; Terry did the signing, constructed the deals, and had brought endorsements and contract negotiations to a high art form.

"We're in good shape," Billy said. "The firm is. You, I don't know about, Terry. There's this buzz about Jonah having his last rites. You're not involved, are you?"

"No, but I wouldn't mind being included. And yes, I've heard it," Terry said.

"Well, is it serious?" Mike asked. He had known and hated Jonah longer than any of them. "Does Val know anything about this?"

"She cut him out of her life ages ago," Terry replied.

"Should *I* tell Mike why?" Billy asked Terry, who nodded. They were both sensitive to what Mike had suffered through with Jonah when he'd been coaching in Fond du Lac and discovered Jonah with his sister. Billy Klein, once a clown but now an adult without hypocrisy, had a grave expression. "I'm no virgin with this kind of behavior. In the sixties, I was a crazy man, too, but Mike, since we're friends talking . . ."

Mike said, "When I met Jane, she was Val's assistant. My wife and I had Jane to dinner a few times. This long-legged, innocent, sweet girl. Go on . . ."

"Jonah bagged her and *turned* her out. He got her into crack and passed her around to his team." Billy shook his head mournfully.

"What a fucking lowlife Jonah's always been," Mike said.

"Yeah." Billy scooped up the last of his bran. "I think Jonah's a marked man, Terry. It's very serious. You know the wiseguy who used to be the oddsmaker and make the sports line in Vegas, Simon Pearl?"

Mike put down his clipboard. "We've all heard of him."

"I thought he'd retired," Terry said, for the connection was disturbing. "Benny La Salle came in with the shakes. I didn't put it together. But he owes Pearl's company a million dollars on some fairy-tale property development. And somehow Jonah's involved."

Without gaiety, Billy said, "Last time I was at Ford, I met Simon. He has a mistress who was also strung out and she was in my group. Something was cooking with him and Jonah. Simon's the financial adviser for some big union pension funds now. He points a finger, they write a check and acquire it."

It was a familiar pattern for Terry. He would see Simon Pearl and try to reach some accommodation for his misguided client. He'd always been a sucker for a boy in trouble.

*   *   *

Sand devils hacked and blundered through the golden hills of the desert, churned through the arroyos, blistering the shuddering cactus and chopping like flak at the slate mountains. The whine and screech of the wind caromed off Terry's Bentley and it veered from side to side. A sea creature, he hated the desert.

Simon Pearl's lavish Tuscany-style villa overlooked the golf course. It loomed over a man-made lake, stocked with waterfowl, fountains, gates, a sanctuary. Beside it were other castles, guarding their barons. Old money, stolen money, young mistresses, and the schemes of untrustworthy traders had found their last outpost in the fertile sands of Palm Desert.

Simon Pearl was a legendary figure with the gracious manner of a man accustomed to playing host. He met Terry with a friendly smile at the arched doorway. He was short and wiry, with a henna tint in his hair and an ebony tan so even that his buffed fingernails gleamed like phosphorus.

"At last, Mr. Brett."

"You sent smoke signals."

"I did indeed."

"I am present."

"How was the drive?"

"Blowing like hell."

"These Santa Anas get everyone crazy."

"I assume they've had that effect on you, Simon."

"The weather I don't mind, it's when people owe me money that I become feral. It has the effect of a wolf-man's bite."

They strolled through acres of travertine marble, statuary, here and there a Rauschenberg, a Bonnard, a pair of Calder mobiles that pranced in the air-conditioning, finally reaching a large family room in soothing pale yellow. Outside the French doors, an attractive woman practiced her putting stroke on the house green.

They were drinking orange juice and Campari, and Simon studied his guest: Terry had clear hazel eyes, looked just above six feet tall, light-bearded with creamy skin, carefully cut blond hair going to gray, and a strong, pugnaciously set jaw. His nose had been broken, and about two inches of scar tissue ran from below his right earlobe along the boneline. Simon knew a gladiator when he saw one. And yet Terry Brett was disarming, with a resonant, persuasive voice. He gave the impression of a straight shooter, the kind of guy who'd be fun to play golf with and have over for dinner.

"Do you know much about me?" Simon asked.

"Only that black clouds surround you."

"At *this* moment, they most certainly do. I hope you can disperse them with your magical legal gifts. Like yourself, Terry, I was once a lawyer and I went to Vegas to set up my practice. But I became fascinated by sports odds. And I had a knack . . . a feel. I could find a middle. The first year I was there, I made myself a quarter of a million and I was invited by some interested parties to join them. I lasted thirty-five years. Then I got bored with it all. They started number-crunching with computers and of course as we all know from chess, computers sometimes lose to world-class players."

Like his art collection, there was an ageless, expansive quality about Pearl. Rich and casual. His gray eyes were filled with wisdom and reflective; but he was infuriated. He had signed on as financial adviser to some union pension funds and was given carte blanche to make investments.

"It suited me perfectly. A Gulfstream-Four, unlimited expenses, a percentage of the pie, and no board of directors to account to, unless something went radically wrong. I assumed full responsibility. Just the sort of thing to amuse me in my golden years. I made some good moves like buying the pension funds a major stake in United Food and Beverage. The stock had a twenty-two-point bounce last year. Now with the cruise lines and resorts we own, it's a very solid package.

"But, Terry, some other investments I've made have turned out disastrously. Unfortunately, there's no insurance against bad judgment."

"It happens to all of us. But I don't think suing Benny La Salle is going to make you well."

"I have no intention of suing Benny. I just wanted you to take notice of me. We have a common enemy."

"Jonah Wolfe."

"Yes. I know that he's your wife's father and there's bad blood between you. The reasons don't interest me."

"I wasn't prepared to disclose them."

"I will disclose mine, Terry. And I want your advice and possibly an alliance. For many years, my reputation was unassailable. All of that changed when I met Jonah one afternoon at La Quinta. We played a round of golf, had some drinks afterwards, and then he said: 'Can I borrow some money?' I thought he was kidding, but it turned out he was serious. Well, I acceded to the tune of a hundred and twenty million dollars of other people's money. I gave him earnest money, angry money, that comes from the sweat of millions of people on assembly lines, teachers, firemen, and yes, even some state police.

"I put this into Jonah's meatpacking plants, which went bankrupt, and a condo development now in fore-closure. A shopping center that went fucking belly-up. My good name can never be restored until I cleanse my-self of Jonah Wolfe."

"You are an attorney, Simon. There are courts that will redress your grievances."

He shook his head furiously. "I said angry money, union money, funny money. Money that was shifted without due authorization. None of this can bear scru-tiny."

Terry was intrigued by Jonah's scam. At present, he knew his father-in-law was broke and barely able to pay the salaries of his team. Jonah had squandered his own fortune as well as others'.

"It's profitless to murder a seventy-eight-year-old man unless you're the beneficiary of a large double indemnity policy that will get you well."

"Terry, these things have to be done as a moral im-perative. It will be an event. Like public hangings in the old days. Let me amplify our position. Each day Jonah wakes up breathing, the people here choke on their break-fast. Their orange juice tastes sour, they can't swallow.

Everyone is constipated. They are running to doctors. Jonah Wolfe has stopped up their works.

"And I am the sickest person of all. I have eczema on my toes and I've developed asthma. All psychosomatic. I have never been ill until recently. There are volunteers who are prepared to throw Jonah off a roof while others will stand on the sidewalk holding up spears so that they can impale him."

Simon sat anxiously waiting for a response.

"The only asset Jonah has is the Los Angeles Stars," Terry said. "And believe me, the National Basketball Association would never allow you and your unions to take over the franchise. If you put him into receivership, it still wouldn't help."

"Terry, I realize the Stars are untouchable."

Terry smiled seductively. "They are not, however, untouchable by me."

Simon liked the direction of the conversation. "Last year there was talk around the league that a few teams were on the block."

"I know. I was approached. I talked it over with my partners at Sports Associates. The prices were too high."

Simon quickly countered. "The head of Amway bought the Orlando Magics for eighty-five million."

Terry wondered if he wanted to leave it all behind, give up the firm he had built, just to settle a score with Jonah. Still, the prospect of owning a professional basketball franchise, even though the Stars were perennial losers, was a challenge he found hard to resist.

"Simon, suppose I bought Jonah's markers for a quarter on the dollar. Nothing would prevent me from taking Jonah to court and suing his ass off. I would then be in a position legally to take over the team, which would be in receivership at that stage."

"That's a very intriguing notion." Simon considered the proposal and smilingly offered Terry his hand. "You will pay us thirty million."

"How would you like a cashier's check tomorrow? You won't look so bad with your colleagues and the orange juice will taste sweeter."

"You've got a deal—with one proviso. When you've persuaded Jonah to sign off, we want him. There are people who've made plans for him and invited their friends for the occasion."

Terry listened with distaste to the homicidal scenario that had been devised for Jonah. Although he shared the general aversion to Valerie's father, the taking of a life would be unconscionable. He could not initiate a pardon, but at least he could stay the execution.

"You can have him only when I tell you I'm ready." With his fox on the run, Terry rode harder. "And Simon, as a token of good faith on your part, you will please ensure that this judgment against Benny La Salle is quashed and his hundred thousand dollars is promptly sent to my office."

Terry was exhilarated when he left the desert community. He was about to become one of America's chosen, the proprietor of a professional sports team.

50

When he left the Port Rivers squad room with half a load on, Sean Arnold, the burly, blue-eyed, bearded Viking, as Captain Barney Laver called him, strutted over to his new fiery red Mustang convertible. His mother had bought it for his birthday. Sean was eager to show his mother his shimmering gold detective badge, which seemed to radiate a power as secret as plutonium, anointing him with the authority of a feudal lord. At twenty-seven, he was the youngest detective on the Port Rivers police force. His advancement had been seeded by his apparent recklessness as a beat patrolman, a street cop, one of the new breed who excited the brass because they gave off a wave of something dangerous and intimidating.

Ah, if his father were only here, Sean thought wistfully, his day would have been complete. But fifteen years ago, his father had been killed by East Germany's secret police. His body had never been recovered. In the deepest recesses of his being, Sean still missed his dad. Throughout his adolescence, there were nights when he cried himself to sleep, longed for the embrace, the companionship, the fine understanding his dad had always given him. He had modeled himself after his father.

"Never be afraid to explore the sorcery of feelings . . . whether you understand them or not," his father had told him.

"How do you actually know you're in love?" Sean remembered asking.

His father considered this for some time. His answer did not disappoint Sean.

"I think you believe you can't live without that person. It's something called rapture."

"The way it is with you and Mom?"

"Yes, absolutely."

Sean had admired his father's courtly manners, his collegiate low-key dress, and he emulated him at the table, always waiting for a woman to be seated, seldom raised his voice, listened attentively. At eighteen, he began wearing some of Dad's old tweed and cashmere jackets. Many of them came from some place in Beverly Hills called Carroll & Company. Out in the coastal resort town of Seacliff where Sean had been born and lived until his dad's death, his friends' parents remarked on how expensive they were. His old man had taste. Sean sought to become a junior version of the magnificent man who had died, sacrificing himself heroically to defend America's freedom.

Wheeling into the lot of The Greenhouse, his mother's gourmet restaurant, he waved at the kids who valet-parked the cars. He stopped at the kitchen door and leaned his head against the mesh grate. He was close to tears, thinking about his old man's courage.

"Man, I'll have a drink to you. Oh, Dad-deeee, I miss you."

Composing himself, Sean cruised into the kitchen, invariably at home with the clatter of pots on the big Wolf range, the aromas of sauces, nodding to the chef and cooks in whites on the line. The dining-room staff eating and gabbing at the large butcher block table were a familiar sight. Sean sniffed the air and tried to guess the specials without looking at the blackboard. His favorite was on, rogan gosh, a mutton curry à la Allison. Among other mysteries, his mother had mastered the subtleties of Indian cuisine.

He had worked alongside her from the age of seven, when the kitchen help at her first diner in Seacliff had consisted of the two of them and a stream of itinerant dishwashers. She had imparted her culinary skills to him. Later he tended bar, constructing magnificent Moscow Mules, Rob Roys, the perfect martini. He could fix the carbon mixture and clear the beer lines, go to market and select the best produce with their deep, earthy smells, examine the meatpacker's range of beef and distinguish between choice and prime by the color and the grainy speckles of fat. He had always fished, and at a glance could pick out the freshest seafood.

Allison was now recognized as a great chef. She knew how to maintain a kitchen. She combined her passion with an understanding of food as a celebration of life, how it brought joy to a birthday or an anniversary. She treated the preparation of a meal as a thrilling event.

The Greenhouse was not merely a stellar restaurant but a food emporium as well. Apart from being a chef of imaginative distinction, his mother had remarkable business instincts. There was a cooking school; a bakery, which specialized in a variety of breads; and a delicatessen, which featured a dizzying array of smoked meats and fish, cured hams, caviar, lines of condiments, herbs, mustards, gourmet groceries all packaged under The Greenhouse label and sold throughout the Northwest to exclusive markets.

Allison was on the kitchen phone with the reservation book balanced on her shapely knee. Sean stood over her as she explained that she was booked solid for two weeks. Her streaked blond hair was twisted in a French roll and she gave off the scent of Fracàs.

She had on dark red leather boots that matched the piping of her Chanel suit. Allison Arnold was a voluptuous woman, with the bountiful, rich, sensuous curves of a Rubens model. Since he could remember, Sean, the queen's knight, had pugnaciously butted in when some dude came on to his mother. After they had lost his father, it drove him crazy when she occasionally dated. He kissed her on the forehead as she was hanging up.

"Are you drunk, Sean?"

"Not yet. I had a few pops with the boys." He took out a set of handcuffs and snapped one on her wrist and the other on himself. "I've got something to show you."

She was startled and amused. "What is this de Sade stuff?"

"It's only six, so you're my prisoner for a while."

Sean led her through the restaurant, fragrant with the flowers shipped in from California every day. They passed busboys setting the blush pink tablecloths with burnished silver and crystal glasses. The Greenhouse was the place to be seen and to eat in, especially now that Mobil had given it a fifth star and *Gourmet Dining* declared it had the best food in the Northwest.

As always before dinner, the Victorian pub bar out front, with its rich mahogany and nautical artifacts, was crammed with the city's luminaries: finagling deals for suspect bank charters, permissions for developments, rezones for skyscrapers. The bigshots were throwing curve balls in their efforts to take over the green belts for factories and housing developments, all of which would be reluctantly denied by the city hall minions who upheld the citizens' environmental theories of ecological purity. Among this group, his mother was regarded as chief witch and nicknamed "Greensleeves."

Commanding a river view, Allison's table was this evening set for six. A Meissen vase overflowed with winter violets and her Lalique champagne flutes glistened beside the Rosenthal settings.

"I put aside a case of Dom 'sixty-one. Cost me a king's ransom. Want a glass, Sean, before your guests arrive?"

"Sounds good, Mom. I love you madly."

The bar waiter brought over a bottle already chilling and poured for them. Poised and unsentimental, she raised a glass. Then suddenly the breath of a tear was visible in her sunny blue eyes.

"The happiest moment of my life was the day you were born, and each birthday gets better."

"You're the best, Mom. My angel."

"Now tell me the good news—you've resigned from the police force."

Sean unlocked the cuffs, reached into his breast pocket, and unflapped his wallet.

"I made detective today! And I'm being sent on a special assignment."

"Oh really . . ."

"Imagine Dad's reaction if he were with us. He would have flipped about me making detective."

The glittering gold badge repelled her. That Sean had chosen a career in the police struck her as quixotic and alarming. When they had moved back to Port Rivers, she hadn't noticed that he had taken to hanging around the police museum and watching every TV crime show. He also immersed himself in novels about secret agents and detectives. She traced this influence directly to Terry. The mere thought of Terry revived her feelings of anguish.

After the breakup, she toted up the times they had actually been together and they came to eighty days in thirteen years. Those moments had been shattered when he had had to run to a phone booth in the middle of the night to call Valerie. Often he had left Allison to catch a flight after they'd made love—even before she could wrap herself in a bathrobe to see him to the car. For weeks afterward she would be forlorn, hating her life, him, their fabrication.

She seldom gave Terry a moment's thought, but with Sean digging up the corpse of her old love, her head seemed to be jammed on a heavy metal station, the volume deafening. When the split with Terry came, she was convinced that she had been ready for it all along. It couldn't go on. She knew that they'd all die on this seesaw. She had to salvage what was left of him for Valerie.

But Sean was so attached to his father that she had fostered the fantasy of their idyllic relationship. The three little piggies in their enchanted cottage on the coast had enjoyed an earthly paradise. She'd do anything not to break Sean's heart.

Sean had fainted while reading the letter from the CIA about Terry's death. Allison hadn't been able to revive him and rushed him to the local hospital. He had remained in shock for a week. What had formerly seemed an awkward adjustment during the beginning of adolescence manifested itself in chains of panic and anxiety attacks that Sean was powerless to prevent.

Out of the blue, he would begin to choke and hyperventilate; his pulse would race; his eyes would roll until he passed out. This condition alarmed Allison. Sean was forced to give up team sports and come to the restaurant immediately after school. She and Pat took him to specialists in Port Rivers and Seattle. Ritalin was prescribed, then discontinued. A year of therapy ensued in Seacliff; the conclusion the doctor reached was nebulous. Allison was told that Sean was angry because of the death of his father. Since he was unable to secure justice or closure because his father's body had not been recovered, his rage had evolved into frustration and ultimately depression, which sought a release in these panic events.

"Why don't you go out and meet some of the guys and play ball," she would say when they returned to Port Rivers. They were staying at Pat's house and he was watching a rerun of *Rawhide* with Clint Eastwood, whose cool, laconic manner he admired. "Did you hear me, Sean?"

"Yes, Mom. My ball-playing days are over," he said without defiance, which she would have welcomed.

"There are new people to meet. It's a fresh start in the city."

"I'm doing fine on my own," he replied unemotionally.

"Find yourself a girlfriend."

At that he turned away from an Eastwood gunfight and his expression evolved into tender poignancy for their condition. "Maybe one day, I'll be lucky enough to meet someone who loves me the way you do Dad."

Almost two years had passed before the two of them, at Sean's insistence, conducted their own memorial service on the bluff of the cliff, which was their favorite eyrie. Sean gradually came out of his deep depression when they moved to Port Rivers. Allison sold the bistro and house and decided to strike out again. Sean needed the companionship of a man to see him through this difficult period. He and Pat had formed a bond and Terry's father doted on him. Sean's condition was ameliorated by the change and apparently vanished as he grew to manhood. But he had lost something, some intangible aspect of himself. At times Allison saw the revival of the old spirit, and this evening marked a resurgence.

"I wish I could say I'm thrilled," she said now. "But you know me. It's always scared the life out of me having you carry a gun. Putting your head on the block."

Sean said, "Can't help it. I love the action."

"You're living in a kid's comic book."

"That's what some people really want their lives to be like."

"I guess."

Her Sean had the intelligence to have selected another profession. After he graduated from River State at twenty, she had been beside herself when he announced that he wanted a career in law enforcement. Retaining her finely tuned sixties radicalism, she talked him out of the CIA and the FBI. This serving your country malarkey had come from Terry.

She raised her glass. "Here's to keeping you safe."

Sean paused. In his soulful eyes she saw Terry's seductive image.

"And to Dad's memory." She nodded, finishing the toast with misgivings. "I've been thinking about him all day."

Allison was tempted to cut loose with the truth. But she had waited too long, and as a designer of lies, she was more culpable than Terry. A slow, mysterious smile played across her lips.

"You're out of reach, Sean, for him or anyone. You're my man for all seasons."

Bonnie Slater, the siren hostess and resident sweater girl, kept peering at them. Her skirt with its strategic thigh slit kept the customers happy when she led them from the bar after an infernal table wait.

"Little Miss Muffin," Allison began, "she's a sweetheart. You two still on?"

"Sort of."

"I really care about her, Sean. She works long hours and studies for her master's degree all night."

Bonnie had a dimpled smile, and her long black hair swished when she meandered over. She demurely lowered her eyes. "Sorry to interrupt."

"That's okay, Bonnie," the boss said. Bonnie was in love. Allison wished her well, but knew she had little chance with her roving bull.

"Happy Birthday, Sean." She handed him a silver-wrapped box and he opened it. A red V-neck cashmere sweater. "I hope it's the right size."

"Forty-two from the waist up," he said, teasingly.

"That's what I bought," Bonnie said.

"You guessed right."

Allison's crowd, the socialites whose parties she'd once catered, filtered in, greeting her, endeavoring to hug her and pass along small-change gossip. She was coaxed up from the table. "Bonnie, have a glass of champagne with Sean."

"It'll get me dizzy and I've got dinner to work."

"The hell with it. Everyone gets snoggered on my brat's birthday. Oh, forgive me, Detective Arnold."

Her *late* husband's father, Pat Brett, slid into his regular groove at the broad-bellied bar and signaled the bartender, who brought over a Chivas Regal on the rocks. Pat kissed Allison, told her that she looked beautiful, and then whispered conspiratorially.

"Did Sean hear anything?"

"From who?"

"You know who."

"You ask every birthday. It's over, Terry's dead! So

please, bury it already." She hadn't intended to sound so harsh, but each year the bitterness rose to the surface whenever Pat made a reference to Terry. "He's got his life and we have ours. And I wouldn't want to change places with him."

Drawn and pasty-faced after recent bypass surgery, Pat Brett's navy blue double-breasted suit hung like an old curtain on his once burly frame. His neck seemed to have shrunk, dangling loosely above an unwieldy Windsor knot. He had always looked important and sounded it, but fatigue had crept in. His weathered skin, the squint lines under his eyes, and a broken nose gave him the presence of a burrowing old fullback, scraping for a yard. He was still a contractor and in his early days one who had been sued from one end of the county to the other. Now, with age, and connections built with fat envelopes stuffed with green, he was the city's royal builder, and the name "Patrick Brett" on a new building meant quality construction even if the job had been bought under the table.

Allison would always be grateful to him. After Pat had bought the derelict restaurant for her from the Aristedes family, disrupting their planned arson, he gutted the place and rebuilt it to her specifications without charging a penny. Nowadays he had become reclusive and didn't see much of her and Sean.

Pat searched for something to say about his missing heir. "As usual, Terry sent me season 'Floor seats' for the Trail Blazers and the NCAA finals." Pat rubbed the loose skin on his big jaw with the back of his hand, reminding her of Terry's mannerism. "Not even I can get four on the floor."

"He always found a way of making connections." She had to change the subject. "I have news, Pat. A big company has invited me to New York to discuss franchising The Greenhouse and distributing my food lines."

"I'm so very proud of you, Allison. Doing all of this alone."

"I had you."

"Sean here yet?" Pat asked.

"He's at the table rubbing knees with Bonnie. What do you think of her?"

Pat gave her a sheepish look. "She's lovely and probably the right one for Sean. But I no longer give advice to men on personal relationships. I gave that up some time ago."

Allison broke into a throaty laugh and joined Pat for a drink. Her somber mood had dissipated. "They made Sean a detective."

"You can't be serious?"

"I wish I wasn't. Can you believe it?"

Pat fretted. "With the money we've got, he'd have the world by the balls if he wanted to do something sensible."

"Sensible? Sean's invited Barney Laver and Paul Cisco for dinner."

Pat was incredulous. "And they had the nerve to accept?"

She nodded. "I didn't want to rock any boats and make Sean suspicious. We'll have to tough it out."

"Sure we will. We're Sean's soldiers." Pat wrapped an arm around her shoulder, snuggling her head close, comforting himself and her. But then the ghost of his son reappeared. "Who would've thought that Terry would never come home?"

"I did. Oh, Pat, let's not go on with this. We do what we have to. My days were numbered. I knew that from the start. Terry was also a victim. *My* victim . . ."

Misty-eyed and still weighed down by the tragedy, Pat said, "My son, my Terry. . . . He was the best."

"I know."

51

Terry arrived at Spago, Jonah Wolfe's favorite spot. Jonah had always lived in a flamboyantly opulent style. In his realm, young women were queen for an evening, a day, seldom a week. Valerie's father had little regard for money or other people's feelings if they intruded on his pleasures. Jonah was at his usual booth at center stage, framed by the huge vase of flowers on the elevated rest behind him. In order to reach any table, diners had to pass his lookout post. Sitting beside him were a pair of young blond girls. Jonah got up. He scrutinized his son-in-law without enthusiasm.

"Terry, when my office gave me your message, I could hardly believe it. This is a first. You inviting me out to dinner?" He played to the girls. "I knew you couldn't stay mad for another twenty-five years." He winked at the blondes. "Who could?" The street-smart young girls tittered. Jonah snapped his fingers and the major domo sped over to him. "Find these ladies a table and please feed them. Nothing, absolutely nothing, with garlic or onions." Wrestling with their leather miniskirts and long legs, the girls wiggled up, and were dispatched.

Val occasionally mentioned Jane Ashley, idly curious about what had happened after Jonah had finished with her. Terry never had the heart to divulge the truth. Jane had been introduced to Madam Alex, Beverly Hills's queenly procuress for call girls. After another fall from grace, someone had mentioned that Jane had drifted down to Tijuana and was working the cribs at the back of tawdry clubs and servicing the boys from Camp Pendleton.

Jonah still practiced a relaxed grace that he lazily cultivated as though he were in line for the throne. His recent skin peel and iron-pumped frame reminded Terry of one those old Charles Atlas ads promising the world through dynamic tension at seventy-eight.

When Terry had first encountered him, Jonah had been sensitive about his tastes—still trying to maintain a good impression—and had paid handsomely to have them suppressed. With age, he no longer cared. His meatpacking plants and insurance company lay in ruins, shells of once-booming enterprises, casualties of his speculative outrages and irresponsibility. The millions had waned in Las Vegas and Monte Carlo, a wraith of the fortune once at his command.

"Still showboating with kids," Terry said.

"Find 'em, feed 'em, and fuck 'em." He looked at Terry with a woeful cast in his bloodshot eyes. "How are they? Val and Aaron, the grandson I never see?"

"Very well."

"It's all very sad," Jonah said.

"You brought it on yourself."

"You and Val got even with me is the way I see it."

Terry ordered caviar and a bottle of Cristal and told the waiter to put everything on his house account. Jonah raised his hands, mystified by Terry's amiability.

"Well, I am amazed. What is it we're celebrating?"

When Terry remained silent, Jonah's impatience and curiosity wore through the veneer of his mournful charm. Terry sat with a poker face, guarding his hand. Jonah reconciled himself to the fact that their meeting would not be pleasant. From their initial encounter, Terry Brett's self-assurance and acuity had spooked him. He was convinced that if Terry had taken the job as his counsel many years ago, his present circumstances would have been more favorable. Jonah needed a warrior by his side, but Terry preferred to go his own way.

"I bartered for your life today and it was very expensive."

Jonah's skin seemed to be stretching over his skull. "What the hell are you talking about?"

"Simon Pearl, remember him?"

"Sure. The investments I made were caught in a squeeze between merchant bankers. In any case, that weasel tried to use me as a Laundromat for his Vegas money."

"That's not the impression he gave me. I'll get to the point, Jonah. I bought your markers at a discount. You are now in debt to me."

"You had no fucking right to stick your nose in my business!"

Terry drank the champagne and ladled some caviar on a toast point. Jonah pushed his plate away. The caviar nauseated him, the champagne gave him such severe indigestion that his chest tightened.

"I decided it was. There are serious consequences involved, Jonah. So stop acting like a diva. You're an old fucking whoremaster. I can bring this to the attention of the league commissioner and the other owners and have them boot you out like a dog. Everyone's very sensitive about professional sports owners consorting with gamblers or people who are deemed undesirable. You're guilty of improprieties.

"Now look at the team. Morale on the Stars is very low and the season is only ten days old. They've lost seven out of eight games. The team's lack of cohesion and the lopsided scores make them very attractive to gamblers."

"I don't even bother to go to the games now. Basketball bores me. These crowds are the dregs."

Terry pressed on. "Just hear me out."

"If I must."

"When the spread runs twelve to eighteen points every game, it's like a lottery. There's tremendous action because of it. None of the games are ever close. It's just a question of how many points the Stars will lose by. You've taken a team that once was something and trashed it."

"I don't have to take this," Jonah said indignantly. "Why are you backing me in a corner?"

"To save your ass. I said that I bartered for your life. I wasn't overstating the case. You took a hundred and twenty million from Simon's people and then told them to drop dead."

Choleric, scowling, hands gesturing in futility, Jonah said, "I will not heel or be blackmailed this time, Terry."

"I've come to you as a courtesy and you don't deserve it. Today, I heard an expression I was unfamiliar with: 'angry money.' Simon Pearl wants you dead. Now, this isn't simply an idle threat that you can ignore. This is terrifying.

"Simon has a collection of psychopaths. He proposes to send a crew of them after you to appease the people who blame him for making an investment in your company. There's a male nurse from Columbus who likes surgery. A chemist from Arkansas who does experiments with acid. This is the meaning of angry money. It's not a figure of speech but your reality."

Jonah was being battered and humiliated, but Terry was hungry and pursued him relentlessly. A bully accustomed to fawning employees, Jonah had never experienced such virulence. He felt heavy angina palpitations slamming into his chest.

"You're involved with them, against me. It's a conspiracy."

"No, I'm your legal creditor. My options are very different and not available to Simon. I will force you into bankruptcy and break up the team by encouraging the players to default on their contracts. They won't show up for games. When you're filing Chapter Seven, I will renegotiate their deals. I can have the courts assign a trustee to take over. You will have nothing. No share of the receipts and intolerable legal expenses. You'll also have someone stalking you to satisfy Simon Pearl's ego."

Jonah placed a nitro pill under his tongue. "What do you propose?"

"I'll take a hike and you can put ten million tax-free in your pocket. You will resign from the Los Angeles Stars with a vestige of dignity. There will be a cosmetic but actual change in ownership. You will not attend any games or make any press statements. You will simply fade from the scene. As far as the media and the league are concerned, your son-in-law, a sports attorney, is the new owner of the Stars. It will be a short squib in the sports section. I will pass league scrutiny and cruise through any investigation."

Jonah fumbled with his pills and drank some water.

"What assurance do I have that Simon won't go through with this threat if I agree?"

Terry regarded the man with repugnance. "You won't understand this, but we shook hands on it. He gave me his word."

The chest pains had subsided. "The reason the Stars

never amounted to anything is that you wouldn't ever let any of your players sign with me."

"You stole Whiz Davis from me."

"He was a bust-out."

"You're to blame, Jonah. He wasn't ready to be a starter as a rookie. If he stayed with Chicago, he would've had a future."

"You always found a way to bust my balls, no matter what I offered."

"You were dishonest and a liar, a man without honor. I made sure we took our players elsewhere."

"I should have had you killed or done it myself the minute I met you."

Terry involuntarily touched the scar on his face. Despite the lack of evidence, he held Jonah responsible. The discolored declivity reflected the very dualism of his life, and of what he had become.

"There was a time when I would've been grateful."

Terry walked over to the table where the two young turnovers were gulping shooters and champagne chasers.

"Ladies, Mr. Wolfe needs some wind in his sails."

52

In the chill air the two men tried to keep out of the slanting sheets of rain beneath the dripping awning of The Greenhouse. They were to take part in Sean's celebration dinner.

"I'm concerned about Sean." The opinion was expressed by Paul Cisco, whose flirtation with the private legal practice handed over to him by Terry a quarter of a century ago had been a fiasco. He had returned to public service and was now in his sixth term as the district attorney in Port Rivers. "Sean's a very sensitive guy, Barney."

"That's what makes him so exceptional," Captain Barney Laver, the new detective's sponsor, replied.

"You're passing up people who have considerable seniority in favor of Sean."

"Paul, I know that. But our Special Investigation Bureau is weak. We need some fire. Which is why I'm sending Sean to L.A. I want him to learn how their outfit operates."

"They say that the Special Investigation Section down there are rogue cops nobody can control. Animals and stonekillers."

"Maybe we can learn how they get away with it."

Paul Cisco was displeased. Licking his lips in anticipation, he watched customers at the bar scooping up the sweet little Olympia oysters and drinking champagne. He was ravenous.

"I don't know how he'll handle those wackos in L.A." Cisco said.

"He'll do fine. He's intelligent."

"Okay, Barney. It's your call."

The two gentlemen who ruled Port Rivers tarried at the reception area, then dawdled in. Neither man could afford the prices at The Greenhouse and they dreaded facing its mistress. But it was Sean's birthday and they could not turn down his invitation.

Though acquainted with Allison for an eternity, they could never be certain of her behavior. She was dangerously mercurial, still very beautiful, and now wealthy. They had injured her seriously, and Sean had no inkling of their malicious folly.

Barney Laver suspiciously two-stepped behind Bonnie. He and Cisco were taken to Allison's table, but blocked at the perimeter where local potentates were paying tribute to her. Sean interrupted his mother and rose for Laver and Cisco like a candidate at West Point joined by superiors at the mess.

"Mother, I'd like to introduce you to the brass. Captain of Detectives Barney Laver, and the D.A., Mr. Paul Cisco."

Allison's brooding eyes were cloaked in shadows while they stood awkwardly at her table. Laver had lost his pompadour and his freckled scalp shone. Paul Cisco's weight had ballooned. His body was shaped like a fire-plug and he wore thick bifocals.

"We met some time ago," Allison said with aloof cordiality. Time had not obliterated the memory or her enmity. But the two men had been forced on her by Sean and she reluctantly fell in with his arrangements. Best to leave the brittle old bones to calcify into dust. She had not encountered either of them for years.

"I'm delighted to see you, Allison," Cisco said, stooping to kiss her hand. "I don't know how we could've gotten in to your restaurant without a royal invitation."

Paul Cisco controlled his office with a sense of urgency. He was celebrated for the timbre of his voice but dismissed as a repertory company Falstaff by the city council.

Barney Laver was sniffing the air and attentively examining the sturgeon grilled with a champagne mustard sauce being served at another table.

"We're honored to be here," Laver said. Her transformation from grifter to grande dame of the city confounded him. "Allison, you look damn good. Life's sure unpredictable."

"It always was, Barney. Less and less meets the eye, and when it does, it's still unbelievable." Allison smiled at last and raised her slender hand, long French-manicured nails fanning the air. "You're making the waiters nervous, gentlemen, please sit."

Pat Brett spotted them and came to the table. He occasionally ran into Cisco on guest day at the country club and avoided him. He was not feeling well and the presence of Allison's onetime antagonists made him irritable. Pat was drinking everything within reach. Allison signaled the waiter to remove his stocks; she was afraid that with one more, he'd begin to reminisce, and she was wary of indiscretions in this company. She instructed the waiter to serve India Pale Ale with the lamb curry, which she had prepared especially for her son.

"I'd like you to please explain these special investigations that Sean's going to be involved in." Allison was worried that it meant something beyond the usual work-day peril.

"Mother, come on, it's hush-hush."

"That's not an endorsement."

She glared at Barney, who was savoring his dinner. He was compelled to explain.

"It's an elite unit of detectives who go after professional criminals. People who've never been caught. These aren't your drive-by shooters. They're very smart."

Sean Arnold felt a rush of excitement. To be included in this remarkable group of daredevils brought him spiritually closer to his father, the two cut from the same cloth.

Cisco took up the cudgels. "Which is why we've established a cadre of unique law enforcement people. And Sean's been selected to be a part of it."

"Sounds like very high stakes poker," Pat added, sharing Allison's misgivings.

Sean looked around the table and spoke with pride of his father's daring exploits in Berlin during the Cold War. "When you see what's happened in Russia and Berlin, well, my dad's dying had something to do with their freedom."

Fortunately, neither Cisco nor Laver had ever known what was going on during the early years when Allison and Chris Arnold were raising their son in Seacliff. They had no reason to doubt the exploits of the departed gladiator. Allison apprehensively averted her eyes, for the direction of the conversation might reveal the truth. Pat might blurt it out. She was tense and grasped his hand tightly under the table.

The conversation drifted into the safety of mundane details. Laver speared the last of his curried lamb. "I remember when your mother was learning how to cook at Milly's place," he told Sean.

"Milly put me in business."

"She gave Allison all the recipes," Pat said with a sigh. "I miss her like hell."

"At least it was fast. She didn't suffer on machines," Allison said of her benefactor.

Milly had withstood Pat's roaming and vague proposals. The two had remained lovers until her recent death of a cerebral hemorrhage. When coffee was served, Allison was relieved that the evening was drawing to a close without incident. The dinner dishes silently disappeared; as she was about to call for the birthday cake, Bonnie signaled her to the reservation desk. Allison slipped away from the table.

"Some woman in the bar's carrying on. Banging back double brandies." Bonnie was skeptical. "Claims she's a friend of yours."

The woman's flesh oozed out of a drooping neckline and a dress that was too tight. Elbows hogging the bar space, she was surly and defiant. Once, she had possessed one of those pretty, miniature faces crammed into a plump frame. Her thick hair was braided back, but there was something unkempt about it. She spoke in a loud, hectoring tone to some men, which softened when Allison approached.

"Allison, Allison . . ." The woman reached out, but Allison deftly avoided the embrace. "I'm so glad, really glad to see you."

"What do *you* want, Georgie?"

"That's not much of a reception."

"What would you expect?"

"You're not still angry?" Georgie asked. "After all this time? Look how well you've done without Terry." Fumes of her brandy breath hissed through the air. "He kept you bottled up in that little dive on the coast for years. His dirty little secret. What kind of life did you have?"

"You're always in my prayers."

"It was for the best."

"Whenever someone tells me they've done something for the best, it turns out that it's best for them."

Allison turned to leave, but Georgie clutched her arm. Her bloated features erupted in sweat and tears. Mascara dripped on her cheeks and she whimpered.

"Come on, don't be so hard on me. Someone brought me in for a drink and went to make a call. The bastard never came back. It's so humiliating."

Allison regarded her with severity. "Your drinks are on the house. I'd like you to get out right now, Georgie."

Georgie obstinately held her ground. "I see you've got the whole crew here. What's the grand occasion?"

"It doesn't concern you. And you're drunk."

"Allison, in the old days I never touched a drink. Earl ruined me, my practice, my life."

Allison felt a resurgence of the anguish that had marred the evening. She was being suffocated.

"I can't keep them waiting."

"Can I come over?" Georgie pleaded. "I won't say a word. Once I was like family, wasn't I? Didn't I go to bat for you when you wanted Terry?"

Allison was accustomed to the distortions of lushes, but this invention transgressed reality. "That's a matter of opinion."

"Oh, Allison, don't. I've got nothing. I'm living in a lousy hotel by the docks and working in Vanities. It's that godawful sex shop Earl's girlfriend, Karen, opened. I'm selling lingerie to hookers."

"How's that possible? Earl's supposed to be loaded and you're a divorce lawyer."

"I haven't practiced in years. I was disbarred because Earl got me into trouble. He took my money, threw me out, and threatened to murder me if I didn't give him a divorce. He wants to marry this whore he lives with. I helped him all during our marriage and when he was in prison for a gambling scam."

"When you do Earl a good turn, he always finds a soft spot. And uses it against you."

"I'm lost, shot, Allison. If Earl doesn't kill me, I'll die on the streets."

Sean was heading toward them. Allison whispered sharply, "He doesn't know anything, so keep your mouth shut or I'll cut your eyes out."

"We're waiting, Mom."

"Sean! Sean!" Georgie staggered off the bar stool and Sean caught her. She braced his face in her piggy fingers and he squirmed away. "I held you as a baby. My, oh, my, what a gorgeous man." She turned to Allison. "Little Baby Sean. Sick all the time."

He was perplexed and displeased by the familiarity. Sean didn't like people touching him, getting close.

"Did you know my father?"

"Sure—" Allison nudged her.

"This is Georgie Conlan, honey."

"We were roommates when I had my condo. Remember, Allison, what a friendly, neighborly place the city was in those days?"

"Not for everyone," Allison interjected.

Reluctantly, she heeled Georgie to the table. Sean was quick to notice a distinct uneasiness among the men, who departed immediately after the birthday cake was served. Sean observed how agitated his mother had become, as though there was some hint of jeopardy.

After the restaurant closed at midnight and they were in the parking lot, he watched Allison giving Georgie some money as she hustled her into a cab.

"What the hell was that all about?" Sean asked.

"She's down on her luck."

"And you're a soft touch." There was a burr digging at him, some elusive component that didn't calibrate. Everyone had frozen when Georgie had appeared. "Is she a problem?"

"No—no. I helped her out. It's not important."

"You sure?"

"Of course I am."

Bonnie was standing indecisively beside Sean's car. Allison knew the feeling well, waiting for a man to make up his mind. The girl began restlessly pacing, suspended.

"The Lady or the Tiger?" Allison asked.

"The Lady, I guess," he said with a relaxed laugh. "I'll stay over at her place."

"So this is getting serious."

"I'm on the fence."

"She's a good girl, Sean."

"Oh, I know. Remember what Dad used to say about me?"

She'd had enough of Terry Brett for the evening. "What in particular?"

"That I was meant to have a special destiny."

"Yes," Allison said with unexpected sadness and nostalgia, "we were all meant to be destiny's darlings."

"He sure was something, that Ace." He kissed her. " 'Night, beautiful. Thanks for the bash, the car . . . and, yeah, my life."

Allison stood rooted to the spot, listening to their laughter, then on the car radio the sound of Sinatra singing, "I brought you violets for your furs . . ." as they drove off.

She felt her chest heave and realized she was crying. The sensation was foreign, disquieting. There had been a thousand nights of tears, but then they had vanished mysteriously and she found a way to heal. Allison pressed her hands to her face, battling to contain herself. But she was overwrought, choking, sobbing desolately.

Oh, Terry, I love you. Wherever you are, I miss you, my darling.

53

For years, Allison had worked to create a life without Terry and most of the time she succeeded in banishing his ghost. Sean had grown into a man she was proud of and respected. Although his choice of a career as a detective rankled her, she still entertained the hope that one day he would come to his senses. The Greenhouse was flourishing and Allison lived regally now.

She had bought the gracious old Van Wyck estate at River Cove. Pat had insisted, fixing a loan at the bank. During sleepless nights, her conservative instincts caused her to waver, but she finally agreed to risk the investment. The house gave her substance and marked her arrival in society. Although it hardly matched the exalted circles Terry and Valerie moved in, her status as a provincial aristocrat pleased her inordinately. The outcast had arrived and she attended charity fund-raisers, was voted Queen of the Firefighters' Ball, and took first prize at the flower show for her pink-blossomed lady's slipper. Like a reformed alcoholic, the onetime hippie Madonna basked in the glow of acceptance.

On their first Christmas together, Allison recalled visiting the place with Terry and exclaiming with girlish awe, *"These people must own the world."* He had replied, *"Very old money. Something we won't have to worry about."* River Cove still had the boathouse Terry had built with his father.

Allison put her imprimatur on the house, furnishing it with Victoriana, Irish linen, pale yellow moiré-covered sofas, wall tapestries, the memorials of a bygone era that she had only read about. Set well back from the street, with a panoramic view of the river, wide lawns, gables serpentined with ivy, old oak trees framing the entrance; with its maze, it had the look of the country houses she had visited during her travels in Europe.

Sean had been reluctant to leave Seacliff; to placate him, she had bought a forty-two-foot sloop so that he could continue his dead father's fabricated maritime tradition. Trolling for Dad. Ultimately she used the boat for gourmet picnics and was able to write off her son's bauble as a business expense.

She loved the house's stateliness, the topiary garden of ivy-covered deer she nurtured, the speckled gray cloudbanks swirling up from the river, the mysterious sounds of barge horns at night, the greenhouse in which she grew orchids that she gave often to her neighbors. What pleased her most was that she had done it alone, believing in herself. Without a family history, she had sought to invent the myth of one, and she saw herself as a pioneer who had tamed the wilderness. Eventually she came to be accepted by the town's old crowd.

Daydreaming, she sometimes lived with the muted expectation that Terry would walk through the door. She nurtured this illusion before the shock of the severance became actuality, mangling her emotions, driving them underground, repressed, gnarled. Eventually the day did come when she was convinced that there would be no reprieve and she would be trapped in the present. She had weaned herself away from happy endings.

Allison snapped out of the murky past. She laid her clothes out on the English four-poster bed. She was going to New York to make the rounds of the restaurants and to meet the executives at United Food and Beverage, who had made her an intriguing offer. She would travel light with one carry bag, knowing she'd come back with three others after a shopping orgy. Apart from the break in routine, what she enjoyed most about traveling was the social and intellectual inventory she could take to determine how she measured up against the elegant women on parade at the finest restaurants.

She knew that she could never compare herself to a true aristocrat, someone like Valerie, whose education and background were beyond her. After all, she was no doctor, just a cook. Still the owners of '21, Lutèce, La Grenouille, and Le Cirque were all her friends. They treated her regally, inviting her to the theater, arranging cocktail parties for her with the city's food writers. It was all good publicity for her jams, mustards, smoked meats, and she worked diligently to build her market. Somehow her loneliness was less pronounced, less an issue, when she was surrounded by courtiers who admired her style and imagination. Along with Alice Waters, she was one of the few women who had broken through in the male-dominated world of restaurateurs, redefining cuisine for Americans.

She picked up the phone and tried to call Sean again at Bonnie's place.

"Well, no, don't bother reporting it out of order," Allison told the operator. "I guess nobody at that end is in the mood for calls. Thanks for your trouble."

It was still busy, off the hook. She remembered those occasions when she and Terry did the same thing.

Allison still savored the pleasure of driving recklessly fast: if not for Sean's police connections, she would have had her license revoked long ago.

"You're not a wheelman at a bank robbery," Sean said with resignation, and yet he admired how skillfully she tooled her Silver Sovereign Jag, the quirky way she refused to conform.

They were driving to the airport. "Why're you going to New York?" he asked.

"I have an important meeting with the CEO of United Foods. I may have to travel with them. My itinerary's on the coffee table. And Bonnie knows where to get hold of me."

"What do they want?"

"There was a convention in Portland and some of their directors drove down and had dinner at the restaurant every night for a week. This was months ago. They looked over my food line in the market. Then they asked if I'd be interested in a new venture."

"You'd give up the restaurant and leave?"

"Honey, they're a twenty-billion-dollar company. Least I can do is listen. Maybe I'll be a consultant, who knows?"

"But you're doing so well," he insisted.

"Sean. It's a challenge. Pat's got a piece of property across from the university. I'm thinking of putting in a rotisserie—only take-out. Big beautiful turkeys, chickens, huge succulent roast beefs spinning happily in the window. The college kids' mouths are going to water. If this pilot works, I might set them up in college towns throughout the country."

"Would United Foods invest?"

"I haven't mentioned this to them." She took his hand. "If you ever decided to leave the crime business, you could run it. We'd really have some fun together." She pressed a set of keys on him. "Honey, please look at the property when you get back from L.A. There's office space above it. We could fix it up. You'd be an executive, build yourself a fortune."

"Thanks for thinking of me," he said with a caustic edge. "I also respond to challenges."

Allison was distraught. Her two men could always hit the nerve, rendering her helpless.

"Damnit, Sean, I have the largest emotional investment of my life in you. I never made you into a mama's boy. I gave you your character, Sean, not your father. And I can't help but feel that you're ruining everything by being a cop. It's all futile, such a waste."

"You don't like cops, do you?"

"I don't like criminals, either."

"Oh, please, Mom, let's not quarrel."

"Let's not."

Sean waved at the patrol car and she pulled into the no parking zone. "I won't see you for a couple of weeks, I guess." He leaned over and held her face close to his. "I asked Bonnie to come down to L.A. with me."

"You knew she couldn't leave even before you asked her."

"I wanted an excuse to get some distance. I don't know if she's *the* one. I'm very mixed up about the way I feel about her."

Allison kissed him and eased away. "I'm not the one to give you advice about this. But do me a favor. Bonnie has lovely qualities. She reminds me of what I was trying to do when I was her age. Taking courses at that JC in Seacliff and working. Making something of myself. For God's sake, don't tear her apart."

"I thought a separation would be some kind of test."

Allison wearily paused. "Did you ever ask yourself why men are always testing women?"

"No."

"So that they can prove that *they* exist."

"It was sort of eerie seeing your mother again," Barney Laver said, looking at the computer screen on his desk, which traced the detectives' progress on their case assignments. "That food shot my cholesterol through the cathedral—into the belltower." He looked up and smiled. "But it was worth it."

"I've been wondering about that dinner, Captain."

Sean had thought about discussing it further with Allison, but when he brought it up, she merely glided out of his grasp.

"She said she started to cook in Port Rivers. Even before I was born."

"That's true enough. Still, I'm glad she doesn't hold a grudge against me and Paul."

"Mr. Cisco?" Sean leaned across Laver's new maroon vinyl sofa. "Tell me about it. I feel like I'm seeing a trailer. I want to see the movie."

Barney Laver fleetingly contemplated Allison's old involvement with Pat's son. They had gone their separate ways. A busted youthful love affair. He never heard about Terry and hadn't seen Pat or Georgie in years. No point in going into it with the kid.

"It was a misunderstanding. We hassled Allison when she first drifted into Port Rivers. And she wasn't the only one by a long shot. She was a knockout—and wild. I think she's even more beautiful than she was in those days. She has an elegance." Laver began his somewhat dissembled and abridged account. "Jesus, she was harmless. But who knew? We were all paranoid in those days. Before she began baking pies at Milly's place, she was giving out these revolutionary pamphlets. Miss First Amendment. The sixties." He snorted. "She was stopping cars with these handouts is all. 'Get out of Vietnam . . . Free Cuba . . . Che Guevara.' That sort of thing. Before your time."

Sean was proud of Allison. She'd always been a gusty lady. Ace, his nickname for his father, and Allison. Mr. and Mrs. Christopher Arnold! What a magical, picturesque team they must have been. Poles apart. The patriot and his hellcat radical hippie.

"Tell me," Sean giddily asked, "did you bust her?"

"Get out of here, God, no."

Laver picked up a dog-eared green file held fast by a rusty paperclip. "Let me lay out your directives in Los Angeles. First, Sean, you're not to carry a weapon—any weapon."

"Yes, sir. Hey, what was all the stuff with that lush Georgie? She and Paul Cisco were law partners?"

"Sean, this is business now."

"I'm listening."

Gone were yesterday's apple pies. Sean leaned forward, intense. Barney was as happy as Allison had been to change the subject. He had expected Billy the Kid walking in with a fast-draw interrogation.

"I'm going to give you my no-bullshit advice. Twenty years from now, I want you to be chief of police, maybe even mayor of Port Rivers. You have leadership qualities. I know character. You have it all."

Sean snapped off a laugh. "I hear the guys in L.A. are terrific. They shoot dogs if they bark or take a dump."

"Ahhh, cut it out. Don't upset me."

"I'll do you proud, Captain Laver."

Barney Laver wondered if he had made a mistake, sending the kid down south. He could shoot out a rat's eye across a room and he had the instincts of a bear hunter, but he had his doubts about Sean when it came to actually shooting at a criminal.

"The Special Investigation Section have a case they've agreed to let you in on as an observer. You're coming in for the chocolate fudge dessert. They're like greyhounds down there. Guys in our Special Bureau still coop and belch their way through these things." He sighed with the frailty and pessimism of a man who had worked profitlessly and for too long. "Sean, I need a star who can also be a team player. Which is why I picked you. You're my rainmaker, Sean Boy. Shake up the team when you get back here."

Sean Arnold was elated by his confidence. This sanctioned his right to lead, to control the behavior of other people.

"We have some ugly people digging into our area. They're a bunch of bikers who did time at Walla-Walla and they're very well organized. Making Ecstasy and Crank. They're also moving girls down from Quebec and Montreal at truckers' stops."

"I've heard as much, Barney. I'll kick ass when I get back, don't worry."

Laver placed his arm affectionately around the kid's shoulder.

"Sean, please don't get yourself hurt in L.A."

54

The ward of the pediatric wing at the teaching hospital was always filled with evidence of God's unspeakable wrath, dying children. Drained by the sight of them, Dr. Valerie Brett had given up trying to balance their pain with logic. These corridors, labs, and lecture rooms had been Valerie's province for many years. Doctors grew accustomed to death; she had grown more sensitive.

She was concluding a talk to her interns on the clinical manifestations of an intestinal obstruction known as intussuception, which was extremely difficult to diagnose.

"It usually occurs in children between the ages of three months and six years. If the child also has gastroenteritis, it can mask the problem. As physicians, you have to watch changes in the patterns of illness and in the character of the pain. There may be vomiting or the onset of rectal bleeding and this should alert you. If it goes untreated by investigative techniques like a barium enema or surgical re-section, intussuception is nearly always fatal.

"I'd like to add one personal note. The practice of pediatrics is one of the most difficult of all specialties. You are dealing with people who are so young that they can't tell you what's bothering them. Be vigilant at all times, don't take any shortcuts. If you don't know, if you're not sure, refer them quickly to a specialist."

Back in her office, she waded through her correspondence and professional papers sent to her for editorial comment. Her afternoon was devoted to the free clinic and the referrals she had spoken about to her students.

Val almost forgot that she herself had been feeling tired and listless for the past weeks and had consulted a personal doctor friend at the beginning of the week. She had been given a battery of tests. It was nothing really, a raised bump below her shoulder blade which Terry had noticed during one of their rare couplings. She ignored it, but then some weeks later, she saw in the mirror that it was turning black and irregular and developing into a skin lesion. When Dr. Lawrence Yaeger's office called and asked her to come in that day, she became rattled.

"I've got a full load."

"Well, he'll see you after office hours. Say about six for a drink."

"Can I talk to him now?"

"He had emergency surgery and he's backed up with patients, Dr. Brett. You understand."

In his waiting room, Valerie was unable to concentrate. She had vast experience with these kinds of appointments with her small patients and their frightened parents. Even the most balanced people recognized the portents of such meetings. Most of the time, the news she offered was serious; occasionally there were tears.

Dr. Larry Yaeger was a tall, slender, sensitive man who was a distinguished surgeon and he had a reputation for excellence and circumspection. She had known him for years and had selected him because she was afraid if something was actually wrong, she would be enveloped by gossip at UCLA.

He rose when she came into his office and uncharacteristically embraced her.

"I'm truly scared out of my wits, Larry. I've never really been sick before."

He looked grave but forced a smile and gently said: "I don't have good news, Val. You know I did an excisional biopsy. Well, I had the lab check it three times."

"Assume melanoma unless proved otherwise," she said.

"Yes, it was positive."

His office walls collapsed then madly expanded and Valerie could not focus on the doctor's face.

She finally worked up the courage to ask the unmentionable, "What about my liver function, the bone and brain scans?" She fought to separate herself as an individual and a physician.

"I hate these reports. They're so impersonal."

"What is it?"

"We found multiple malignant nodules, with diffuse metastatic lesions. As a colleague and a friend, I'm so terribly sorry to give you this news. Val, you more than anyone know, we're not immortal."

The shock waves were thunderous. It was as though his soft voice had been attached to giant speakers. After a moment, she caught her breath. "Will I make it through Christmas?"

"I hope so."

"Is it very aggressive?" He nodded. She lost her self-control and began to rock in the chair, despondent and fearful. He put an arm around her. "No chemo, no surgery?"

"No, they won't help."

"Then what is there?" she asked, knowing the answer to her question. "I have so much to do. My students, my life with Terry. Aaron."

"You and Terry have to seize the moment."

He wrote her prescriptions for Seconal and Demerol. The sleeplessness and pain, quiescent so far, would come in a violent rush, a barrage, engulfing her.

At home, Val sat in Terry's dark study, clenching a large glass of scotch. She was surrounded by autographed photographs of sports figures he had represented and befriended. In many ways, this was the idealized boy's room, with footballs, bats, baseball gloves, and basketballs lovingly signed by his victors. Among Sports Associates clients and their families, Terry occupied a place of honor.

She heard him at the front door. He set down his attaché case on the hall table, rustling envelopes and magazines. He strode into the room, thumbing through *Sports Illustrated*. As he was about to switch on the light, he became aware that she was there.

"Val? Why're you sitting in the dark?"

"I must have dozed off. I just felt like being cozy with you."

"What a lovely surprise. I thought you'd be late after your lecture."

"I took off early."

He put his mail on the desk. "I'll light a fire. Get you a drink, babe. . . . Oh, you have one."

She wondered how to begin. How could she withhold the facts or be valiant?

I am a doctor, a professional. I know about these things. I can deal with . . .

But the voice within drowned out the search for poise. She was about to lose it all. The sun, laughter, music, the trees outside, the flower garden she had nurtured, Aaron her child. He was still her child. Almost greater than the fear of death, Valerie reached a state of panic imagining the loss of Terry.

"Billy's taking Christmas skiing reservations for Aspen. I told him we're in. I had to. His house is awful, twenty thousand square feet, a Tyrolean chalet. But he's so proud of it. The photos he showed me are horrible. Mike and his wife are staying at their condo. I guess we're stuck. Billy brought in a German chef. Can you believe we're going to be eating smoked goose and sauerbraten for Christmas. Did I forget herring?"

Terry threw on some pinecones and eucalyptus and switched on the gas burner. In a moment the room was bright with flames and comforting to Val. With a drink, he sat opposite her in a leather wing chair and they tapped glasses.

"I don't want to go skiing. Could we do something insane and go to Venice instead?"

"Venice?"

"Yes. We'll stay at the Gritti Palace again. Like we did on our honeymoon."

Terry frowned. "The weather's rotten this time of year. Rains all the time."

"Oh, come on. We'll get loaded at Harry's Bar."

He was puzzled by the request but let it go. "I haven't told anyone at the office yet. But Valerie, finally, I will be taking over the Los Angeles Stars."

"How? Don't tell me, you actually saw Jonah?" Ah,

her father was a subject she could get her teeth into and afterwards spit out the gristle. Jonah was good for her. He made her angry, took her mind off herself.

"He's dead broke."

"It couldn't happen to a nicer guy," Val said.

"I finessed myself into a deal. You know I've always wanted a team."

"There must be some trick he's got in store." She was confounded. "He actually sold it to you?"

"Darling, he didn't have a choice."

"I hope you took him over the coals. Terry, do you have enough money to close it?"

"God, yes, absolutely. My net worth, which doesn't include your money, is about two hundred million."

Yet another diversion presented itself before she had to make her nightmarish disclosure.

"My money. Is my trust secure?"

" 'Course it is." Terry was baffled. "What makes you ask?"

"I don't know. It's been so long since I've even thought of money and with you spending millions to buy out Jonah, I simply wondered."

"You can stop wondering. Prior to dividend distributions, your trust is in excess of six hundred million dollars." He was amused. "We may still avoid that damn *Forbes* list if I can snow them for another year."

The amount startled her, struck her as unfair, unjust, meretricious. What had she ever done to accumulate such a fortune? Terry had made it and managed it. Half of it should have been his.

"When Aaron marries Kit, she'll be sitting pretty."

"Val, forgive me, but I don't follow your drift."

She went to the bar in the corner of the room and poured herself another large scotch while he quizzically watched.

"I'll do that. I thought I was the bartender."

"Aaron will inherit from me?"

"Of course. From both of us. And the children's hospitals and our charities."

As she came toward him, Terry snared her in his arms

and settled her on his lap. She kissed him and buried her face against his.

"What's this all about, Val? Are you reading *Death in Venice* or Swinburne again? Is something wrong?"

"Have I given off any signals?"

"I'm not sure. You're kind of distant. . . . Venice? Valerie, what is it? It can't be *that* serious."

She could hold out no longer. The chill of death gathered around her, molding her thoughts.

"But it is." She was weeping. "Oh, Terry, my Terry," her voice broke, "I'm *going* . . . for good . . . and soon."

He was astonished and paralyzed. For a moment he could not look into her eyes.

"Valerie, what do you mean?"

"I have melanoma and it will ravage me."

He gasped. "There have to be treatments. There *must* be!"

"There are none for what I have."

He was befuddled. Suddenly, the certainty hit him with the impact of a bullet. He shuddered, stricken, sobbing openly, and she found herself consoling him, drawing him close.

"Come on, Terry. The hell with the rain." Freed of the secret, she grew stronger. "I want to hear Vivaldi's *Four Seasons*, see the Giorgione at the Scuole di San Rocco and have you hold me in your arms."

"Don't I hold you?"

"Yes, but in Venice it was different. Please let's go. . . . We'll visit Pia's palazzo and her chef will make us the gnocchi and fegato. I had a letter from her last week. She'll be eighty on the twenty-seventh and everyone from my old school will be there for the party."

Terry was unable to control his emotions. "Don't go on, Val. I can't bear it."

"I'll tell Aaron about my condition when I'm ready."

Terry wiped his eyes with the back of his hand and with abject desolation leaned his head against hers, holding her tightly in his arms. "This time Venice will be the honeymoon we should have had, darling."

"Without ghosts, Terry."

"Yes, Val," he said shivering.

Their anguish was a voyage of desolate winds searching for a wall to immure them.

Terry failed to convince Valerie to resign from her duties at UCLA. They had lunch the next day in the doctors' cafeteria. He had never before been there. When he spied her in a discussion with a group of worshipful students, he realized that this was a bad idea. Out of desperation, he was pressing her. She beckoned him to join the group and gave him the amiable Valerie smile, behaving as though nothing was wrong.

"You're magnificent. But you piss me off."

"I told you not to come. It would bore you."

"Nothing you do bores me," he said, clutching her in his arms at the elevator door.

Terry found it impossible to concentrate at the office; he skipped meetings, kept his door closed. Cruising back home down the Wilshire corridor, he decided to see Aaron at Kit's apartment. She lived on Beverly Glen in a fourplex with peeling green paint. Terry had dropped her off months ago when Aaron had been on call at the hospital. Kit had given him a drink of supermarket gin and filled it with cloudy ice cubes. She thought he could be useful. She had wanted to represent one of his players for a TV movie, but Terry had him sign with another theatrical agency. If things didn't work out, he would have had to kick Kit's ass, and this would cause problems with Aaron, who had started dating her. But Kit was pushy and he had his client turn her down directly.

Kit had risen from the dustbowl of Oklahoma but her behavior suggested lemonade on the porch, rides in convertibles to the lake with admirers, the confidence of a belle. She still flounced with sass. Mischievous and saucy, she had the allure of one of the flamboyant Guess girls. Terry was pleased that his son had selected a woman who was interesting and experienced.

Aaron, in a tux with a clip-on bowtie dangling, opened

the door. Terry had taught him how to tie bowties, but his son preferred shortcuts.

"We're going to a film premiere," Aaron explained. "This is a nice surprise, having you drop in finally. How're you doing, Dad?"

"Where's Kit?"

"Picking up Mom's dress at the cleaners. Is Dr. Brett on the warpath about me and Kit again?"

Behind Aaron were cartons stacked up to the wall, books slanting on the shelves where he had begun to plant them in some wayward order. The bed was unmade, Kit's lingerie soaking in the kitchen sink. Terry balanced on the arm of a sofa while Aaron rinsed some mugs and gave his father a drink in one of them.

"Let me tell you that I like Kit. She's aggressive, spunky, a go-getter, and in lots of ways your opposite. That can be very stimulating in a relationship."

Aaron laughed. Despite his determination to appear older, the mature psychiatrist, he seemed like an embarrassed boy trying on a man's clothing.

"Go on, I'm starting to enjoy things. But leave this when Kit comes in."

Aaron always imposed rules and it annoyed Terry.

"This isn't some psychiatrist session, so please don't talk to me like a patient. And if I sound hostile, it's because of your attitude, not mine."

Aaron finally secured his bowtie. "Well, let's begin," he said blithely.

"Your mother never wanted you to hang out with rich society riffraff and dopers, and you got the message early. The fact is, she has certain standards of morality, which she tries to impose on other people. It makes them uncomfortable. She's one of those old-fashioned straight shooters."

"That's obvious."

Aaron slipped on his flea market knock-off wireframed Armani specs, ready to listen to this patient's complaints.

"Why don't you buy yourself a decent tux? You can afford it."

"Photographers are not on my trail. I don't care. We're going to a movie and I can get some sleep. What's on your mind?"

"Okay. I want you to *tell* Kit to give up this dump because you've decided to move into the guesthouse."

Aaron waited and looked at Terry with a hint of anger. "That would be very imperious. I don't order Kit around. Kit and I still have things to work out. The other thing is, she won't take any crap from Mom. And neither of them will compromise."

"Kit will compromise her position to please the man she loves," Terry said. "I'm an expert in this territory."

His son was attentive. Terry thought Aaron's raven dark eyes had the force of lances and must have been disconcerting to some patients. In his gaunt features there was a lazy, handsome quality that might have been more pronounced if his manner weren't condescending. Nothing was ever straightforward for Aaron. He interpreted reality as a coded transmission, a series of symbols.

"If this is some kind of collusive effort with you fronting for Mom, you can forget it, Ace."

"What the hell're you talking about? Since when have I interfered with your life?"

Aaron retreated. "What's got you so pissed off, Dad?"

"Don't give me any shit, Aaron. I have something catastrophic to share with you." Terry could hardly breathe. "Your mother is lost to us. She's dying."

Aaron seemed in a spell, then his head snapped back as though from a hard blow. The impending calamity registered shockingly on his face and Terry almost wished he hadn't revealed Valerie's condition.

"Oh, Christ, don't tell me, God, no, no!" Aaron slumped into a chair. "She didn't want me to know?"

"No."

"Oh, Dad . . . Dad, are you okay?"

"Now that it's sinking in, I am devastated. I feel a sense of despair like never before. I don't know what to do."

"How bad is she?"

"Melanoma."

"How aggressive is it?"

Terry foundered before announcing the verdict. "Weeks, a few months. It's going to be very soon, Ace."

They held each other like a forlorn couple.

"And I've been quarreling with her."

"She won't hold it against you, Aaron. You know as well as I do, she loves you more than anything. There's lots to talk about and I think with you moving back home, it'll be easier."

"Of course. What will you tell Mother?"

"That Kit lost her lease and you want to stay with us until you can find a condo or a house."

"Will Mom believe it?"

"I've sold her before," Terry said. "The problem is Kit."

"I'll deal with Kit. In any case, I'm fed up living here."

Terry was burnt out but pushed on. He had to make Aaron face up to what lay ahead.

"Aaron, there are some other things I'm bound to mention as a lawyer. We've always lived comfortably, bought what we liked, but we avoided flash. No limelight. I shun press interviews. We keep a low profile. Your mother is a modest woman. Oh, sure, she likes to spend a buck on high-fashion clothes, but she's earned a very good living and so have I. Actually, I've made a fortune—millions in a business that was a fluke."

"Are you serious? That's outrageous."

Terry suppressed a laugh. It was all hollow to him now.

"Your mother inherited a fortune before I met her." Aaron's cool professional demeanor gave way to surprise. "Some years ago, I took over her trust and made strategic investments on her behalf. I had this small-town, stubborn pride about myself and I excluded myself from her will—against her wishes, I should add. Half will go to you, with myself and Billy Klein as trustees."

"How much is it?"

"After what she's set aside for charitable contributions, something like three hundred million."

Aaron took on Valerie's self-effacing innocence when

such matters were brought up. He seemed to be surveying the room for a place to hide as Terry elaborated.

"Three hundred million? Dad, what do I do?"

"You can try to follow your mother's example. Live quietly, not talk about it or showboat. Complete your residency and try to do some good for other people."

Aaron shook his head fretfully, searching for some grand design in the universe.

"The way I've talked to patients about death . . . everything sounds ridiculous. Bullshit." His voice had a broken string. "Dad, I love her so much. I wish I knew how to handle this."

"You're a good guy. I love you, Ace."

"Nobody like you, Dad. You're the *real* Ace."

With the dress she had borrowed from Valerie and grocery bags spilling from her arms, Kit heaved open the door. She was about to drop everything when Terry caught a sack of frozen pizzas.

"Terry? How lovely to see you. I'm sorry we're rushing out." Kit had on a black velvet cape and Valerie's low-cut Venetian lace evening gown. Thick reddish-blond hair piling into her face, Aaron's Primavera might have leaped out of a fashion magazine. Smelling of something tantalizingly sweet, she kissed Terry. "I tried to call Valerie to thank her and kept missing her."

Aaron remained on the fringe, immune to their small talk.

"Kit, you can thank her when we have dinner."

"Whenever you like."

"We're going to be seeing a lot of each other from now on."

"I'm no match for someone like Valerie. You'll help smooth things over, won't you, Terry?"

"I've always been on the side of love, Kit."

"You make me melt."

"I'm casting bread on the water for my old age."

In the hallway, Terry held on to his son. "Think about setting a wedding date very soon."

55

Four days into his assignment with the Special Investigation Section (SIS) in Los Angeles, Sean found himself deeply frustrated with the case. All the shadowing, the lurking in bar corners, sitting in dirty vans checking surveillance equipment, watching video monitors, logging the team in, the diet of cold, greasy junk food, frazzled his nerves. Under surveillance were two men and a woman from North Hollywood. The men had been out of prison for a year. The woman, Brenda Leighton, who lived with them and acted as their spotter, had never been convicted. They specialized in following wealthy people home and robbing them. They were heavily armed and suspects in dozens of such crimes. Several of the victims had been ferociously beaten and two had been shot.

Sean and the SIS were camped outside Spago on the Sunset Strip observing Los Angeles's patricians. In their wake and equally as grand as this aristocracy was its embellished sewage: well-turned-out and fashionable hookers who looked as though they were Vassar graduates, beau monde pimps, and the cream of this detritus, nimble drug dealers, with fistfuls of cash, wheeling out of Porsches.

"I think our suspects need a goose," Sean told Commander Browning, who gave him a grizzled Irish stare from darkly creased eyes that never seemed to have known sunlight.

"Do they?"

"Yes, sir. I'd like to go inside, order champagne at the bar, try to pick up a hooker. I'll make sure everyone hears that I'm in the music business. And I have a mansion in Bel Air. The woman they've got as a nose is still exploring. Let her find me, Commander Browning."

"The problem with that, Sean, is that you've got nothing worth stealing."

Browning liked the kid's refreshing offbeat inventiveness, his instinct for confronting trouble. Maybe he should send this young hotshot in.

"You'd have to set me up with a house there. And give me a roll. Believe me, I'll rattle the cage."

"It'll take too much time," another detective observed.

The principle of arrest and conviction of dangerous felons was contrary to the SIS code. In their world, the very notion of apprehension or the concept of a trial was a violation of their self-styled charter.

"Look," Sean persisted, "I'm a new face. No one in L.A. knows me. Let me stir the pot."

Browning nodded. "Okay, Sean, go in, keep quiet, and work the bar."

Sean left the unmarked van and noticed two valets, also detectives, and two cars with men inside, watching him.

He had never been to a restaurant as celebrated as Spago, which his mother spoke of with reverence. He passed through a large, perfumed crowd and bullied his way to the bar. He observed Brenda Leighton, a sylphlike blonde, go to the telephone. She was the finger in the crew. Had she spotted anyone?

"Give me a split of champagne," he called out to the bartender. When he was served, Brenda had returned. Her head bobbed up like a swimmer and she made eye contact with him. It was clear to Sean that she was extremely sharp. Sean lifted the split from the bar and through the mass of bodies offered it to her. She smiled and looked away.

He continued to drink and went through another split, careful to avoid her gaze. A combo of women, yoked to a pimp, examined him. He counted three pairs, all with an individual blocker, an older woman who acted as a bodyguard and could shoo away any man who didn't smell of money. An hour later a middle-aged couple, apparently well known, started past the maître d's station.

They were waylaid by a group of suck artists who shook their hands and kissed the woman.

Sean casually watched them from the window, as the valet helped them into a Rolls-Royce. Brenda scrutinized them, then headed for the ladies' room. He laid a hundred-dollar bill on the bar and told the bartender he'd be back. He strolled outside, stretched, and whispered to a valet.

"I've got the license of the Rolls."

The valet signaled the detectives' cars. Sean got into the backseat of a blue Mercury beside Browning.

"We could be in business, sir. Brenda just called again."

"I owe you an apology, Sean. Your sleepy little village is going to have a real pro on its squad. I'll vouch for that."

A van and a convoy of detectives' cars crept along Sunset Boulevard toward the beach while Browning ran the Rolls license through the DMV.

"It's registered to Nathan Burkman. He's a jeweler in Beverly Hills. He lends his trinkets to movie stars for Oscar shows and charity benefits. He's got a condo on El Camiño and a house in Malibu."

"Maybe our gentlemen are going to visit him for an appraisal," Sean said.

Other SIS cars in communication entered from Temescal Canyon and were now ahead of the Rolls on the Pacific Coast Highway. Huge concrete walls with steel mesh wire had been constructed during the previous rainstorms. It was an annual event on national TV, as audiences sipped beer and watched boulders and mudslides ooze down the soft, brown-cropped mountains, carrying multimillion-dollar homes from the eroded beaches into the ocean.

In silence, they passed the Malibu Colony and its security post. The shopping center was alight, and ahead of them, a Dodge van pulled out and trailed after Nathan Burkman's Rolls-Royce.

"Could be them," Browning said. He had Burkman's address and informed the cars in the escort to stop before they reached his house and reconnoiter on the beach. No one was to intercept either the Burkman car or the Dodge following it. Over the radio, Browning was informed that Burkman had pulled into his driveway and was opening his garage. The Dodge had passed the house and then turned around. It was parked on the verge of the road and two men had gotten out, wearing backpacks.

The men were spotted walking through the treeline and then vanished.

Browning and Sean with three other detectives' cars met a hundred yards short of Burkman's house.

"Now what? Are we going to take them?" Sean asked.

"Jesus, Sean, you think we've got twelve officers here to arrest these comics for B&E or unlicensed possession of a firearm?" Browning snapped.

"Kid, we're not in the business of entrapment," another detective informed Sean.

"Or to read them their rights," said another member of the team.

The detectives opened their trunks and seized Bonelli shotguns and cartridge bandoleers. Browning signaled them to move to the beach. Sean trotted alongside and had out his cherished Commander .45. Now that he was about to see action, he was horrified by the detectives' plan. They were going to wait until the Burkmans were robbed, beaten, possibly murdered, and they had no intention of intervening.

Over the radio came the calm voice of a detective:

"Suspects have entered the house . . ."

As the team of men crept along the beach, another squad was hiding in the Burkmans' front garden. Sean and the men saw the blinds being closed. There was a muffled scream followed by a dread silence with only the grate of the wind and the monotony of waves clapping the beach.

Sean waited apprehensively and studied the impassive faces of these detectives who might have been in a duck blind waiting for the birds to take flight. After a half hour of sweating, they watched as two men dressed in black left the house, climbed over the deck, and dropped onto the beach.

The SIS had them sandwiched. With a faint call of "Police" from Browning, spotlights were turned on and a rampage of gunfire ravished the silent beauty of the beach.

Sean stood back. The two men were armed with Uzis and fired furiously, but then they dropped their weapons and raised their hands. It was to no avail. The crossfire of sharpshooters with shotguns cropped them like grass. Sean dashed over their bodies and sprinted into the house.

He saw the elderly jeweler hog-tied to a kitchen chair. He was bleeding heavily from a series of knife wounds and Sean untied him. He helped him to a sofa.

"Where's your wife?"

"Upstairs."

As Sean ran up the spiral staircase, he shouted to the detectives storming in, "We need an ambulance!" The attractive woman he had seen hours earlier was naked, hanging upside down from a chinning bar in the gym. He undid the wires on her ankles and eased her into his arms. Her breathing was labored, eyes rolling, and her color jaundiced.

"Get a medic or we're going to lose the woman!"

Sirens, flashing lights, and mobs were already outside the house. Paramedics bolted into the room. Sean watched them take her vital signs and then lift her onto a stretcher. His head spinning, in a flood of light, he followed them down to the ambulance.

The team of shooters smugly surrounded the body bags of the two men, which were heaved into the back of an open coroner's wagon.

"Did you give some first aid?" a detective asked sardonically.

"He did fine," Browning said. "Somebody's got to look after the civilians. You've got chips on the table in this town."

"You're right, sir," said another detective, his shotgun

crooked in his arm. "How do you do things up your way, Sean?"

Before Sean could reply, Browning interceded.

"Let's do the reports and meet down at New Otani in Little Tokyo. Do you like sushi, Sean?"

"I used to."

"I'd like you to join us. We're going have ourselves a feast and raise a little hell."

"What about Brenda? Does she walk?" he asked.

"Let's not be greedy. She's got two policewomen tagging her."

"Hey, Sean, if you're lonely, invite her along and see if she wants to party."

56

Aaron could not even begin to address the shock of his mother's imminent death. After a film premiere that he found stultifying, he slowly composed himself. Later that night, when he and Kit were in bed, Aaron decided he could not reveal the true reason for initiating a move back home.

"I've thought this out carefully, Kit," he had informed her after Terry had come up to her apartment. "Living here is interfering with my residency. I need the space we can have at the guesthouse at home. It's too disruptive here."

"Why? I don't understand." Kit was sulky and puzzled. "I thought we cut a deal."

"I was trying to placate you. The real reason you don't want to move into the house is that you're afraid of my mother. So let's confront the issue and see if you two can work things out."

"Why do I have to stick my hand in the fire? She intimidates me, Aaron. The few times we met were enough to convince me she doesn't think I'm right for you." Kit's face was pinched with misery. "She looks at me like I was rough trade. And what has this got to do with your training?"

He took a quantum leap into the unknown depths of his subconscious, exposing the snares he had reluctantly discussed with his mentor at his therapy sessions during his training.

"There are deep, unspoken attachments between my mother and me. I guess it all came about when I was a kid. My father was always away recruiting players to represent. We hardly ever saw him. Thanksgiving, even Christmas, he'd be at some basketball tournament or spring training with one of his major leaguers. Now I recognize how absolutely compulsive he was about his business. Terry bought into the success racket and nobody could get him off the swing.

"What I'm trying to say is that there are elements in my own makeup which are also at war. In conflict, Kit. This has to do with unresolved issues within my family. I've grown up puzzled about my parents, their relationship, their mysterious past. If I don't go back home, I'll feel I missed something valuable, and I won't have another chance to be close to them again."

Kit had discovered harmony, a new balance when they were together. Now he was taking that away from her. Only in the area of their intimacy was she in charge, transcendent. She had been astonished by his inexperience. Oh, he understood everything medically, but he demonstrated a degree of awkwardness, sheer greenness, that was endearing. He had never had a long-term relationship with a woman. She did not attribute this naïveté to fears of disease, but rather the controlling influence of his mother.

"I don't get it. Your parents strike me as happy and devoted. What do you expect to find out about them?"

The imminence of Valerie's loss had set off a chain of events that rocked Aaron.

"I'm not sure. But something's always nagged me. I can't put my finger on it. There's so much left out, gaps. People who choose to become psychiatrists have a tremendous curiosity about themselves. There's nothing ac-

cidental about the decision. In a way, you are your own
first patient, a detective investigating your own mind,
your behavior."

"I love you, Aaron, and I'll do my best to help you
work this out."

Aaron showed Kit through the guesthouse adjoining the
bright crown over the ocean bluff which his parents had
built as a citadel to shelter their love. During Terry's
absences, he had been very lonely as a child, but when
he was about twelve, they saw more of each other. Now
that Terry was regularly home, his mother, always bur-
dened by her practice, seemed to blossom again.

He led Kit into the main house for drinks in the library,
a paneled, baronial room of deep dark brown leather
chairs, a pair of nineteenth-century Chesterfields beside
the crackling fire which Terry was stoking. Above them
was a circular gallery containing thousands of rare books,
leatherbound classics, medical and legal volumes. Even
the syncopation of a Bach Brandenberg Concerto unnerved Kit. Looking pale and somewhat worn-out, but
splendid in a dark green suit, Valerie was drinking sherry.
Kit never liked the taste and asked the butler for a vodka
on the rocks. On the walls were a gallery of Impressionist
paintings. Kit recognized a Renoir that she had once
bought as a print for her first apartment.

"I hope you're settling in," Valerie said.

"I'm not organized. I don't seem to have the time."

"Nor does Aaron," Valerie replied quickly, as though
to establish immediately who was more important.

"We'll all pitch in. Kit, this is going to be your home,"
Terry said pleasantly, "so please feel free to ask the staff
to get whatever you need. And if you want a particular
dish, some down-home cooking, we'll have it."

"Chicken-fried steak?" she asked and was met by Valerie's censorious eyes.

"Love it," Terry said with relish. "Or I did until Val
had it officially declared a poison. When I traveled to
recruit players down south, I lived on that sort of food
and barbecue."

Kit took a big belt of her drink. "It's going to take me a while to get used to living without a Laundromat, broken toilets, and frozen food."

Aaron hugged her. "We'll try to survive without Mrs. Paul's Fish Fingers and meatloaf!"

Terry noticed how quickly Kit had downed her drink; he took her glass and refilled it. He wanted to put her at her ease. "I know it might be a little overwhelming at first, but Val and I want you to be comfortable and happy. So if we're not around, you're in charge, okay?"

"I am?"

At dinner over champagne and grilled salmon, she and Valerie loosened up, or at least Kit thought Valerie was less of a prosecutor until she got caught out.

"Exactly what kind of shoes does your father manufacture?"

"He sells them."

"Oh, I see."

"Retail," Aaron shot in. "He's a nice guy. I met him when he came for a visit a few weeks ago."

"He has a shop?" Valerie continued.

"Yes. He sells cut-rate shoes, off sizes, slightly damaged. His customers are mostly blue-collar, like me, Valerie."

"Does your mother work with him?"

"No, they were divorced years ago and he raised me."

Kit's grittiness reminded Terry of Allison and how abrasive Pat's inquisition had been when they first met. Terry's sympathies were engaged and he gently prodded Valerie under the table, but she moved with the deadly stealth of a cat approaching a hummingbird. Aaron reacted with a sense of urgency.

"Speaking of fathers, Dad, how's yours doing?" He had to take the pressure off Kit. "My granddad, Pat. I guess I met him a couple of times. For some reason, this family hasn't done well with fathers. Do you ever hear from him?"

The question exploded in Terry's brain. As the attention turned sharply in his direction, he became nervous.

"No, not in years. I don't even know if he's still alive."

Valerie consoled him. "Don't get down about it, Ter."

"Oh, I'm not."

Valerie had found her cause. "It's been our misfortune to break with our fathers. Mine is depraved. He seduced a girl who worked for me many years ago. She was like a younger sister. I thought I might help her through medical school." Valerie's eyes clouded. "You won't be meeting our fathers, Kit."

Terry remained silent, and with dinner over, brandies in hand, he and Valerie walked the young couple back to the guesthouse. Valerie had not finished with fathers. Again she took up the cudgels, turning to Aaron.

"Your grandfather, Pat Brett, asked your father to do something dishonest about a criminal offense he was involved in. It was a monstrous conspiracy. From my point of view, he's an absolutely despicable man. He was certainly no friend to me."

Terry knew that nothing could have been further from the truth. His father had a righteous cause, defending his relationship with Allison and Sean. Terry tried to struggle out of the bad dream.

"It was a question of deceit," Terry said, "and the truth is, I was responsible for his actions." Aaron was somewhat startled by the dejection he observed in Terry. "It's too late to fix and too obscure to elaborate on."

"So much for family history," Aaron said, puzzled but circumspect about an old feud.

When they had gone, Kit kissed Aaron outside the guesthouse. "Aaron, I'm not even curious. That's one of the advantages of a southern upbringing. You don't ask questions."

Leaning on Terry's shoulder after they had said their good nights, Valerie touched his hand sympathetically and they started back to the house.

"You don't think of the old times—the other life—do you, Terry?"

"No, the slate's clean."

"Regrets?"

"Never."

Every day the ruin of Valerie became more tangible,

and at unbearable moments like this when they were close, she so brave and uncomplaining, it seemed to Terry he had lost gravity, descending in a free fall through the galaxy of his old lies. The time he had stolen from her with Allison could never be restored.

"Terry, did you tell Aaron about me? Is that why he came back?"

"I think he missed *you*."

The E.R. staff at Daniel Freeman Hospital had been alerted, and by the time Sean reached Marina del Rey, Nathan Burkman was already in a private room and fully conscious. He beckoned Sean to his bedside. He took Sean's hand and pressed it against his lips.

"You were the one who got Mimi and me out."

"Yes, sir. They cut you pretty good, Mr. Burkman."

"I don't care. The plastic surgeon is on his way. How's my wife?"

"She's going to be fine. They put her on a defibrillator and her heart contractions are back to normal."

"Thank God for people like you. You're still a boy."

"That's why I grew a beard."

"What's your name?"

"Sean Arnold. I'm not from L.A. I came down here on a training course with the SIS and they took me along tonight."

"What happened?"

"These people followed you and your wife from Spago and we got a call," Sean said, sticking to the official version mandated by the SIS command. "These men were specialists, and before we knew it, they'd broken into your house."

A flush of surprise brightened Burkman's sallow skin. "You were outside?"

Sean nodded. "We couldn't go in after them because they might have held you hostage or killed you and your wife."

"I see," he said, accepting the logic. "Sean, have you got a girlfriend or a wife yet?"

"No, but I'm getting close."

"You in love with her?"

"Yes, I think so, Mr. Burkman."

"When you propose, don't buy her a ring. Come down to Beverly Hills and pick out something for her in my store. I can't have *you* getting robbed."

"We'll see, but thank you, sir."

"I've got to do something for you and your squad. Do you like basketball?"

"I love it. I go to as many Trail Blazers games as I can with my uncle Pat. He gets us floor seats."

"So do I. The owner of the L.A. Stars is a customer of mine. I usually take clients. The team's not doing too well. They're playing the Bulls tomorrow night. It'll be a runaway, but Michael Jordan and hot dogs is the best I can do. I want you to use my tickets. Take the guys with you. I've got six seats."

"Okay, I will."

"Bless you. I hope your father appreciates the kind of son he has."

Book VI

THE FLOWERS OF SECRECY
AND SHADE

57

In the pantheon of gods hanging on the walls of Dr. Saul Greenman's office, Freud was king. He gave Jung and Adler their due with smaller photographs, but the two framed letters he had bought in Vienna when he was a student were written by the master.

A bear of a man, the size of a linebacker, Dr. Greenman had a caustic, hard-driven manner. The sound of his bass voice made the residents he trained and supervised quake as they heard their work hit by a sledgehammer. Greenman was surveying the diagnoses on Aaron's current cases. He shoved away the stack of files on his desk and stood for a moment beside his young resident.

"This forensic case you've submitted to me for review and approval in regard to the criminal procedure law troubles me. Let's hear your reasoning from the patient's personal history as well as your clinical observations."

Aaron felt he had already made a gaffe.

"The case was well worked up and provided a current diagnosis and was discussed at the medical staff meeting. This is a follow-up. The individual was found by the courts to be not responsible for his acts by reason of insanity and the patient was hospitalized for psychiatric treatment."

"I know that; go on."

"The patient committed an ax murder on his father because he *thought* he overheard a physician tell him that he had terminal AIDS. It's hard to believe, but the patient claims he subsequently perpetrated a mercy killing."

Exasperated, Greenman broke in, "Pardon me. Let's get this straight, Aaron. Your patient's records reveal he had sustained a head injury and there's documentation of heavy cocaine abuse prior to his violent behavior. He also had a history of chronic alcoholism."

Aaron felt cornered. "He was worked up at Atascadero

for organicity with negative findings. He was found to be not psychotic."

"Really?"

"I placed him on Antabuse. With successful results, Dr. Greenman. He is still a recovering alcoholic. My diagnosis is dissociative disorder. I've concluded that the patient has an intermittent explosive disorder."

"I don't agree with that. My feeling is that he had a toxic psychotic episode associated with drugs and alcohol and that clearly rules out a dissociative disorder. The other thing, Aaron, your current diagnosis in no way reflects the patient's history of severe psychotic episodes. Don't you see that this has to be included to maintain your perspective and for treatment strategies?"

Aaron shrank back from Dr. Greenman's withering eyes.

"Let's throw the books out. I don't give a damn about an elegant diagnosis or even about what criteria you're using. Anyone who tells you that he's hacked up his father with an ax to relieve his pain and it's a mercy killing is psychotic in my book. Crazy!"

Preoccupied, Aaron stared out of Dr. Greenman's office window at the campus below where groups of students were dashing into Westwood.

"Aaron, I'd like to push on to the aspects of major depressive episodes as they relate to hospital admissions."

Aaron's mind strayed to his own mother. Valerie would be completing her morning panel on the uncommon infectious diseases of childhood at the medical school. Would he have time to meet her for lunch? He agonized over the physical changes, her sallow skin, bloodshot eyes, the way she was piling on makeup as though this would conceal the tumor ravaging her.

"Something wrong with you, Aaron?"

The thought of lying to his supervisor crossed Aaron's mind.

"I'm having a generalized anxiety reaction—as we speak. My father used to have them." Aaron tried to humor himself out of the bind. "Maybe it's genetic."

Dr. Greenman took Aaron's pulse, felt his carotid artery and looked at his pupils.

"Lie down. Tell me what's happening. Am I being too tough on your work? It's passable as it stands. But I've come to expect more from you."

Aaron could not determine what was appropriate behavior. Should he bottle up his emotions or let them flash out like shells from the mouth of a cannon? He slunk down in a deep leather sofa and reflected on the green, untroubled moments of his childhood when he was not haunted by his mother's loneliness.

"You seem disturbed, Aaron. What are you worried about?"

"Right now . . . Saul, I'm concerned about crying in front of you."

"Nobody's immune to these events. Don't be guarded. Talk to me, Aaron. What's going on? Are you having some form of father transference? Are you feeling hostile toward me, him . . . us?"

"I'm having sexual problems. There's no question about it," Aaron admitted. "Since I moved Kit in against her will, things have gone sour with us. I've become impotent. She feels rejected. It's reached the stage where she's getting desperate."

"Is this all of a sudden or is there another reason?"

"Why do you ask?"

"My recollection from our previous discussions is that you were crazy about Kit and she was driving you up the wall when she was still getting over that actor guy? Doesn't Kit appeal to you now? It happens. We want a woman desperately, we get her, and we don't know what to do. Frankly, I'm still not clear about why you moved her into your parents' place."

The painful conflicts crawled in and out of Aaron's mind like spiders.

"My mother's dying," he said. "Melanoma, advanced. And she's getting weaker every day. It's so fast. I can't look her in the eye. We haven't discussed it. She knows I know and we can't find an opening through the wall.

It's like she's performing some ritual. Burying herself psychologically before the end."

Dr. Greenman could not mask his own shock and personal distress. He reached into his drawer and poked at a cigar that had been there for ages.

"Valerie, dying of cancer? Christ, she's my friend and my kids' pediatrician." As his confidante, Greenman had discussed his divorce and second marriage with her when the prospect of becoming a father late in life troubled him. She had reassured him. Valerie Brett was the most balanced woman he had ever met.

"Maybe we can make some assumptions about your temporary impotence. Your mother has implicitly forbidden you to be intimate with another woman at this time. It would be disloyal to her. You'd be cheating. And your repressed incestuous feelings are streaming up to the surface. You want to be close to her, nurse her, return to a time that was comforting for both of you. So you've got yourself into a double bind with the women. And of course your father's around. His is the voice of authority and the supreme representative of prohibition."

"I was thinking of asking for a leave of absence."

Greenman's face flushed and his voice rose. "No, forget that. I'm turning you down flat. If you're going to be one of my boys, you better learn how to live through rough times yourself. Because the people you're going to be treating will be going through hell. And you're going to persuade them to function, hold a job if they can and not murder anyone. Let's address ourselves to your problem, not take a powder on it, Aaron."

Greenman let a little time pass without prodding as Aaron struggled in the emotional current but was helplessly drifting toward the maelstrom, in dread of exposing the very core of himself.

"According to my father, my mother doesn't want me to know what's going on. It's our secret."

"This seems kind of surreptitious for people as enlightened as your parents—certainly your mother. So they have a conspiracy. And you and Terry have another one, your ignorance. Good guy, bad guy, and you're in the middle with a dirty secret. Well, we know there are no *dirty* secrets, just secrets."

"My mother wants to bow out elegantly, with style."

"Perhaps in another sense, your mother wants you to retain a certain innocence, and of course it's doubly ironic since you're both physicians. She's being protective, Aaron."

"Do I call her on it?"

"Your mother's not irrational. She's taken a position. She has an image of herself, false or accurate, that she feels compelled to maintain. If she were under your care, would you advise her to tell her family that she's dying?"

"I'd leave it up to the patient."

"Why?"

"It would be an invasion of privacy."

"Now you sound like a psychiatrist. Your mother has great dignity. She made a choice to end the journey on her terms. She couldn't conceal it from your father. But as far as you're concerned, she had an option. We know how horrible melanoma is. Let her do things in her own way."

Aaron felt something terrible explode from the dark landscape within him.

"I think my mother wanted me to be her lover." The moment the words were out, he found that a burden had been lifted, but in its place, a distasteful guilt poisoned the admission. Tears baffled his vision. "All those years when my father was traveling, I was my mother's date. Her escort, her armpiece, her friend. I became a doctor because of her. I always felt that she was on the verge of opening up to me. But she held back."

"Is there some chain of circumstances from your early years to lead you onto the Oedipal track? We all have this boxcar. And as you know very well, we uncouple it."

"I got the feeling my mother was never sexually satisfied in her marriage. She never complained about my father. There's a distance between them. Something's missing from my father—emotion. What affect he reveals is stunted. Yet he's very caring at the same time.

He's an extremely friendly man, but that's as far as it goes. He holds back. I've never known how to deal with it."

"Have you discussed it with him?"

Aaron shook his head with regret. "I don't think he really understands how to love. We're close but not intimate. He has this barrier.

"And I'm terribly worried about him. He's one of these people who seems to take care of everyone and not himself. He avoids closeness. My mother hasn't got much time and I'm afraid that the moment she's gone, I might find out that he's one of those men who's been screwing around with some bimbo."

Dr. Greenman considered the mass of material his protégé had stored up. He was disappointed more in himself than the young man. He had been with Aaron for almost two years and had been reasonably convinced that Aaron was steady and that there was nothing significant he was holding back.

"Your father's in his prime. What's he supposed to do, go into religious orders? Disavow the world? He's very successful. There are going to be women gravitating to a man like him. You've got your life with Kit; let him live his. You're not his conscience or his monitor. He doesn't have to account to you."

"My father was made of iron. Nothing was ever wrong. He was perfect. At least I thought so, until the other night when we were talking about his father. He clammed up and became emotional. I saw a degree of affect that was healthy. Then it was gone, repressed. Maybe he was really thinking about losing my mother."

For a long moment, Dr. Greenman studied him.

"Your mother's dying, but your father's the one who worries you. What does that mean?"

Aaron tried to consider the problem objectively. "I'm not sure. Okay, a reversal of roles. I'm grieving for my mother as my father should be because I want to take his place." Aaron then took the emotional leap he had been afraid of. "I feel like I'm about to be an orphan. My mother raised me. I didn't get to know my father until

my teens and even now there's something elusive and
mysterious about him."

"Good. But just remember, he's the one who will be
lost after such a long marriage. He'll need you to nurture
him. I think your sexual problem with Kit will pass. What
appears to be happening is not so much connected with
an Oedipal predicament as it is with the guilty pleasure
of enjoying yourself with Kit while your father is being
denied his sexuality with your mother.

"Subconsciously, you're gratified about having the up-
per hand—the son becomes more powerful and potent
than the father. At the same time, it's inhibiting you.
There's always a powerful degree of ambivalence connected with our fathers. In a sense, it's 'Oh, how the
mighty have fallen.' "

Aaron listened as his mentor poked around in the elusive mercurial byways of his psyche.

"Even though you're a physician, accepting the death
of your mother is an intolerable strain. Val is a wonderful
human being. It's difficult even for me to accept the idea
of being without her."

"The lost symmetry in my life—"

"No, it's not *life*. What you're holding on to is the
illusion of childhood, and that's been over for a long
time."

58

From her suite on the twelfth floor at the Carlyle Hotel
the glinting lights of Central Park spread out before
Allison like a birthday cake. In between meetings with
the directors of United Food and Beverage, she had gone
on a shopping rampage. Boxes from Ralph Lauren, Barney's, and Bergdorf's were stacked high on the settee.
She wished Sean had been with her on this trip. In a
paroxysm of maternal frustration she had bought him
three suits, two sports coats, Turnbull & Asser shirts, ties

at Sulka. He'd be *GQ*'s best-dressed cop in the entire Northwest.

Rushing to dress for dinner with the company chairman, she couldn't get Bonnie off the phone.

"Sean's given me an ultimatum."

"Bonnie, you can't walk out of the restaurant on a Friday night."

"I have to fly down to L.A."

"Where is Sean? Isn't this training job over?"

"No," she whimpered. "He's in some hotel in Santa Monica."

"God almighty, the zipper on my dress is jammed and I have someone coming in five minutes. Help!"

The doorbell rang, and she told Bonnie to hold on. It was room service with a bottle of Krug Champagne and armloads of flowers. Allison frantically signaled to a maid in the hallway to help her. While the maid with a pin was trying to liberate the material in the zipper, Allison listened to cadenzas of blubbering at the other end.

"Bonnie, don't, don't do this to me!" The zipper finally hummed up and Allison reached for her bag and tipped the maid. "Thank you. No, that was the maid. Listen to me, will you. Even though he's my son, make him sweat it. Men don't like it when it's easy and there are no exceptions to that rule. I know for damn sure!

"I've got to run, Bonnie. Stand your ground and don't let him push you around."

"Thanks, Allison."

In the doorway, Frank Grace stood smiling, an elegant man in a double-breasted suit holding an orchid.

Frank ignored the last of her conversation and opened the champagne, brought her a glass, and explored her figure with the eye of an appraiser, taking in the sleek new décolletage of her glamorous black velvet Lagerfeld dress.

"You're ravishing Allison. A knockout."

"Thanks, but I'm forty-six and a little old for this."

"Nonsense. You're in your prime."

"My prime? Is that what you call the third act in New York?"

"The minute I met you, I said, thank God I'm divorced. Cheating's so time-consuming and you have to keep taking showers in the afternoon."

"Please, try someone a little younger."

"Not any more. They're like commercials, short, sweet, and with temporary life stories." He was a New Yorker with no rough edges, very cosmopolitan and very direct. "You're so lovely, Allison. I can't believe you don't have a dozen men baying at your door."

"I lost interest in baying men a long time ago."

"Let's see if I can reignite it."

Flustered but pleased, she said, "I was really under the impression that this was a business dinner, Frank."

He offered her his arm. "Consider it due diligence."

"I will if you calm down and write me a lovely, large check."

59

The contractor's boy from Port Rivers had written out a personal check for ten million dollars to Jonah Wolfe. Terry had never imagined he would be wealthy enough to realize his dream of owning a professional basketball team. He had been satisfied living vicariously through athletes, gaining their friendship and helping them achieve stability. His partners were gloomy, for without Terry at the helm, making the right investments, coddling contracts, knowing when to push and when to play possum, the future of Sports Associates lay behind them.

"I have to make a total divestiture of my interest in the company to avoid a conflict of interest and get league approval," Terry advised his solemn partners. "What I intend to do is to assign my fifty percent equally to you both. We can work out some formula for payment. Take all the time you need."

Mike Summers had conflicting emotions. He was delighted that Terry had wrested the team away from the man who had seduced Karen, his young sister. Karen had made the connection that changed his life. Terry had taken him under his wing, and an obscure coach from a small town had become not merely successful but a celebrity in his own right. He was already feeling lost without Terry.

"You finally bagged your big game."

"Like everything I've done, Mike, it was a stroke of luck."

Billy Klein had been silent and remote. "Frankly, I'm ready to throw in the towel," he said now. "Sure we can get lawyers, form committees, promote people from within, but there's no one here with your vision. I'd hate to hang around watching everything we built fall apart without you."

Terry and the two men had forged a brotherhood.

"Maybe we're all ready for a change and another challenge." Always anticipating, Terry projected another scenario. "I bought the Stars at a fire-sale price because Jonah's in deep trouble. I'll need help rebuilding the team. What would you think of coming in with me? Mike would be general manager, Billy president, and I'd keep it all greased."

"What about the hundreds of people we represent?" Billy asked. "Do we bail out on them?"

"Absolutely not. We look for a buyer, finesse an unobtrusive takeover from IMG. I'll give Mark McCormick a call. One of you should hang around during the transition."

Like a boy learning a new game, Terry thrust himself into planning and constructing an incredible change in his company. It eased him away from the level of reality that he and Val faced. His first order of business would be to relocate the team, for the Los Angeles market could not support the Lakers and the Stars. He had settled on Long Beach, the freeway access, the confluence of sports-starved cities that had been ignored by Jonah Wolfe.

"I'm going to try to cut a deal with the Convention Center in Long Beach," he informed them.

"The demographics are good down there," Billy agreed.

Terry listened to his partners begin to create their scenarios.

"You'll have Orange County and still be fed by San Diego and L.A. It's an easier run from there than Anaheim."

"Once I develop some fan support and show the community I'm willing to spend money on quality players, and I bring in a new coach, I'll raise the money privately to build a stadium on the ocean. That way I won't have to go cap in hand to the municipal authorities and have city hall shysters leaning on me for kickbacks. We'll own all the parking and food concessions and I'm not going to soak the public. They're tired of getting ripped off. If I get us in the play-offs in four–five years, I'll have something they can all be proud of."

"They'll love you down there," Mike said. "It'll give them a reason to buy season tickets. And Billy, you know the cable operators. I'm sure we can fix a national TV deal."

Terry raised his hand and stopped their brainstorming. At times they became unruly. "The thing is, I don't know how the hell it could possibly work without the two of you working with me."

Billy and Mike looked at each other. Terry Brett had made them.

"We're in," they both said.

"Well, gentlemen, let's read Jonah his rights and boot him out tonight."

At the last minute, Mike decided not to accompany them to the closing. "I'm afraid I might commit murder and Jonah's not worth it."

Heading for Wolfe Auditorium downtown, Billy skirted rush-hour traffic on the surface streets through the gang-controlled moors of East Los Angeles. Terry had recruited young athletes in these wastelands, visited their ratholes, bought families food, paid utility bills. He and

Val had anonymously contributed to parks and play-grounds, but no palliative they could offer altered the misery of the inner city. The boy's world Terry had in-habited during the day with Billy and Mike collapsed. He was a man accustomed to a shield and he dropped it as he passed the burned-out shells where the disenfranchised practiced another form of commerce in their crack bar-onies.

Restraining his tears, Terry confided in Billy. Val was withering before his eyes.

"You're going to lose Valerie!" Billy said again. He was appalled and distressed. "Sorry to go on. I still can't grasp it. When I saw her a few weeks ago, she looked great. It's ghastly." He paused, ruminating. "Wild, when I think I was the one who introduced you two."

"When was that?" Terry asked through the foggy mists of recollection.

"You were staying at my place at the beach." They had not discussed the events for more than two decades. Terry's eyes were remote cavities. With some conster-nation, Billy continued, "Then you were beaten up, and the girl you were going to marry was murdered."

"That period is still a blur."

"It was a bad time for you."

Terry grappled with the murky vision of it all. He had been a man searching for Allison and had encountered his involuntary destiny with Valerie.

"Around Christmas, Val and I are taking the Concorde to Paris and then we'll go on to Venice. We had our honeymoon at the Gritti Palace and she wants to go back."

"And then?"

"There is no *then*."

"I'm talking about you, Ter."

"After Aaron marries Kit, I'll probably sell the house. Or give it to them if they want it. I couldn't bear to be in the house Val built for us without her. I'll find myself a condo in Century City. I won't need more because I intend to travel with the team."

"In some ways, it's a pity you've been so faithful to

her and never chased. At least you'd have a housebroken body next to you."

Never chased! The keeper of secrets winced at the remark.

It was still light when they turned into the personnel parking section of Wolfe Auditorium. Wheezing school buses on bald tires skittered to a stop beyond them. Orders from vigilant teachers blared out as they urged their charges into ragged lines.

"Looks like there may be a crowd."

"Yeah, there'll be close to a full house."

Excited youngsters in natty blazers, hollering, trooped off the yellow-bug death traps. Priests and nuns from the parochial schools broke up the bickering between bullies and their victims.

Billy looked at his watch and had a change of heart. "Terry, when Jonah signs the stock transfer, I'll give him the check. I hope there aren't going to be any last-minute glitches."

"With Jonah, you never know."

Billy hugged him. "Mind if I split?"

"No."

"I want to get home to my wife and hold her."

He and Billy trooped down the sweaty, dank corridor, paint-flake walls decomposing all the way to the Stars locker room, rank with defeat, the doomed dreams of boys who had hoped to create history under the aegis of Jonah Wolfe. Instead, season after season, they recorded two decades of subjugation by other teams with inspirational coaches and enlightened owners. It was a cathedral of failure. Even Jonah's glass-doored office had a shabbiness, walls and mantel devoid of awards and trophies.

Jonah stuck his head out with a victor's confidence.

"Billy." He shook hands jovially. He had no ax to grind with Billy Klein. He offered his hand to Terry, but then dropped it against his side. Terry had decided not to disclose Valerie's condition to her father. An unsettling merriment in Jonah's eyes removed any desire for sharing a confidence.

No one spoke while the documents were executed, the stock ownership transferred. Jonah's debts to Simon Pearl were retired, "paid in full."

Billy was anxious to leave. Jonah spooked him and he had no wish to witness the Stars being mauled by the visiting Chicago Bulls.

"I'll catch you at the office tomorrow, Terry."

Jonah had a jauntiness that repelled Terry and he refused a drink. "I'm trying to arrange an orderly transition. I told the coaches and the team this afternoon that you would be the new owner as of tonight."

"Then they know they've got to stop doggin' it or else they can head for Europe and play for Milan."

Jonah pounced on him. "You enjoy having people in that position, making them sweat it. Well, Terry, you won. Come on, walk me out to my car. I've got a parting gift for you."

In the gloom of dusk, he followed Jonah to his Rolls Corniche. Fans were streaming through the turnstiles. Jonah opened the passenger side of the car, reached into the glove compartment, and removed an old yellowing envelope.

"What's this about?"

"When we first met, you were representing that donkey Earl Raymond."

Jonah was treading on dangerous ground. The name set off a haunting fugue within Terry.

"I recall the circumstances very clearly."

"The thing is, Earl truly hated you. When you were his roomie last year in college, you high-hatted him, made him feel worthless. When he got you on my case and you relieved me of a half a million dollars, I thought you needed to be paid back in kind.

"So I got in touch with Earl and explained the situation. Yeah, I was paying up. Earl would have his stake for the future. Make some deal for a bar. But I needed a favor and I was prepared to pay ten thousand for it. I sent my plane up to Port Rivers." He smiled. "Earl has always been for hire.

"He flew down to L.A. with a character by the name

of Warren Paris who also had a grievance against you. Remember him? A business associate of Earl's. Warren was afraid of you, Terry. You have a remarkable talent for inspiring great passion in your enemies. It's your tenacity—your holier-than-thou fervor—which mortal sinners like Earl Raymond and myself couldn't tolerate."

Terry had listened to bluffers before and ignored Jonah. "I wasn't exactly granted immunity when character defects were dished out. I haven't taken holy orders. We both started out as lawyers with, I assume, a goal and principles."

Jonah Wolfe's mouth opened and he roared with laughter. His buff caps and implants were naked and the roof of his mouth was like a cave.

"A goal, principles?" he asked incredulously, spitting out the words like phlegm. "I had an objective. To get into Val's mother's pants and fuck her silly so that I could get my hands on her fortune. Those beer barons had millions and I was peddling dead meat, gristle in ghetto markets."

Terry was startled by Jonah's abrasive glee. "Jonah, as far as I'm concerned, I ruined *everything* when I forgot why I became an advocate and turned myself into a shabby blackmailer. Why? To beat you for money. I fell on my face when I held you up for Earl Raymond."

"Did you ever, Terry." A look of orgasmic pleasure swelled the plastic seams of Jonah's face. He got in and started the engine. "I know you're a collector of rare old Polaroids, so I thought you might like to have this keepsake from the old days."

Terry took the manila envelope, flipped it over, and touched the yellowed crust of Scotch tape on the back.

"Ter, you extorted money once from me. The second time, I took the precaution of photographing my models with their permission. Earl Raymond and Warren Paris are wearing bellhop uniforms . . . they're holding the stocking masks I bought. By the way, when you look at the pictures in the light, those are my Lalique champagne glasses in their hands. Earl and Warren were in my house. The three of us were celebrating beating you to a pulp. Enjoy the team, Terry. You paid in blood for the Los Angeles Stars and bought a pig in a poke."

Terry recoiled from the photograph as though from a live wire.

Misty rivers, the gloomy sound of rain, Allison's voice and Earl's laughter echoed through his mind.

60

Valerie had been reading Swinburne, her favorite poet, as well as Plato's *Dialogues*. Plato had explained with eloquently controlled emotion and logic the nobility of Socrates' death in the *Phaedo*. She agreed with the lofty principles. Yes, a philosopher can accept death without trepidation. Death separates the body from the soul and the object of life is to liberate the soul so that it no longer relies on the body. In life, the body intrudes on the soul's enterprise. Immune to morality and rationality, the passions interrupt the quest for wisdom and goodness.

" 'Socrates held the cup to his lips quite readily and cheerfully he drank of the poison . . . ,' " she read aloud, then closed the book and her eyes.

She had been reading voraciously: the Bible, the Koran, the *Upanishads*. In none of these holy texts had she discovered a remedy to cope with the diabolical pain she was enduring. There simply were no answers. Her spirit was enriched, her soul tranquil, but the periods of mental clarity were becoming fewer. She was drifting into the void of another drugged afternoon stupor.

The disease seethed with fury, rapaciously consuming its host. It had moved rapidly through the parietal lobe, spreading with the wildness of a forest fire. She was developing serious neurological imbalances. Valerie had no doubt that her mind was going and she clutched frantically at sanity. The headaches were blinding, the respite brief. The quality of her life was deteriorating by the actual minute. Her sleep was barely made possible by Seconals and punctuated by visions of her brain dying.

That morning before Terry had left for the office, she had seen the look of frustration on his face. There was nothing he could do. He made well-meaning, absurd suggestions.

"I can't let you go on this way," he said. "Heroin is supposed to be better than morphine. Valerie, I'll get it for you!"

"I don't need anything but you." Her cheeks had receded, compressing into a strange mask, so alien to her bright, hopeful good nature. "You can't be too thin or too rich. Well, I'm both." It brought a smile to her face, this sophomoric gallows humor at her own expense. But her throaty laugh had a brittle clack like hail hitting the pavement and Terry was devastated.

"I'm supposed to close the deal with Jonah and meet the team tonight. But I can skip it. I want to be with you, my honey."

Her fingers glided over his face and she held him at a distance, fearing the pain of an embrace. Her bones were fragile, the nerve endings shrieking.

"Go, please. I insist on you having this moment of triumph with Jonah. Throw him out of his office." Bristling with hatred, a blush of color appeared on Valerie's face. "Frankly, Terry, I would've let him sink without a trace and pushed him into bankruptcy."

Nothing promoted vitality like the joyless war within a family, he reflected.

"There was no other way. Valerie, would you be up for a little dinner at the Bel Air afterwards? We'll celebrate. It's an early game. Five o'clock start."

"You bet." Anything to please Terry. She'd increase the witch's brew with more morphine. What did it matter? "Call me when the game's over."

"I'll see if I can round up Aaron."

Terry's voice evaporated.

Was she dreaming or was someone touching her hand, holding her wrist? A figure sat down beside her. Valerie stirred, and through the bleak cloud of drugs, thought she saw the figurines on the Meissen lamp begin to dance.

Aaron's lips pressed against her forehead and she pulled away, troubled that she might have bad breath. Dying people had an odor about them. She knew it well.

"Your pulse is a little irregular." He took his stethoscope from his medical case. "Mind if I listen."

"This new flu strain is going around." She was still groggy and having difficulty focusing. When Aaron moved to the side, she lost sight of him.

"Is that what you think you've got?"

He pressed the scope against her chest and back. He could not reveal that Terry had told him she was dying, for Valerie would feel doubly betrayed.

"Whatever's going around with the kids, I seem to catch nowadays."

"You develop phantom symptoms, I know." In pique, he dropped the scope, renouncing the role of psychiatrist for that of her devoted son.

He lay on his father's side of the bed and took in the room. Salomé's boudoir with its veiled four-poster, gauzy curtains, exotic perfumes on the dressing table, all combined to produce a world of intense femininity. Designed for seduction, it had seldom been used for this purpose. Aaron recalled how often he had fallen asleep on the deserted outskirts. His mother had an aversion to clutter, but now patient files were mixed up with her teaching notes and the ward charts for grand rounds drooped off the table.

"Mom, why didn't you trust me?"

Their time together would always be a game of exquisite entrapment. It was ending abruptly, and Valerie searched for a direction.

"I was afraid you wouldn't be brave enough."

"Really? I was the *man* when Dad was away."

It was too late for absolution and she said, "I'm sorry you felt that way."

For Aaron, life had been a penance, the pleasure principle stillborn; feeling responsible, she was now committed to candor. She struggled off the bed and reached her dressing table.

"What actually was the situation with you two? I really have to know for my own peace of mind."

She pondered, dabbed on Bal à Versailles, and made an attempt to dress her face for a night out.

"He loved me in a way. But there was this shadow from his past that hovered over him. I nursed him through a bad period and he was very grateful and loving. He's not to blame.

"People can get along without the blarney of romance. By caring, giving their friendship. That's about it, Aaron. I'd hoped to complete this term with my students. If the dean knew about my condition, he would have forced me to leave."

As always there was a magnanimity to her reasoning. He kissed her with tenderness.

"You're my queen. If I can make it easier . . . do you follow me?"

"Yes, yes, I understand."

"I love you totally. Without reservation. But no surprises."

The phone rang and Valerie answered on the third ring. It was Kit, trilling excitedly, momentarily relieving the gloom.

Valerie replied, "Oh, you've made a film deal? Kit, we're going to meet Terry at the Bel Air for dinner after the Stars game." Valerie looked up at Aaron. "Please come. What? Of course. I always mean what I say, Kit. I like having you around more and more."

61

The Los Angeles Stars games were invariably poorly attended, and the ragtag of players Jonah Wolfe had recruited played listlessly. It would be another futile season for them. The Wolfe Auditorium downtown was

badly in need of repairs and its bleakness discouraged
fans. But this evening with Michael Jordan taking the
floor, the excitement of seeing the world's greatest player
had brought out even cynics.

Sean had garnered Commander Browning and four
other grateful detectives. Their seats were behind the Chicago Bulls bench. Sean had made peace with himself
about the SIS tactics, but was determined that detectives
in Port Rivers would never conduct themselves in the
same lawless manner. He tried to lose himself in the
game.

To everyone's surprise, the L.A. Stars broke to a quick
start and were hot, jumping to a 10–4 lead. The crowd
sensed a change in the team. It was meshing, fighting for
rebounds, moving purposively down the court. No wild
passes heaved out of bounds. The Bulls were being out-
hustled by a band of stooges.

Sitting behind the Stars bench, Terry tried to concentrate on the game, but the grotesque image of Earl Raymond continued to flash through his mind. With the score
16–6, the Bulls called a time-out and their coach furiously huddled with his team, gesturing wildly at diagrams
held up by his assistants.

The crowd cheered when the first quarter ended with
the Stars opening a twelve-point lead, 36 to 24. Lathered
with sweat like out-of-the-money nags, the Bulls were
confused. Jordan had been held to six points. Thrilled by
the action, everyone was humming. Several of the Stars
glanced over at Terry and smiled.

But all Terry could think of was Earl Raymond, the
mercenary ghost rider attached to him. Terry finally
cleared his head. He drifted onto the floor and stood beside his warriors.

"You like what you're seeing, boss?" asked one of the
guards, a graceful kid with bullet-tapered legs.

Terry forced himself to connect with their excitement.
"Eat 'em up. I want blood!"

Across the floor, Sean and the detectives were already
on their third beers and eating hot dogs. At times like
this, Sean felt a camaraderie with these gunslingers. At

half-time, with the Stars leading 55–48, they all went outside to smoke and chat.

"Believe me, Barney Laver is going to get one helluva report, Sean," Browning said, lighting up a cigar.

"I appreciate that. For my performance or these seats?"

"Both; you got balls under fire," another detective, and one of the shooters, agreed.

"I'm grateful that things are quieter in Port Rivers."

"They may be for now, but when the gangs move in, it'll change like the rest of the country."

"There's no safe haven any more," yet another added gloomily. "It's a thing of the past."

As the second half began and the game unfolded, the Stars lost their energy. Chicago relentlessly attacked. Watching Michael Jordan make a steal, beginning his leap to dunk from the foul line, everyone stood up and applauded, astounded by his effortless grace. The Bulls continued to move ahead, but the Stars were playing gamely. With two minutes left on the clock, the Bulls were ahead by sixteen points. Michael Jordan left the floor. Sean and the detectives were on their feet, as were the entire Stars bench. He had scored forty points in the second half alone and it seemed as though he hadn't been trying.

"You missed the sushi last night, Sean. Tonight is Chinatown," Browning said. "The brass is going to be there and I want to introduce you around."

The chillingly familiar face of a man standing behind the Stars players flashed instantaneously across Sean's field of vision. The image hovered, then crazily bounced through his mind, distracting him for a second.

"You got a flight home tonight, Sean?" another asked.

"Early tomorrow."

"I'll catch up with you later, Commander."

"We'll be at the Plum Tree Inn on Broadway."

"Got it," he replied, distant and troubled. The man he had fleetingly glimpsed was familiar. Peeling across the floor toward the Stars bench, Sean spotted the man now standing at courtside, fist raised, cheering the team on. As the game ended, he embraced the players. Sean's

heart stood still and he shivered. He could have sworn it
was his dead father.

The man's sporty collegiate appearance and the resemblance must have been an illusion. But as Sean closed
the distance between them, he was overwhelmed by the
singular thought that this man being treated with such
intimacy by the players and coach must be Chris Arnold's twin brother. The lights were spinning and the fans
rammed into him as they were leaving.

Arms linked, the high-fiving players rushed into a tunnel that led to their dressing room. Sean tried to get a
grip on himself. In a giddy daze, he trailed after them.

Since his birthday, he had been thinking about his father. A flood of memories, highlighted by games they
had watched together on TV, fused into this eerie association. Basketball and his father were mystically joined.
Now Sean recalled Chris explaining that his missions in
foreign countries, the months aboard ship and his undercover work, prevented him from watching ball games of
any kind. Chris Arnold had been an expert on sports. He
could watch a football player or major leaguer and find
the flaws in a quarterback's ball handling or a pitcher's
delivery.

How often had he said, "This kid's throwing with his
arm and not using his legs. He'll have shoulder problems
and a short career." He had an uncanny ability for anticipating which play would be called when they were
watching a football game. However, his expertise in basketball was supreme. The nuances of this simple game
had found their poet in his father's descriptions.

"All the good athletes have superhuman ability, their
field of vision, their reflexes, their refined senses, all they
possess is beyond us." They had been watching Dr. J.
performing his death-defying leaps from the foul line to
slam-dunk balls over taller opponents. "But the great
ones have character."

It was the strangest feeling Sean had ever had in his
life, this pleasurable double vision, the present and his
good recollections united. He went through the players'

tunnel. The flaking green ceiling with its old rusted fixtures cast spokes of burnished light into his reverie.

He was making a fool of himself by following this man. What was the point of it? Somebody reminded him of his old man. A security guard confronted him outside the players' dressing room.

"Help you?"

"Not really, pal." Sean leaned forward aggressively. He displayed his badge and the guard backed off. Sean yanked the bottom of his jacket back, revealing his shoulder holster. He was about to leave, but the man's identity nettled him. For his peace of mind, he had to resolve this. "Hey, there was a guy who went in with the team. Late forties, early fifties. He was wearing a gray tweed sports jacket, crewneck sweater, navy, I think. Joe College look. Do you know him?"

"No, I didn't see him."

"Do me a favor and check if he's inside."

The security man squinted in the dim light. "Is there a problem?"

"No, I just want to ask him a question."

After a moment, the guard ambled out with a beer in his hand. "I saw him leave through the private exit. It's for personnel."

"Where does it lead?"

"The parking lot."

Sean pushed off the wall. Suddenly a nerve was touched, some interior suspicion about being tricked, falling for an evasive action. Nothing he could pinpoint. Bursting past the guard, Sean ripped through the dressing room with the fury of a linebacker blitzing. Players and coaches were astonished and complained about the lack of security. Sean flew out the door before anyone could act.

He observed a dark Bentley pulling out. He ran toward the car but it was moving too fast, weaving through the lot. Sean sprinted to his rented car and had it slamming over the speed bumps. He ran a light and turned onto a freeway. They were heading west to the beach.

"License, SPORTS . . . Oh, Sean, get your head in gear!" he said to himself.

Keeping a vision of the Bentley with its smoked windows in his mind, hitting freeway shoulders and MUST EXIT signs, he slewed and twisted through the traffic gridlock. The Bentley was four cars ahead of him, thrusting at eighty on the fast lane, smoothly pulling onto yet another freeway, then heading north on the 405. Sean gunned the gas and was behind the slick car, the traffic easy, the night clear. He tried to visualize the man's face as though it belonged to a criminal. He had to get close to him, see him undistracted, in good light.

By the time Sean trailed the Bentley to the entrance of the Bel Air Hotel, he was embarrassed and disgusted with his behavior. The valet who took his car asked him if he was staying at the hotel and he said he was meeting someone for a drink. He received a parking stub and watched the man walking under the canopy, then turning right. Sean crossed over a stone bridge and paused in surprise at the sight of an illuminated pond presided over by swans in discord.

With its slouching elderly waiters, the darkly paneled hotel lounge bore the whispered wealth and airs of an English club. A graying pianist played something of Cole Porter's. Several tables were occupied by softly spoken people dressed with the understated elegance of the hidden aristocracy.

The man went into the dining room, bent down to kiss a pretty woman who had an anemic frailty about her. Sitting alongside her was a rumpled, slender younger man, wearing round wire specs and a creased blazer. He stood up, shook hands. A heartbreakingly beautiful woman sprang into the aisle and hugged the younger man, who slid into the booth out of sight.

The maître d' greeted Sean with a smile tainted by obsequiousness. "Will you be having dinner with us, sir, or are you joining someone?"

"No. I thought I recognized . . . I'm waiting for someone. I haven't got a reservation."

"We're fully booked. I might have a table break in

about thirty minutes. How many will you be?"

"I'm not sure." Distracted, gaping at the diners, Sean was not paying attention to the maître d's growing impatience and concern. "A man walked into the dining room a minute ago . . . over there." Completely losing his cool, Sean stupidly pointed. "He's sitting at a table with a young couple and an older woman. Do you know his name?"

Something about this bulky, bearded young man's intensity and agitation perturbed the maître d'. "I'm sorry, I don't."

"Can you get me a table near him?"

"Is there a reason why?"

"Never mind."

Kit was growing more comfortable in the company of the sharp-tongued dragon lady. Valerie struck her as wan, fatigued, altogether less formidable. Terry was a gallant old-school sweetie who invariably took her side. With the deal she had closed earlier that evening, her career would be blossoming. Life had become easier. She proudly looked across the table at the Brett men in deep low conversation. Within easy reach was a bottle of Cristal attended by a diligent waiter who filled their glasses constantly.

"The Brett family always seems to be celebrating," Kit said.

The room was spinning, but Valerie shared the girl's excitement and her pain had subsided. "I hope your life is filled with these occasions."

"What a lovely thing to say, Val. Imagine, me! Little Miss Nobody, putting together a package and making a fortune for the agency on a deal. Actually, I've spent a year on it, nursing a script, signing the right actress for the role and getting the director to leave a big agency to come aboard with me. Then closing the deal at Warners."

"I still don't quite follow how this works."

Kit was giddy with pleasure. She could explain the mysterious ways of the film business. She actually knew something more than Dr. Valerie Brett.

"The script went for five hundred thousand, the actress's price is two million, this director gets three. That adds up to five and a half million. At ten percent, I should get five-fifty in commission. But because I represent the three elements, I waived the commissions. I then was able to negotiate four percent of the film's budget. If for example it's fifty million dollars, the agency would receive two million dollars. It's called a packaging fee and we can't collect client commissions as well as this. So I have three very happy clients. The partners at the agency are thrilled with me. But even more than the money, this could be a wonderful film."

Valerie reached over and gripped Kit's hand. The girl's passion, her exhilaration, assumed a deeper emotional form than Valerie had believed possible. For once Valerie had diagnosed someone superficially. Kit wanted to shine in her eyes and convince her that Aaron was not throwing his life away.

"All I'm bringing to the party are the reckless hopes of an outsider. Mine is a business of freebooters, pirates, and lowlifes. I know I have no right to your son. But he is my rainbow."

"And mine."

"Can he be ours?"

Valerie was touched by Kit's sweetness. Aaron would be in safe hands.

"Of course. I feel I can trust you, Kit."

"Then why didn't you like me?"

"Candidly?" Kit nodded. "I thought I wanted Aaron to have someone . . . innocent. But that would have been a disaster."

"Who would he have learned from?" The two women laughed.

Terry relaxed, delighting in the joy of being with his son, Valerie, and Kit. The bad thoughts of Earl and Jonah slowly dissipated in this family atmosphere. How many more evenings would he have Valerie? He noticed that she was forcing herself to eat the Dover sole. His heart was breaking as he visualized the vital, athletic young girl she had been. Murdering him on the tennis court, tacking expertly on her sailboat, giving him a head start then outriding him on a bike. Like a rare old friend, the Colnago she had given him was something he had grown to cherish.

Aaron tilted forward and signaled for attention but was nervous.

Terry nudged him. "Come on, Ace."

Aaron had a sheepish smile. "Mother, while you were talking business, the two romantics at the table were making plans."

"Like what?" Valerie asked, feeling her son's energy.

Aaron kissed Kit's hand and she lowered her eyes. "Like a wedding."

Terry kissed Valerie. "Your mother and I'll be there, Ace."

An easygoing baritone version of "Memories" glided in the background when Sean returned to the bar and took a table framing the dining-room entrance. He ordered a double Stoli on the rocks. Reflecting on this mystical occurrence, as though analyzing a crime and the motives behind it, a series of questions was triggered. What was driving him? The man couldn't possibly be *his* father. Why had he followed him? Why wasn't he with Browning and his team or heading out to the airport? He had checked out of the hotel. His bag was packed and in the car.

Three doubles later, Sean looked at his watch. The man and his party would be finishing their main courses; Sean quickly made a decision to walk by their table. He'd pretend to be lost. No, it was absurd, getting out of hand. But he found that he couldn't control his curiosity.

The man was already on his feet and the younger man was helping the thin woman out through a side door. In the dim light, she was wobbly, possibly drunk.

"Aaron!" the man, extremely agitated, called out.

"It's okay, Dad. She'll be fine. We'll be home in five minutes," the young man said. They quickly assisted the gaunt woman through an emergency exit. The very pretty girl at the table was behind them. Sean picked up the charge slip on the table. He looked at the first five digits. It was a platinum-coded American Express card, initialed "T. B." He examined the merchant copy. It was in the name of a company called Sports Associates.

He trotted out to the front of the hotel. The Bentley was outside, purring at the curb. Sean caught up with the group. The man was behind the wheel, but Sean distracted him and prevented him from leaving. Hawk-eyed, he leaned into the open window.

"I'm with hotel security. Can I do anything to help?"

"Thanks for your concern. My son's a doctor," the man said gratefully and drove off.

The scar on the man's cheek, the broken bridge of the nose.

How could they be replicated? Was this an optical illusion Sean's mind had manufactured and imposed on this innocent man?

The voice . . . This is not happening, I'm imagining it!

There was no sign of recognition. Sean was merely a stranger. The incalculable shock to his system froze him. Heart racing, not knowing what to do, Sean finally tossed five bucks at the valet and leaped into his car.

The man had my dad's voice.

Sound waves echoed mysteriously, reentering Sean's mind. Whenever his father spoke to anyone, he made that person the center of the universe, and his manner always carried a sense of privacy, sureness, control. What had always fascinated Sean about his father was that his every utterance had the force of a deep confidence that provided him with a mission to perform.

The experience was bizarre. He seemed to float outside his body, encompassing two separate realities. Alarmed by this paralyzing split within himself, he saw himself as a young child clinging to his father.

"Dad! My God, you're alive!"

62

Nothing in his experience had prepared Sean for this encounter. It was apocalyptic in its furor. Despite his police training, he could not suppress his conflicting emotions, which screamed for an outlet. With tears streaming down his cheeks, wailing from the depths of his soul, Sean curled behind the wheel of his car.

"Ace, how could you do this to us?"

He caught up with the Bentley as it passed Bundy Drive on San Vicente, and headed to the beach. This was familiar territory to him, a route he had used for ten days to get into Brentwood. The Bentley slipped into Ocean Place, a narrow road over which a canopy of great trees threw off the scent of eucalyptus.

The large, gabled brick house stood in its own grounds on the crest of a hill that overlooked the beach below. An old wooden gate, left open, swung on creaking hinges. Beside it a rusted sign dangled, with the words VIGILANT PATROL. No phony "Armed Response" to greet an intruder. So much for security, the detective thought.

The man and his son had been too concerned with the sick woman to notice they were being followed. To the east of the property an apartment over the large garage had on lights, and a couple were watching a TV program.

Sean clashed with himself. *I'm losing it. Now hang in!*

His mind seemed to hold up a telescope to the psychic planets of the past. The conjunction of Allison and this foreign being dreamily soared through his consciousness, forming an alliance that was no longer distant.

Did his mother know Chris was alive? No, she couldn't have. She had mourned too long. Strong, resourceful, balanced as Allison was, such a trauma might destroy her. Sean tried to imagine any woman being told—seeing with her own eyes the man she had loved, the father of her son—that her dead husband was alive!

" 'It's okay, Dad. She'll be fine.' "
" 'My son's a doctor.' "

The words shrieked. *His* son? Sean was *his* son. How could Chris have another one? Had he adopted this guy or married someone before Allison? After her? Had there been a secret divorce? Sean continued to grapple with his warring emotions. He despised the young man who had stolen his father. His mood turned to resentment, frustration, the anger swelling within him.

This man wanted to play games, fuck with people's heads, their lives. He'd soon discover that he had met his match.

Sean left the car, opened the mailbox set in a brick post, and found a solitary envelope. A bill from Tierra, a landscaping company, was made out to "Dr. V." Marine navigator, spy, and now a doctor. This con artist was posing as a quack. Sean wondered how many other identities Christopher Arnold had assumed.

"After the champagne I guess I needed some air," Valerie said, laughing. "I wasn't always such a cheap drunk. How I miss those tequila nights with you, Terry." She was settled in bed propped up on a bank of lace pillows. At the doorway, Terry and Aaron huddled. "Will you guys stop clucking over me." They approached her and Aaron gravely sat down on the bed and took her pulse.

"Her skin color's better. The pupils are still dilated but that's the morphine."

"Morphine?" Valerie nodded. Terry was irate. Like a man caught in a blinding snowstorm, his inclination was to put up his hands as a shield. Too many things were striking him at once. "Even I know it doesn't go with alcohol."

"Oh give it up, honey and don't be a nag. I want to hear what happened with my father. Come to bed."

Aaron's face screwed up, the hurt child being chased from his parents' bedroom, their mysteries inviolate.

"I really do like Kit," Valerie said, accepting a kiss from Aaron. "I had no idea she was so tenacious and smart. I was wrong. She's very impressive."

"Thanks, Mother. Good night. If there's a problem, just buzz me."

In his dressing room, Terry wrenched the old curled Polaroid out of his breast pocket and under his desk lamp examined the smug expression of Earl Raymond. Beside him Warren Paris was glassy-eyed, drunk, drugged. He was irrelevant, for Terry's venomous wrath was exclusively reserved for Earl.

"If you're still alive, we'll have our day, Earl. I promise you that."

Terry went downstairs to his study, opened his safe, and slipped the photo into the tattered folder which contained the relics of his Seacliff misadventure. A picture of Sean aged ten stuck to his fingers. Sean was on a horse holding the .22 rifle he had bought him for his birthday. Terry was beside a Palomino with a deer tied across the saddle. He had shot it that morning. Allison had taken the picture. Some weeks later, on another of his sporadic trips to his other family, they had dined on saddle of venison.

Maybe once Valerie was gone, he'd look up the boy, see if he could help him out financially, get him a job. He'd been a wonderful son, steadfast, adoring. Terry closed the safe and returned to the bedroom.

"Leave it alone."

"Terry, who're you talking to?"

"No one, sweetheart."

Sean checked into the Century Plaza Hotel. Peeling off his sweat-soaked clothes, he was shivering. He had bought himself a bottle of Stoli and took a pull from the bottle as he unpacked his bag. First thing in the morning, he'd head down to Parker Center and use the SIS computers. Once he had T. B.'s information on the mainframe, he'd put this guy's ass in a sling.

The torment of the discovery again intruded. He threw himself on the bed and struggled with the pain of betrayal. The big lie had an enduring shelf life, as it warped his mother and himself. The ineffably somber visions of the two of them returned. He and his mother would huddle together, sitting in the dank, chilly old movie theater in Seacliff, and his mother would burst into tears out of the blue.

He, the fatherless child, would walk lost through town, shunning his classmates and friends, avoiding people, sucking up the unbearable loneliness of having loved a human being so deeply and to have lost him to an all-powerful, unknowable God. No one had the right to punish him with such perverse cruelty. The knell of vengeance tolled through Sean's brain.

He was at Parker Center by seven the next morning and decided to call Bonnie. Her sleepy voice took on a sense of urgency.

"Sean, Sean, how are you? I've been worried about you. I miss you like hell."

"I'm fine, Bonnie. The case is dragging on. I'm in no danger. It's mostly office work, hacking the computers between two states to check out information on my *suspect*."

He pronounced the word with relish, adding an emphasis.

"Why do you sound so remote?"

"Do I? Hey, how do I get in touch with my mother?"

"She's on one of the company's cruise ships." There was a pause. "I wrote it down at the restaurant. The *Magellan*, I believe. She'll be arriving in Fort Lauderdale, then flying home in a few days. She's really excited. It seems they made some terrific offer."

On the computer screen a Social Security number from American Express appeared, followed by a name:

TERENCE SEAN BRETT

"Sean, are you there . . . Sean?" Bonnie asked.

"Yeah." He examined each letter of the name over and over again. It was as though spikes had been driven into his eyes. A feeling of nausea overcame him.

"Your mother gave me two weeks off. She'll work Christmas. How's that sound? We could go to Hawaii. Or do you have to get back to work?"

Without thinking, he hung up, stared at the name until he became dizzy. It was incredible.

Christopher James Arnold was Terry Brett!

His uncle Pat's dead son. The level of the conspiracy perpetrated against himself and his mother shocked him. His mind shifted back. During his childhood, he had seen Pat and Terry together many times when they were all in Seacliff. He had never seen them together in Port Rivers. He had never been to Port Rivers with his father. Did Pat know Terry was still alive?

Sean fully realized why the old man had shown so much interest in him and, of course, how they managed to sit courtside at every basketball game. The season tickets were worth thousands of dollars. A man would have to be a celebrity or a multimillionaire friend of a team owner to get seats like that. Terry certainly was connected. That explained how he maneuvered behind the Stars bench and had access to their dressing room.

The audacity of his father's scheme was breathtaking. Sean realized he couldn't take anyone's word for anything. This had now become a criminal investigation. The puzzle of Terry-Chris brought out the fine logical qualities that had enabled Sean to make detective. The screen filled up with information from both California and Oregon.

BRETT, TERENCE SEAN

Attorney, passed bar in both states. Chairman of Sports Associates.

In the sports pages, Sean had read the names of Billy Klein and Mike Summers for years. They represented major athletes and made colossal contract deals for their clients. In Port Rivers, Terry's law firm had been called Brett & Conlan. Georgina Conlan. She was the woman whom his mother had met in the restaurant. She had been his father's partner.

He ran Terry's address through the computer: 456 Ocean Place; he discovered that a Dr. Valerie Brett and a Dr. Aaron James Brett also lived there. Then he matched it with physicians on file. Both were at UCLA Medical Center. The woman was a professor of pediatrics and the son was a resident in psychiatry.

"Act like a cop, don't just jump in. You've uncovered a crime; build a case with hard evidence," Sean told himself.

Sean signed out a laptop computer, which the clerk had to clear with Commander Browning. "Give Detective Arnold *anything* he wants," he heard over the squawk box.

He would orchestrate a time of reckoning. The quest for truth was a hallowed undertaking. Suddenly, Sean was overwhelmed by a mysterious illumination that sprang through his soul. The special destiny his father had implanted into his childhood had found its moment, its anvil.

63

Sean had Bonnie send down by Federal Express an old blazer with a bold red speckled lining. It was a favorite sports coat the impostor had left behind, and which Sean had worn during the period when he wished to live in his father's skin.

"Whatever you do," he told Bonnie, "please don't mention it to my mother. I'm going to surprise her."

When he learned that Allison had returned from her New York trip, he phoned her.

Enthusiasm unbounded, Allison had delicious tales of New York and the high seas, the riches that awaited them. She sounded like a rookie the Dodgers were bringing up from the minors to pitch opening day. Sean's conversation was brief, the busy detective. His mood had changed and now he wondered if his mother was privy to this fantastic treachery; could she know that Terry-Chris was alive and well, living in splendor and reclusive prominence?

Two days later, Sean walked through Beverly Hills and located Carroll & Company, an elegant haberdashers. Its stolid, gracious, low-key English air was a relief from the shrill boutiques and designer flagships that lured visitors to the area. He took a voyeuristic pleasure in the surveillance of his father. Once inside the shop, Sean handed his father's ancient blazer to an incredulous salesman. "I want this mended and I don't care what it costs."

"You'd be better off buying a new one."

"I know that. But it's for Terry Brett. It has sentimental value. I work for his firm. He asked me to drop it off. He's very attached to it."

"Well, that's different. Him and Aaron," the salesman said familiarly, "two of a kind. They hate to give up anything. I'll call the tailor."

Sean looked at the salesman with an air of quiet brooding. "Terry and Aaron sound very close."

"Been waiting on them, twenty years or better. Aaron—oh, it's *Dr.* Aaron now—he's his old man's sunshine."

Map in hand, studying the area, Sean took it as a sign of fate that he was only one block from his quarry's office on Century Park East. After handing his cleaning to the valet, he sat down on the sofa and stared out the window. Theatergoers were heading into the Shubert and he wished he too were carefree and about to spend an evening seeing a musical with Bonnie. That's what normal people did. They had dinner, went to a movie or show, stayed home, watched TV with a pizza, then hopped into the sack.

Sean plugged the laptop and modem into a portable phone he had also signed out, which enabled him to access the mainframe at Parker Center. He spread the computer printout on the coffee table. A thunderbolt of rage threatened to devour him and he was afraid of the violence his discovery had unleashed.

It was three in the morning when Sean reached the Port Rivers airport. A freezing rain pierced his skin as he slithered across the roadway to the taxi stand. He gave the driver Bonnie's address.

When he slid the key into the lock and banged into Bonnie's bookcase—a new, as yet partially assembled one—Sean executed a figure-eight and fell flat on his face.

Stance perfect, distance police academy reference, firing position just a little high, Bonnie said:

"You dropped into the wrong place. My boyfriend's a detective. I hope there's a reward out for your ass."

Where common sense failed, the lurid movies about serial killers had persuaded Bonnie to ask for instruction in firearms.

"A plus, Bonnie."

A table lamp light laced the room. She was aiming his old .38 special at him.

"You! What am I going to do about you?" Bonnie gripped herself in bewilderment. She shivered in her long white flannel nightdress.

He got up, nodded, walking to the shelf that contained the collection of liquor they brought home from the restaurant. He filled a large balloon with cognac.

"Were you up?"

"No. But my reflexes are good." She made a move to him, then thought better of it. "Thrilled to see me?" Furiously, she· sucked in her breath. "Looks like you screwed your brains out in L.A."

He was on a different curve. "Even when you've been good, women think you haven't." He collapsed. "Bonnie, I had a real bad time."

She cupped his face in her warm palms. "You look terrible, Sean. Tell me what happened?"

In bed she tried to nurse away his silence. Afraid to antagonize him, she stroked him vigilantly. Like a nomadic cat he might hiss, claw out, wound her. He retreated into the dark corridor of his mind, eventually slipping into a thin restless sleep.

They rose early and walked by the river past Founder's Park down to Old Town and along Bucaneer Square. The dragon arches of Chinatown and the dinky restaurants remained along with the customhouse architecture which had been fought for and preserved by Allison and her Greensleeves followers. The storm last night had cleared the air, turning the sky peacock blue. The bustling sunlit streets were sharply defined by a background of flat barges towed by tug artists gracefully easing past the returning fishing boats.

The city's craftsmen were flourishing. Potters clattered their wooden boxes of mugs and vases. From everywhere smells of the food bazaar curled into low-drifting hazes. The middle-aged hippies had become mustard chemists, chili champions, vintners, jam queens, beer brewers, sausage designers. Then there were the certifiably crazy bread people, who baked their loaves with everything from prunes to pickles. Sean was in his element, for when he and Allison had been repatriated to Port Rivers, they had been a part of such street festivals. She had made friends with produce, fish, and beef suppliers and they had helped her get started.

Sean had been trying to explain to Bonnie what was swarming through his mind, but held back.

"I don't understand what's going on with you, Sean." He hadn't come near her, definitely signing off. "I feel like I'm losing you."

"Bonnie, something happened."

"Was it your assignment?"

"No, it was strictly personal."

"Oh, God no!" she said tearfully. "I knew it was another woman! Goddamn it, I trusted you."

He moved close to her, huddling in the folds of her firm thighs, and pressed his chest against her breasts. He tasted her sweet, racing breath.

"Bonnie, I have many quarrels. But none with you. I love you, darling."

"Do you mean that? I'm so confused by your behavior."

"There are some things I have to do. I may blow my career on the force. I expect to make enemies."

"You're going to walk around wearing a wire? Is it police corruption?" she asked, agog.

"No, nothing like that." After a moment, he went on, "I can't ever rest until I solve this. My peace of mind is at stake."

Her earnest face was taut with apprehension. "I'm not sure you want me to ask more."

"I don't."

She began to cry in relief. "I'm with you, Sean."

"When this is over, will you think about marrying me in June—maybe around Rose Festival time?"

She kissed him with that secret unforgettable enchantment a loving woman dreams of and caresses.

64

Sean located his mother in the Patrick Brett Wing of Good Samaritan Hospital. The old tear-down specialist had donated a million-dollar contracting fee to the hospital. In the intensive care unit, the wing's patron, eyes in the gray netherworld, tubes coming out of him, looked as mummified as tripe. A doctor, one of the old-timers, and three hawkish young guys leaned over the bed and charts.

"No more blood-thinners."

"An angiogram—"

"It's too risky."

Face tight with foreboding, Allison turned away from the bed. When she saw Sean standing at the far end of the room, she rushed to him and wrapped her arms around him. In her tight jeans, red turtleneck, and old sneakers, Sean imagined her young again and with Terry.

"I'm so glad you're home. It's been awful, especially since such good things have happened to me. Now Pat, of all people, can't share them."

Sean had counted on talking to Pat man-to-man about Terry.

"What happened?" he asked in frustration.

"I called Pat the other day. He wasn't at the office and he didn't answer at home, so I drove over to his house. I found him groaning on the floor. I think he had a stroke. I got the paramedics and they brought him here."

The lead doctor, a tall, angular man with a shock of gray hair and a bony, philosophical face, interrupted them.

"Allison, the cardiologists say operating on his hip is out of the question. The stroke was relatively mild on the right side and he has intermittent coherence. He'll fade in and out."

"This is my son, Boyd. Dr. Flannigan looked after me and operated on my busted leg many, many years ago, Sean."

Sean looked quizzically at the doctor and shook hands. "You never mentioned breaking your leg."

"She sure did. It was a real mess for a while. Fact is, Allison, I never thought you'd walk without a limp."

Every scintilla of information, even this innocent revelation, heightened Sean's suspicions, hacked his nerves. Had everyone in town known he was Terry Brett's son—except him!

Gunning back to River Cove in Allison's Jag, she resumed her crusade about his leaving the police force and joining her in the new venture.

"I met a real gentleman in New York. His name is Frank Grace. He's the CEO of United Foods. God, he wined and dined me for a week."

"Is it serious? Like marriage?"

"No. That won't happen again."

"I wish I could understand you, Mom. Since Dad died, men have surrounded you. Some nice guys, too. Why've you always pushed them away?"

The question upset her. "I had something with your father that was rare and irreplaceable. When it was gone, I realized, as a woman, I had no more to give."

"You never talk about Dad any more."

"I know what he meant to you and how much his loss affected you."

Sean cast a cold eye on Allison. "Yeah. I never asked, but was it really that great for you with him?"

Allison stopped for a light, closed her eyes, and nodded. "It was the Garden of Eden . . . priceless."

In the vestibule, a flotilla of boxes from Ralph Lauren and Barney's were lined up like officers on deck.

"These are pre-Christmas presents."

He opened a box and uncovered a banker's double-breasted gray pencil-stripe suit. "I'll be the only cop in the country who ever gets into *Vanity Fair*."

"We've got to change your image for United Foods. If I ask nicely, maybe they'll offer you an executive job. Come on, Sean, loosen up. Was Los Angeles such hell?"

"I kept busy. It wasn't an easy situation for me. When were you there last?"

"Some years ago. I seldom go."

"I'm sort of puzzled. You keep up with every change in food but not Wolfgang Puck's restaurants in L.A.? They've been the rage for years."

She looked at him with a shade of curiosity. "I'm glad your work as a guardian of the law hasn't stopped you from keeping up with trends in cuisine."

They headed for the kitchen, their shelter.

"What're we going to do about Uncle Pat?" he asked when she was amid her hanging copper pans, the Aga stove a battlement against the world.

"Pat lived, he had pleasure, he made choices, despaired, knew grief and gave some. He's in God's territory." She sailed into another refrain. "I assume you came in last night and stayed with Bonnie." He nodded. "There'll be hell to pay if you wreck that girl."

"Stay out of my business," he said sharply, and she flinched as he contemptuously dropped a Turnbull & Asser shirt on the floor.

"What the hell's bugging you?"

He set a small trap. "I have been thinking about a change in career." She glowed, picked up the shirt, deciding to forgive him. "It was a real shock coming home to find Uncle Pat in this condition. I feel like I'm losing my grandfather."

"You are," she said without hesitation, "that's how he thought of himself."

Her candescent blue eyes, the open concerned face, were not those of a liar. He no longer wondered if Allison was deceitful. She'd have a heart attack or fall into a depression if he told her:

Your husband, Christopher James Arnold, is alive! He lied to us. His name is Terence Sean Brett and he is married to an heiress. She is a doctor and they have a son my age who is a psychiatrist.

Like him, Allison also found ambiguity and deception alien. Everyone knew where Allison stood. She couldn't possibly have any idea that Terry was still around.

"Pat turned out to be a true friend when I thought I had none," she said, unwrapping Sean's gifts.

Sean's speculations surrendered to the prospect of shouldering his mother's pain. After Terry had deserted them, Sean remembered the lonely, hardworking life she had constructed. At the same time, the detective in him considered her a suspect. He studied everything about his mother—tone of voice, eyes, expression, posture. She whirled through this quadrant with the breeze of innocence.

"I'd hate to see Uncle Pat in one of those old-age homes."

Nettled by something unspoken in the air, Allison regarded Sean with impatience. "Don't worry, he won't be. Now give it to me straight—are you quitting the police force?"

"I'm thinking about it. I've got to consider the two women I love," he said, with smooth persuasion.

"Oh, Sean, you'd make me so happy!"

"I'm taking some time off now. I've got a month coming to me. But there's a case that's been nagging at me. I'll have to see it through. After that I may entertain offers."

Allison posed him in front of the mirror in the living room. Sean looked at their images. There was a splendor, an overflowing sensuality that Allison exuded, which embraced everyone in her orbit. How did a man leave such

a woman? Sean's mind re-formed the image of the gaunt
Dr. Valerie Brett, her starved, death's-head features. It
was too fantastic to contemplate. To Allison's delight, he
continued to try on his clothes in an effort to lure her
into an indiscretion.

"Mother, before Bonnie dropped me off at the hospital,
we stopped by the restaurant. There was a call from that
woman I met. Georgie?"

"I hope you didn't give her our home number."

"No, I knew you didn't want to see her again."

He had answered the phone and told Georgie that Allison would be traveling—indefinitely.

65

Jonah Wolfe threw himself a gala farewell cocktail
party at Seventy-Two Market Street in Venice. The
team, their harems, various wives, hairdressers, coaches,
flacks, along with a string of Jonah's former kickknacks,
attended. There was also a new face. Jumpy, with good
reason, Jonah had hired one of his former players as a
security guard. Eddie Diamond, known as Elbows during
his playing days, was six foot seven and approached each
day as if he were going up for a rebound. When he'd
muscled people in the league under the boards, he said,
"They be hearing the Pony Express hoofbeats in their
heads for a week." Off the court, people still jumped out
of his way.

Terry had ordered the team not to attend the party if
it was going to be a press bash and he had hired security
people to keep them out. Jonah had hoped his retirement
would be on network news, possibly spawn an ESPN
special. He was deeply upset when Terry laid down these
conditions.

"Terry," Jonah pleaded, "can we please forget all the
shit? It's my last night. I was wrong to get Earl and his
pal to hurt you the way they did. I was vindictive and in

those day I always had to get back at people. It was intoxicating."

"Jonah, what I'm about to do is also intoxicating."

Amid the waiters dishing out Ceviche and tasties, Miss Ringsider finalists in Day-Glo Brazilian string bikinis carried signs: JONAH WE LOVE YOU. Jonah's kingdom may have collapsed, but he was behaving as though this were an investiture.

To celebrate the abdication, Terry invited Simon Pearl, his hangman, along as his guest. With pony glasses of chilled Chinoco, the two men approached Jonah. The guest of honor was busily stroking a bosomy young woman who wore a string bikini. Jonah released his hold on the temptress.

"You recall meeting Simon Pearl, don't you, Jonah? You fucked him and his pension fund out of a few million. And now they can't pay retirement benefits or health insurance." Jonah's liver-spotted face crumbled. "Simon wanted to wish you farewell," Terry said.

"I thought all of this was over," Jonah said.

"Whenever Terry decides it's time, I will send a visitor to say bon voyage on your final cruise," Simon Pearl observed. "Then it will be Judgment Day."

Terry shoved Elbows out of his way. He dragged his host by the lapels and forced him to sit on the bar. This seemed a gesture of goodwill to the assembly, prompting a speech.

"Terry, please don't do this," Jonah whispered. "*You* can talk Simon out of murder."

"Maybe you can hire a lawyer who can persuade him."

En route to Simon's jet at LAX, he divulged the facts he had gathered for Terry.

"That guy you called me about last week, Earl Raymond . . ."

"Yeah, I hope he's not invisible."

"Oh, no, Terry. No one's invisible today. Earl did time in Walla-Walla. He tried to fix some college basketball games. Small potatoes. All very amateurish. He's got some kind of bar and a bookie joint. I heard he also peddles drugs with a biker outfit he hooked up with in prison."

Away from the airport terminals, the car stopped outside a private hangar where a Gulfstream waited. As he was about to go up the plane's steps, Simon regarded Terry with bewilderment. He placed his hands on Terry's shoulders.

"How can someone like you—a man I admire—have a beef with some lowlife like this Earl?"

"Her name was Allison."

Terry telephoned Valerie from his car to check on her without being obvious. But of course his concern was evident. As the Bentley whirred down the freeway on the drive home, Terry thought about the depth of Val's commitment to him and how she had rescued him. For the first time he considered his actual, corporeal life without her, and the outlook was unspeakable.

Then the prisoner of the past stealthily crept out and scaled the mountainface. He would track Earl Raymond down. A good, successful lawyer prepares, and someone bent on murder required a blueprint. Jonah and Earl would pay perilous reparations.

Terry thought about looking Allison up. Coursing through his mind, she reappeared, resurrected, duplicated and cloned in his rearview mirror. Her luminous blue eyes were flooding the headlights behind him. Had Allison returned to the drug life? Would she need rehab? Was she in prison? She might be stoned on crack. Or had she taken the reverse path, running a soup kitchen for some do-gooders' group?

He'd give it a shot and try to find her so that she could lead him to the son he'd lost. What had become of Sean? He'd try to mend fences with the boy and explain why he had been forced to leave. He hoped Sean was successful and happy. If the young man needed help, Terry would find something for him: a front office job working for the club, or encourage Sean to follow his personal destiny.

Terry pulled through the gates of his house, parked the

car. As he was approaching the front door, he began to weep tears of shame for thinking of Allison and Sean in such a contemptible, needy way.

By the time he reached the bedroom, he had pulled himself together. He looked at Val, took her pulse. She was in a deep, drugged sleep, a gray wraith. He kneeled at the bedside.

66

Obsessed by his father's twisted identities, Sean's compulsion to continue the investigation caved in to depression and lethargy. His powers of concentration vanished. He felt battered, in shock, floating into sleepless stupors. Immobilized by his discovery, the world was out of focus. He had to escape from his mother's innocence. He lived in dread of blurting it all out.

Bonnie was reading a ski article on a new method for mastering moguls. In a purple outfit, which Allison had bought her, Bonnie was dressed for a day ski trip to Mount Hood. She gave Sean a funny look when he offhandedly told her at the last moment that he had to finish some business downtown. She choked on his indifference, defenseless against his moods.

She and Allison watched him leave without comment. Sleeves rolled up and in her navy-striped French apron, Allison was in the kitchen with her looseleaf book open, devising recipes she had promised to test for her future partners. She deveined some shrimp and dried them. All concentration, she mixed a coconut batter and then began to create a lime-curry sauce, adjusting it constantly with a drop of white wine. Finally, she added a hint of Scotch Bonnet hot sauce and seemed satisfied.

"Why'd Sean leave?" Allison asked.

"I don't know or understand his behavior any longer."

Drying her hands on the towel around her neck, Allison came out into the breakfast nook where Bonnie sat hunched over. Dark rings puffed Bonnie's eyes, pinching the skin. The gaiety she'd exuded had vanished and her face had developed a formation of hard angles.

"What about taking that cruise? I can get you guys on free, first class, outside cabin, top deck. These suckers will give me anything. They're serving expensive boring dinners and nobody eats in their restaurants. The Caribbean Islands. You two need to sit yourself on a beach, drink Margaritas, and"—her eyes danced—"have long naps."

"Just keep dreaming, Allison. Look, I'll go anywhere. For months I've been up till three–four every night studying for exams. I'm not complaining. Until I met Sean, I was handling my life very well. My brain is no longer functioning. I'm exhausted. I've pleaded with Sean for us to go away. He agrees, then forgets I'm alive." Her eyes had a haunted expression. "Something *shocking* happened to him in Los Angeles. I don't know what it could be. He's so torn."

"He's in love with you, Bonnie. I know it."

"I'm beginning to wonder. May I speak candidly? It's very personal. I could never bring up this subject with my own mother. . . . Please."

Allison was less broad-minded nowadays. She'd closed herself off. The very prospect of sex had become irrelevant.

"Go ahead."

"Sean's lost his desire. And I don't know what to do to help him. He wants to talk to someone, but not me."

Convertible top down, smiling at the shark-toothed cloudline over the Cascades, Sean reveled in the speed at near-freezing temperature and drove downtown. The sky was calm and a fresh, blustery wind sculled down the coast, traipsing along the river, goosing some sailboats. He had some time before meeting the district attorney. Paul Cisco had ordered a command appearance.

Sean parked at the courthouse beside the Astor monument and looked at the town with cold eyes. Port Rivers had been a charming river-flanked mosaic when Sean was growing up, home to old settler families, truck farmers, salmon fishermen, Greeks, the Chinese. Its naturalness, easy coastal mores, and distinctive appearance had attracted a sharp group of entrepreneurs, property traders, shills, cunning factors, and lawyers. He thought about Pat with pride, for his grandfather had resisted their blandishments and fought along with his mother to maintain the town's character; but they could not prevent the stampede of hucksters.

Strolling around Riverbed Place, Sean decided to drop into Karen's Vanities, the shop Georgie worked in. Drifting through the tools and inventions of a hooker's boudoir, a listless fashion show of sorts progressed. Eerie businessmen killing time, who could afford the prices, dashed in and out to glimpse the willowy college-girl models grifting for some Christmas cash. Sean slithered through mannequins in satin Teddies, biodegradable panties, appliances, and enough leather for a court of queens.

He found himself in the dressing area. Suddenly springing out of a huddle of girls bound in garter-belt contraptions, Sean faced the sweat-dripping pudding chins of the shop's commandant.

"Men aren't allowed in the changing area!" The woman's voice resounded with the depth of a cannonade. Eyes viperous as a headmistress, she burled forward, using her menacing bulk.

Sean backed off. "Oh, I'm sorry."

The woman peered at him. "Hey, wait a minute. Aren't you"—Georgie bullied up against him with maudlin affection—"Sean?"

"Madam Conlan? Of course, right," he said, sucking her in. "We spoke on the phone the other day. I'm still waiting for my mother to check in." He was all warmth and kinship. "I'll give her your message soon as she does."

"You're a sweetheart. I'll walk out with you."

Before wariness intruded, he disarmed her. "You were looking to rent an office. There's one available. It's upstairs over a take-out shop Allison plans to open across from the university. Pat owns the property. He said it would be fine. No first and last. Pay as you roll. I've got the keys."

"You really are a fine young man." Georgie could not withhold the extent of her self-disgust. "Me working here as a saleslady, maid is what I am. I can't imagine what you must think." She grimaced and chronicled her finer hours. "Once I was an attorney who commanded respect. Before 'lawyer' was an ugly word."

"Please, please. Stop. I don't form opinions instantly, or judge Allison's old friends."

"Having to start over at this stage isn't much fun."

"These things happen." Sean drizzled soft soap. "It couldn't have been easy in those days for a woman to hang out a shingle on her own."

She caught herself, imprisoning her distress. "It wasn't." She fretted, apologetic. "Nobody cares."

"I have a meeting at the courthouse. Afterwards, when you're through here, maybe we can have a drink and I'll run you over to see the office."

Sean crossed the triangle to the courthouse. Georgie Conlan had been pathetically grateful to him. He had mixed emotions about duping the poor thing. Once again he was fired up; resolve propelling him, he shook himself out of the doldrums. He'd check into the marriage license and the registration of Chris Arnold's Commander .45.

In the district attorney's office, Paul Cisco expelled fumes of garlic from a luncheon with the Greek American Service Patriots. Waving the GASP presentation plaque he had been honored with and hacking at some underling on the phone about a bail demand, Cisco tilted his hunter trophy head toward the sofa.

"Oh, Sean, my boy, if only these idiots could try a case. Maybe you should go to law school." Cisco took his hand. "I could probably wrangle something. Think about it."

Sean wondered if Cisco was ridiculing him. He could become another social-climbing shyster like his father.

He would dump Bonnie and get into the pants of some rich scarecrow.

"That's a very interesting suggestion, sir. But the real money's in private practice."

"I tried it years ago for a short time but went back to public office. The money was good," Cisco admitted, "but kissing the asses of felons was beyond me. The bullshit you have to force-feed yourself." He flaunted his head like Pavarotti conscripted to sing with the local glee club. "Everyone's supposed to be entitled to a defense even when you know the bastard raped a girl or shot someone in a robbery. I couldn't buy into that racket."

"Makes you want to puke," Sean, the acolyte, agreed. "I can't picture you in that role, Mr. Cisco."

"My practice lasted about a year or so."

"I admire you, sir. Weren't you the assistant D.A. before that, though? I'm interested in how people make decisions. Did you just quit and start your own law firm?"

Sean paused to let the district attorney summon up one of his arias.

"My wife goaded me into it. The grass was supposed to be greener." He regarded Sean with avuncular warmth. "Actually it was a complicated set of circumstances. I guess it doesn't matter after all these years and I'm sure your mother harbors no ill will toward me. At least none was evident at our dinner."

Sean masked his purpose and affected indifference as Cisco rambled on. "Allison can get to people."

"I'm an authority on that."

"Well, there was this phenomenal young criminal lawyer, absolute stonekiller in court. I've never seen anyone with a legal mind like his. You're up against someone pointing an Uzi at you. He was Pat Brett's son, Terry, he had the belly for it. He could've gotten Ted Bundy off.

"Terry was quite taken with your mother. And as things go, for some reason they fell out. Allison was certainly a show-stopper even then. She was far-out—this town's dazzler and then some." Cisco paused, savoring his reflections. "The point I was making. This hotshot

Terry and I had been adversaries in court. Pals outside. He was one smart, good-looking guy, and a charmer. Then he freaked out. People have breakdowns and he had one—just about lost his mind. Dumped everything one day. Picked up and turned his practice over to me for a buck. My wife said, grab it."

"Oh, so Pat did have a son?"

"Yeah, sure. Well, you see, Terry Brett got it into his head that there was a conspiracy against him. The sixties was a time of conspiracies. Naturally, there was nothing to it. He broke with everyone, including Pat. I lost track of him."

"I guess it was that woman, Georgie Somebody, who brought all this up."

"Georgie Conlan was Terry's partner. And later mine. She had a helluva divorce practice at the time. But then she loused it up with this bum she was desperate to marry. Earl Raymond, ball player buddy of Terry's. A real loser. Georgie was this classic cliché, the forgotten woman. She started drinking, coming into the office at all hours. Earl Raymond could do anyone in. I must admit it was sad seeing Georgie like that at your birthday dinner."

"She's been phoning my mother."

"Georgie calls everyone until Earl comes down to drag her back to his roadhouse. She's deeply disturbed."

Sean tried to wiggle Cisco into a more vulnerable position.

"I'm sort of surprised that you'd never been to The Greenhouse for dinner."

"Sean, on my salary, I can't be forking out a hundred a head for dinner. I have retained my idealism, despite my shitty salary. But I enjoy self-respect. And that's what counts in the world my conscience rules."

The conversation devolved into more practical matters. Judge Barry Walsh was the dean of the law school. Paul Cisco and he were old friends. "I think he'd like you." Cisco rose from his desk, clotted with files. He turned to the window, savoring the river view. "The reason I asked to see you must remain confidential."

Sean gave him a nasty spin.

"I grew up in a household in which covert missions took place all the time."

"Really?"

"You never knew that my father was an undercover agent with the CIA?"

"Not until you told me."

Paul Cisco clearly had no inkling of Terry Brett's double life. He clapped his pudgy hands together, embracing the information with enthusiasm.

"My dad was killed on a secret mission in East Berlin when I was a kid. In those days, he was a hero."

Like Terry, his son propagated deceit, sowed lies in the fertile mythology he had inherited.

"What a background! Sean, I must confess that I was deeply concerned about Barney sending you down to L.A. This SIS outfit is something I've been opposed to because these people act outside the law. I'd find myself more often than not defending *them* rather than prosecuting felons.

"More to the point, I was skeptical about a new detective being given such an assignment." He smiled. "Especially someone without more seasoning. But I read Commander Browning's report on you. And I changed my mind. Here, I thought, was a young man I could mold eventually into an attorney and who in the meantime could join my staff as an important addition to my investigation team. It would keep you out of the line of fire. I'd cut you good hours. You could go to law school."

Sean said after a moment, "What an offer. I'm overwhelmed."

"Five thousand a year more than you're getting and an expense account that won't be subject to quibbles. And a title: 'Special Investigator for the District Attorney.'"

"Mr. Cisco."

"This is obviously very sensitive. What is essential is that you don't mention this conversation to Captain Laver." Cisco's eyes were swimming offshore in polluted waters. "Politically, there would be fallout. Nuclear in its intensity with the city council."

"It's a very attractive offer, Mr. Cisco." He laid out his snare. "The thing is, I'm working on a case. On my own time. That's why I took my vacation now. It looks small and obscure, but my gut tells me it could be very hot. I could really use your help."

Cisco had his calls held. "Speak, son—"

"Would you prosecute a bigamy case?"

Cisco laughed, then thought it through.

"Delicious. I've never had one. What a change of pace. It'll send the media reeling. They've had it with serial killings. The *National Enquirer* would pay for that. I'd be on supermarket racks before an election. Is there more?"

Sean wondered what had happened to the real Christopher James Arnold or if such a person ever existed.

"This bigamist might have committed a murder. You see, he took over another man's identity and may have murdered him. He's a very wealthy, prominent person living under a false name in Los Angeles."

Spittle gathered at the corners of Cisco's mouth in anticipation of the feast. Sean thought the man was about to embrace him.

"Exquisite. You leave clouds of glory in this modest, provincial office. I am at your disposal, my son."

Beyond the detectives' squad room, in the chilly basement of the dank Hall of Justice, Sean sat at a bank of computers and fax machines. Like the collective unconscious of deeds and events, the mainframe gushed forth information and delivered what Sean had been searching for.

A copy of a marriage license dated December 18, 1966, appeared. The parties were Allison Desmond and Christopher James Arnold, both of Seacliff. Witnesses to the happy historical event were Milly Canfield and Patrick Brett. Born out of wedlock, Sean now realized that his own date of birth had been fraudulent. This incremental lie infuriated him. Everything his father touched, he tainted.

He compared this document with the earlier record he

had of the Los Angeles wedding of Terence Sean Brett and Valerie Holland (widowed, née Wolfe) on September 12, 1966. Terry was one musician playing two instruments at the same time.

Sean found himself perplexed by the mystery. What lay below the surface? What possessed Terry to marry Allison three months after he was already legally married to Valerie? Obviously, he'd knocked Allison up. Terry certainly could have paid her child support. Had she threatened to go to Valerie and expose him? Blackmail him. No, not Allison. More than likely, Terry had been sleeping with his flower child and the heiress at the same time, neither the wiser. He'd cut a deal, but Allison paid the pound of flesh.

Terry had been very sharp in his unscrupulous shadow life. He had surgically separated his two wives and children, banishing friends, his own father, so that neither existence would overlap or intrude. This feat of creating separate compartments was a remarkable one. Truly a double agent.

But Detective Sean Arnold knew Terry wasn't infallible. The registration of the Commander .45 license came over from records, disclosing that his father had skidded on black ice. The pistol was in Terry Brett's name. Another check established that the real Christopher James Arnold had been a career merchant mariner who had died at sea. Nothing, any longer, about the secret lives of people was secret.

Many interesting possibilities occurred to Sean. He recognized the bold symmetry of his destiny. The crime, its enforcer, and punishment had come together in a holy trinity.

Book VII

FAMILY REUNION

67

Shielding herself from the fury of the rasping wind, squirrel collar curled up, Georgie huddled in the lingerie shop's entryway, slapping her gloved hands together. Smiling genially, Sean took her arm.

"It's happy hour, how about it? Then we'll go to your new office."

"Oh, yes, yes."

Sean took her to the Surf Landing. With its panoramic view of the bay, even then in the gray vaporous fog, the mitered islands took on the refulgence of matched pearls. Stevedores were unloading cargo; the gull cries echoed along the waterfront. Sean waited before turning over the gray ashes of the past.

Georgie was a deeply serious drinker and downed several big Cutty Sarks before he returned from the chafing dishes with pinched meatballs and dried chicken wings. Georgie attacked these scraps with ferocity.

"I had quite a session with your old associate."

"Lead ass Cisco. An extremely finicky lawyer. He couldn't build the bridge from the D.A.'s office. I don't think Paul ever believed any client he represented might be innocent."

"Maybe that's why he couldn't handle private practice."

"My perception is somewhat different," she said. "He is an individual who needs a title to define him. We had a rocky year together. Come to think of it, everything's been rocky for me for a very long time."

He consoled Georgie with the prospect of a rebirth.

"Divorces are still in style. They're big business. If you're a guy and you wave a fist at a woman, she'll be running to you. Counselor Conlan, you'll be back on your feet in a few months."

"Counselor . . . if only." She belted back her drink and

Sean gave the victory sign to a waitress he knew. "The thing is, Sean, the first *choice* people make in marriage is everything—" Georgie stopped when the waitress removed her assemblage of glasses. ·"Thank you, Sean. Once a marriage goes wrong, nobody fully recovers. It's over, no matter what they say or think they feel. There's always the imagery hanging over them, haunting the present. Ex's and alimony, kids who hate. At the best of times, optimism is a luxury."

Sean touched Georgie's soft hand. She eagerly took his hand as they spanned in the perfect reciprocal warm feelings of drink.

"I guess you'd know." Sean remained the sympathetic listener, fearing that a premature question, an untoward suggestion about Terry and Chris, would spook her and she'd bolt. "Paul Cisco mentioned you had a problem with your own husband. . . . Is it Earl, that his name? Sorry I've been calling you Miss Conlan and it should be Mrs. Raymond. Shouldn't it?"

The drinks had inflamed Georgie. Her revelations of domestic horror with Earl Raymond fulminated in a recital. Through reconciliations, separations, new tries, old agonies, their marital slaughterhouse had been opened for viewing.

Sean knew that Terry Brett and his old buddy Earl had much in common when it came to abusing people. Battling through the roiling seas of Earl's infidelity and betrayal, something briefly captured Sean's attention. Earl had been in prison.

"Walla-Walla?" Sean asked.

"Earl was a spotter for the sportsbooks in Reno. They'd pay his expenses, and, depending on the quality of his information, pay him a thousand a month. He'd travel the Northwest looking over young players and romancing other men's wives. Whatever. . . . Well, he's up in Seattle and he tries to fix a basketball game! They slammed two years at him. I wish it had been life without parole."

"And you were working at the place he had?"

"Yes." She raised a finger and more drinks were already waiting on the waitress's tray.

"You ran the Paradise Inn when Earl was away chopping wood?"

"I had to. It ruined my law practice. Some time when you want to catch yourself a criminal, you take a ride up and bust Earl. Now *he* wants a divorce, but I'm going to sweat him until I get the property settlement I want. One day, I expect he'll kill me."

A voice within Sean roared—Tell me about Terry Brett!

After eight o'clock, Georgie and the fossils of chicken wings were slipping off the continental shelf. She was in no condition to see the office he had offered her. He suggested dropping her off and made another date. He bought her a carton of Kools at a 7-Eleven and some Diet Cokes. She was sloppy with gratitude. Sean had to cut through the fog of evasion and her rancid whiskey breath. The impulse to ask the question snaked out of him like an adolescent erection.

"When's the last time you saw my father?"

"Pardon?"

"Chris Arnold."

"Huh? I never heard of him. Thanks for the Kools."

"He was my dad. I can't believe you never met?"

"No . . . I never . . . actually, Allison and I stopped seeing each other way before she met him."

"Why's that, girls' beef?"

"Nah, she hated Earl."

Sean pulled up at Georgie's hotel and caught her as she was about to get out. If she had been a suspect, he would have been controlled, patient. This behavior was counter to his training and experience.

"What about Terry Brett? Couldn't he help you out?"

"No. Not anymore." Tears came flooding down her cheeks. "He was the noblest man I ever met. Gave me my break and made me his law partner." She slurred on. "He was Paul Cisco's nemesis. Terry wanted to ruin Paul, which was why he handed over his practice to him. He knew Paul couldn't hack it and would make a fool of himself."

Sean, the detective, knew Georgie had prepared a scenario for him. Lawyers lied.

She lumbered to the entrance, and Sean saw a tall man limp out of the shadows and intercept her. She took his hand and he led her to a cream-colored Rolls-Royce.

In a loud voice, Georgie pleaded, "Oh, Earl, please let's try to work this out. Take me back . . ."

"Sure, sugar. Come home with me. We'll go to the beach house."

"Is Karen still there?"

"She's moving out right now."

"Earl, I love you."

After packing a bag at home and jamming in some of Terry's old possessions, Sean headed for the police property department. He collected a kit of burglar tools that had been confiscated, then strode out to the vehicle depot behind the courthouse. He walked through the yard with a rookie who had pulled the cold-ass night duty. Sean examined vans, campers, a few RVs, seized from drug dealers. Ultimately they would be sold at the department's public auction. In the meantime, the best of them had been worked on by the police mechanics and set aside for official use. He looked at the paperwork on a hi-tech Warrior conversion fitted with a pair of bunks, sink, pullman kitchen, microwave, tinted windows, and a turbocharged modified V-8 engine.

"Pull the registration and slap on a set of plates."

The sleepy cop picked up a clipboard and began filling out a form. "On whose authorization, Detective Arnold?"

"The district attorney, Mr. Cisco."

"Purpose?"

"Special assignment."

On the way out of town, he passed Bonnie's town house. A light was on in the living room and he felt a powerful urge to stop. To comfort her and to be comforted. But the quest for enlightenment devoured him and he plunged into the demons of night.

68

Sean stopped at Printland in Santa Monica for the business cards he had ordered. Then he reclaimed the navy blazer he had left to be mended at Carroll & Company. He also rented a Lincoln Town car. The van might arouse suspicion while he covered the territory necessary to complete his dossier. He had been shadowing his targets. It was important to determine if Terry had shared his secret with anyone. Had others been involved in the plot? What would Jonah Wolfe do when he found out his son-in-law was a bigamist?

Jonah was coming off the golf course at Hillcrest with a scrambling 88. He was headed toward the card room when a steward from the club intercepted him.

"Someone to see you, Mr. Wolfe."

"Who is he?"

"Here's his card." Jonah read the name:

CHRISTOPHER J. ARNOLD, JR.
NATIONAL BASKETBALL ASSOCIATION
SECURITY INVESTIGATIONS
WESTERN SECTOR

"A league snoop," Jonah said with disdain. "Where's my security man?"

"I haven't seen him around."

"Oh, yeah, I sent him to get himself outfitted and pick up the plane tickets."

Elbows would be at The High and the Mighty reluctantly selecting his wardrobe. It had taken double pay to get Elbows to accompany him for a ski holiday. Not for the first time, Jonah had been told, "African Americans hate cemeteries and snow."

Jonah would be leaving for his final Christmas fiesta

in Aspen. He would put the house up for sale and expected to net out five million, which, with the ten Terry had paid him, would be his nest egg. He planned to move to Puerto Vallarta where the buck went a lot further and virgins were for sale.

"Show Mr. Arnold out here."

Since Simon Pearl's threat, Jonah had been vigilant. It would be safer to meet this man on the practice putting green in view of the members and caddies. Jonah signed a chit for his caddy, opened up a pack of Titleists, and practiced his putting.

A tall, burly, handsome young man with a well-trimmed beard and deepset knowledgeable eyes measured him for a moment. He was wearing a shabby blazer, rep tie from the dark ages, and a button-down blue shirt.

"I'm happy to meet a sports legend, Mr. Wolfe." On the face of it, Jonah would not be likely to cover up for Terry, but as a detective, nothing would surprise or scandalize Sean in the corrupt society Terry moved in. "I hope you can help me resolve a few questions about Terry Brett."

Sean slipped a hand in his pocket to activate the tape recorder he'd wired himself with. Cisco would want this kind of evidence for a grand jury indictment.

"Mr. Arnold, you just hit the daily double." Jonah warmed to the interview. "Ask away."

"I have information that Terry Brett used an alias when he lived in Seacliff."

Jonah was intrigued. "Seacliff? I thought he was from Port Rivers. But nothing about him would surprise me."

"Did you know Mr. Brett was married to a woman by the name of Allison Desmond?" Sean consulted his notes. "They were married on December 18 in 1966."

"What?" Jonah's eyes protruded. "How could that be? He was married to my daughter Valerie then."

"I know that. Unfortunately, there's no record of his divorce from Miss Desmond."

"My God, I don't believe this."

The discussion continued in this fashion for several

minutes, Sean chipping away, Jonah attentive. Terry had impressed people with his straight-arrow façade, but behind the Eagle Scout lurked a malevolent opportunist whose treachery, according to Jonah Wolfe, was unrivaled.

"Terry's diabolical. But he'll probably manufacture some explanation for the Desmond woman."

Sean pondered his next move. "Mr. Wolfe, another name keeps coming up. He was supposed to be a friend of Brett's. I wonder if you can tell me what the relationship is between him and Earl Raymond."

"Earl?" The name froze Jonah and he was troubled. "I don't get it!"

"Sorry to have upset you, sir. But Earl did play for the Stars. What exactly occurred with Brett, Mr. Raymond, and yourself?"

Face ashen, Jonah asked, "What's this all about?" Something now seemed dubious about this young man. "You're not from the league, are you?"

Sean slowly broke into a smile. At first it was beguiling, then it became deeper, ironic, and ultimately disturbing.

"You're right. I'm not who you think I am. I'm somebody else."

The admission terrified Jonah. He was now convinced that this man was a killer sent by Simon Pearl at Terry's instigation. Jonah noticed something—a wire appeared to be trickling out from under the man's threadbare blazer. The puff under the armpit outlined a gun. This man had waited for his bodyguard to leave him alone.

Jonah clutched his chest, then wildly sprinted down the eighteenth fairway.

"Hey, we're on the same side," Sean called after him, but Jonah was already out of earshot.

Heart pounding like a bellows, sucking in air, Jonah dashed into the range of a foursome hitting their shots. The arteries massed, throbbed in his forehead, something stabbed his carotid artery as he darted from side to side in a panic. The spasm came with swiftness. He clutched his throat, gagging on blood. His chest being pounded by an ax, the aorta exploded, and he fell face-down into a sandtrap.

From a distance Sean watched a group of men rush from their golf carts and attempt to revive his fallen ally.

At the Sports Associates office, a middle-aged receptionist routing calls on her computer eventually found time to tell Sean that both Billy Klein and Mike Summers would be away until after the new year. Sean was about to ask for Terry when the woman explained he was no longer with the firm.

"Why don't you leave a note and your phone number? And Mr. Brett will get back to you."

Sean stared blankly at her. "Never mind."

Back in his hotel room he switched on the TV. Jonah Wolfe's death of a massive coronary at the Hillside Country Club was reported on the five o'clock news. A profile of the controversial sportsman would be coming up on the sports segment.

As Sean was calmly considering his notes, and the next move to advance his case, he called the UCLA Medical Center. He learned that Aaron would be on duty from eight that evening. He wanted to see his brother face-to-face in his natural habitat and find out what he knew about their father. Suddenly, Sean noticed a tightening in his throat and in a moment he could not swallow.

His fingers tingled and began to tremble. He had no tranquilizers to relax him. Sweat dripped off his forehead and his left arm developed a numbness. Something had triggered an anxiety attack. Sean tried to calm himself, but his autonomic nervous system had been activated, and he knew that once this fright alert ensnared him, he was lost.

He took his racing pulse and in fifteen seconds the throbbing veins in his wrist had registered 30; his heart was going at 120 beats a minute. This hadn't happened to him for many years and whenever it occurred he was powerless to reverse it. The fear of a heart attack immobilized him. The panic reached a crescendo and ripened into an overwhelming state of terror. He dizzily searched the desk drawer and found a paper bag, rolled the edges into a cuff and breathed into it slowly, desperate to restrict his hyperventilation. The saliva in his mouth had dried and his tongue reflexively crawled over the roof of his mouth.

With the bag over his mouth, he staggered into the bathroom and turned on the cold water. As he reached for a glass, it fell from his hand and shattered on the tile floor. He peered into the mirror and observed his pupils dilating wildly. His color was sallow and he corkscrewed to the floor, curling under the sink. He lay there for hours, semiconscious and in dread.

69

With a burst of energy, Valerie managed to conclude her final course in pediatrics at the medical school. As she packed her briefcase and left the lecture hall, she was grief-stricken and sinking into the sump of depression. She would never be back and reflected sadly on the end of her career.

Terry had called her at the office earlier that afternoon with the news of Jonah's death. There had been a long silence at her end.

"I'm relieved," she said finally. "There was no unfinished business for any of us."

In a sense, Terry regarded Jonah's passing from natural causes as a dispensation, for it removed the pressure of guilt that he might have had if Simon Pearl had been called upon as his instrument. He thought of Earl. The coast would be clear shortly.

"Do you want me to make arrangements for a funeral?"

"No, Ter, I'll do it." There would be a cremation, Jonah's ashes thrown to the wind at Malibu. "I'm not going to be a hypocrite and hold a memorial service, either. None of us would attend, so why bother?"

He found her logic severe but cogent. "I'm meeting Aaron at the Hamlet Gardens before he goes on duty. Val, can you join us?"

"I'm very tired. I'll catch you at home."

Aaron was rushed and the restaurant crowded, so they ate salads at the bar before his shift began.

"This sure is a troubled family. Mom had nothing to do with her father and you don't speak to yours."

Terry flared up. "I'm not a psychiatrist. But just because you're related to someone doesn't mean you have to like them. People are individuals, and when they injure you, maybe it's better to avoid them."

"But these are such fundamental relationships, so integral to one's life. How will you feel if your father goes and the two of you still haven't been speaking?"

The question exacerbated Terry's raw nerves.

"Friendship is all that counts with me. I've given mine to many people and been rewarded. Look, the thing is, when someone constantly goes up against you and undermines your life, you're better off without them."

"Sorry I brought it up. Still, I don't agree. There is no scenario I can imagine that would turn me against you."

Terry lost his defensive posture. "I appreciate that, Ace. How's Kit doing? I haven't seen her in days. And I miss not having her around."

"She went to Vegas with a client who's doing some TV special. She's due back tomorrow."

It was one of those easy infrequent father-son evenings that Aaron had missed when he was growing up. Recently, his father seemed to have more time for him. They veered into the rich, happy territory of his future with Kit.

"I realize now it's pointless to rush your marriage," Terry said. "Your mother's condition . . ."

"Dad, we want Mother at the wedding. I need her there. Kit's going to arrange for her father to come up from Oklahoma. And there'll be one other couple, my supervisor, Dr. Saul Greenman, and his wife. I had to explain the situation to Saul."

Terry's face clouded with displeasure. "Why'd you do that?"

"My work was going to hell and he demanded a reason. He helped me over the hump. Jesus, I was thinking of taking a leave of absence or resigning. I've talked this out with Kit and she's all for it."

They planned a small private ceremony at home before Christmas and at some future date they would have a reception at the Bel Air Hotel and invite their friends.

Aaron looked at his watch. "I've got to run. If Kit calls, tell her I've pulled the graveyard MOD tonight and I'll have to sleep at the hospital."

It was almost midnight at the UCLA emergency ward and slow for a Wednesday night. Two heart attacks; a man with a skull fracture after a beating in a bar; a twelve-year-old gunman shot by the police; four coke overdoses; a teenage girl's suicide attempt—wrists slashed with a kitchen knife—after she revealed she was pregnant and her parents threw her out.

Aaron was finishing with the girl and wrote "P.C." on her chart. Since she hadn't volunteered, a physician commitment for observation was necessary. He had her sedated. The duty nurse came into his small cubicle as the girl was wheeled out and took his completed chart.

"Dr. Brett, we've got a strange one. Everyone's pretty nervous around him. He had a panic attack and claims his father's to blame and he made threats."

"Did you do a workup?"

"Full physical and chemistry profile. Complete blood count."

"What about the urine drugscreen and breathalyzer?"

"Right here, Dr. Brett."

She handed him a chart. Christopher Arnold, Jr., twenty-seven, had been cleared of somatic problems. The urinalysis showed no alcohol or drugs in his system.

He was brought into Aaron's glass cubicle by an orderly. In a checked hospital gown, the man's muscled arms and barrel chest stretched the garment. His glacial blue eyes were fixed on Aaron. The fact that the patient had come in of his own free will was already a positive sign. Aaron was friendly but cautious.

"Please take a seat, Mr. Arnold, and let's talk about this."

After his anxiety attack had subsided, Sean intended to wait for Aaron to complete his shift, but once again he found himself overwhelmed by the circumstances.

"I had a panic attack that lasted almost three hours."

"Have you had them before?"

"Not for about thirteen–fourteen years."

"So, you have a history of them. Have you had any previous psychiatric history as an inpatient?"

"When I was thirteen, I was in the hospital for a few weeks. I had a couple of years of therapy after that."

"Did your physician come to any conclusions?"

Sean searched for physical correspondences in his half brother, a voice intonation, mannerisms that would link them. Aaron had a deep, well-modulated voice, and was a sensitive, delicate man, with fine, thin fingers, the hue of his skin darker than his own. He had cavernous eyes, bright with acuity, and of such a deep brown that they appeared black. His hair was longish, thick and curly. His angular features and aquiline nose had little of Terry about him.

"He said it was depression. My father vanished, but I believed he was dead. I was lied to."

Aaron shook his head. "I see." He scanned the chart. "What brings you to L.A.?"

"Business and . . . I saw my father."

"That must've been a shock."

"Sure was. Frankly, I don't know what to do about it. He committed bigamy: there was my mother and this other woman he married in Los Angeles. I've tracked down the whole family."

"What a situation," Aaron said sympathetically. "What kind of job do you have?"

"I'm in law enforcement. I'm a detective. My father is a felon."

"Sounds like it. Is he under arrest?"

"Not yet."

Sean lapsed into a regression. He was six years old, wearing a sailor suit, playing in the pond by the house in Seacliff with a sailboat that Terry had given him. He was waiting for his father.

"The fact is, Dr. Brett, when I was a kid and these episodes began, I was first diagnosed as suffering from some trauma which developed after the shock of my father's death. Later on, I had a tremendous rage building up inside me because I felt that my father's death deprived me of the greatest human being I'd ever known. My mother tried to replace him, but she couldn't. I was told that my dad worked for the CIA and that he was murdered by East German secret agents. Do you want to know what I think happened?"

"Yes, please go on."

"My teenage rage was channeled into depression and then these anxiety attacks displaced it."

"You've got a really good fix on yourself."

Sean's head fell forward and he became emotional. "I'd like to think so, but I don't. The problem is I feel violent now. I'm terrified . . . I might kill him."

Aaron made a note: *Shock activating psychic mechanisms. Patient states he intends to murder his father. Intermittent hostility as defense. Murderous impulses could be acted out.*

"You came here for help, not to commit murder. So let's discuss these feelings. That's the important thing." He waited a moment as the patient composed himself and reluctantly nodded. "What's your reaction to these thoughts you've been having about your father?"

"I visualize my father begging me for mercy."

"Are these thoughts interfering with your ability to function as a detective?"

A bitter, biting, howling jeer filled the room. "Interfering! My fucking sex life's a wreck. I've got a beautiful fiancée and I can't get an erection!"

Aaron thought briefly of his own situation and the fragility of men. Hand trembling, he wrote: *Castration anxiety. Patient has unconscious retaliation fantasy for his murderous impulses and this is intra-psychically affect-*

ing his sexuality. Positive sign. Superego and defense mechanisms in play, inhibiting active response, manifesting itself in impotence.

"Have you been in contact with your father?"

"No, I've been following him."

"He has no idea that you've located him?" Aaron asked.

Sean stared at Aaron. "I'm building a case against him."

"That's a better approach. As a detective with a knowledge of the law, it would be more satisfying for you and your mother to have this man arrested and tried in court. Murder is not the resolution to justice."

"You're right, of course. I should just keep gathering evidence." Sean could not contain his curiosity and needed to probe Aaron. "Have you ever known loneliness, Dr. Brett?"

Aaron smiled. "I don't think you've come here to listen me."

The detective in Sean asserted itself. "Just answer the question!"

"Is it so important? Okay, sure I've had my days of loneliness. Now you're at bat. What made you come here for help?"

"My compass has gone haywire. I had to leave Port Rivers, come back to Los Angeles, and now I can't find a way home."

Patient flees home and at the same time seeks it.

Aaron was becoming increasingly worried and wondered if he ought to contact Dr. Greenman. No, that would be bailing out. He had to see this through on his own.

"When I was at school, I used to look at my friends' fathers with envy. Once, after a baseball game and I hit a grand slam, one of the fathers came over to congratulate me and I kissed him. The guys taunted me for ages after that. Man, it was so painful."

Convinced of the truth of the story of neglect and desertion, Aaron felt a degree of sympathy for the young man who was almost his own age.

"You wanted approval from your father. Your feelings were good, universal, natural. We all want magic and perfection from our fathers."

Sean gradually regarded his antagonist in a different, more generous light. He responded to Aaron's humanity, his patience. His empathy embraced Aaron and he thought: *This son has been cheated too, and he must've been smart enough to know it. That's why he became a shrink. He's looking for answers.*

Aaron made some final notes on the chart. "I think you ought to come back to the clinic. There's a crisis service twenty-four hours a day." He wrote the number down. "I'm going to prescribe a two-milligram dose of Ativan for you. It's a tranquilizer. Take two twice a day. Don't drive, don't drink, and don't use any drugs with it. You could get a serious cross reaction."

Sean nodded appreciatively and extended his hand across the desk. Normally, Aaron, like all psychiatrists, avoided this with patients, but it seemed appropriate in this case. Aaron shook his hand.

"When do I see you again?"

"You'll see my supervisor, Dr. Greenman."

Sean rose from the chair and thundered, "You don't really give a shit about me, do you? Trying to palm me off on somebody else. Look, pal, the minute I leave, I know where to find my father, and believe me, I'll make him pay for what he did to me and my mother. It'll be slow and painful for that bastard!"

Aaron confronted him. "Really? Well, that's quite a position you're putting me in. Chris, take it easy. I'm the resident O.D. My job is to help you over an immediate crisis and to refer you. It's the process of therapy that can help you, not a single individual with some miraculous cure. All these pent-up feelings you've stored up will take time to resolve."

"I want *you* to be my doctor."

Aaron looked at him severely and walked out to the corridor. There were four more cases waiting.

"That can't be arranged." He handed him the prescription slip. "Our pharmacy will fill this fast."

Still balking, Sean felt deeply ambivalent toward
Aaron. He made an effort to ingratiate himself, smiled
warmly, and started down the corridor, past the familiar
sights of bleeding, injured, keening, mad people he himself had encountered, as a cop, in emergency rooms in
the middle of the night.

"Okay, *Ace,* I get the picture."

Aaron was startled. He turned and charged after Sean.
"What did you call me?"

"Nothing, Bro, you're an ace is all. I feel a kinship.
You're a shrink. Don't you understand that?"

Before Aaron could reply, a nurse intervened, waving
charts and assisting another patient.

"Dr. Brett, is Mr. Arnold going to be discharged?"

Sean was already walking and winking at Aaron.

"Yes, discharge him."

"Love you, man." Sean called out. "I'm the black
knight."

70

This would be another Christmas of grief for Allison.
The holidays from Thanksgiving to New Year's had
the effect of capsizing her, for they reminded her of the
shell of a life she inhabited, the abstinence from sex,
the failure to connect, the abyss of time without Terry.
She wrestled with these thoughts, never far below the
surface, especially with "Jingle Bells" and snow in the
air.

Bonnie was poker-faced and had a flu pallor when Allison met her. Bonnie ordered a pot of herbal tea and sat
with her eyes averted. Sean had been gone a week and
they hadn't heard from him. At first, the women were
joined in anger toward him, but this had given way to a
sickly fear that prompted Allison to act.

"How're you feeling?"

The response was a hacking cough. "Death took a holiday." Bonnie regained her breath and wiped her brow with the back of her hand. "Sean asked me to keep it quiet until he was finished with some case and told you. But it doesn't matter any more. Allison, he asked me to marry him. We even made plans to have the wedding during Rose Festival."

"That's wonderful. I'm going to give you a reception that—"

"—Look, Allison, I've never been burned like this before. I've done my crying. I feel humiliated. I won't be a victim for him or anyone else." Allison was familiar with those brave, fruitless words. "I'm glad you called. It's better than writing you a letter. I won't be coming back to The Greenhouse."

"You need the money to pay your tuition."

Voice choked with phlegm, Bonnie's eyes flared. "I'll find another job. You see, Allison, when it comes to it, you'll side with Sean. He won't have any trouble finding himself someone else. He's probably with a girl in L.A. I finally realized his marriage proposal was a song and dance. Sean has no sense of loyalty or the least idea of what it is a woman gives. It's not cups of soup or sex. Maybe you ought to sit him down one of these days and explain that. The other thing is, he's so protective of you and you of him. In some way, maybe that's why he wanted to be a cop. So he could keep the guys away from you, banished to the badlands."

"Bonnie, please, I promise we're going to find out what this is all about."

"Find out for yourself, not me."

Allison made some calls and learned that Paul Cisco would be in court, trying a case. The courtroom smelled of old sandwiches and galoshes. Cisco, wearing elevated heels, a gray pinstripe suit, had just finished addressing the jury. The judge looked at his watch. "This court will adjourn until two o'clock."

Cisco and his colleagues were gathering their documents when Allison's long fingernails tapped on the district attorney's attaché case.

"Yes? Ahh, it's you. What's up?"

"Have you got a minute?"

"Literally a minute, Allison."

"What's going on with my son?"

"Frankly, I'm not sure. He's on a case in Los Angeles."

"With that special team?"

"No, he told Barney that something turned up accidentally while he was on the other investigation. I let him sign out for a camper van and he drove down."

"I spoke to Barney. He claims he doesn't know a thing about this."

"That's true. I'm not sure I do either. I've just given Sean his head on this one."

"Paul, please, tell me, is he in trouble?"

To wipe away her tears, Cisco gallantly took out a handkerchief dried with Bounce that made Allison sneeze.

"No, certainly not." He paused. "I'd never make you cry again, Allison."

Terry dropped in for a drink at Dan Tana's restaurant, which was one of his favorite watering holes. He sat down with the owner at his table in the bar.

"A curious thing happened, Terry. A guy came in asking a lot of questions about you."

"What did he want to know?"

"He was trying to weasel odd information about you."

Terry was bemused by this peculiar set of circumstances. "Was he a ball player?"

"I don't think so."

"Did he give his name?" Dan Tana shook his head. "What did he look like?"

"He was about six-one, blond, one-ninety, muscled, beard. Hard to tell his age. Maybe thirty. Good-looking guy. Very smooth, sort of a con-man type. He had one of those stares that worry bartenders and cops. That's about it, Terry."

"Thanks, Dan."

Terry had anticipated a league investigation, but this surreptitious method puzzled him. It was unusual. In fact,

Terry had spoken to the NBA office only a few days before and been told that no one had any doubts about his ability to take over the Stars. A financial statement would be required as well as a personal interview and a vote by the other owners. All of this was pro forma.

According to Elbows, this same investigator had come to Jonah's golf club and spoken to him just before his heart attack. Some time later he had appeared at the Sports Associates office asking for Terry. He hadn't left a message.

Later that night, when Terry was home in bed with Valerie, she snuggled up to him. Spirits elevated, she appeared improved, her color back; even the weight loss seemed arrested. He held her in his arms with hope.

"You're such a good girl. Val, don't leave me."

She shook her head. "Terry, you were the man of my dreams. Even during the bad times, I felt lucky to have you." She kissed him with affection. They would be leaving shortly before Christmas and have New Year's Eve at Harry's Bar.

"I forgot to tell you, Aaron's going to ask Dr. Greenman for a week off and join us with Kit. A double honeymoon. How's that sound, Val?"

Once again her eyes had a youthful, magical glow. "I'd love that. A wedding on Christmas Eve, and Venice after."

The ringing of the phone interrupted them. Terry picked up the receiver.

"Hello, Simon. No, it's not too late. I appreciate your calling." Terry listened for a moment. "Yeah, well, Jonah didn't suffer, he made others do that for him—including his daughter. Ashes to the wind.

"Simon, there's some character cruising around—supposedly investigating me on behalf of the NBA. They assured me that he's not one of their people. I wondered if he was one of yours? No, okay. I just thought . . . I don't think it's serious, just a nuisance. Thanks for calling."

Valerie glanced over at Terry. "He contacted my office too, asking about you, and spoke to my secretary. He didn't leave a name or explain what it was all about."

"It's probably nothing."

Val picked up her book, and Terry resented even this moment away from her. He moved close to her in bed, and she looked up with a pale smile.

"What're you reading?"

"My old Swinburne. It's his tribute to Baudelaire."

"You used to read to me years back and I was enthralled by the sweetness of your voice."

She touched his hand and leaned against his chest. Her fragility distressed him. But her voice was still deep and girlish with innocence.

> . . . Or they loved their life through, and then went
>   whither?
> And were one to the end—but what end who knows?
> Love deep as the sea as a rose must wither?
> As the rose-red seaweed that mocks the rose.
> Shall the dead take thought for the dead to love them?
> What love was ever as deep as a grave?
> They are loveless now as the grass above them
> Or the wave.

He closed his eyes and tried to visualize her as she once was.

"Terry, what's going to happen to you . . . afterward?"

"I don't know. I can't imagine. The prospect is unbearable."

Val held his strong hand in her raw-boned palm. "Terry, it's time for a moment of candor."

"Haven't we had them since I came back?"

"I want to talk about that. You and your lost life."

"I don't want to hear."

"I have to say some things about it. I don't want them buried with me. Allison loved you, and you loved her and the boy very deeply. I know it's been a source of distress for you."

The cold wave of Sean's loss swept over him. For a moment he was adrift, imagining Allison's shadowy face; her poignant smile, masking her pain; the lambent deep blue eyes resigned to his departure back to Val. This image was quickly obliterated by the callous, snarling voice of a manipulative hustler. He had loved the young Allison and despised the malicious mastermind who had entrapped him.

"Val, please stop."

"I have to get this out. Terry, I want you to see them when I'm gone."

"I can never do that."

"It's the only way you'll heal the wound. Yours and theirs."

"I have no idea what's happened to them—even if they're alive. I've thought about Sean a lot lately. He was such a good kid. I don't know if I ought to try to look him up. Help him, if he needs it. But there's Aaron to consider, and he comes first. At least I know for sure he's my son."

"Allison couldn't help herself, none of us could. You're not the bad guy. You did what you thought would be honorable for them, and now, I can't fault you. You see, Terry, at this point in what time that's left for me, I see things so much more clearly. It's like a perfect X ray of the soul. Terry, go back to her. I want to know that you'll be with a woman who really loves you and deserves you."

"That's impossible, Val. People change."

"I know that you've never stopped loving her, and I respect you for it. Give her back her life."

"No."

"I'll rest easier."

"Val, please."

"*I* have to release you because I really believe Allison let you go for me."

Sean's mood alternated between fury and despondency. He was agitated, and he concluded that Aaron had simply disposed of him as Terry had. *Here's a pill, take it, and the years of suffering and loneliness will disappear.* Sean wanted to connect to Aaron, but at the same time, he was overcome by the compelling need to upset the symmetry of his life. How would Dr. Aaron Brett, psychiatric resident, handle pressure? Aaron was what the newspapers would refer to as a "scion," the heir to a fortune: Terry was a multimillionaire; Dr. Valerie Brett was loaded; and Grandpa Jonah Wolfe had probably left his grandson an enormous estate.

Had Aaron ever had a cloudy day in his life? Had he worked in kitchens chopping off fish heads; had he humped furniture in the rain; had this prince of psychological knowledge and enlightenment ever had an anxious moment? Sean was determined to squeeze and churn him through the wringer.

It was a gray morning at the beach, with a whining wind. Sean ordered corned beef hash and eggs and coffee at the Ocean Drugstore, a neighborhood mom-and-pop place, a few booths with cracked black vinyl, a five-seat counter, pharmacy in the rear, magazine rack with no skin slicks. Homey, clean, deliveryman packing up prescriptions, short-order cook stroking toast with a butter brush. These establishments had become rare in a world of Save-Ons and Denny's.

"Crisp up the home fries, please," Sean asked the waitress. "And would you bring some Tabasco?"

Sean turned to the *USA Today* sports section. On the road, the Stars were 2 and 7. Karl Malone had mailed them forty-two points the previous evening in Utah. Next stop Phoenix, to be electrocuted by the Suns. He doubted if that basketball genius Terry Brett could shake the team out of its stupor.

Slouching and with bloodshot eyes, Dr. Aaron Brett muttered good mornings to everyone and plopped into a booth. A mug of coffee was put down. He unzipped his briefcase and took out a stack of files.

Sean's plate arrived, the hash still hissing from the grill. "More coffee?" the waitress asked. He nodded. As she poured, he was aware of Aaron staring at him. He decided to ignore Aaron and began to eat.

Let him sweat it, grind and bleed. Fine, he'll think I'm crazy.

A shadow cut across the table. "What are you doing here?" Aaron glowered at him.

"Pardon?"

"I saw you in emergency a few nights ago." Sean motioned for him to sit but was shaken off. "I asked you a question."

"Oh, it's you. How're you doing, doc. I'm having breakfast. I was going to write you a thank-you note. But I forgot your name. What a state I must've been in."

Aaron could not exclude the possibility of a fortuitous meeting, but his reaction was that he was being set up by this man. As Sean reached into his pocket, the lapels of his shiny blazer spread its wings and revealed a leather harness holding a revolver with a large black grip. A small yellow envelope was thrust on the table holding the Ativan pills.

"I didn't need them. You did such a good job that I went back to the hotel, had a drink at the bar, and decided to forget it all." Sean dabbed a forkful of hash into the egg yolk. "Let sleeping dogs lie, right?"

The veins stood out on Aaron's forehead. "What brought you to this locals' spot?"

"Chance," Sean said airily. "Your pancakes are coming. Want to join me?"

Aaron realized he was in the power of an armed man. Yet he knew that to accept the invitation would reveal weakness. He had no choice but to maintain his distance.

"I've got some work to do." He had to address the issue of his patient being armed. "You doing some detective work?"

"In a way."

"Does your father live around here?"

"A five-minute walk."

"Have you seen him?"

"I'm waiting for the right moment."

"Have you called him?"

"No. He's busy at the moment. I'll wait till things calm down and give him a buzz."

"That's a good idea."

"Why don't you sit down, Dr. Brett. Come on. If

you've got my records, maybe I can clear up a few things."

"I don't have them."

"Okay. No big deal." Sean resumed eating while Aaron stood his ground. Sean opened a flip-flop wallet. His gold detective badge caught the light. "The reason I'm here is because the suspect I'm pursuing is in the area."

"You're a little far from your jurisdiction."

"So is the suspect." Sean took out a card. "Call the SIS, Dr. Brett."

Aaron looked at him quizzically.

"You don't know who they are?" Sean continued.

"No, should I?"

"It's the Special Investigation Section. An elite unit in the LAPD who go after elite criminals. If you think I'm a liar or some wacko, ask them about me."

"This isn't a poker game. I don't have to call any hands."

"No, I will."

"I'm sorry I forgot your name," Aaron said.

"It's Chris Arnold. . . . It happens frequently to me. Especially when people don't want to see me."

"Are you working with this elite group to extradite your father for his crimes?"

"The process goes something like this: First there has to be a positive identification, and then a warrant has to be issued so that an arrest can be made . . . provided he doesn't resist."

Aaron was uncomfortable and retreated. Sean read him easily.

"I see," Aaron said. "This all sounds sensible. Violence in families—"

"—Don't tell me *my* business. I didn't tell you how to treat me. I want you to understand something, Dr. Brett. I'm a responsible law enforcement officer. I had a crisis. I was fortunate to luck into you. I was acting impulsively like a child, and I was very angry. That's an explosive mixture. And, no, I haven't seen my dad yet."

These remarks were delivered in a crisp matter-of-fact

manner which defused the situation for Aaron.

"I'm happy I was able to help."

"Well, you did. Look, since fathers have been such an issue with me, and you're a psychiatrist, I'm curious about something. How's your relationship with *your* father—assuming he's alive?"

Aaron observed the agonized look in his eyes but decided not to prolong the encounter. He had his exit.

"Excellent."

"He's devoted to you, I'll bet," Sean snarled. "Well, with a doctor-son, someone he can be proud of, respect, who could blame him?" Sean cupped a hand over his eyes, fearing that he might break down. "Yeah, I'm dead sure *your* father appreciates you. Which is more than I can say for mine."

71

There would be no trip to Venice, and Valerie knew she could not attend her son's wedding. They were fantasies designed for Terry and Aaron. The dying had to eradicate their pain for loved ones, she reflected while she injected a syringe of morphine into her vein. Prop them up, give them a sense of security. A witness to the vigils in hospitals, she had marveled at this perverse phenomenon. Provided the patients could speak, they were the ones offering comfort to their mournful families and friends.

With great difficulty, breaking down repeatedly, she finally managed to write notes to Terry and Aaron. She had also given serious consideration to Kit's place in their lives. She had misjudged the girl. She was not coming to Aaron on bended knee. She had substance and dignity; if her past was perhaps too full of actors and former lovers to suit Val, it no longer mattered. Terry had been right: Men rhapsodized about virgins and purity, but in fact they sought out the Allisons of the world.

When Val went down to the kitchen, Terry's favorite dinner at home was being prepared and the air had the tantalizing fragrance of cilantro and garlic. Maria was scoring the leg of pork and mixing the molasses marinade for carnitas. Valerie dipped her finger into a bowl and tasted a new batch of rich, bloodred salsa.

"It's delicious. Even hot enough for Mr. Brett. I have to meet Kit. Is Antonio busy or can he drive me to town?"

Valerie banged into the counter and bashed her hip. Once she could find her way around the kitchen in darkness, but now in broad daylight she was clumsy, prone to accidents.

"Of course. Are you all right, Señora Brett?"

"I'm fine. I have to get my contacts prescription changed. I'll get around to it eventually," she said vaguely.

When Antonio opened the door of the Mercedes, Valerie was disoriented. Everything was a blur. She hadn't even been aware that they had already arrived at Chanel. Kit came toward her; for a moment Valerie didn't recognize her.

"Valerie, what's wrong?" Kit took her arm and escorted her into the boutique.

"I'm okay. Damn contacts are giving me a problem." She opened her purse, found her pill case, and slipped a Dexamil bullet into her mouth to counteract the morphine. "Do you like Chanel, Kit?"

Kit tossed her head back, laughing with the brash unself-conscious ease of being twenty-nine and strikingly lovely. "Who doesn't?"

The speed rushed into Val's bloodstream and her mood was elevated. "Well, now you're going to dress like a star."

"How do you mean?"

"Life begins with a classic Chanel suit."

"Valerie, give me a break—they're three or four thousand."

"You don't have a mother or sisters, so I want to be

a surrogate. I don't know what your plans for a trousseau are, but let's start here."

Kit protested, then accepted this act of generosity. Dancing back to the office, she visualized the Gucci shoes, Ungaro dresses, Chanel suits, a Lagerfeld cocktail dress, the Armani skirts and jackets that would be delivered to the house. In the elevator going up to her office, she said aloud: "Please, God, don't let her die. I want her for my mama."

The atmosphere at Theatrical Artists was convivial; the Christmas office party had begun early, troops had left the front lines, ferreting out of the backroom cubicles into a spotlight of champagne. Prancing buoyantly in a new perfect-fit royal blue Chanel blazer, Kit was already giggly and passed up a hit from the coke hawks dealing from the mailroom. No, her Christmas didn't need to be any whiter. She gaily drank some champagne with the partners who remembered the deals she had closed during the year. It was bonus time and Kit knew she was not among the hostages who would be pink-slipped out of the place. They were sniffing around her too much. Jasmine, the sinewy Eurasian receptionist and gossip virtuoso, waved to her from across the room.

High on herself, Kit kissed Jasmine. "What have I missed?"

"The best two hours of my life. Have I met a guy!" The receptionist failed in a disco turn and two feet of jet black hair whirled into her drink. A producer helped mop her up with paper napkins. All at once, a gallant, knightly figure, carrying drinks, carved a path through the merrymakers. "It's Kevin Costner in a Robin Hood beard. My stars said, 'Dress up, venture out, and don't wear panties.' He wants to sign with me."

"Jasmine, you are not an agent."

Jasmine's hero cautiously handed them drinks. He smelled good when he leaned toward Kit.

"This is Captain Chris—"

"—Arnold."

"Kit, meet one of Aaron's closest friends."

Kit shook his hand warmly. Trust Aaron, Dr. Silence, to wheel these treats out for her. The man had startling blue eyes, which focused intently on her. He struck her as somewhat reticent but powerful, secure in his physical prowess.

"Are you an actor?"

"You kidding? Miss Fortune Cookie gave me the come-on. You know, I should be a movie star."

"She has her enthusiasms. . . . Chris, how'd you know I'd be here?"

"Aaron told me. We met for breakfast at the old pharmacy on Ocean. I was coming into Beverly Hills and since he's on duty, he suggested I stop by and meet the future bride."

Sean scrutinized her carefully but not overtly. She was hot, exuding a carnal essence; he liked her lilting southern voice, sharpened by her trade. She had immaculate skin, just a touch of blush and lipstick. Her figure combined sinewy lines and the kind of urgent femininity that appealed to him. He wondered if his brother could handle her.

When he related how he had been dropped into Bosnia behind the lines with his Special Forces unit, she became enthralled. Even more engaging was his reluctance to admit any act of valor. He and Aaron had known each other for years but lost contact when Chris had gone to West Point and Aaron to medical school.

"I never doubted Aaron would wind up in medicine. But a psychiatrist? Spending his time with wackos? Who can figure people?"

"He followed Valerie's lead."

"Not Terry's."

"No, I don't think Aaron ever considered law. And what Terry does is like black magic. He has an amazing capacity to sign these athletes, make multimillion-dollar contracts, and stay in the background."

"It won't be quite so easy to avoid the publicity now that he's the owner of the Stars."

"Terry wants a winner, not personal glory. He's extremely self-effacing." He gave her a somewhat surprised look. "I'm probably not telling you anything you don't already know about him. He is without question the smartest man I've ever met. And he wears his intelligence gracefully. He listens to people and he always knows the right way to do things."

They'd had enough of the office champagne, and when Sean suggested dinner at Trader Vic's, she readily accepted. She relished Chris's stories of Aaron as a young man, how he came to the aid of anyone who was injured. He had great medical knowledge even as boy, Chris informed her. He held up his hand.

"I didn't even realize my finger was broken until Aaron looked at it. Well, he set it right on the spot and I went back to football practice."

They both sucked on their straws from a gourd of Scorpions, and he casually linked fingers with her. She did not withdraw and he could tell by her smile she was getting high.

"Is everything working out okay?" he asked.

"How do you mean?"

His thigh leaned into hers. "You and Aaron. I don't mean to probe. You know how it is when you care about someone."

She was comfortable with this staunch protective friend and allowed herself to open up.

"This is going to sound odd, but in some quirky way, you know who you remind me of?"

"No idea."

"Terry. You've both got a way of concentrating only on the person you're with. I mean, a bomb could go off and I don't think either of you would turn your heads." She giggled. "I feel like you're taking my picture."

"Do you like it?"

"It's lovely."

"I'm overwhelmed by the comparison to Terry. Unfortunately, he always considered me a nobody. He never wanted Aaron to hang out with me and kept us apart. He thought I'd be a bad influence on him."

"Really? I think Valerie's harder on people than he is."

"Maybe being as pretty as you helped some. I'm not telling tales out of school. But Aaron had trouble with sex when we were growing up. We used to cruise together and Terry didn't like that."

They picked at their food, and in the spirit of the moment Kit dropped her guard. "When I first met Aaron, my God, he was the most inhibited man I'd been with." Her eyes lit up knowingly. "I cured that real quick."

"I'll bet you did." Sean picked up the scent. He touched her cheek and ear with the back of his hand. He'd flap his wings with a version of the real truth. "Lucky I'm engaged—that we both are." He smiled pleasantly. "I, we, could get into a helluva pickle, Kit. It's a good thing I love Aaron like a brother."

She frowned. The second Scorpion had just about done her in and she was torn between resisting the advance and surrendering to it. A year ago, before she met Aaron, she would've been in the sack with Chris.

"I feel foolish. You're a very attractive man and I hope you and your fiancée are going to be our friends. I think I'd better get home now."

He stood up, took her hand solicitously. "You okay to drive? Cops are red-hot around Christmas, point eight and they book you. I'd be happy to drop you."

"What about your alcohol level?"

"I have connections; they don't arrest heroes." He hugged her. "Now, Kit, don't forget to give Aaron a big squeeze for me."

No question, Chris Arnold had turned her on. As Kit slowly undressed, the juices were flowing, her thighs taut with longing. She took a shower to cool down, fiddled with her nails, but the desire remained with her. When Aaron came through the guesthouse door, his exhausted pallor failed to extinguish her hunger. She thrust herself at him and seductively kissed his rough cheeks.

"You smell intoxicating," he said. "You're gorgeous."

"Thank you, Doctor. I've been waiting for you. If you touch me, I'll come."

"Give me a few minutes."

"Try five. Honey, I had a lovely day with your mother. She's so thoughtful. It took me completely off guard. I feel like she's adopted me. Then when I went back to the office for the Christmas party I met your old friend and we had a great dinner at Trader Vic's. *Qué hombre.*"

Aaron blinked with interest. "Which friend?"

"Chris, Chris Arnold."

The image of his troubled patient flashed through the channels of Aaron's mind.

"Who did you say?"

"Chris. Chris Arnold, of course. He dropped by the office just to meet me. Real lady-killer. Special Forces in Bosnia."

"Kit! Kit! I don't know him!" She backed away as though from a slap. "I treated him in emergency the other night. I think the guy may be a psychopath!"

She trembled. "Aaron, you're frightening me."

"I can't help it. The situation is alarming."

Eyes vast with panic, Kit pressed her head against the wall. Sheets of night air hissed through the window, enveloping them. She held on to Aaron, their fear palpable, inhabiting the room.

"For some reason he's decided to invade my life. And I don't know what to do about it!"

Aaron had concluded that Chris Arnold could be dangerous and that the situation for Kit and himself had become perilous. He was up most of the night preparing a memo on Chris Arnold. He marked it URGENT, and left it with Dr. Greenman's assistant the following morning. He caught up with Greenman leaving the platform in the lecture hall after he had completed a grand rounds colloquy which had been devoted to the Freud-Jung letters.

"I've got to meet my wife and kids. Walk me to my car."

Greenman lit a cigar that soured the air around him. They strode briskly across the campus, thinned out by Christmas holidays.

"You read the memo."

"Yes. The problem is, this Chris character hasn't done

anything illegal—anything the police can act on. Even if he threatened to murder you, there's nothing anyone can do. But the fact remains, he hasn't actually menaced you or made any threats. He is a pest and probably unstable."

"I'm not comforted by your conclusions, sir. I considered that there was a superficial element of transference when I saw him in emergency. We're about the same age. His father abandoned him, mine didn't. He wants to identify with me. I had no idea that this would develop into a full-blown transference reaction."

Greenman hesitated, wanting to reassure Aaron, who seemed about to give way to the pressure.

"Aaron, the point is that he hasn't hurt anyone. He had a chance to do real damage with Kit when they were out together. She was vulnerable. If the man is psychotic, who knows what could have happened?

"He talked himself out of murdering his father, he returned the Ativan. This is not irrational behavior. People fantasize about their psychiatrists, they want to be friends, they want a quick fix, they believe we can wave a wand and get rid of all the poisons they've accumulated.

"This Chris is a role player. First he's a secret agent in Bosnia, then he's some kind of detective. These roles have special meaning. He wants the power and authority to counteract yours. He's really reaching out for help. This man admires you." They had reached the faculty parking lot and the sparkle of the noon sun belied Christmas. "He wants to be you, which is why he went after Kit. He claims you as a friend, not an enemy. If you're afraid of him and he knows it, he'll beat you.

"I'm not trying to minimize the problem. But from your workup, what strikes me is that he'd like you to think he's *in control*. Psychologically, this is a reflection of the inadequacy he feels. Aaron, it makes me bristle to have my residents whipped by strays who wander in and try to take control. You're in the driver's seat, not this character."

At the root of Chris Arnold's behavior was a desire to demonstrate that he was more powerful than Aaron and could manipulate him. Why, Aaron pondered, had this man set up such an elaborate scheme to outwit him? What lay behind it? What was the design, the blueprint behind Chris Arnold's behavior? Aaron suspected it was not a haphazard choice that this stranger had made.

"He's trying to make an asshole out of me."

"Could you possibly come up with a more scientific diagnosis? Look, Aaron, I've had this sort of thing happen to me occasionally. All you can do is go on with your work and be careful. It'll go away."

Dr. Greenman opened the door of his new silver BMW. Before getting into the car, he ground out the cigar butt on his attaché case, wrapped it in cellophane, and shoved it into the case.

"How's your mother doing?"

"Fighting like a lioness."

Valerie had picked a loving way to part from her staff at home. Antonio and Maria had been with them since Aaron was an infant and they lived as family. Although they both knew that she was seriously ill, they never crossed the boundaries of propriety.

Antonio wore a dark blue suit and a striped tie. His black shoes were spit-polished and with his shock of cropped gray hair he looked as prosperous as a Mexican grandee. Valerie had given Maria one of her Armani dresses. The soft gray loose cut suited her.

"You both look very elegant."

"Señora Brett, are you sure you can manage alone?" Antonio asked.

"Of course I can. Look, you two don't get out much and this is one of your Christmas presents. So don't argue." She had used her connections to secure twelfth-row center-aisle orchestra seats for *Phantom*, and made a dinner reservation for them at Spago. "Just have a good time. And do it in style. Take my Mercedes."

From the camper across the street, Sean watched the car come down the hill from the house. He waited. Sometimes people forgot something and returned unexpectedly. He'd give them fifteen minutes.

Valerie gathered herself in a warm winter robe over her white silk pajamas. She sat down in her favorite armchair by the fire in the bedroom and pressed the CD remote. Rachmaninoff's mournfully romantic Symphony No. 2 filled the room. The music captured the fatality of her mood. Her fingers stroked the top of the wood table and grazed a bottle of 100mg Seconals. She had filled a prescription for sixty of them that afternoon. She reread the letters she would be leaving.

My dearest Terry,

Regrettably, I am not able to blunder through another year with you or make our date in Venice. While there is still something left of my body and spirit, my will, I've decided that this is the way it must end for me. I know you did your best to fulfill my unrealistic dreams and I'm grateful. I've had a good life with you and I thank you for giving me a remarkable, loving son. Please think about our last discussion. You can't reclaim the past, but you can rebuild your life.

My darling, if there's a Venice on the other side— and there must be one—I'll see you there for a Bellini at Harry's Bar. We'll listen to the music and walk arm in arm through Pia's garden . . .
Love from everywhere,
Val

My darling Aaron,

I think you knew this was inevitable. My condition has deteriorated considerably in the last few days. I am disoriented and confused so much of the time. I have revised my harsh opinion of Kit and wish you both the beautiful life I enjoyed with your father. I would like Kit to have my grandmother's engagement ring and jewelry. It is a memento of the

Bach family. It has brought me luck and a blessed marriage.

I am proud of the fact that you chose medicine as a career, but even more importantly that you are a loving, caring man. Our money has not shaped you. Weaker people might have been destroyed by this vast wealth. In the last resort, we Bretts have character.

Not many mothers can have been as fortunate as I've been. I have had a son who will walk with kings.

Love and luck,
Mother

The front door of the house was locked. Sean adroitly slipped a slender knife into the Baldwin and picked it. The house was dark and silent; a chill of anticipation coursed through him. He would see the other side of Terry's life. He shone a flashlight around. The dining-room table might have been Chippendale—Allison could have identified it, but he didn't need her to tell him that the paintings on the walls were original Impressionists.

The kitchen was a large, country-style affair with a breakfast nook overlooking the pool and rear garden where there was a tennis court. He walked through and found himself in an enormous living room. This opened onto a two-story, galleried library, crowned by a stained-glass skylight. For a few moments, he stood in awe, looking up. He might have been in a cathedral or a palace.

He crept into Terry's study. The walls abounded with photos of famous athletes Sean had seen play. On the large English desk were pictures of Valerie when she was younger and a photo-collage of Aaron, tracing his boyhood through school graduations. Sean sadly sat down in the green leather swivel chair and rested his head on the desk.

"And where's my picture?"

He eased himself up from the chair and looked through the mahogany bookcases. There was a Bang & Olufson stereo that had the appearance of sculpture. He opened some cabinets and found rows of albums with press cuttings.

Nothing, however, connected his father with his life in Seacliff. Terry had found a final solution to his past. Moving along, Sean discovered an old-fashioned Mosler safe with wobbly tumblers. He checked for an alarm connection and found none. He fiddled with the tumblers, then brought out a high-speed drill from his case of burglar tools.

Listening to the lyrical Adagio, Valerie gazed into the crackling fire. She poured herself a glass of water and reached for the bottle of Seconals. She opened the lid and filled her palm with capsules. They reminded her of jelly beans. She was distracted by an odd humming sound, which seemed to be coming from Terry's study downstairs. He couldn't be home yet. She had spoken to him an hour ago and he was ending a meeting.

In the library, Sean found an envelope spilling over with crinkly photos in the safe. He shone his light on a picture of his parents. His mother, a mere girl, had a skittish look, an air of diffidence. Terry had an enigmatic smile that struck Sean as assured. They were young and in love. On the back was a stamp from Timberline Lodge dated 1966.

Sean uncovered a treasure trove: a driver's license and Social Security card made out to Christopher Arnold; scraps of paper, a torn letter from someplace in India. There were other photos of the house in Seacliff and Allison's Bistro. He discovered one of his father and himself and tenderly fingered the curled border. Nothing his father had done made any sense to him.

"My God, Dad, you didn't forget me," Sean said with a sense of confused elation. "You must've loved me!" he bellowed.

Valerie had been disturbed by the whirring sound and clearly heard the strange man's voice. Short of breath, she wobbled from side to side, fighting the chaos of the pills, the fading in and out, the visual distortions. Heartbeat wildly irregular and losing her thoughts before they could be born as words, she plummeted down the stairs.

Sean heard the music from above and the heavy thud of a body reeling down and hitting the wooden floor. He dropped the flashlight, and, in a fluid motion, rolled behind a sofa. He spied a leg jerking spasmodically. A long, heaving sigh whispered through the room.

Silence.

A plant light on a timer suddenly sprang on, illuminating a tall ficus. Shaking, Sean whirled up, pointing the Commander .45.

He stared at the body.

This sad drunken woman sends out the servants so she can get loaded and stash her bottles. She hears me and rushes down the stairs. I pray for your immortal soul.

He pumped her chest, opened her mouth, pressed his lips against hers, and breathed air into her, until he was sweating. There were no signs of life. She was gray as melted wax, emaciated, her bones toothpicks. He gently closed her eyes. He rolled up the sleeve on her robe and saw a long chain of jaundiced skin, mottled track marks. In death, this frail worn-out figure, Allison's nemesis, evoked his pity and contrition.

Aaron's mother, Terry's other wife, was gone and they would mourn her.

Sean walked around the room, groaning. Ten minutes later, gloomily checking through the house, he found a half-filled bottle of Seconals in the bedroom and put some in his pocket. Valerie's medical bag was a cornucopia of drugs—syringes, morphine, Demerol, Xanax, Tuinals, and more reds. He thought she must have had cancer or some kindred disease of unendurable pain.

He read the mournful notes she had written and was profoundly grateful that he had not been the instrument of her death. Something larger, an inscrutable pattern, had brought them together at this moment.

72

Shortly after ten, Terry's Bentley climbed over the worn speed bumps, then slid into its home port. He stretched, picked up his briefcase, and got out. Valerie's Mercedes was out, which he took as a good sign. Perhaps there could be a medical miracle.

Sean quietly rose from the side terrace steps. On the cobbled path he nervously glided past bags of leaves rolling ghostlike in the wind.

Terry headed for the front door. Sean was there blocking his way. Terry smiled at the bearded young man and his demeanor had a quizzical sense of forgetting somebody's name. A ball player? Possibly a messenger, he decided, when he saw an envelope in his hand.

"I hope you haven't been waiting long."

Actually, I have been waiting—quite awhile . . . "You can't quite place me, can you?"

"Should I? Are you the one who's been asking questions about me." Terry was surprised but hospitable. No danger. "Want to come in for a drink? And you'll get it from the horse's mouth."

"I guess it's my beard." Sean did a little turn. "Do the blazer and rep tie look familiar?"

Terry moved closer to the lamplight. "Are you sure you've got the right address? I'm Terry Brett."

"Terry? I thought your name was Chris Arnold."

Stunned, Terry peered through the darkened windows, praying that no one was home.

"Do I know you?"

"*Dad,* we've got to talk about a lot of things. It's long overdue."

Terry trembled, dropped his briefcase, and listed; bewildered, he grabbed for something to support himself. He leaned against a brick column.

"Sean? Oh, my, my God! You're here."

"Are you a little dizzy?"

"Yes, I think so."

"After someone's committed a crime and been caught, it's a natural reaction. When the brain gets the news, it forwards it through the central nervous system. Everyone gets shaky."

Terry sucked in air. Allison, of course! She had finally told Sean and no doubt given herself the best of it.

"You seem very knowledgeable about behavior."

"Not as knowledgeable as Aaron. Are you sure you still want me to come in for that drink?" He allowed Terry a moment. "No? Well, I didn't think so. I suggest we head to my van and take a ride. Talk about things."

The ground still moving under him, deep cavernous rumbles along the fault line, Terry docilely followed, waited as the van door slid open, climbed in. Sean started the engine and pressed the automatic lock, but Terry didn't notice.

"I've been thinking about you," Terry said. "I often do, but lately . . . oh well."

"Really? Well, you know how gullible I am. I believe everything you tell me."

"There were reasons. Good ones. You've made a terrible mistake. I'm not your real father."

Sean began to laugh. "Come on, give me a break, Ace." Sean shook his head with amused disbelief. "Cut it out. How're you doing? Where've you been? Were you MIA? East Germans capture you or did the Russians send you to a gulag in Siberia?" Sean gave another harsh laugh. "On my birthday I even raised my glass to toast you. My American hero. The absurdity of it. I'm still choking on it."

"How many years has it been since I've seen you, Sean?"

"You tell me."

The vitality he remembered was gone from Terry's face. Jaw limp, eyes bloodshot, his head wearily flopped back on the cold seat. Sean sensed his thoughts. Rough day, wife dying. Now him! A nightmare.

"There's an ice cooler behind you, Dad. Grab yourself a beer or a real drink."

"Thanks, you're very considerate."

"Well, Jesus, you do look beat."

"I am. Where're we going?"

"Oh, just for a cruise. So we can shoot the breeze."

It was a clear run to Newhall where Sean picked up the Interstate, which would take them back to Port Rivers.

"I can't stay too long," Terry said as they seemed to be driving aimlessly.

"Nothing's more important than right now. It may cost America its freedom or the Chinese might drop a hydrogen bomb. But America will survive for a little while without you. Right?"

Terry felt the nails digging in and knew he deserved it. He'd check on Valerie after they had a drink. Sean had always been a sweet, malleable boy. He'd be reasonable.

"I will have a drink."

"Let's do it."

At the Valencia signpost, Sean spotted a golf course off the road and pulled into a quiet residential street fronting it. The TVs were on to the eleven o'clock news and the Christmas tree lights were being switched off.

"I'm your Christmas present. How do you like that?"

"Best one I could have been given."

Terry now clearly beheld the young man's features. He was a replication of Allison. He laid his head on Sean's chest and Sean felt the tears on his cheeks.

"Don't! Stop it, will you. Come on, let's have a drink. I've got a bottle of Stoli. But this calls for champagne." Sean wrapped the bottle with a towel, expertly lifted the cork. "How's a 'sixty-one Dom sound? It was left over from my birthday."

"You're really something."

"I do a great steak tartare."

"You're a cook, too?"

"Only occasionally—for hangovers."

"Lalique glasses?"

"Why not? I don't get to visit my father that often."

"If only I was. Sean, Sean, I'm so sorry. You can't imagine."

There was no reason to trust Terry or believe him. Trapped within Sean was the strangled primal scream, clotting his throat with its venom.

The hunter and his unwary prey were joined together. The situation appealed to Sean. Terry had no idea that the dynamics of their roles had been reversed and neither his wealth nor his influence would count with his son. Lulled into a false sense of security, Terry was ready to return to his house when they finished the champagne.

"I really do want to see you and try to get to know you again. And explain what happened. Now I've got to get back."

"Dad, you've put me on hold all my life. The time you've recklessly squandered."

"It's been no joyride for me."

"Spare me. It's over." The policeman's manner was sure, authoritative. "Let's establish the ground rules here. I'm not some fucking hired help you can walk over. If you're not cooperative, it's going to be a very unpleasant trip for you. You're not in charge any more."

The van roared off, and Terry noticed that the door handle had been removed on his side.

"Where are we going?"

"Home."

"This doesn't make any sense."

"You have no choice."

As they sped through the night, the distance between them increased. They had become prisoner and guard. Sean tuned the radio to the police frequency to listen to calls, then switched to the CB and picked up the shuck and jive of truckers talking about hookers, dope, radar traps.

"Why're you doing this?" Terry asked, fully roused, after what seemed an eternity of silence.

"I want to understand what happened."

"Did you see my picture in the paper when I bought the Stars?"

"Yes. But I hardly recognized you. You could have gone on playing hide-and-seek forever. As it happens, I spotted you at the Stars-Bulls game a few weeks ago. Remember, when a man was running after your car? That was me."

"You? Were you running from the cops? Do you need help—a lawyer? Have you broken out of jail? Look, I can try to fix things with the police."

"Man, you are something. You need the lawyer, not me." Sean flipped open his wallet and his gold shield glinted. "*I* am the fucking police. You're a felon. And you're under arrest for bigamy, fraud, and impersonating a CIA officer. I've got all your phony IDs as well. I'll give you your rights if you like. I have the California and Oregon codes. If you're not familiar with them, you can read them. I'm sure you'll have a very convincing explanation for Paul Cisco when he files charges against you with the grand jury."

"Are you extraditing me?" Terry asked with incredulity.

"In a manner of speaking."

"Legally speaking, you haven't got a leg to stand on. Is there a felony warrant which the attorney general of Oregon has filed with the state of California?"

"Any way you cut it, Mr. Brett, you broke the law, and the two states can decide which one of us did the right thing."

"You're quite an investigator. Sean, come on! What do you hope to accomplish by doing this?" Terry had a horror of this ill-fated voyage back to the past. "Is your mother still alive?"

"Very much so."

"I wonder what she told you about me."

"She has no idea I know or that I'm bringing you back."

"Allison may not thank you."

The first mention of her name sounded strange coming from Terry. Sean strained to hear them talk from this great distance of years. Their voices had always been muted, evasive. And yet his father had kept the picture of them from Timberline.

"We'll have plenty of time to hear all about it," Sean said, with sinister composure. "To get things in sync."

"You're not going to like it, Sean."

"Oh, Daddy, sit me on your lap and tell me a story."

Peeling off the miles down the tortuous Grapevine, through the San Joaquin Valley in the foul dun of night fog and into daybreak, Sean gave vent to the emotions of the lost boy deprived of his rightful ascension.

"Do you know that after you 'died,' everything was always out of whack, nothing was ever right for me? You were my idol. Do you know what we've lost, what can never be regained?"

Our innocence, Terry reflected, battered by the young stranger's grievances. *But how could it have been different?*

"Can you stop at a service station? I've got to use the toilet," Terry asked.

"There's a head in the back."

Sean nosed into a truck stop in Visalia. He eased Terry over the seat into the back, took out his handcuffs, and hooked him onto a metal rail. He tore off a piece of duct tape and was about to slap it across Terry's mouth.

"Is this necessary?"

"I have no reason to take your word for anything. I've got to gas up and—"

"I'd like to call Valerie."

"She'll have to wait—the way I did."

"She'll be worried. Please. She's very ill."

"I'm sorry to hear that."

"Be reasonable. She's dying of cancer." Sean scowled at him. "For Chrissake, the police are bound to be looking for me already. I wouldn't just disappear."

"Wouldn't you?"

Stubble-bearded, washing with his right hand, the left handcuffed to the rail, Terry pressed his head against the tinted window. Sean paid for the gas. From a distance the resemblance between them was imprecise. He favored Allison, and yet Terry thought he recognized some part of himself. Sean had the iron pumper's solid broadness, a heavier beard, but the earnest expression in his blue eyes and crisp gestures belonged to Terry and seemed an apparition of what he had once been. Terry considered an escape, but he was discouraged by the prospect of battling with the armed, enraged Sean.

I must let him play his hand or God knows what he'll do . . .

He realized how well Sean had planned everything. The small head in the rear of the van was supplied with Neutrogena shampoo and Colgate toothpaste, both his brands. What most upset Terry, though, was the presence of what he had left behind years back: an old double-edged Wilkinson razor, the Yardley shaving soap mug, his Kent hairbrush, the *Pour Un Homme* aftershave cologne.

Reeking of gasoline, Sean poked his head into the camper.

"Want a bacon and egg sandwich—coffee?"

"Sure. Can I go with you?"

Sean hit the lock and slammed the door. When he returned and undid the handcuffs, Terry rubbed his wrist and wanted to deck him. He pushed up against Sean.

"Whatever you've got in mind, I don't think we're going to live through it."

"Me neither, *Dad*."

73

At dusk they reached the outskirts of Stockton's dry frozen fields. Sean decided to inspect the place as a campsite. He and Terry had been arguing ferociously. Sean cuffed him again.

"Sons remember the promises of fathers."

"Am I going to ride handcuffed? There is the dignity of prisoners and the common decency offered them. I'd like to stretch my legs."

Sean unlocked the cuffs, went around to his door, and helped him out. He unholstered the .45. Terry stared at the automatic.

"Seen it before? Well, Terry, I guess you were too busy running to take it along. It's still registered under your real name."

"Don't you think I know that? I left it behind. Your mother and I fought for it."

"I don't know whether to believe you or not."

"Try being a detective. Now let me call Valerie."

Sean thought of Allison waiting years for a call that never came and the wretched blankness in her eyes when he mentioned his father. Now he understood her reluctance to discuss him. At the edge of the fields, Sean noticed a flickering Cantina neon sign.

"We'll make a deal. Call Martha, your secretary. Short and sweet. Tell her you're fine and had to leave town unexpectedly. You've had plenty of practice doing that."

The pay phone was beside the bar. Sean got some change and two Corona beers. He was sure Terry would get cute. He'd memorized Terry's phone numbers and stood by as he dialed his home number.

Just what he asked him not to do and what he'd expected. Aaron's voice. He gave Terry a hard look and forced him to share the receiver.

"She's dead." Aaron said. "Dad, where are you?"

Sean slammed his palm over the mouthpiece. "Just listen!"

"Dad, you there? I said, Mom's dead. She took an overdose of pills."

Terry flinched. "I heard you, Aaron." He grunted. "Was it suicide or accidental?"

"Suicide." Aaron's voice quavered.

"Oh, Jesus." Terry shook his head in anguish. "Maybe she's finally at peace. Not in pain."

"Yes, Dad, I feel that way. There are complications. Some detectives want to talk to you."

"Why?"

"The safe in your study was drilled open. Someone broke in and we don't know what's missing."

His eyes accused Sean. "I see."

"She left notes for both of us."

"Was it definitely suicide?"

Sean heard and nodded.

"Yes. Dad, you haven't told me where you are." Aaron's voice grew higher. "I'm very concerned about you."

The receiver was yanked from Terry's hand.

"Hi, Ace, I'm deeply sorry about your mother. I'm sure she was a good woman. You have my sympathy and condolences. I know what it's like to lose a loved one."

"What? Who is this?"

"It's me. Your favorite patient."

Aaron was dumbfounded. "You!"

Terry flopped down at a table. The lurking owner brought over a bottle of home-brewed tequila.

"Yeah. I've got the original Ace with me. We're catching up on old times."

"Now, listen, Chris, I don't know what this is about. We've had a tragedy in the family. Don't do anything you'll regret. Let me help you."

"I appreciate that, Bro. Now you listen to me. Remember the problem I came to you with? Well, if you call the police and tell them about this, Dad's going to be very hard to find. It's up to you. Professor Greenman can't help you over this crunch. Just be cool. I'll stay in touch."

Aaron was shaken by these convulsive events. Kit came beside him. Fearfully, she waited for him to regain his self-possession.

"What is it?"

"That guy's kidnapped my father."

She was rocked. "The man pretending he was your friend?"

"Yes, I just spoke to him."

She wavered and pressed a hand against the desk to support herself.

"It's a nightmare, Aaron. How can this be happening? Let's call the police."

"I can't let them know. The reason this Chris came to emergency was because he wanted to murder his father. Now he's threatened to kill Dad. He's armed, bragging, laughing at us. He's had us under surveillance. He even knows Dr. Greenman is my supervisor."

Kit struggled to comprehend the dementia of the man. "Why, why would he kidnap Terry? I can't make sense out of it. Aaron, how can you have an enemy who's a total stranger?"

Aaron forced himself to pull together all his experience—the books he'd read, courses he'd taken, the years of study—in an effort to construct some plausible profile.

"I've never come across anything like it. This guy is acting out some imaginary sibling rivalry with me. Maybe he had a brother he doesn't see, or who's dead. Something set off the fantasies he's stored up. I don't know how he found a point of identity with me. The problem is, when you're deranged, you make the rules. It's your universe."

Sitting at a small corner table against the wall, Terry drifted into another world. He and Sean had done most of the bottle of tequila when the cheerful owner swaggered over carrying plates of salsa and hot corn tortillas.

"*Hombres,* tonight there is *chile rellenos* and *carne asada.*"

"Sounds good," Sean said. "We'll order in a few minutes—"

I have him all to myself. I don't have to share him with anyone.

Sean raised his shooter glass. "Never thought the day would come when my dad and I would get smashed and have dinner together." He touched Terry's hand. "It's strange and breathtaking. Like meeting God."

Terry roused himself from his desolate, black reverie and looked at Sean. Sean smiled at him with adoration;

despite the situation, Terry felt a wave of compassion for the misguided young man.

"Your patronizing manner toward Valerie is deeply offensive to me. You don't know how good she was!"

Sean's manner altered, assuming the sweetness of a subdued child who has managed to get his own way.

"I apologize."

"I will tell you everything, Sean, about your mother and me. Now, you're not going to threaten me or force me to do things against my will."

Sean filled their tumblers with tequila. "Okay, let's do it in an honorable way."

During his recitation of how he met Allison, Terry experienced a split within, seeing himself also in the image of Chris. As he described the two men to Sean, the schism was so real that he actually thought he might possess a double. He tried to hold on to Terry, the attorney, and found him being strangled by Chris, the dead seaman, who had become his phantom.

Sean was riveted when his father finally reached the point of Allison's departure. He examined the contents of the envelope he had lifted from the safe and found the torn bits of his mother's letter sent from India, which he pieced together like a jigsaw puzzle and read.

Sean was unsettled. "Allison left you?"

"Yes. She was right to go. Everyone in town—my father, Barney Laver, Paul Cisco, and even Georgie—turned against her."

"Now you want me to believe that my mother conned you into taking Earl's case against Jonah?"

"That's exactly what happened."

Sean was baffled. "Our history would have been different. You never would have met Jonah Wolfe and been beaten up. You would have married Allison, no matter how Pat felt about her."

"That was my dream. But I took on a dirty case. I had a sense of it from the beginning. It was like cleaning out a drain. You put your hand down and then you're sucked into it. But I loved your mother so much, I would've done anything for her."

"You couldn't turn her down."

"I had things to prove to her." Wearily, Terry picked up the bottle and poured a drink. "Or maybe it was meant to be this way. I don't know any longer. I've thought about it for years and tried to work it out. There's no solution. We're in the area of human character, the mystery, the chaos of it."

Sean examined the yellow, dog-eared photographs in the envelope of himself, his mother, Chris, his dad. One picture puzzled him.

"Who're these two guys in bellhop uniforms?"

Terry grimaced. "Earl Raymond and a friend of his. A present from Jonah. I'll get to them."

"What made you come back to Port Rivers and Allison?"

"You, Sean, both of you," Terry said helplessly. "You have no idea how painful this is and how torn I've always been."

Guiding Sean, they traveled in a free fall through the galaxies of memory to the place they had once called home.

The events of his birth in India, followed by Terry's bigamous marriage to Allison when she returned to Port Rivers, stunned Sean. Everything about his life was fraudulent, even to his birth certificate and delivery at Good Samaritan Hospital. Like disease, nothing could deter the power of the first lie. It grew, multiplied, spawning deadly colonies of new fabrications. He had maligned Valerie, the woman who had saved his life. His actions horrified him. But through the chain of remorse that shaped his thinking, a new force emerged, which defined his role in the tragedy of the Bretts and the Arnolds. He was free to exercise his choice, and he faced his newly won freedom with awe. Unless he willed it, acted, nothing was inevitable now that he was free to learn the missing key to the story.

Sean scaled the tenebrous reef, sorting through its artifacts, and the shattered family's misfortunes. Why had his father left Allison?

Terry had dozed off. Uncoiling his legs from the springs of the van sofa, he looked around, disoriented by his surroundings. His body stuttered to life. He peered out the window and discovered that they were in a trailer camp. He had to go home and bury his beloved Valerie.

Sean was stretched out on a bed, staring at him. He had driven the back roads as far as Gold Beach on the Oregon coast and was within striking distance of Port Rivers.

"When you were asleep, I moved into this RV park and hooked us up," Sean said. "There's hot water and the pressure's fair. Some of your old clothes are in the van closet. Get cleaned up and I'll take you back home."

While Terry showered, Sean fixed coffee and unwrapped some churros he had bought at a lunch wagon on the camp grounds. It was comforting to have Terry close to him, sharing confidences. Terry fascinated him. He still struck Sean as a magician.

"What happened to you when you got back to Los Angeles with Valerie?"

Off dangerous ground, Terry grew expansive as he soaped himself in the narrow shower stall.

"My brief career at O'Callahan & Klein was intolerable and I took a hike. But the real reason for quitting was that I found a way out. I could travel without suspicion and spend time with you and your mother."

The conversation took Terry's mind off Valerie and funeral arrangements. He slapped on some aftershave, slipped into a pair of his old JC Penney khakis and a denim shirt. He embraced the young man with mournful sadness.

"Sean, I'm so terribly sorry about all of this."

"I want you to know, I do still love you." Gnawing at Sean was the reason for Terry's desertion. "Tell me, why did you die? What made you take it that far?"

Terry had been waiting for this.

"I can't and I won't discuss it. There's no law that says what goes on between a man and woman has to be revealed to anyone. It's between your mother and me."

"I thought as much."

"Now be a good guy and take me to the nearest airport."

Sean had anticipated this demand. As Terry combed his wet hair, Sean opened two Seconal capsules and stirred them into the coffee before he handed the mug to Terry.

"Yeah, I'll get you back. Why'd you and Pat fall out?"

Terry glared at him reprovingly and dug in. He drank his coffee and Sean poured him another cup.

"That's it. Look, I've told you everything I'm about to."

"I'm sorry. But I'm not little Sean now, I am a detective."

Terry stretched languidly. He felt odd, something beyond a hangover. His mind drifted off course, lost its perimeters. The Seconals wove into his system.

"I'm getting sleepy, got to get to the airport. Val's alone . . ."

"Ace, everything's out of kilter. I have to get to the bottom of this. No matter how much it hurts."

Terry couldn't keep his eyes open any longer. "Home . . . take me home . . ."

Sean helped him back onto the bunk. The old familiar scent of Terry's aftershave brought him home as well.

"We'll be there before dark."

Aaron was crippled by indecision. His father had been missing for almost a day. He was afraid to leave the house in case Chris Arnold called. Aaron was now absolutely convinced that he was dealing with a sociopath. Kit and he were up all night, prisoners in a nightmare. He was drinking scotch and she was the voice of reason, calmly bolstering him.

"Aaron, I don't believe Chris is a killer. He's very strange. It was like he knew all of us. And he's getting his rocks off. I don't know why. But it's a game to him. He talks about murdering his father, then it's let's pretend, 'Who am I today?' "

The phone rang day and night with demands for Terry from the office. Valerie's colleagues and students at the medical school were asking about the funeral arrangements for his mother. Her body lay at Forest Lawn and her mourners floated in limbo.

Detectives arrived with suspicions and brought along forensic technicians. It was night when they began to question Aaron about relations between his parents. They were imputing a motive to his father's disappearance. Where was he?

"Did your father have a girlfriend?"

"You've got a nerve asking me that," Aaron shouted.

"Maybe your father *assisted* her in the suicide?"

"Shit, the notes are in my mother's handwriting."

They wouldn't let him or Kit rest.

"There was a robbery here."

"But nothing's missing!"

It added another mystery to what they were already calling "the case." In Terry's safe, two hundred thousand dollars in cash and four million in bearer bonds was stashed. His mother's bedroom jewelry safe had not been touched. This again stymied the detectives. They gossiped among themselves. They were all astounded by the Bretts' wealth as well as the thoughtfulness of the thief. A broad-beamed lieutenant got involved.

"I understand the burglar left a fortune behind. None of this makes sense."

"My father was away on business. He always travels. And he got stomach poisoning on his way home."

"Where was he?"

"I think Chicago," Kit said.

"Dr. Brett, does he know your mother's dead?"

"I told him. I think he collapsed."

"Do you have a number for him?"

"No. Maybe he's in some airport motel."

When they were alone, Kit nervously wandered around the room. She straightened Aaron's books, ordered a pizza, switched on the TV and tried to alleviate the tension. She would do anything to cheer up Aaron. She picked up an Oakland Raiders helmet she found on a bookshelf and read the legend:

SUPER BOWL XI, RAIDERS 32, VIKINGS 14
ROSE BOWL, PASADENA, CALIFORNIA

Wearing the helmet, she sought to divert him. "I didn't know you were a Raiders fan."

He was angry and irrational about his father and the absences that always came with an excuse.

"I never was. The helmet was a gift from my father one Christmas. His idea of a joke." Aaron lay in the hollow of her shoulder and she cradled him in her arms. "Kit, something terrible is happening."

74

Terry groped around in a warm dark room. He heard the sound of ice crunching and striking the doors below, where a sailboat nested for the winter. The echo of a ferry whistle in the distance and the honk of a tug sailing through cold gluey air told him he was back in Port Rivers.

"What am I doing here?"

"I wanted you to see my place, Dad. Allison lives in the big house."

The light was switched on. Dressed in a English tweed jacket, Sean had transformed himself into a young country squire. He had champagne in a bucket, the flowered Perrier-Jouet.

Terry was still groggy from the pills. "This is . . . the old River Cove boathouse on the Van Wyck estate."

"You're right. I wanted to have a drink with you in *my* home. Pat rebuilt it and made an apartment for me."

"Sean, what're *you* doing in this house?"

"My mother owns it. She bought it with help from my grandfather, Pat. The house was part of an estate sale.

Some woman called Joanne had died and she'd inherited it." Everyone had a name now, an identity. Dad, Grandfather, the communion of family relations made Sean happy. "Mom sold the bistro in Seacliff and we lived in an apartment on University Heights the first year. Then while she was looking for a restaurant location, she heard about Aristedes's joint in Old Town. She caught them just before they were about to torch it for the insurance. Grandpa gave them twenty-five big ones and rebuilt it for her. That's a little of our history."

Sean handed a glass of champagne to Terry.

"If I drink this, where do I wake up next? At a slave auction? India?" Sean sipped both of them and allowed Terry to select either glass.

Sean was still nettled. "I need to get to the bottom of this. There's a piece missing."

"Can't you just leave it alone, Sean?"

"No, it's consuming me—You know you're going to have to come clean," he insisted.

Lumbering to the bed, Terry felt cornered, without resources. How could he make amends to this troubled boy? Terry realized that he could not rewrite history. Sean poured more champagne and paced the room.

"Your double life goes on for years. Everyone's in the dark, but everyone's content. Quite a feat. Then some time after my thirteenth birthday, you arrange your death. Why?"

"You'll hate what you hear."

"Double agents are betrayed all the time. But you weren't. Why, why?"

"Your mother and Pat knew I was alive."

As he related the events of how Valerie discovered his life in Seacliff, Terry's remorse was intensified by Sean's attentive silence.

"In all the confusion, I didn't know what I was doing that Christmas. I hadn't been with you and your mother except for a weekend that summer. And Pat and I hadn't seen each other for three years. So I made up a story about some important basketball tournament that I had to attend to sign a player. That was for Valerie's benefit. I completely forgot that she'd made plans for us to meet my partners and Aaron in Aspen. I twisted his arm to go to ski school so that he would have something to do over the holidays.

"When I got up to Seacliff, I realized that you were the one supposed to get ski lessons. I was so happy to see you and your mother that it all went out of my head. Even to the fact that I got your Christmas present mixed up with Aaron's. Through someone at the NFL office, I managed to land you a Raiders Super Bowl helmet, and Valerie had ordered a microscope for Aaron."

"The microscope and the chemistry set! Jesus, Dad. And a stethoscope."

"When you were asleep that night, Valerie arrived. I guess a blind man could have followed my trail."

The roles of Allison's unforgiving husband and Sean's father entwined Terry so tightly that the past seemed to rise up like some primeval beast, tearing him apart even now. He looked at Sean's distraught eyes. He could change nothing. The paths he had chosen were all crooked, leading nowhere.

"Valerie threatened to expose me, and that would have meant a jail term, which would have affected all of you. I didn't care. I was prepared to take my medicine and not leave. Your mother wouldn't have it. She was afraid for you, all of us. We had a violent argument. Then she said the reason she got involved with me in the first place was so that I'd take Earl Raymond's case. She'd been his girlfriend. They'd cooked up a scheme to use me. She clawed me apart and it broke my spirit to think she'd been so cynical and dishonest.

"I went for the gun you've got. My old Commander .45. I was going to kill us, her and then myself. We fought for the gun and she won." Terry's emotions clashed, but he faced his young judge without flinching.

"I was forced to sacrifice you and it was an unspeakable settlement which your mother can never make up to you."

"My mother?" Sean asked in horror.

"Yes, Sean. You're Earl's son, not *mine*. That's why

I left. And rather than tell you the truth, I sent a telegram and wrote a letter on CIA stationery which was made for me by a forger in Port Rivers. He was a specialist, a legendmaker who once worked for the CIA."

Released from the bondage of memories and finally able to give a genuine account of what had occurred to the person who had suffered the greatest harm assuaged Terry's own wound. In a perverse way, Terry found himself grateful to Sean for having kidnapped him. Whether he'd been right to marry Allison or wrong to abandon her was no longer at issue. The conflicts that had raged within Terry surrendered at last to a fragmentary peace of mind.

"And what happened with Pat and you?"

"I went to see him immediately after Allison told me who your real father was. Pat broke down when he had to choose between you and Allison, and me. There was no other way. Valerie knew he'd lied to protect me and never spoke to him again or allowed him to see Aaron."

Sean was overwhelmed by the hunger for redemption that emanated from Terry. "I don't know how any of us survived this. . . . Valerie had to swallow this humiliation and Aaron never knew."

"No, Aaron was given a pardon. We all buried it."

"I see. I do forgive you," Sean said. "It's like a dream having you home. But my pain won't go away."

"I realize that." The mood of reconciliation and the retrieval of his honor gave way to despondency. "Now you've got to let me go back and bury Valerie."

Sean also nurtured guilt about this woman who had been wronged and had made many generous sacrifices.

"I feel awful about Valerie," he said remorsefully.

"I understand why you reacted as you did."

Sean held the faded old Polaroid snapshot of Earl and Warren in bellhop uniforms which Jonah had taken of them, celebrating their triumph. The image intruded on Sean's consciousness, darkening it with a more ominous coupling. Earl and Allison. Sean, too, wondered if he heard Earl laughing at them.

"You never suspected Earl of engineering this?"

"No. Let's leave it, please, Sean."

He sensed Terry's rage. "I can't. Why didn't Earl tell you about him and Mom when he got sore at you about splitting Wolfe's money?"

"I've often wondered. He's not confrontational. He was afraid of what I might do. Cowards only bark alone."

Terry reached for the ancient Harris tweed sports jacket his son had kept. He noticed that his old penny loafers were shined and the blue button-down shirt was pressed along with his fraternity rep tie.

"You must have had your doubts about Earl when you were roomies in college."

"I was lame and he could fly. Looks and athletic ability cover up a lot when you're as impressionable as I was. I think I might have taken his case without your mother's cooperation. He had Georgie on his side as well, and I was real fond of her."

"Georgie. I saw her last week. She's a wreck."

"Is Earl still around?" Terry asked.

"Yes. And Georgie's terrified of him, but she goes back to him for more abuse." Fitting in the last piece of the puzzle, Sean shook his head with renewed purpose. "Earl Raymond sure did a number on this family. Some people really do get away with murder. Let me ask you, what would you like to do about him? If you had the chance."

Terry was guarded. Sean's question was dangerous and he didn't trust his reaction. He was becoming too volatile.

"Let it go, Sean."

But Sean couldn't. Perhaps Terry could tolerate it, but Sean found the malevolence of it unbearable. Earl was the devil.

"I have to check in downtown at the station. Call Aaron and make your arrangements for flying to L.A. I'd really appreciate having dinner with you before you go. It's been so long since we've had a real evening together—in public. I'll meet you at a restaurant. The Greenhouse, it's in Old Town."

"Okay, sure, whatever you say."

"Grandpa Pat's with us in the house. You could see him."

"I'd like that. Is your mother home?" Terry asked nervously.

"I'm not sure if she's even in town. She's been flying back and forth to New York. Some company wants to buy her out. I haven't been paying much attention to what's been going on."

"Does she know you found me?"

"No. Look, if you don't want to see her, I can understand. Oh, Jesus. Why don't I leave it up to you?"

Sean helped him on with the new cashmere overcoat Allison had bought him in New York. "It may be a little big for you, but it's warm."

Sean shook his head with disbelief and considered the circumstances. Gone was the anger and resentment he had harbored against Terry. His childhood recollections, the reverence for this man, had not been in vain.

"It's a miracle having you here for Christmas."

"Having had you for a son—even for that short time— was a privilege."

"You're really a good man, Ace."

"As long as you think so, because that's all that counts," Terry said.

The fresh air revived Terry, the clean bite of snow flurries, the wind harping through the familiar bay inlet where he had sailed so many times in his youth a lifetime ago. They crossed into the old mansion and Terry walked cautiously through the oak-paneled halls, pausing at the entry of the ballroom. Joanne Van Wyck had kissed him under the mistletoe on her Sweet Sixteen party and told him that she loved him. He had spent many days and nights with her and her brothers.

Sean led him to a room where the door was open. A nurse sat with a box of chocolate chip cookies, reading a copy of *People* magazine, and she nodded to them.

Staring blankly at a basketball game shimmering on TV, Pat was propped up in a hospital bed. Lost in the frozen realm of illness, the wizened figure of Terry's father seemed childlike and innocent.

"My mother brought him here while I was away. He'd rather die here than the hospital. He drifts in and out."

Terry approached the bed and sat beside Pat. He picked up the bony hand and kissed it.

"Dad, it's *me* . . . Terry."

Pat's eyes, wandering through thick bifocals, were determined to focus. His lips wrenched at sounds. Spidery fingers grasped Terry's wrist.

"Terrrrr . . ."

Terry sat on the bed, leaned close to him. "Yes, Dad?"

"See-ee Allisooooooon . . ."

Pat had fallen into a tranquil sleep and Terry left his bedside. He walked through the living room, poignantly aware of Allison's warm touches—the velvet sofas facing each other in front of the fireplace, the antique tables, the bowl of potpourri, her china collection begun in Seacliff. Under a mast of gleaming copper pans in the kitchen, fragrant with herbs and fruit, he picked up the phone and called his house.

Aaron's voice rasped, fearfully, "Oh, Jesus, Dad, you're alive! I've been worried sick about you."

"I'm really fine now," Terry said reassuringly.

"Has that maniac let you go?"

"He's not a maniac, Aaron. He had his reasons and I'll tell you about them when I get home."

"Is this nightmare over?"

"Yes, it is."

"Where are you?"

"Port Rivers."

"What are you doing *there*?"

"My father had a stroke and I had to see him before it was too late. The most important thing is us putting your mother to rest. We have a family plot at Forest Lawn." There was a pause and he heard Aaron explaining to Kit. "Call the mortuary and have Martha contact our friends and your mother's colleagues. I'll catch a flight back late tonight or tomorrow morning."

Leaning against the counter, Terry felt uneasy, an invader in the secret kingdom of the woman he had loved. In a sense, nothing had changed; he was still trying to occupy two places at the same time.

75

Propelled by turbulent, uncontrollable rage, Sean turned north on the fork outside Port Rivers and drove to the Paradise Inn. He had become fixated by the fact that Earl Raymond could go on living outside the law, free to destroy people with impunity. He'd break the stranglehold Earl had on all of them.

Haunted by the scars on Terry's face, Sean found himself glancing at the old photo of Earl rejoicing after having savagely beaten him. The smirk on Earl's face made him wince. Earl had changed the history of the Bretts, for Terry would have married Allison, and Sean would have had the family he had been entitled to.

Sean knew that there was nothing more honorable than bringing a family together or more rewarding than obliterating what had pulled it apart.

You murdered my childhood . . .

For several years, in partnership with some bikers he had met while in prison at Walla-Walla, Earl Raymond had been manufacturing Ecstasy. Simple and cheap to produce, its properties as a feeling enhancer made it something of an aphrodisiac and a hallucinogen. Earl's cost was about a dime a dose. On the street, it went for ten dollars a hit. The profits in the tax-free kingdom were colossal, enabling him to live in a mansion on the beach and to travel the world.

This evening the kingdom was in danger and Earl himself was ready to abdicate. He slewed his cream Rolls-Royce into the Paradise Inn and nervously looked at the seductive raven-haired woman beside him.

"I still can't believe it? What do we do next, Karen?"

His long mustache, sallow skin, eyes laden with livid booze bags gave him the aspect of a nomad battered by desert winds.

"Settle down, it'll all be fine. I'll fix everything."

When Earl had hooked up with Karen Summers, the lost sister of Mike Summers, in Las Vegas years back, she was working conventions as a hostess. He and Karen did a number of those conversational takes of what a small world this was. They had originally met through Mike when Earl and Jonah Wolfe had come up to scout players in Wisconsin. She had been the young girl Jonah had seduced and photographed.

Earl was quick to realize that the vagaries of life had played a crucial part in bringing them together. If not for Karen, he would not have had his stake. Ever superstitious, Earl regarded this temptress as a charm, a lucky coin, which the gods had dropped in his palm. In spite of the problems this caused with Georgie, he was reluctant to part with Karen. And then he didn't dare.

"Earl, stop dreaming. You've got to function."

Earl lifted his left leg out of the car. Lame and arthritic, the ridges of the metal brace clawed at his knee like a bear trap. He reached into the backseat and yanked out his malacca cane. He had closed down for his annual Christmas vacation and he and Karen had planned to fly to his condo in Scottsdale for the holidays.

Everything had changed when he brought Georgie back to the house. This time he was prepared to discuss a divorce and offer her a reasonable settlement. Finally in a position to dictate terms and free to testify against him and Karen, Georgie was squeezing them, using all of her skills as a divorce lawyer. With a drug lab on the grounds, they took her threats seriously.

"Earl, now take it slow. Pretend nothing is wrong," Karen barked.

He hobbled into the warmth of his deteriorated palace.

"Hey, Earl . . . Karen . . . didn't expect you folks. Get you all a drink?" Bruce, the caretaker, asked.

"We'll help ourselves." Earl leaned on the butt-burned

bar. "Going to check out the liquor inventory. You got some time off coming to you. Be back the week of the first."

"You sure?" Bruce was one of those lethargic, well-meaning men who performed simple tasks with the care of a watchmaker repairing a Rolex. "Is Georgie going to need me?"

"No, she went down to Florida," Karen said.

"You haul ass, I'll lock up."

"Okay, Earl, thanks."

They waited until the caretaker's battered red pickup was grumbling down the dirt road. Karen looked through the kitchen and the backyard while Earl filled a bucket glass with Yukon Jack and banged it back.

"Give it a rest," she said, looking lynx-eyed at him.

Tremors wove through his hands. "Needed a jumpstart, angel."

"I'll say. Now back the car up to the furnace house."

He was still vague about the details of Georgie's death in their beach house. He had awakened that afternoon from a drugged sleep with Karen and found Georgie's body in the kitchen. Karen insisted that they dispose of it. Earl had been terrified about driving with Georgie's body in his trunk.

"How did this happen, Karen? Did you murder Georgie?"

"Your mind really is in reverse, Earl. You went and picked Georgie up in Port Rivers the night we dropped off the Ecstasy. You brought her back here and let her stay with Bruce. Then she had him drive her to the beach house and she started carrying on. She threatened you, and said she was going to tell the cops we were dealing drugs."

Earl stared hollowly, trying to recall.

"Earl, we'd been smoking crack and you went crazy. You dragged her into the kitchen. She picked up the steam iron and you whacked her. You handcuffed her. Then you went at her with a meat cleaver."

Earl was too frightened to argue. The dim, drugged, repressed memories returned. Georgie was pleading. He had only helped Karen to cuff her. Karen had slapped duct tape across Georgie's mouth and it was Karen who had picked up the cleaver and hacked at Georgie.

"Karen, I can call some of the bikers to get rid of her."

"Where are your brains? They'll have a hold on you and you won't ever shake them. We did this and only we know what happened. It's our business."

The reality shook Earl once again. He was aghast. "Burn her?"

"Well, do you want a funeral with a preacher or what?"

Earl sucked on the mouth of the Yukon Jack bottle and finally lumbered outside. He backed up the car slowly, following Karen's signals so that the rear end fit snugly into the doorway of the furnace house. He released the catch of the Rolls trunk and it whispered open.

Used for the drug laboratory's chemical waste, the furnace behind them was a Hercules of industrial strength with massive steel jaws. Earl eased out Georgie's body with strangely reverential consideration. She was wrapped in a heavy shower curtain that tangled in Earl's western boots and the body rolled out. A bloodied leather knout was lashed around her throat; the arms and legs were ribbons of raw flesh. A chunky silver braid was dislodged from her matted hair and dropped to the ground. In their haste to get her out of the house, they had forgotten to remove the handcuffs.

"You have the key to the cuffs?" Earl asked.

"Are you serious? Let's just burn her!"

Sweat beads dribbled into Earl's eyes. "I can't go on."

"You better, mister."

His sighs became staccato gasps. "Turn it to high, I guess . . . maybe medium. Don't want this sucker blowing up."

Karen flipped the gritty knob and they heard a thudding bang as the pilot light rose and the metal expanded. The fire came alive and viperously bit the jaws of the furnace. He and Karen cautiously fed the body in headfirst. The flames chivvied against Georgie's skin, which sizzled, then was swallowed in a series of searing rasps as the flames engulfed her hair. The scent of sizzling flesh was overpowering.

"How long you think this'll take?" Earl asked.

Hard laughter played in Karen's devious brown eyes. "Lots to cook. She spent years stuffing that fat face."

Earl thought he'd chuck, but tightened his gut. They went back to the bar. He held Karen close, taking comfort in the firm flex of her body.

"I can't take any more of this, Karen. Let's get out. This could all be a jinx. How about I sell the Paradise? The bikers would grab it."

With a look of perfect innocence, Karen kissed him. She handed him a tab of Ecstasy and folded some lines of coke on the bar.

"Earl, you murdered your wife awhile ago. You're in charge. I just follow wherever a man leads me."

Sean drove through dense pine forests that gave the area a primeval cast: Isolated hardscrabble farms were masked by the trees, connected by dirt roads leading to serpentine canyons, some winding to logging camps. A beacon of light fulminated, spreading through the dark twisting back road.

EARL RAYMOND'S PARADISE INN announced itself as a capital of pleasures, the outpost of the damned, offering Lowball Poker, an XXX Film Arcade, Adult Motel, Bar, Dancing, Disco. It would no longer be paradise for Earl.

The sign suddenly went off.

Sean stopped his car and got out at the pink-arched entrance. His sawed-off twelve-gauge Remington was packed in his briefcase. His boots scrunched on the frozen lot. It was gray with an icy-clad drizzle and a screeching wind spread out the snow-heavy pine branches like bat wings.

He sniffed the air, which had an odd, sweet, pungent, nose-tickling odor like sarsaparilla or root beer, then he breathed in acetone and wondered if the place was being used as a dump for toxic waste. From behind the road-house, an acidic dark jade funnel of smoke hissed out of the chimney of a small building, filling the air with cinders. The cream-colored Rolls-Royce was parked up ahead.

Sean prowled around, passing a TV satellite dish, poking his head into a stale cabin with an unmade bed and wall-to-wall tarnished mirrors. Alongside the cabin was a long, narrow building with a sloping tin roof. Inside were condom machines, and the walls featured posters of porn stars. He checked a storeroom. A mass of beakers and glass tubing lay on a workbench and the concrete floor was littered with large empty containers of Isosafrole, the precursor used in the manufacture of methyldioxide amphetamine, which he recognized immediately as Ecstasy.

At the end of the arcade, a door led outside to the hut housing the furnace. Up close, he knew it was the stench of flesh burning. A dull piece of metal was on the ground and he picked it up, turned it over, and saw the initial G. on a haircomb. He peeked through the door and the furnace snapped and settled, cooling down. He found a torn piece of darkly stained shower curtain, its metal eyelets encrusted with blood. He switched off the furnace and saw a pair of red-hot handcuffs shackled to an ashy bone.

Carrying his bag, Sean went into the bar. Mounted on the walls were the heads of black bear, large bucks, and rusty ancient firearms. Beyond the bar was a stable of video games, pool tables, and a row of slots.

The blender was on. Earl was moping on a bar stool, head down, and Karen was behind, her back to him. Startled, she turned and whipped out a .357 Magnum which had been delivered by a spring trap below. She held it with knowledge, securely.

"Hi, cutie, lost your daddy?"

Earl stirred, wheeling around on his stool. "She's a deadeye with that, so don't think of anything but stating your business. Now who the hell are you?" Judging by the heft in his flak vest, Earl was also armed.

"My name is Christopher Arnold. I didn't mean to surprise you. I'm looking for Mr. Earl Raymond."

"And what do you want with him, boy?" Earl snapped.

"I have a business card in my briefcase. If you let me

get it, you'll understand. You are Mr. Raymond?"

"The place is closed," Karen said, the gun never wavering in her hand.

Sean reached into his briefcase and withdrew a card, which he placed on the bar.

CHRISTOPHER J. ARNOLD JR.
NATIONAL BASKETBALL ASSOCIATION
SECURITY INVESTIGATIONS
WESTERN SECTOR

"So what's this got to do with me?"

Dissolute, bloated, Earl was only a shadow of the grinning young man in Jonah's snapshot.

"I'd like to talk to you. It's been a very, very *long* trip, Mr. Raymond. A man by the name of Terry Brett recently acquired the Los Angeles Stars—you may've read about it."

"I do keep up with basketball. He probably had to kill Jonah to get the team."

"Mr. Wolfe died of a heart attack."

Karen said, "Jonah Wolfe! Jesus, Earl, you never mentioned it." Her eyes glinted with delight. She leaned forward attentively. "Jonah, what a case he was."

"You see, sir, the league does an investigation on all new owners and your name came up on the computer."

Earl guffawed, waved at Karen to ease up, and motioned Sean over to join him.

"Hey, Karen, this is a riot. Let's loosen up. I think we can spare a few minutes. Sit yourself down, Chris, and have a Ramos Gin Fizz. Karen makes the best one in the 'Western Sector.'"

Sean saw the coke crumbs under the bar lip. Earl was in an expansive skydiving mood and clearly high, smirking, tickled by his recollections. Karen remained vigilant, finally putting down the Magnum within easy reach.

"Terry, praised be his name, he made me a rich man."

Sean tasted his drink, raised his glass to Karen. "It's terrific." He took out a notebook. "From our documents, Mr. Raymond, you were his roommate at USC."

"Asshole buddies. I used to give him my girls."

Sean winced. "Really?"

"But I never liked Terry. He's was very arrogant, used to rag me. He treated me like I was a moron. After college, he worked on a case for me and stole my settlement money. I was injured in practice."

"Can you prove that?"

"I doubt it. But it's true."

Sean turned a page of his notebook and pretended to refer to some questions.

"Do you still see Mr. Brett?"

"No, and I don't expect to. How'd you find me?"

"That's what I'm paid for. The other person I'm trying to locate is your wife, Mr. Raymond."

A jumpy silence altered the atmosphere, squelching Earl's good humor.

"What's she got to do with anything?" Karen snapped.

The two of them were too high-strung. Sean prepared to leave and call Captain Laver from his car. He had stepped on a live wire. But at the last moment, he pressed on.

"From our report, I understand she was Mr. Brett's law partner at one time." Sean waited them out. "Maybe she can shed some further light on his past dishonest activities."

"She's down in Florida. Hates the cold. Been there since Thanksgiving," Earl said, tapping his cane on the bar rail.

"Would you have an address for her?"

They were responding badly to the pressure, but Sean couldn't let up. Karen had her hands on her hips defiantly. "She moves around. Try Mexico or South America while you're at it."

"South America? I heard she was in Port Rivers just a few days ago. And not doing too well. She's working in a shop called Karen's Vanities and living in a skid row women's hotel."

They were both staring at him. "Anyone know you're up here visiting with us?" Karen asked.

"I check in regularly."

"Who the fuck are you, really?" Earl said, pressing up close to him and spraying him with spittle.

"Allison's my mother."

Earl's boisterous laughter had an acidulous peal. "You're kidding."

"No, I'm dead serious." He stared at Earl's coarse features, searching for a resemblance. "I heard that you and she had a son."

Earl cackled again and his yellow teeth hiccuped over his bottom lip. "Then it'd be the second fucking immaculate conception. What do you take me for? Allison didn't have a nickel. She was a bust-out hippie. We never had anything going. I wouldn't have pissed on her if she was on fire."

Sean yanked Earl's cane away and cracked him across the face. "I'm a detective with the Port Rivers police. You're both under arrest for suspicion of murder."

"Shoot the bastard, Karen!"

Karen moved swiftly, lunging over the bar for her gun. Sean kicked her feet from under her and she slammed down, hitting her face on the brass foot rail. As she screamed, bleeding on the floor, Earl slipped his hand inside the flak vest, but Sean jabbed the Commander .45 between his eyes. Sean's finger quivered on the trigger. He had come prepared to kill Earl Raymond only to discover he could not commit murder.

76

Terry asked the cabdriver to stop when they were about to pass his old house. In the driveway, a concrete seam with filmy ice glistened and gaped; the basketball backboard over the garage had lost a hinge and tilted on its side, and the rusted hoop clattered in the hurly-burly river wind. The shutters were nailed like coffins. What had been the front garden he had worked in with Pat appeared to have shrunk, and in its place was an unfamiliar weedy patch of marsh. He got back into the taxi and continued the fugitive trip.

The downtown restoration of Port Rivers had been another flattening of an old seafaring American town, plundering the character that Terry had been attached to from boyhood. Cheap, ugly superstore chains had moved in and the streets overflowed with evening shoppers, who found themselves dwarfed by HMO and financial office slabs. The sinkholes had at last been filled. A new, glittering, neon-emblazoned bus terminal had been constructed, flashing departures and arrival times. The marine welding shop had been converted into a gleaming steel-fronted micro-brewery.

In Old Town, he was more comfortable. The courthouse and his former office on Buccaneer Square were still intact. Most of the names of the outlaws had changed. The streets meandered down to the river. Art galleries, boutiques, confetti ribbons of clubs and restaurants had displaced the lofts and deserted factories. Outside The Greenhouse he peered through the window, trying to get his bearings. Was this the old Piraeus?

The restaurant was crammed full of well-dressed, well-heeled attractive people with the snappy chatter of deals pending or about to be done. Beside a large fireplace, carolers in eighteenth-century costume were singing "O Come, All Ye Faithful" with the crowd in the lounge. Terry waded through an oyster bar and into the main dining room. A glassed-in terrace outside overlooked the port where ships with Christmas-light necklaces winked in the distance. There were several groups ahead of him.

"Two for dinner, please."

"Do you have a reservation?" the young, pretty hostess asked.

"No. Please put my name on the list. It's Brett."

"Okay, I'll see what I can do. Excuse me, Mr. Brett, I have to seat a party."

With her back to him, a woman in a long dark green velvet dress, laughing at some bawdy remark, had turned away from a group and stopped laughing with suddenness. The glass of champagne in her hand swayed. No

matter how long it had been, Allison could never forget
the mellifluous chords of Terry's voice. She gradually
moved closer to him, hoping that the noise from the bar
had deceived her.

She strode up and then wavered. His head was turned
away, and he looked into the room. Then she took his
arm, and they were face to face, both shaken and shocked
by the encounter.

"It is you, *you*, Terry."

His eyes explored her and he grasped for something to
say.

"Allison. I never thought this would happen . . . that
we'd see each other again."

Allison was too surprised to think, to redeem the past.
Beyond the creases on Terry's face, she detected something still loving, which had lingered and harkened back
to the secretive visits of another time. She was unable to
mask the temblor of pleasure his presence gave her.

People brushed by them, leaned over, searching for
their names on the reservation chart, spoke to Allison,
and she apologized for delays.

Her long blond hair was upswept and held fast by a
gold butterfly comb. She was stately, with a ripened elegance, and a grace that he had not recognized before.

"What are you doing here, Terry?"

"Waiting for Sean. Allison, I'm happy and sad to see
you. You're more beautiful than I ever could have remembered."

Allison simply nodded, taking him in, shut in by the
glaring darkness of his absence.

"I never told Sean a thing."

"I know that. But I have. He found me."

Impatient diners called out "Allison," shook her hand,
crowded around, boxing them in. Her desire and passion
for him was reawakened, the attraction no longer soiled.
She wanted to hold his hand, to kiss him and have him
rub his fingers over her lips.

"I'll get someone to take over for me." Allison's eyes
circled the room. A bar waiter came by. "Bring this gentleman a double Herradura shooter . . . make it two." She

hesitated. "Terry, don't be gone when I get back."

He was reminded of her agitation during his clandestine visits to Seacliff. He smiled cautiously. "I won't move." He picked up a menu.

THE GREENHOUSE
ALL RECIPES CREATED BY ALLISON
ARNOLD, PROPRIETRESS

A vision in green velvet, Allison whirled through the customers in her emeralds and pearls and returned with the hostess.

"Bonnie Slater, this is Terry Brett." Allison's strong fingers entwined around his. "He and I were once young together." Allison gave Terry a melancholy smile. "He was the love of my life."

Bonnie's eyes studiously wandered over Terry, like someone reading a map under a car light. She had never observed Allison quite so high-strung with any man. Allison spirited him away, weaving through the clusters in the bar where the new, young aristocrats were drinking champagne, snapping their braces, and making promises to girls with skeptical eyes.

"Come on, Terry, I'll fix you dinner."

"This was Aristedes's joint?" Terry asked.

"Yes. He's still remembered. I make a variation of his spit-roasted baby lamb." She smiled. "Mine doesn't slide off the plate. Your jacket and tie look familiar."

"Sean saved them for me." He paused and looked at her intently. "I've had the adventure of my life with him."

"It doesn't surprise me. He's been very truly crazy lately."

"I'm the reason."

They sat at a handsomely curtained alcove table. "Where is Sean?"

"He went to the police station to check in. He should be coming here soon to have dinner with me."

"Did he just run into you and Valerie when he was in Los Angeles?"

"No, that's not quite how it happened."

"Valerie doesn't know?"

"No. She died two days ago. I'm going back for the funeral. Tonight if I can get a flight."

In silence, they drank at the table, the only one he observed with a lace cloth and white roses.

"Val's dead. . . . Something sudden?" Allison asked, not quite believing it.

"Cancer."

"I'm sorry, Terry, genuinely."

"I know you are. So am I." He changed the subject. "You're so very successful."

"I am now. I couldn't have done it without Pat."

"Allison, what you're doing for my father goes beyond kindness."

"He deserves it and more. I couldn't imagine him alone in a hospital room. After all, we are family."

On her left hand she still wore the wedding band she had given Terry and which he had flung at her. He would never forget the words it represented:

Mizpah. "The Lord watch between me and thee, when we are absent one from another."

Impulsively, she touched his hand below the table. With a long, pained look, she dropped her head on his shoulder. It was no time to be vindictive.

"I wish I knew how I could've done things differently. I feel my life's been bartered with everyone else I dragged down with me," he admitted.

Allison found herself retreating, searching for a safe haven. "Terry, please don't. I'm in absolute dread of stirring up emotions I buried the night we broke up."

He felt an uncontrollable charge of anger twisting through him.

"Allison, you know I wouldn't have left you and Sean. There was never any question of how I felt. What you told me about you and Earl killed me. We had nowhere to go."

Tears streaming down her face, Allison cupped her face in her hand and shook her head submissively.

"Please, I beg you, please, stop," she implored him.

"I didn't mean to upset you."

"Terry, when you love the way we did, you make sacrifices whatever the cost. You married me bigamously. The risk you took was beyond anything I could have conceived. The day of our wedding, I promised myself if there was ever a problem, or even a chance of you going down, I'd stand aside.

"You were trapped when Val came through the cottage door. And I was afraid for you. You'd been suffering so much. If it all came out, it would have broken you again. And Terry, we both owed Val. There was no escaping that."

She leaned over and held Terry tightly. The treacherous yearning, the desire to be beside him, possessed her.

"What are you trying to say?"

"Terry, you needed a reason to get out of the situation. I gave you a motive. The life we had together was a mirage . . . our mirage. The one I'd wanted when I was a kid. But Valerie finding out about us wasn't enough for you. I had to play into your weakness and make you think the worst of me. Earl!" She uttered his name with a rancorous jeer. "I never gave him the right time. There was never any plan at all for you to take his case against Jonah. I made it up. I was frantic about saving you. I had to force you to give me up. I sacrificed Sean, wrecked him and myself for you. And it was worth it. I'd do it again."

Terry was humbled. "Is this true about Earl? I need to know. For Sean's sake. He's so confused and I have to go to him honorably. Tell me, tell me."

"There's nothing to tell. I was *never* with Earl. I had to convince you I was, that *he* was Sean's father. That was the only way you'd ever leave us."

The revelation beamed brightly all through dinner. Terry sensed a foundation within himself, something tangible, all of it planted on solid bedrock. The horizon fluttered along the shoreline like the lighted ships in the harbor in which nothing was fixed.

When the restaurant closed, he accompanied Allison

to her office. She had made a nest in the back, furnishing it with chairs and sofas from the house in Seacliff. She wheeled a trolley of brandies in from the bar. She reached over and selected a flagon of Armagnac and poured two snifters, rolled them around, and handed one to Terry.

"I don't know how I'll stand up if I have another."

"Don't worry about anything right now. I'll drive you to the airport."

Allison realized how much she had actually liked Terry. There was a struggle as she drifted in and out of their past.

"This is velvet fire, very special."

"Everything about you always was," he said.

Apart from the kitchen staff clearing up and Bonnie reconciling the checks on the bar computer, they were alone.

"I consider myself a fortunate man. I have two sons and they're both talking to me."

"I don't think you've done badly at all."

Bonnie came by with the night deposit bag. Allison noticed she was wearing fresh makeup. "I'll drop it. I'm passing the bank."

"Have you heard from Sean yet?" Allison asked.

"Yes. He's at headquarters now. He had to make an arrest on some old case. He said it was no big deal. I'm going to meet him for coffee. He sounds like himself again." She stared at Terry with a hint of puzzlement and smiled. "Good night, Mr. Brett."

When she'd gone, they drank slowly, together and yet alone, constrained but personal. Terry listed forward and wrapped his arms around Allison's shoulders. Her cheeks were warm and her perfume familiar. She resisted her instincts and moved away. Then, almost tearful, she pulled him close and pressed into his chest, feeling the mold of his body.

"Allison, I have so many things I want to say to you."

"I wondered if you ever thought of me."

"I've never been in doubt about my feelings for you."

"And Val?"

"Of course I loved her. I would have left otherwise."

"It's crazy, Terry, but that makes me happy. I didn't want Val to have you without you caring for her. I can't tell you how much she meant to me. We were never rivals."

Allison removed the wedding band she had given Terry and he had thrown at her. "Put this on her finger, please."

She took the comb from her hair, which slid down her shoulders. She embraced Terry, kissing him with a lavishness that brought them back to the bloom of their springtime.

"Wherever I was, Allison, nothing could stop me from thinking of you. You were always alive for me in my dreams."

She shuddered and lay her head on his lap and he stroked her hair. "Terry, darling, I love you. I always have and I'll never stop. Forgive me for what I did to you."

Terry leaned down and studied her face with reverence. "We've both learned some terrible lessons. I thought there was some element of honor in deception."

"No, there isn't."

They both rose, and holding each other, walked back through the empty restaurant. He put on the coat that Sean had given him and helped her on with a green velvet cape.

"My car's in the back. I'll take you to the airport, Terry."

"Thanks. I have to get going."

She said good night to the porter and once outside, she shook her head with wonder. They seemed to float to her Jaguar and then stopped suddenly when a red Mustang squealed to a halt in front of them. With the engine still running, Sean burst out of the driver's side. He saw his parents' linked arms and approached them with euphoria.

"I made my last arrest tonight," he said buoyantly.

Terry shook his hand and they embraced. "That's a relief."

"For both of us," Allison pitched in. "I guess your father was a good influence."

"Yes, Mother, he definitely was." He held Allison's car door open and when Terry slipped in beside her, Sean gazed at the of two of them with a sense of piety. "Will you come back, Dad? Or do I have to file extradition papers?"

The question made Terry laugh and his amusement was contagious. "Count on it," Terry said, embracing Sean. Now I know where you got your sense of humor," he said. "You won't need a felony warrant, I'm giving myself up."

77

It was cold and luminously clear in Los Angeles. In a black flannel suit, Terry sat in the front row of the chapel listening to Aaron conclude the eulogy for his mother. "I'd like to read my mother's favorite passage. It's from a poem by Swinburne":

> *For winters rains and ruins are over,*
> *And all the seasons of snows and sins;*
> *The days dividing lover and lover,*
> *The light that loses, the night that wins;*
> *And time remembered is grief forgotten,*
> *And frosts are slain and flowers begotten,*
> *And in green underwood and cover*
> *Blossom by blossom the spring begins.*

Terry walked outside the chapel with Aaron. They shook the hands of the many people who had come to say their farewells to Valerie. She had been a woman shaped by solid values, which could never be conditional or altered to suit others, and the source of her strength was her character. She had despised her father for falling short. She had been married first to a young man who had cheated on his medical exams, later to a man who had cheated on her and whom she forgave. Terry had been privileged to have had her love and loved her in return.

He had been exposed to the wondrous secrets of women, how they felt, breathed, sounded, but he had ignored their inner life until now. His duplicity had not made anyone feel better and sooner or later it strangled everyone. He knew he could never again be tripped up or have a justification for lying. That morning, he had told Aaron exactly what had happened. Aaron was an image of his mother. Terry detected disapproval from his son, but he had experienced a sense of liberation.

Aaron was incredulous. "It's hard to understand how you two could go on after that."

"Maybe it strengthened us," Terry replied. "I can only guess. Your mother was the most generous person I've ever known."

"And what about this woman, Allison?"

"I don't feel that there's a betrayal involved any longer, Aaron. The truth is, I could *never* find a negotiating principle in a condition like mine. I'm talking about the alchemy of love. My heart doesn't fathom logic or reason. I'm a deeply flawed man. Maybe there are other people out there without sin. I'm not."

Aaron shook his head with anger. He was about to move away from Terry when he realized that what he really wanted most was to be held in his father's arms.

"How could you have married this woman?"

"I loved her and she was the mother of my son. It was beyond me to find a middle ground with myself. I had a divided heart, and when it's your own, you fail yourself and everyone. Now I can't bargain or haggle with you about my emotions. I've done that long enough."

Aaron turned to Kit, who was ill at ease. She had listened quietly with her mouth agape, but she was a young woman who like Allison had lived through hard times. Kit tried to topple the barrier that Aaron had already erected and dissolve his bitterness.

"Aaron, your father is trying to explain and maybe you'll learn something about people."

"Will I? Speaking professionally, I'm relieved to finally

know the truth, Dad. As your son, I'm disappointed in you. You see, no matter what you eventually decide to do, we can't all be friends and pretend that this is one happy family."

"I know that."

Terry backed away and was about to leave when Kit sharply reproached Aaron. "That would be a disastrous mistake, Aaron. I don't think Valerie would have liked you to behave this way, especially now."

If Terry hadn't appeared to be such a model of probity, with Val backing up his performance, Terry's imposture would have been obvious to Aaron. He could now reconcile his own emotional turmoil and the enigmas of his childhood. Allison and Sean had been the missing parts of the family.

"Dad, it's going to take me some time." He grasped Terry's arm. "What're you going to do now?" he asked with desperation.

"I'll go back to the house to see all our old friends. After that, I'll be leaving for Port Rivers to be with *my* father. I'd like you and Kit to come. It would mean a great deal to him and me."

Over a mask of snow, Christmas Day had fleeting moments of sunshine, and the Van Wyck estate appeared to rise up with the permanence of a cathedral. Its maze, which led to the glistening riverpoint, furrowed by ice, had been cared for by its mistress. Pat sat in his wheelchair on the sunporch. He had been saving his words, his good times, like the property he owned. But he was vigilant.

The house was now full, and strangers, who were family, his blood, surrounded him. Aaron was taking his pulse and wore around his neck an old-fashioned, untrustworthy stethoscope. Two young women were drinking red wine and showing each other new cocktail dresses still on hangers. Sean was behind the bar, stirring a martini the way Terry had many years before.

His son and Allison walked toward him, both smiling,

and Pat imagined them when they were young and living with him. He closed his eyes, and their images lodged like ghosts in his mind, before vanishing in their own chariot.

ACKNOWLEDGMENTS

I wish to express my gratitude to a host of people who patiently read the manuscript and offered their counsel.

My modern-day Athenas, Lori Cohen, Patricia Fuller, and Alice L. Birney did their best to guide me through the mazes of a woman's sensibility during the time periods my characters lived through. I hope some of these ladies' wisdom has been imparted to my people.

My doctor friends provided invaluable information regarding medical procedure. Dr. Benjamin Cohen took me through the byways of pediatrics. Dr. Lawrence Yaeger marched me through surgical techniques and treatments for diseases. And finally Dr. L. G. advised me on psychiatric protocols and the training of residents.

Susan Crawford offered yet more practical advice and encouragement.

Ellis Amburn, once my editor and now a distinguished biographer, assiduously went through the book and spared me both folly and public humiliation.

Natalia Aponte brought her editorial perspicacity, insight, and perseverance to bear and helped to shape a work that has occupied five years of my life.

Michael Viner and Deborah Raffin are friends for all seasons.

Get caught reading.

Jake Lloyd reading ENDER'S GAME.

A Message from the
Association of American Publishers